Heartbeat:

Constable along the Lane and Other Tales of a Yorkshire Village Bobby

Nicholas Rhea

HEADLINE

First published in this edition in 1995
by HEADLINE BOOK PUBLISHING

10 9 8 7 6 5 4 3 2

ISBN 0 7472 5159 2

Typeset by CBS, Felixstowe, Suffolk

Printed and bound in Great Britain by
Cox & Wyman Ltd, Reading, Berks.

HEADLINE BOOK PUBLISHING
A division of Hodder Headline PLC
338 Euston Road
London NW1 3BH

Nicholas Rhea is the pen-name of Peter N. Walker, formerly an inspector with the North Yorkshire Police, and the creator of the *Constable* series of books from which the Yorkshire TV series *Heartbeat* has been derived. In the three *Constable* books in this volume, *Constable by the Sea*, *Constable along the Lane* and *Constable through the Meadow*, Nicholas Rhea recounts more of the amusing incidents which happen to the colourful and eccentric characters encountered by a country constable, stories which have provided the basis for the adventures of PC Nick Rowan, played by Nick Berry, in the TV series. Peter N. Walker is also author of *Portrait of the North York Moors*, *Murders & Mysteries from the North York Moors* and *Folk Tales from the North York Moors*. He is married with a family and lives in North Yorkshire.

BOOKS BY PETER N. WALKER

CRIME FICTION
The *Carnaby* series pub. Hale:
Carnaby and the Hijackers (1967)*
Carnaby and the Gaolbreakers (1968)
Carnaby and the Assassins (1968)
Carnaby and the Conspirators (1969)
Carnaby and the Saboteurs (1970)
Carnaby and the Eliminators (1971)
Carnaby and the Demonstrators (1972)
Carnaby and the Infiltrators (1974)**
Carnaby and the Kidnappers (1976)
Carnaby and the Counterfeiters (1980)
Carnaby and the Campaigners (1984)
Fatal Accident (1970)
Panda One on Duty (1971)
Special Duty (1971)
Identification Parade (1972)
Panda One Investigates (1973)
Major Incident (1974)
The Dovingsby Death (1975)
Missing from Home (1977)
The MacIntyre Plot (1977)
Witchcraft for Panda One (1978)
Target Criminal (1978)
The Carlton Plot (1980)
Siege for Panda One (1981)
Teenage Cop (1982)
Robber in a Mole Trap (1984)
False Alibi (pub. Constable 1991)
Grave Secrets (pub. Constable 1992)
  *reprinted Chivers (Black Dagger) 1993
**   "   "   "   " 1994
WRITTEN AS **CHRISTOPHER CORAM**
pub. Hale:
A Call to Danger (1968)
A Call to Die (1969)
Death in Ptarmigan Forest (1970)
Death on the Motorway (1973)
Murder by the Lake (1975)
Murder Beneath the Trees (1979)
Prisoner on the Dam (1982)
Prisoner on the Run (1985)

WRITTEN AS **TOM FERRIS:**
Espionage for a Lady (pub. Hale 1969)
WRITTEN AS **ANDREW ARNCLIFFE:**
Murder after the Holiday (pub. Hale 1985)
WRITTEN AS **NICHOLAS RHEA:**
Family Ties (pub. Constable 1985)
EMMERDALE TITLES:
WRITTEN AS **JAMES FERGUSON:**
A Friend in Need (pub. Fontana 1987)
Divided Loyalties (pub. Fontana 1988)
Wives and Lovers (pub. Fontana 1989)
Emmerdale Book of Country Lore
(pub. Hamlyn 1988)
Emmerdale Official Companion
(pub. Weidenfeld & Nicolson 1988)
Emmerdale's Yorkshire
(pub. Weidenfeld & Nicolson 1990)
The *Constable* series pub. Hale
WRITTEN AS **NICHOLAS RHEA:**
Constable on the Hill (1979)
Constable on the Prowl (1980)
Constable around the Village (1981)
Constable across the Moors (1982)
Constable in the Dale (1983)
Constable by the Sea (1985)
Constable along the Lane (1986)
Constable through the Meadow (1988)
Constable at the Double (1988)
Constable in Disguise (1989)
Constable among the Heather (1990)
Constable beside the Stream (1991)
Constable around the Green (1993)
Constable beneath the Trees (1994)
Constable in the Shrubbery (1995)
Heartbeat Omnibus I (1992)
Heartbeat Omnibus II (1993)
Heartbeat – Constable among the
    Heather (pub. Headline 1992)
Heartbeat – Constable across the Moors
    (pub. Headline 1993)
Heartbeat – Constable on Call
    (pub. Headline 1993)

CONTENTS

Constable
by the Sea

1

And the sun went down
And the stars came out far over the summer sea.

Alfred, Lord Tennyson, 1809-92

It was the first week of July and I was on a slow train which was carrying me to the seaside. Mine was not a holiday trip, however, but a police duty engagement. I was on my way to Strensford, a picturesque and sometimes busy seaside resort on the north-east coast of Yorkshire. Graced by miles of smooth, yellow sand, Strensford is famed for its kippers and the fact that the bright summer sun both rises and sets over the sea. It is also known for its towering cliffs with a ruined abbey gloriously perched on top, and the haphazard cluster of red-roofed cottages which crowd around the harbour side, at times touching the water.

A few years ago, I had started my police career in this town, but much as I liked Strensford, I hadn't volunteered for this return visit. Who would volunteer to leave behind a loving wife and four tiny children? It is at times like this policemen realize that their wives are angels and models of patience and understanding – well, most of them are!

It was Sergeant Blaketon who had said, 'Rhea, I put your name down for coastal duties. You could do with a change of scenery and the chance to do some real police work; it'll do you good to cope with daft holiday-makers, drunken locals and masses of cars all heading for the same

parking space. So I've volunteered you for this duty.
Fourteen weeks, it is. Each spell of duty is seven days on
followed by two days off. You'll be working shifts, so you'll
get home once in a while.

'You'll be in uniform, helping the local lads to cope with
the summer rush. Report at Strensford Police Station
prompt at 9 a.m. a week on Monday, and take enough stuff
to last you a week. Digs will be found and food will be
provided. It'll be no holiday, mind you, so don't go thinking
it's a doddle.'

It didn't matter whether or not I wanted to volunteer –
I was on my way, but one thing did please me. For three
blissful months or so, I'd be free from the domineering
presence of Sergeant Oscar Blaketon. That pleasing thought
was the one bright spot in the gloom which would follow
departure from my little family.

I was familiar with the coastal problems. I'd served my
police apprenticeship at Strensford and knew that during
the winter months the town literally died. Lashed by fierce
north-east gales, high seas, dense fogs and intensely cold
weather, the little resort simply ceased to appeal to anyone.
Even its own residents grumbled about the treatment it
received from the uncaring weather. As the claws of winter
chased away the holiday-makers, Strensford's streets and
hotels emptied, its beaches became deserted and its shops
closed their doors against the Arctic blasts. To walk those
blustery streets on a Sunday in winter was tantamount to
trekking to the North Pole.

This was in direct contrast to the summer months,
when the town changed beyond all belief (even the fogs
were a few degrees warmer). Holiday-makers swamped
the place. Boarding houses and hotels re-opened, the
amusement arcades dusted their machines, camping sites
bustled with activity and the shopkeepers gave their

premises a new coat of paint. Lines of traffic flooded into the town; bus-loads came for the day and train-loads came for longer periods.

Even foreigners came to Strensford in the summer. Flat-capped folks came from the West Riding of Yorkshire, and beer-swilling Geordies came down from the north. Scots folks arrived for two-week stretches to spend a little cash, Europeans passed through, and it was even rumoured that some from the south of England ventured this far north.

And as if to please all those visitors, the sun occasionally broke through the summer fogs to bathe the town in a warm, pleasing glow.

From the police officer's point of view, this annual influx presented severe problems. In the winter, the resident constables were bored out of their minds due to a lamentable lack of activity, whereas the hectic summer months pushed them to their limits and beyond. There just weren't sufficient officers to cope with the plethora of problems the visitors managed to generate.

It is widely known in police circles that when people descend *en masse* upon a place, they produce problems. Those problems are bewildering and awesome in their range and complexity, and it is invariably the police who have to deal with them. At the seaside, they range from simple things like children getting lost or vehicles travelling the wrong way along one-way streets, to mammoth worries like people leaping off cliffs to end their lives or ships going down with all hands. The coastal constable sees a lot, learns a lot, copes with a lot and, in despair and disbelief, shakes his head a lot.

I was aware of all these factors as my train neared the end of its journey. I was to become, however temporarily, such a constable. For the next few weeks, which embraced the height of Strensford's summer season, I was to be a constable by the sea.

After a very early morning start, I had caught this train, the only one which would allow me to arrive at Strensford Police Station by no later than the stipulated hour of 9 a.m. This train was also the local train, for on its long tortuous but incredibly picturesque route through the Strensbeck Valley of the North York Moors, it gathered masses of children from the dales and villages and poured them into Strensford to be 'eddicated' as the dalesmen put it. Once in town, they dispersed daily to their secondary schools or to the grammar school.

In those days, railway carriages were divided into individual compartments, each of which seated about ten people, and so I had entered one which contained nothing that looked remotely like a rampant schoolchild. Schoolchildren can be very wearisome as travelling companions. Instead, my fellow passengers were a sober bunch of people from the villages, people whose livelihood was earned in Strensford through earnest toil in its shops, offices and factories. As I'd entered, they had stared at me briefly; for one thing, I was a stranger on the train, and secondly, my mode of dress was an obvious mixture of civilian clothing and police uniform.

I had deemed this necessary because I had to be at the police station no later than 9 a.m., and the train arrived at Strensford at five minutes to nine. This meant I had no time to change, so to save time, and to prevent a possible disciplinary charge by being late, I had donned my best uniform and wore it beneath a civilian mackintosh. Thus I sported large black, polished boots, dark blue serge trousers, a blue shirt and black tie, all of which were clearly visible and which announced that I was a member of the Force. My tunic was nicely concealed beneath my raincoat, while my hand luggage comprised a bulky holdall, a small suitcase and some bags of assorted necessities.

One snag was that police uniforms are the most difficult things to pack, consequently my cumbersome greatcoat was slung on top of my holdall, between the handles, and for the time being my police cap on top of that. These were all on the rack above my head. I had a second tunic slung over my suitcase and had other bags and belongings draped around it. I reasoned that, even though my luggage was bulky and a nuisance, I could cope with it during the short, brisk walk from the railway station.

Sergeant Blaketon reckoned it was only a two-minute walk, but I knew the train could be late. Fortunately, this one was on time, but even so, I would have no moments to spare once the train halted at Strensford. Believing in early preparation, I stood up and began to gather my belongings as it rattled beneath the huge viaduct on its final mile or so. I was determined to have my things off the racks and securely clutched in my hands by the time the train halted. Then I'd make a dash for the barrier with my ticket at the ready, and I would gain the town's streets before the other passengers clogged the exit.

'Ah wouldn't bother,' said a man in the corner opposite.

'Pardon?' I wasn't sure he was addressing me.

'Ah said Ah wouldn't bother,' he was pointing at my unwieldy collection of belongings. 'Getting them things down yet. You'll not beat 'em.'

'Beat 'em?' I suspended my work and placed one hand on the edge of the rack as I questioned him.

'Aye,' he said. 'The kids. Schoolkids. They'll be out afore you, like a horde of bloody rampaging cattle, they are. It's a bloody stampede. We allus sit tight till they've got clear. It's safer in the long run.'

The other passengers clearly agreed with this middle-aged chap in the sports jacket, for they nodded and smiled at his words of common sense. But I couldn't afford to wait – it was already six minutes to nine.

'Thanks,' I smiled at them all, and at him in particular. 'But I've got to be at work prompt at nine o'clock, not a second later. I'll get through the crush. But thanks for the warning.'

After all, I told myself, I had been in the RAF during my National Service, and that experience had taught me a lot about rushing for trains, rushing off trains, galloping heavily laden along busy platforms, changing stations with seconds to spare, battling through rush-hour crowds – we servicemen had done it all, and that expertise was going to be my salvation this very morning.

I stood at the carriage door and lowered the window so that I could operate the catch from the outside. As I did so, I breathed in the clean salt air, air which some believe contains ozone but which in fact is a heady mixture of evaporating brine and kipper smoke. Even so, the blast of fresh air which blew into my face and ruffled my hair had a definite tang of the wide-open sea. It was clean and refreshing, beautifully pure and enervating. It held a promise of excitement and romance.

We were now reducing speed; the train had arrived at the outward end of the long, curving platform and was braking. There was the clash of brakes, the squeal of iron wheels on iron rails, the clanking buffers all accompanied by the shuddering motions of a heavily laden train being forced to a halt. We entered the station buildings, and the roof appeared in view; slowly, we cruised to a halt.

Quickly, I opened my door. The train was still moving, albeit very, very slowly. I gripped my assorted baggage just as I wanted it, and I could see the deserted barrier near the head of the train. There was no reason why I should not be first through. A forlorn ticket-collector stood there, his dark blue uniform prominent against the greyness of the station's stonework, and there was no one ahead of me. The way was clear.

With my customary agility and my practised RAF leap, I descended from the still-moving train, and in spite of my luggage, my legs had no trouble adjusting to a rapid running motion. I was on my way, and my luggage bobbed and bounced as I ran. I was running towards the ticket-collector at the speed of the slowing train. I could see him waiting for me, even though he did seem to be an awful long way off.

I'm not sure what went wrong with my strategy.

I became aware that I was being rapidly overtaken and simultaneously surrounded by noisy, galloping schoolchildren. Hats, scarfs, satchels, waving arms and bare knees were all about me, all heading in the same direction but with even more speed and urgency than I could muster. I was vaguely aware of countless stomping feet, many shrill voices all raised in unison and an unseen determination by each one of them to be first through that ticket-barrier. I was probably unwittingly involved in a daily race for some kind of momentary, childish glory.

I was unavoidably swept along by the thrusting crowd; this was mass movement at its very worst, for even if I'd wished to turn around, it would have been impossible. I had no choice but to go along with the stampeding mass of school-bound youngsters, and as I galloped along with them, I realized that they had also to be in class by nine o'clock.

To add to my impending and inevitable delay at the barrier, my uniform greatcoat, which had been lying on top of my holdall, had gradually slipped, and its tail was trailing on the platform. It was gathering dust as I ran, and with horror I realized that my cap was also working loose. Being swept along as I was, I could not halt my onward rush to rectify matters.

And as these doom-laden realizations impressed themselves upon me, disaster arrived. As I pumped my way through the crowd, I trod upon that loose coat tail. My running motion was rudely interrupted and I was launched briefly into mid-air, then went sprawling to earth in an entanglement of arms and legs, some of which did not belong to me. As I fell, I lost my grip on the holdall; I recall that it bounded, or was kicked, from my grasp, and it disappeared among hundreds of stamping feet as it was bundled along by the moving mass. My cap broke loose too and went bowling along beneath a tumult of feet as I lay on the platform with a multiplicity of shoes pounding my back, head, arms and legs. The surging crowd moved on. I tried to get up; I couldn't. Each time, more feet pounded me back into the ground. And then, quite suddenly, it was all over and there was peace.

I struggled to my feet and saw that a mass of children had come to a halt around the unfortunate ticket-collector, but their number was reducing rapidly as they squeezed through the barriers and ran for their waiting buses or hurried to their schools.

My battered holdall was lying midway between me and the barrier, and my trampled greatcoat was spread open nearby, something like Walter Raleigh's famous cape, except there was no royal personage to walk upon it and no puddle to justify its position on the ground. It was smothered in the thick grey dust of the railway station.

I had no idea where my cap had gone.

I dusted down my trousers and mackintosh and then began to make my slow, somewhat painful way to the barrier, retrieving my holdall and greatcoat *en route*. I got there eventually, by which time the last of the children had passed through. Their disappearance through the narrow gap was rather like sand slipping through an hourglass, and their final departure produced an air of sudden peace and tranquillity.

'Your cap,' grunted the ticket collector. It was perched on the gatepost at the barrier, buckled, bruised and very dirty. 'They're animals, the lot of 'em. Bloody animals. No respect.'

I smiled ruefully as I handed in my ticket and lifted my cap from its temporary resting place. As I did so, I became aware of a man beside me.

'Ah said thoo shouldn't have bothered.' It was the man from the railway carriage, and he was shaking his head. 'Thoo hasn't saved any time. See? We've caught thoo up.'

Through the gap in the wall which was the exit, I could see the police station, a red-brick building on a hill about four hundred yards away. The ticket-collector noticed me looking anxiously at it.

'By lad,' he said. 'You'll need a bit more about you if you're going to be stationed in this spot! 'Specially with summer coming on. Some o' these day-trippers eat young lads like you! Now, next time, stay on this train till yon school-rush is clear of this barrier.'

'Ah did warn you,' muttered the fellow in the sports jacket, and now I could see the other passengers heading this way.

'Thanks.' I tried to show pleasure at their helpfulness, but my back hurt and I felt a real mess.

It was one minute to nine as I left the portals of the railway station, and I struggled across the street with my battered load. I took a short cut across the forecourt of the bus station, hurried through a back street near a cinema and climbed the short, steep, cobbled hill towards the red-brick edifice which was Strensford's police station, a building erected in Victoria's reign.

I was puffing and panting by now, with sweat pouring off me. My perspiration had gathered a good deal of flying dust during my tumble, and I knew my hands and face were stained and dirty. My hair was hanging limp and I could feel the mess I was in. My cumbersome baggage had made things worse. Items trailed from it, my cap kept falling off, and the infuriating coat insisted on slipping to the ground.

Eventually I arrived at the entrance, which was along a level cul-de-sac, a side-street leading off the cobbled hill, and which was marked by a blue sign saying 'Police'. There was a row of bicycles parked against the wall but no outward sign of activity.

I entered to memories of my early days here and hurriedly descended a dark flight of steps into the ageing bowels of this curious old place. I found myself at the hatch over which was a notice saying, 'Enquiries'. I peeped through – there was an office full of policemen, so I walked in as I'd done much less confidently a few years ago.

'Rhea!' bellowed an all-too-familiar voice in my ear. 'You're late! Three minutes late on your first day's duty. And look at the state of you! Has there been a train crash? Have you been fighting drunks already, Rhea? And that uniform! And you should not be wearing a mixture of civilian clothes with your uniform . . .'

Sergeant Blaketon had also come to Strensford for a spell of coastal duty. I let him ramble on but did wonder how he had managed to arrive on time and why he had not brought me with him. I was to learn later that he had instructed one of the Ashfordly constables to drive him over in the official car, a privilege not permitted constables. Man and car had returned to patrol duties around my peaceful patch at Aidensfield.

'You're on nights, tonight, Rhea,' Sergeant Blaketon was saying. 'So you needn't have got dressed up like that. Now, your digs are at the Breckdale Private Hotel across the street. Go there now. The rest have already arrived. Settle in, they'll explain things to you, then report back here for duty at ten tonight. And Rhea, be smart and be on time. In fact, be early. Ten minutes to ten, on the dot.'

'Yes, sergeant.' Quite suddenly, I wasn't looking forward to being a constable by the sea.

My first night's duty wasn't too bad. I knew my way around the town and had no real difficulty adjusting to this changed routine. Even so, there was a marked contrast between plodding a beat around farms and villages and treading featureless streets. Now my time would be spent visiting public houses to quell any possible fighting and to ensure they closed on time, or checking numerous shop doors to make sure they were locked and secure against prowling criminals.

It was the latter task which almost landed me in more hot water with Sergeant Blaketon; the incident occurred during my second night on duty.

By way of an excuse, I ought to add that I had been very tired even before embarking on that second tour of eight foot-slogging hours. Having arrived at nine o'clock on that Monday morning, I had been awake all that day and, without any sleep, had performed an eight-hour tour of night duty that night. I'd collapsed into bed just after 6.30 the following morning but had not slept at all. For one thing, I missed Mary; for another, a strange bed was not conducive to peaceful slumber, and the routine sounds of the hotel were not the best at lulling me to sleep. Finally, I was called down to lunch at one o'clock, so my sleep total was practically nil. It was not the best recipe for another tour of night duty.

When I began that second tour, therefore, I was almost asleep on my feet even before parading for duty and put on what I hoped was a wide-awake appearance during the briefing in the muster room. Sergeant Blaketon was duty sergeant that night, and I caught him eyeing me once or twice as he informed us about the night's work. There were unoccupied houses and shops to care for, likely trouble-spots outside dance halls and clubs, and a spate of burglaries by villains using stolen cars.

'Are you all right, Rhea?' he suddenly asked.

'Yes, sergeant,' I said, looking puzzled.

'You look bloody awful,' he commented. 'Pale and tired. Is this townie style of bobbying too much for you?'

'Not at all!' I tried to sound very confident in my response. 'I'm fine.'

'Right,' he addressed the entire complement of tonight's officers. 'To your beats.'

I had been allocated No 2 Beat, which comprised the town centre, and this meant I had lots of shop premises, office blocks, restaurants and pubs to check during the first half of my tour. Those mundane tasks would pass the time rapidly until my 2 a.m. break.

To be honest, those first four hours flew past; I was so busy checking all the property for which I was responsible that I had no time to feel tired. This was aided by cheery home-going drinkers who always stopped for a chat with the patrolling policeman. Their good humour helped to while away the long night hours – as long as they were not troublesome. It is fair to say that very few of them did cause real trouble – we would often place a cheerful drunk into a taxi to help him home, the 'penalty' being the taxi-fare, but they rarely caused anything more serious.

At 2 a.m., therefore, I adjourned to the station, where I

thoroughly enjoyed my sandwiches and coffee.

The worst was to come. The second half of a night shift is always a trial because, even with an adequate amount of sleep, there is that awful period between 3 a.m. and 4 a.m. when the patrolling constable is at his lowest ebb. There are times when he is literally asleep on his feet, when he is walking like a robot, when he is not seeing anything and when he doesn't know anything. It is a ghastly time and few escape it. Having been denied my fair share of sleep, that low ebb hit me hard. I was patrolling the second half of my beat, refreshed with coffee and sandwiches, and the time had reached 3 a.m. Daylight was not far away. But at five minutes past three, by now feeling exceedingly weary, I found an insecure shop door. It was not locked, although the shop lights were out and there did not appear to have been a break-in. I checked all the external windows and the back door, but it became clear that the shop-keeper had forgotten to lock his front door.

This discovery kept me awake for a while, and I knew my next task was to search the shop for intruders. This was in the days before police officers enjoyed the support of personal radio sets, so I was alone. Snapping on my powerful torch, I entered the shop and began a thorough search in the darkness. It was a furniture shop on two storeys, and I made a meticulous search of every conceivable hiding place. There was no intruder, the till had not been forced and there did not appear to have been a break-in.

The simple solution was to lock the offending door by dropping the latch, and then get the key-holder out of bed to ask for a check of his premises. This was always done, just to be sure that all was well. This rude awakening had the added effect of making the key-holder more careful in the future about locking up. But this lock was of the mortice type, and there was no key in the lock. I could not leave the premises insecure – there might be a shop-breaker lurking in the night, so I picked up the shop's telephone and rang the police station.

Sergeant Blaketon answered.

He listened to my story then said, 'Right, Rhea, I've checked the key-holders' register and that furniture shop belongs to a chap called Raymond Austin. He lives out at Oakdale, and that's a good half-hour's drive, then he's got to get dressed. I'll ring him now and get him to lock his shop. You wait there until he comes – it could be three-quarters of an hour; check it all over just to be sure nothing's been stolen, and then make sure he locks up.'

'Yes, sergeant.' I replaced the telephone and resigned myself to a long wait. But there was one advantage about having to wait here – it was a furniture shop full of comfortable seats.

I closed the front door but did not switch on the shop's lights and with the aid of my torch selected a comfortable settee upon which to wait. It was nicely out of view of the windows – not that many folks would be passing by or window-shopping at this time of the morning, but I did not wish to be stared at during my lonely vigil. I settled down on the lovely soft surface of the settee, and in the warmth of the evening my eyes began to close and my head began to nod. My head jolted alarmingly as I fought to keep awake, and in an effort to do so, I walked around the shop once or twice, but the inevitable happened. Eventually, I fell asleep.

When I awoke, daylight had arrived. The summer dawn arrived early on the coast, and when I checked my watch, it was four o'clock. Four o'clock? It took me a few minutes to gather my wits and to realize where I was, but then I recalled with horror that I was still in the shop and that I must have nodded off. I hurriedly left my cosy resting-place, shivered and walked around for a minute or two, checking the time and wondering where the key-holder was. Surely it was time he was here! If there'd been a problem, Sergeant Blaketon would have rung back.

I decided to have a look up the street, just to see if he was anywhere in sight. I went to the front door. It was locked. I shook it, tugged it, I hauled on the handle, but it was as secure as a fortress.

With my heart sinking fast into my boots, I realized what had happened. Mr Austin must have driven down from Oakdale and arrived at his premises while I was slumbering out of his sight; he'd simply locked his door and departed. I was now locked in.

I walked around the shop, my heart thumping with worry, and I knew that I'd be in real trouble if Blaketon discovered my lapse. Sleeping on duty was almost a cardinal sin. I told myself to be calm as I wandered around, seeking a window which might open, or a key which might permit me to leave. But none of the windows was of the opening kind, save for a small one in the toilet, but that wouldn't even admit a cat. And I could not find a key hanging anywhere.

There was only one solution – I'd have to ring the station once more and hope that Sergeant Blaketon was out of the building. I'd ask whoever was on duty to ring Mr Austin again. I'd have to ask him to drive back into town to release me. I had to be out of the shop before six o'clock, otherwise I'd be late for booking off duty, and that would get me into severe trouble . . .

Then it dawned on me that if the station duty constable could ring Mr Austin, why couldn't I? Perhaps I could cover up my crass stupidity! I looked up his number in the directory which lay by the phone, checked my watch and realized he'd almost be back home. I knew he'd be horrified if he was roused again, so I wanted to catch him before he got back into bed. I was aware that he was liable to write a letter of complaint to the Superintendent, but it was a risk I could not avoid.

I rang the number. The telephone rang for a long, long time but eventually a woman sleepily answered.

'Oh,' I said apologetically. 'This is Strensford Police. It's PC Rhea speaking. Is Mr Austin there?'

'No, he's gone to his shop. Your office rang about it.'

'Ah, well, it's urgent. We need to contact him.'

'Well, I'm sorry, but he left well over an hour ago, to lock up his premises, he said. It had been left open.'

'Yes, well, he has locked it, but something urgent has arisen and I thought he might have returned home by now.'

'No, constable, he said it was hardly worth while coming all this way back, so he said he was going fishing off the pier end. He said he'd stay there until it was time to open up at half past eight. He often gets up early to go sea-fishing, constable; he loves every minute of it. That's where you'll find him, sitting on the end of the pier with his fishing rod.'

'Oh, well, I need him urgently but can't reach him . . .'

'What's wrong, officer?' There was alarm in her voice.

I took a deep breath. 'You're going to laugh at this, Mrs Austin, but I'm locked in your shop! I can't get out,' and I explained how this terrible thing had happened.

She burst into laughter and I felt an utter fool. Finally, she said, 'Look, there's no need to worry. Look in Ray's desk, right-hand drawer, in an old toffee box. There's a spare set of keys with a bobbin attached. Use them, and pop them back through the letterbox when you've got out.'

'Thank you!' I breathed. 'Thank you. You don't know how relieved I am!'

'Then come back into the shop one day and tell me. I

work there too – there'll be a cup of tea for you, and I know my husband would love to meet you . . .' and she chuckled loudly as she replaced the telephone.

I did find those keys, and I did let myself out, then I tried to resume my patrol as if nothing had happened. But I reckoned the story would surface one day – so I'm telling it now, without exaggeration. I made firm friends of Mr and Mrs Austin, but I often wonder if Sergeant Blaketon ever knew about my lapse.

That morning, as I booked off duty, he asked, with a twinkle in his eyes, 'Is everything all right, Rhea?'

'Yes, all correct, sergeant,' I assured him.

2

O well for the sailor lad
That he sings on his boat in the bay.
Alfred, Lord Tennyson, 1809-92

To walk the early morning beat in Strensford is an enchanting experience. Such is the appeal of the harbourside and the beach at the dawn of a summer's day that holiday-makers and local residents alike stir themselves from their slumbers and journey to the sea, there to explore the coast and to witness the daily routine of the fishermen. These sturdy, hard-working men may begin their work at any hour of the day or night depending upon the timing of the tides. Sometimes they return to shore in the light of a new dawn, and sometimes they rise even before the sun to busy themselves about their boats or at the nearby fishmarket.

There are times when the undulating waters of the harbour are hidden beneath a floating, constantly moving platform of fishing boats. Men clad in thigh-length waders and thick, dark-blue jerseys known as gansers move from boat to boat with astonishing ease and confidence, while the boats themselves are moored both side by side and stern by prow. They form a solid, gently swaying platform which reaches midway across the water, and from many of them spirals of blue smoke rise from tiny chimneys as their motors idle with a strangely fluid sound. There is the scent too, the distinctive scent of the sea and of fish and fishing, a scent not unpleasant here on the quayside.

In the summer, some of the boats belong to the local fishermen, but others do come to Strensford as visitors. Some hail from English ports, others come from Scotland, Holland and Scandinavia, but they all seek the shoals of herring which visit Dogger Bank and inhabit the North Sea.

The visitors invariably live upon their boats, sleeping, eating and working within the spotless confines of their accommodation below deck. During their annual visit to Strensford, these ships are a combination of miniature floating homes, factories and fishmarkets. The men on board are dressed for combat both with the sea and with fish, for here you'll find sou'westers, gansers, thigh-length sea-boots and one-piece pale blue denim tops with long sleeves and no buttons.

And always, there is the ever-present scent of fish, the glistening fish scales, the huge boxes of cooling ice and buckets of fresh cleansing water. Cool wetness and fish seem to be inseparable, and in those days boxes of preserving ice were manufactured at local ice factories.

To witness the careful work-a-day preparations by this multinational fleet is fascinating. Daily they brave the wrath of the grey North Sea in boats which seem too small and flimsy when viewed from the staiths but which are sturdy enough to cope with their tough, thankless task.

It is this unique activity which so captivates the holiday-makers, and we policemen who then patrolled the town were privileged to see this routine during our normal duties. And in spite of seeing it time and time again, it never lost its appeal. Sea fishermen live in a self-contained world; it is a unique way of life which is an echo of the past. There was never any overt urgency in their behaviour, just a steady, methodical style born of generations of hard-working men whose chosen career faced nature at its most severe.

Sometimes at night or in the very early dark hours of the morning, the same fleet would position itself far out at sea to undertake its work. From the shore, it could be seen as a distant town of gently moving lights, all arranged in straight lines like formal streets. I've known motorists high on the moors be puzzled by the appearance of the 'mirage' of a new town out in the blackness of the night-time sea, but those are the lights by which these men work to drag from the deep their full nets of struggling fish. And, when the night's work is done, they will return to Strensford to unload and sell their catch, to prepare their boats and equipment for the following day and then to embark once again, depending not upon the passage of time but upon the sequence of high tides and a knowledge of the movements of the herring shoals, or the availability of whiting, cod and other fish.

Although visitors did sometimes join local boats for paid fishing trips, I never anticipated stepping on board any of them, either British or foreign.

But it did happen.

The first time was when I was on early duty, my beat taking me along the harbourside.

My 6.35 a.m. point was at the telephone kiosk in the Fish Market, and on this occasion there was a call for me.

'It's Stan in the office,' said the voice. 'I've a pleasant little job for you.'

'Fire away.' I took my notebook from my tunic pocket and opened its pages on the coinbox so I could write in it.

'It's from a Mrs Maureen McPherson.' He spoke slowly, allowing me time to take down his words. 'From Aberdeen,' and he gave me the address.

'Yes,' I said, having noted these details.

'Her son, Ian, is a crewman on the fishing boat *Waverley* – it's in our harbour all this week. It's registered in Aberdeen, you'll find it easily enough. We've got a request message for him – tell him that his mother rang. It's to say that his wife, Joan, has given birth to a baby boy. She's in the maternity hospital in Aberdeen, and both are doing well. Maybe he'll give his mother a call as soon as possible?'

'I'll be delighted,' I said. The delivery of these so-called 'request messages' was a task we often undertook for those people who did not have a telephone. On this occasion it was a pleasant message, but more often than not we had to deliver news of deaths or severe accidents. News of a happy birth was a very welcome change.

I went cheerfully about my task and soon found the fishing boat. It was moored midway along the harbourside and lay beyond a further three, well into the centre of the full harbour. All seemed at rest, for there was no obvious work going on.

I climbed down to the deck of the nearest boat and by stepping across other decks soon reached the *Waverley*. There was no one on deck, so I tapped on the cabin door, where I was greeted by a thick-set fisherman in the customary heavy navy-blue sweater. In his late forties, he oozed power and authority, a formidable man to cross, I guessed.

'Good morning,' I said as he opened the narrow door.

'Wha' is it?' There was more than a hint of suspicion in his gruff Scots voice. 'It's no' bother, is it?'

'No,' I said. 'It's good news. Is Ian McPherson below?'

'Aye.'

'Could I have a word with him?'

'Here?'

'Yes please.'

'He's busy, doon the galley, but Ah'll fetch him.'

I watched his broad back disappear below and waited until a younger man arrived. He was dark-haired and swarthy, if a little more slender than the previous one. He'd be about twenty-six years old but was almost a carbon-copy of the older man. He was powerful too, thick-set with a strong chin and deep chest. I reckoned he and his father could cope with any kind of 'bother' as they called it.

'Hello,' he said.

'Ian McPherson?'

'Aye. Ah'm Ian, that other was ma dad.'

'Oh, well. It's good news. I've got a message from your mother. It's to say you're a proud dad, Ian. A lovely baby boy, born in Aberdeen maternity hospital. Your wife and baby are both fine. I was asked to inform you. Oh, and you've got to ring your mother.'

His dark eyes misted at my news, and this was followed by the quivering of his bottom lip, both signs of a happy new father. This tough, stolid Scotsman was doing his best not to show any emotion, but he was losing the battle.

'Congratulations,' I said.

'Aye,' he wiped an eye with the rough sleeve of his ganser. 'Look, officer, come along doon. We'll need to celebrate de noo.'

It was rather early in the morning to be drinking, I thought, but I did not like to appear churlish in his moment of happiness, so I followed him downstairs into the tiny, cramped galley. It was spotlessly clean and tidy. I noticed the table was laid for five breakfasts, and as I reached the end of this tiny table, Ian shouted.

'Hey, fellers. Listen to this! Ah'm a dad, a new dad, a little lad, so we've got another crew member, heh?'

Four men rushed in, one of them still in pyjamas, and

they slapped him on the back, congratulated him and praised him. Then they turned to the man I'd first met and offered him their congratulations on being a new grandfather. I did likewise.

'Ah've fetched the constable doon for a celebration,' said the new father. 'Set him a place, Donal.'

One of them set a breakfast place at the end of the table and offered me a stool; I sat down, feeling a little bewildered by this turn of events, but Mr McPherson senior said, 'This is a family boat, constable. My lad and oor cousins, that's who we are. It's oors and oors alone. Noo we've a new man to grow in tae the business, and tha's good. Verra good. You'll be welcome to celebrate wi' us, seeing 'twas you who brought the good news. You'll take breakfast wi' us then?'

'I'll be delighted,' I said, wondering how I'd manage two breakfasts in one short morning. The hotel would have one ready when I returned around nine o'clock.

They busied themselves in the cramped little galley, and then a bottle of Scotch appeared. It was placed in the centre of the table, and six glistening cut glasses were positioned at each of the breakfast settings. Then, as if at some unseen signal, the whole crew of five settled around the table, the pyjama-clad cousin having dressed by this time.

Then Ian's father, whom I took to be the captain of this boat, surprised me by saying, 'Constable, we say grace de noo.'

And they did. Those five hard, rugged Scotsmen bowed their heads as Mr McPherson said grace.

Afterwards he poured a generous tipple of whisky into each glass, and we toasted the health of the new baby and his absent mother. At that, one of them left the table and brought the first course of the breakfast. It was porridge, unsweetened, thick and eaten with salt.

I stayed there too long; I drank too much of their whisky and ate far too much of their plain but wholesome breakfast, but I was pleased I'd eaten a Scots breakfast on board an immaculate fishing boat with such a caring family.

But the most memorable sight was of those five tough seamen with bowed heads meekly saying grace before they ate.

Another opportunity to go aboard a boat occurred when the daughter of the proprietor of our digs, the Breckdale Private Hotel, asked if I could obtain a clog for her. Anne, tall, pretty and blonde, asked me at lunchtime one day.

'A clog?' I must have sounded surprised.

'Yes, a real clog, a Dutchman's clog, one of those wooden ones. I'd love one of those.'

'Why do you want a clog?' I asked.

'To bring good luck,' she answered. 'A real clog, as worn by a Dutch person, brings good luck.'

I'd never heard of this superstition. I knew that fisherfolk the world over were highly superstitious – the local ones, for example, believed that if the family kept a black cat, it would ensure the safe return from sea of the man-of-the-house. But once at sea, the word 'cat' had never to be mentioned because it would bring ill fortune, although some felt it sensible to keep a black cat on board. In the event of a shipwreck, this was first to be rescued.

Other forbidden words included *drowning*, *witch*, *death*, *pig*, *dog*, *rabbit* and *rat*, as well as references to clergymen and words for various parts of the human body!

If, on their way to their boat, the fishermen met either a cross-eyed person, a woman wearing a white apron, a clergyman or a hare, there was nothing that could be done to avert a sea-faring disaster other than to turn around and go home. There is still a belief that sea-birds contain the souls of the drowned and that their cries are the cries of the dead who are warning the living against the storms and hidden dangers.

But I knew nothing about clogs bringing good luck. A similar superstition was that if a person carried a fisherman's sea-boots to him, they should always be borne under the arm and not over the shoulder, for fear of bringing bad luck. Another belief in some places was that old shoes should be thrown after boats as they left port as a means of either bringing good fortune or, I suggest, getting rid of old shoes!

So far as I know, Dutchmen's clogs did not enter this little world of ancient beliefs, but because of Anne's sincere request I promised to do my best to acquire one for her. So, whenever I worked a harbourside beat, I examined from a distance the decks of the Dutch fleet, albeit never really expecting to see a discarded clog.

But one morning, about 6.15 a.m., I espied the very thing. It was a large, yellow-painted clog made of wood, with the familiar upturned toe, and it looked exactly right for Anne. It looked huge from where I was standing on the staith, but it was lying on the prow of a Dutch fishing boat, resting on a pile of coiled rope as the fishermen busied themselves in preparation for sailing.

My heart leaped at the sight. I'd never really expected to find Anne's treasure, but there it was, and it looked like a cast-off because it had a hole in the sole. The hole was about the size of a half-crown, well over an inch across, and I wondered if clogs were re-soled like shoes. If so, how was it done? Then I wondered if it was a true cast-off or whether it was there to be thrown for good luck, after some departing vessel in times to come? Or perhaps it would be thrown overboard as rubbish?

But I could not let this opportunity pass without making some effort to obtain that clog, even if it meant buying it as a present. The first problem was how to gain legitimate possession of it.

Possession would then present the second problem, i.e. how to convey it back to Anne via the police station while I was dressed in full police uniform. This was even more of a problem because the eagle-eyed Sergeant Blaketon was on duty this morning.

But first things first. I would make an effort to get my hands on that clog. I knew the boat was preparing to sail so I dared not wait until the end of my first period of patrolling, and I was due back at the police station at 9 a.m. to report 'off duty' for my refreshment break. I had to get that clog immediately so I could hand it to Anne when I arrived at the hotel for breakfast. I stared at it for a long time as I debated the best course of action. I know that my mesmeric stance caused many early-strolling visitors to peer over the harbour rails, probably wondering why the constabulary was paying so much attention to a Dutch fishing boat.

In the midst of my thoughts, a man emerged from the cabin. He noticed me, and I waved my hands to indicate that I wished to speak with him, but he just waved back and went about his work. I decided I must be bold so I descended the steep stone steps which led down the side of the harbour wall to the level of the boats. I crossed one or two swaying decks before I arrived at the Dutch boat. The man was busy with some fishing nets.

'Good morning,' I said, realizing I was speaking loudly as one tends to do when addressing foreigners.

'Hooye morhen,' I think he replied, but I could see the worried look on his face.

It was then that I realized that in other countries the relationship between the police and the public wasn't quite the same as that which existed between the British bobby and his public. By arriving on his boat without permission, I had probably put the fear of God into this poor fellow. He probably thought I was going to impound his vessel, arrest his crew or arrange a Customs search.

'Do you speak English?' I asked.

He shook his head and continued to wear a very harassed expression. The last thing I wanted was to frighten him, and it did cross my mind that, if I antagonized him too greatly, I might have to swim back to the police station.

'Does anyone on board speak English?' I tried.

He raised a finger as if in understanding and disappeared below; I could hear a jabbering of tongues and then five men emerged. My heart sank into my boots. I'd done it now . . . I had no chance against five powerful Dutchmen.

'Good morning.' I tried the Englishman's traditional approach, the one which seems to be used in any situation.

It brought no reply. They stood and stared at me in the way that cows stand and stare at those who picnic in their fields.

'Does anyone speak English?' I spoke slowly now, if a little too loudly, my voice rising in pitch as if to betray my fears.

'*Ja*,' said one of them after a long pause. 'I spik Engles.'

'Ah,' I breathed a sigh of relief. Now for my strange proposition.

'My-girl-friend,' I said slowly, thinking the true relationship would be too difficult to explain. 'She-wants-a-clog-to-keep-for-good-luck,' and I pointed to the clog I'd earmarked.

'Clog?' asked the English-speaker. 'Schoenen?'

I smiled and nodded furiously, then continued very slowly. 'Yes, she-believes-that-a-clog-like-that-brings-good-fortune-to-her. She-has-asked-me-to-find-a-clog-for-her. I-saw-that-clog-and-thought-it-might-not-be-wanted . . .'

'Ah!' beamed the English-speaking fellow. 'I understand. She likes charm, hey? A charm? The clog, it will be a charm for her? For luck? She want this charm?'

'*Ja*,' I tried, and once more nodded furiously, hoping the reason for my presence would be fully understood.

Now they were all smiling and laughing, and I sensed a deep feeling of relief among them.

'Yes,' said the English-speaker. 'Yes, she can have the clog.'

He gabbled something at the others in his own tongue, and they all smiled and laughed, and I knew how they felt. Relief swept across them and, I must admit, across me.

'Come,' said my new friend. 'Down below, with us. For breakfast? I will get you the clog now.'

And so I joined them all below deck, where I enjoyed a large mug of coffee in their spotless galley. They presented me with the worn-out clog, and once they discovered I was friendly, I found out they could all speak a smattering of English.

Soon afterwards, I left with the huge clog. It must have been a size 12, and I now had the problem of hiding it for the next couple of hours or so, as I smuggled it back to Anne via the police station. I couldn't take it directly to her because the hotel was a long way off my present beat, and to be found absent from one's beat was to risk a disciplinary charge, especially with Sergeant Blaketon on duty.

My cape provided the answer. When on patrol, even on summer days, we carried our voluminous capes by folding them flat into several folds and then slinging them over our shoulders. They were ideal waterproof garments, and when worn about our bodies, they also concealed a great deal. I've known policemen do their wives' shopping at times, and then smuggle it home beneath their flowing capes; they can hide fish-and-chips at supper time, Christmas presents at Christmas time, and I once knew a constable who smuggled a custard pie home beneath his cape. So, by draping my cape around my shoulders, I would be able to conceal the large, wooden clog from prying eyes.

Although it wasn't raining and although it wasn't particularly chilly that morning, I completed the remainder of the first half of my patrol with my cape concealing the clog. I carried the clog in one hand, with my thumb tucked beneath the button of my breast pocket for support, and none of the passing citizens seemed to think it odd that I should be dressed for rain.

I entered the police station to book off and decided I would make a quick dash to the counter and poke my head through the enquiry hatch without entering the office. I would call, 'PC Rhea, booking off, refreshment break,' and then vanish before anyone could forestall my dash from the building or ask silly questions.

But I hadn't bargained for Sergeant Blaketon.

He saw me before I saw him, and called out, 'Rhea, just a minute!'

My heart sank. Now I had to enter the office, and there he was, with his back to the fireplace, beaming almost villainously as I walked in. The office man, a senior constable called Stan who was local to Strensford, was seated on a tall stool at the counter, and he flashed me a brief but sympathetic smile.

'Ah, Rhea,' Sergeant Blaketon said. 'Anything to report from No. 1 Beat this morning?'

'No, sergeant,' I smiled. 'All correct. I'm just heading for breakfast.'

'No trouble on the Dutch fishing boats then?'

'Trouble, sergeant?' I wondered how much he knew, or

how much he had seen. I had not noticed him on the quayside.

'Trouble, Rhea. Bother. Mayhem. That sort of thing, the sort of thing that might require the presence of a constable. Nothing like that, was there? Nothing to report?'

The crafty character must have seen me on the deck of that boat, or else he'd been talking to someone else who had seen me. I thought I'd string him along to see what he was aiming at.

'No, sergeant.' I decided that brief answers were the best.

'Oh, I just wondered, I heard that a young constable had been seen on board a Dutch fishing boat this morning. That's your beat, so I wondered if it might have been trouble of some kind.'

'No, sergeant,' I said, and I knew I was blushing by this time. 'No trouble.'

'It was you, though, wasn't it, Rhea?' he persisted.

'I did go on board for a chat, sergeant, just a friendly chat. Passing the time of day, you know.'

'Ah!' he beamed. 'So my information was correct. But there was no trouble, no complaints, no problems?'

'None at all, sergeant.'

'Hmm. Well, that's all right then. So long as there is no trouble. So you'll be off for your breakfast then?'

'Yes, sergeant, I must be off. The hotel likes us to be on time . . .'

'Not raining on your beat, was it? Or cold?'

I thought fast. He was moving to the subject of my cape now, so I smiled and said, 'It was a bit chilly, sergeant, a breeze off the sea, you know. It can blow a bit chilly on the harbourside at dawn.'

'Yes, so it can.' He paused, and at that precise moment the telephone rang. The office constable answered it and said, 'Sergeant, it's for you. The Superintendent.'

As he moved to take the call, Sergeant Blaketon looked at me as if he was going to say something, but already I was moving towards the door. I bolted out of the office and was hurrying towards the exit of the police station as I heard Sergeant Blaketon in an animated conversation with the Superintendent. I'd been saved literally in the nick of time.

But before I reached the door, a voice halted me. It was Stan, the PC on office duty.

'Outside, quick,' he said as he bustled me out of the station.

'What's the matter, Stan?' I almost shouted.

'Have you got a bloody clog off that boat?' he asked me, eyeing the bulky shape beneath my cape.

'Yes,' I said. 'Why? It was given to me.'

He laughed. 'Then get to hell out of here, and quick! He was after it, he wanted it, that bloody sergeant you've brought over from Ashfordly. He noticed it there last night but there was no one about to ask, so he was going to have a word with the skipper this morning. It seems his wife has always wanted a genuine Dutch clog to put on her mantelpiece, but I can't think why . . . Anyway, it had gone by the time he got down to the harbourside this morning . . .'

'I'm going!' I said, and I almost ran to the hotel. Anne was delighted, and I got a double helping of sausages that morning.

The next time I boarded a fishing vessel occurred after a spate of shop-breakings in Strensford. In those days, the crime of breaking into shop premises to steal goods was popularly known as shop-breaking, but since 1968 all such 'break and entry' offences have been grouped together under the single heading of *burglary*.

Whenever we paraded for a night shift during that short sojourn at the seaside, we were reminded that someone, probably a lone operator, was breaking into shops all over the town. The stolen property was not particularly valuable, like cameras or radio sets, nor was it particularly useful, like food or clothing. Most of the attacked premises were the tourist-souvenir type of shop, selling cheap oddments such as jewellery, watches, ornaments and knick-knacks of the kind no truly discerning visitor would take home. They were all close to the harbourside too.

On one occasion, for example, three flying ducks in plaster were taken, and we did wonder if the thief ran a boarding house. Almost all the boarding houses in Strensford at that time had plaster ducks flying up their walls, and some had gnomes in their gardens.

The CID reckoned the breaker was a youth, perhaps a visitor to one of the holiday camps or caravan sites, but whoever he was, he always escaped. Their reckoning was based partly on the fact that he must be slim and agile to be able to wriggle through some of the skylights which were his chief source of entry, and another part of their logic was that the mediocre stuff he stole would hardly appeal to an adult. It would certainly not appeal to a handler of stolen goods or an antique-dealer.

Throughout those warm summer nights, therefore, the uniform branch maintained observations upon the streets, but we never caught our man.

More shops were raided, more junk was stolen and eventually the Chamber of Trade, and the *Strensford Times*, began to ask what the police were doing about the sudden and unwarranted major crime wave. The local superintendent had the sense to issue a statement to the paper: 'We are maintaining observations and are utilizing all available manpower in an attempt to curb this seasonal outbreak of crime. We believe it is the work of visiting criminals.'

This series of shopbreakings occurred long before the days of collators who assembled and disseminated crime-beating information, and long before the police had computers, which could assess crime intelligence. As I read the Occurrence Book each day, however, I did become aware that the shops were raided on the same nights that we received calls from some sleepy residents that a horse was loose and roaming the streets. It had been heard several times in the dead of night, but no one had actually seen the horse. There developed a theory that the shop-breaker was a horseman and that he carefully studied the movements of the police before committing his crimes.

In an attempt to gain more information, I took several Occurrence Books, which were logs of all daily events, and checked them meticulously for (a) calls about horses loose at night in Strensford and (b) shop-breakings which occurred around the same time. And a pattern did emerge. The breaks were occurring around two o'clock in the morning, the very time the policemen went into the station for their mid-shift break – this made it seem they *were* being observed. Furthermore, all the occasions when the horse had been reported were around the same mid-shift time.

Then, by one of those strokes of fortune by which great crimes are solved, I had to compile a list of the times of high tides for the information of Force Headquarters – someone over there was compiling a Spring Tide Early Warning System. As I listed the times known to Strensford, I suddenly wondered whether the raids could be linked with tidal times. I was really thinking of the swing bridge across the harbour which opened at times of high tide; high tides occurred twice a day, with about twelve hours in between each high water. I did wonder if our horse-riding villain came across that bridge into town, so I carried out my survey over several months.

To cut a long story short, I did not voice my opinions to anyone else but decided to carry out a spell of observations whenever my night duty coincided with a high tide which occurred around 2 a.m. The tide was almost full for some time both before and after the official high-tide time; this meant there was often full water while the policemen were having their mid-shift meals . . . and that meant the fishing boats were under preparation for sailing. My mind was working fast.

'Sergeant,' I spoke to Sergeant Blaketon at the beginning of one night shift. 'Can I work a harbourside beat tonight but take my break later than normal, say 3 a.m.?'

'Why, Rhea? What are you scheming now?'

I was in two minds not to tell him, but I felt he would not grant this odd request without knowing the story, and so, in the peace of the sergeant's office, I explained. To give him credit, he did listen.

'Right,' he said. 'Do it. And I'll be there too. We'll see this out together, Rhea. We'll show these townies that us country coppers can arrest their shop-breakers!'

We arranged to meet at 1.45 a.m., and together we would seek a place of concealment from where we could overlook the swing bridge, the harbourside and quays, the herring boats and the main thoroughfares into town.

That night, high tide was at 2.33 a.m., and as we watched from an alley overlooking the harbour, we could see the lights of the boats as their crews were preparing to sail to the herring grounds. And then we saw him.

A tall, lithe young man left the shadows of the harbourside and made his noisy way into town. A Dutchman, in clogs. Clip-clopping into town.

'There's the horse, sergeant!' I hissed at him.

'Where, Rhea?'

'The clogs!' I snapped. 'They sound like a horse walking at night, when the streets are empty. This is our breaker, a Dutch seaman!'

'Right, we need to catch him with the evidence. Wait here until he comes back with his loot.'

That was true. We had no evidence yet, certainly not enough to convict him, and so we simply waited and then, some forty minutes later, we heard the clip-clop of his return journey.

'Nice work, Rhea,' beamed Sergeant Blaketon. 'You'll get high praise for this one. Now, when he's past us on the way to his ship, we go and nab him. Nab him *before* he gets back to his boat – I'm not sure what the law is about arresting foreign nationals on board their own ships. But the arrest is yours, so do it on British soil.'

But as the tall, young Dutchman passed us with a carrier bag full of his ill-gotten gains, he heard our movements. He started to run. Even in those clumsy clogs, he covered the ground at a remarkable speed, and he sounded like a horse at full gallop. I was sure we'd get more complaints about galloping horses, but right now Blaketon and I were hard on his heels.

The Dutchman beat us to his ship. He slithered down a harbourside ladder and reached his boat as we reached the harbour's edge. Then, before our very eyes, he threw the offending bag into the harbour, where it sank immediately.

'Our bloody evidence!' snapped Sergeant Blaketon.

But the youth was doing something even worse. As Sergeant Blaketon stood and watched, he removed both his clogs and threw them one by one over the side of the boat. Each landed with a splash. One filled with water and sank, while the other sailed away into the darkness.

'He's thrown his clogs away!' gasped Sergeant Blaketon.

I felt very sorry for poor Oscar Blaketon at that point, for we could not prove our case. But I do know that someone from CID had a word with the captain, and all the shops, save the final one, had their goods returned. The sixteen-year-old boy was a kleptomaniac. There was no prosecution because of international complications but the shop-breakings did come to an end. And so did reports of horses galloping through Strensford at night.

But Sergeant Blaketon still hasn't obtained a real Dutch clog for his mantelpiece.

3

He that is robbed not wanting what is stolen,
Let him not know it, and he's not robb'd at all.
William Shakespeare, 1564-1616

When patrolling the quiet streets of Strensford during
those warm summer nights, my mind turned frequently to
the initial police training course I had undergone. I recalled
the essence of lectures about all manner of fascinating
things, and one of the subjects was crime. It was a subject
which intrigued all the students, and some went on to
become clever detectives.

One aspect of crime which was discussed at length was
that which is known in Latin as *mens rea*. It is a curious
phrase which refers to the state of mind of a criminal, his
criminal intent in other words. It is that guilty or
blameworthy state of mind during which crimes are
committed. During our lectures, we were given questions
which endeavoured to show us the difference between an
intent and an *attempt* to commit crime. We were told that a
person's criminal intent was rarely punishable – a man can
intend to commit burglary, rape or murder, but the mere
intention to do such a thing, however serious, is not in
itself a crime. On the other hand, at attempt to commit a
crime is illegal.

We wondered if a person could be guilty of an attempted
larceny when it was impossible to commit the full crime.

One example of this is a pickpocket who dips his hand into a man's pocket to steal a wallet, but the pocket is empty. Thus he cannot complete his intended crime. So is he guilty of attempted larceny? If the pocket had contained a wallet, then most certainly the attempt could be completed, if not the full crime . . .

Many academic questions of this kind were discussed, and it is fair to say that few of us ever dreamed we would be confronted with real examples of this kind of legal puzzle. In the world of practical policing, crimes were committed, criminals were arrested and proceedings were taken. The academic side of things was left to the lawyers.

At least that's what I thought until I came across Hedda Flynn.

Although my time in Strensford was short and somewhat fragmented, due to the shifts I worked, I did begin to recognize those whom I saw regularly. In the main, they were local people going about their business or pleasure in their small and charming town. Hedda Flynn was such a person. He caught my attention when I noticed he was beginning to loiter around the entrance to St Patrick's Roman Catholic Church and that he chose to do so at a time the local churches were experiencing a spate of offertory box thefts.

Several boxes had been broken into during the early summer months, the technique being by the simple medium of using what police described as a 'blunt instrument' to force open the lids. This was probably a screwdriver. The cash contents, the amount of which was invariably unknown, were stolen. Although these crimes were comparatively minor, they did present problems.

No community, whether in a town or a village, likes its church to be attacked in any way, and these crimes were considered very distasteful. It was felt they were the work of a travelling vagrant, because none of the boxes contained a large amount. The task of forcing the wooden lids and removing the contents would often result in the theft of only a few shillings, hardly a major crime.

Some good Christians argued that if the thief was so poor that the funds within the offertory boxes were vital to his existence, why not let him take them? After all, wasn't the Church there to provide for the poor? If the fellow had asked the priest or vicar for some money, it would probably have been given. This was an argument which did not impress the police. In their books a crime was a crime, whatever the reason for its commission.

As a form of crime prevention, we toured all the churches and chapels within our Division and suggested to their priests, vicars and ministers that they make their offertory boxes more substantial and secure. We even suggested they enclose them within the walls of their churches or make them of metal, then cement them into the floor. Some did this.

One who did not follow our advice was Monsignor Joseph O'Flaherty of St Patrick's Roman Catholic Church, and it was his offertory box which I suspected was an object of great interest to Hedda Flynn.

There was a time when I considered arresting Hedda under the Vagrancy Act of 1824, for that quaint old statute created an offence of being a suspected person or reputed thief loitering with intent to commit a crime. Certainly, Hedda had undertaken a good deal of loitering, usually around lunch-time, but his intentions were unknown. There was no evidence that he intended to commit a crime, nor could he be described as either a suspected person or a reputed thief. The law lays down quite specifically what is meant by 'suspected person', and Hedda's behaviour had not quite lifted him into that category. In fact, he was a very decent fellow.

Having noticed him once or twice, I carried out my own
discreet enquiries and learned he was a married man with
two small children. He worked behind the counter of a
gentlemen's clothes shop in Strensford for what was
probably a pittance, and he would be about thirty-five
years old. He was a small, dark man whose own clothes
hung from him; they appeared to be several sizes too large,
and I guessed that, as a child, his mother had always
bought him clothes which were too large, so that he could
grow into them. I reckoned he never had grown into them
but that he still hoped he would.

His thin, sallow face with its bushy eyebrows and dark
troubled eyes gave him the appearance of a haunted man,
and it was clear something was troubling him. Was he a
lapsed Catholic who wanted to return to the faith?

On the other hand, I wondered if his conscience was
troubling him. I wondered if he was fiddling the till at
work, or whether he had another woman in tow, or, of
course, whether he was the offertory box thief who was
plaguing the district.

I decided to speak to Monsignor O'Flaherty about
Hedda and about the risks to his offertory box. I had seen
the box in question – it was a simple wooden container
screwed to a table at the back of the church, and it would
be a simple matter to force the lid with a screwdriver and
remove its meagre contents.

I knocked on the door of the presbytery and was admitted
by the priest's housekeeper, who showed me to a study
littered with books and watercolours. Some stood on the
floor and others filled every possible space on the wall. I
waited, intrigued by the smell of the place and its wonderful
array of books and paintings.

The Monsignor came in, smiling and happy. He was

dressed in a clerical grey suit with a carnation in his buttonhole. He was a very rounded man with a rosy red face and thinning grey hair above very bright and twinkling blue eyes. He looked like a man who enjoyed life.

'Ah!' he smiled. ''Tis the law. You'll be having a drink then?'

'Good morning, Monsignor,' I said. 'I'd like a coffee please.'

'Coffee, is it? I was thinking of something more congenial, like a dram of the morning dew? So is it coffee or whisky, or perhaps both?'

'Just coffee, Monsignor. I'm on duty.'

'So it's official, then? You're not coming to see me about your spiritual welfare or to get married or something? Haven't I seen you at Mass?'

'Yes, but this is police work.'

'Then sit yourself down, son, and I'll arrange the coffee. Sugar? Milk?''

I requested both, and the tray soon appeared with coffee for us both and a glass of his 'wee dram'. While we drank them, he learned my name and something of my own family background. The introductions and pleasantries over, we turned to the purpose of my visit.

I began with the attacks on offertory boxes and put forward various suggestions for making them less vulnerable to thieves. He listened attentively and said he had seen reports in the *Strensford Gazette* about the other attacks.

'But, you see, I always make sure there is a collection plate on the table at the back of the church, close to the door. And in that plate, there is always a few coins; either the faithful put them there or I do, so if a thief does come, he'll grab that money and he'll leave the box alone. Now, I don't mind him taking those loose coins, and indeed, I'll seldom know whether he has or not, will I? It's only

copper, but it could be food for a starving man. And our
offertory box has never been forced open.'

I admired the sheer logic of this and now recalled the
large wooden collection plate which was always on the
table near the main door. It often had a half crown or a
florin in it, with an assortment of smaller coins, such as a
sixpence and one or two pennies.

'There is something else, Monsignor.' I emptied my
coffee cup and he refilled it from the percolator.

'Go on.'

I told him about Hedda Flynn and my suspicions. He
listened and then smiled in understanding.

'Hedda is a good man,' he said. 'A very good man, a
faithful member of my congregation and as honest as the
day is long. He would never do anything wrong to anyone,
let alone steal from the church.'

'He does linger about the back of the church.' I had
come across this very Christian attitude many times before
but police officers are cynical and distrustful. 'I feel I ought
to warn you of his activities.'

'Thanks anyway, constable, but I know Hedda. And I
might add, I know his wife too. Now there's a holy woman.
Mass at half-seven every morning. Benediction twice a
week. Generous to the church, generous to a fault she is.
Wonderful wife for Hedda, wonderful mother for her
family. A church helper, too. She does the flowers for the
altar, cleans the church – she's a saint, constable, a true
saint. Hedda is a very lucky man, very lucky.'

I felt I had fulfilled my purpose. I had drawn his atten-
tion to the risks and I had even named a suspect. Perhaps
I had been wrong to do the latter, for it was clear that the
Monsignor thought a lot about the Flynn family, although
I did wonder why, if Hedda was such a good Catholic, he
hung around the back of the church at lunch-time rather

than enter to kneel and pray. But it was time to go.

Before I left, Monsignor O'Flaherty showed me some of his books and explained that he collected watercolours by the local artist Scott Hodgson, hence his massive assortment of his, and other artists', works.

Within a week, two more offertory boxes had been broken into, each in parish churches in nearby moorland villages, and even I felt that Hedda could not be responsible for those crimes. He didn't have a car, and I knew he had been at work during the material times. But he continued to hang around the back of St Patrick's . . .

Then came the day I decided to do something positive. It happened because late one Friday afternoon I chanced to be walking past the main door of the church, in full uniform, just as the small, untidy figure of Hedda was vanishing inside. He had not seen me, and so I crossed the street and climbed the wide and steep flight of steps up to the entrance.

I must admit that my heart was beating; I wondered if I was about to arrest a thief actually in the act of committing his crime and found myself tiptoeing across the threshold and into the interior of the large building with its subdued lighting and hushed atmosphere. I had to find out what he was up to.

The large, ribbed door was open, as it always was during the daytime hours, and I sneaked inside. I removed my uniform cap and found myself in the shadows of the rearmost part of the church, my soft-soled boots making no sound on the marble floor. And I could see Hedda at the table which bore the offertory box. He stood with his head bowed in the silence of the empty church. The box had not been touched, but he was gazing down upon it, both hands resting on the table.

I did not know what to do. He had committed no crime,

not yet. I waited. He stood there, almost as if in prayer, and then turned to leave. He moved quickly, almost abruptly, and suddenly found himself face to face with me, my uniform buttons catching the multi-coloured lights of the stained glass windows.

'Oh, Holy Mother of God, you gave me a fright, so you did, standing there like that,' he said.

'What are you doing, Mr Flynn?' I asked.

'Doing, officer? Nothing. I came to say a prayer or two, that's all. Why should that interest the police?' There was bravado in his voice, but I could hear the tremors as he spoke.

'Mr Flynn. We have been having a lot of cash stolen from offertory boxes in recent weeks. We're keeping our eyes open for the thief . . .'

'My God, you don't think I'm the thief! Oh, Jesus, now that is terrible. Really terrible . . . No, I'm no thief, sir, never in a million years. I mean, look, the box has not been touched . . .'

'Then what were you doing?' I had to press home my questions now. 'If you were praying, why weren't you kneeling in one of the pews?'

He hung his head, and I saw tears in his eyes.

His small, drawn face had a haunted look, a desperate look which I could see clearly now that I was so close to him. It did not take a clever person to realize that he was sorely troubled in some way. I still wondered if he had intended to break into the offertory box and whether his strong faith, coupled with the atmosphere of the church surroundings, had defeated him.

'I need to talk to someone,' he said, looking around, but we were alone in the vast emptiness of the church. 'I wanted to talk to Monsignor but he thinks such a lot of Teresa.'

'Teresa?' I asked, hoping my voice sounded gentle and encouraging.

'My wife,' he said, wiping his eyes roughly with his sleeve. 'She's a . . . well, they say she's a good, holy woman, you see, but . . .'

'Go on,' I spoke softly now, cognizant of the atmosphere in which we stood and increasingly aware that he was about to unburden himself of a massive problem of some kind. And now I was sure he was no thief.

'Well, you're a Catholic. I've seen you at Mass,' he said. 'So that makes it easier, you'll understand what I'm saying. I must talk to someone, I'm getting desperate . . .'

I wondered about moving outside but realized the church probably provided the best surroundings for whatever he wished to say. I smiled at him and said, 'Well, Mr Flynn, here I am, and I am very happy to listen to you.'

He told me that he received £15.17s.6d weekly as wages from his work at the clothes shop, with an annual bonus paid at Christmas which came to around £30. He said it was just enough to live on – he could not afford luxuries or holidays, but because he could buy his clothes at reduced prices, he could manage to support his wife and his family.

'But, you see, constable, I give Teresa all my wages, except for the 17s.6d. I keep that for myself – I like an occasional drink, and sometimes I take her to the pictures. She gets the £15, and we use the bonus for Christmas presents.'

'Go on,' I said.

'Well, as I said, she is a good Catholic woman, a very good one. In fact she's besotted with her religion. It's become a mania . . .'

'How do you mean, a mania?'

'Well, I give her my wages and I've found out she's not been paying the household bills – you know, food, rent, rates, heating, that sort of thing. I've discovered that for nearly three months now she's not paid anyone. I've had the grocer on to me – that's how I found out, and she's run a big bill up at the Co-Op. The Electricity Board is shouting for payment, and others too.'

'So what's she been doing with the money?'

'She's donated it all to the church, constable. Here, to this church. I found out that she comes on a Friday afternoon, straight after I've given her the money over lunch, and she's been putting it all into this offertory box. All the housekeeping. £15! Damn it, it's hard enough to find five bob every week for the collection, but to give the lot, my entire income . . .'

'You've mentioned it to her?'

'Yes, of course.' Tears were streaming down his face now.

'And what does she say?' I asked.

'She says the Lord will provide.'

'Can't you explain that the system doesn't work like that? Surely she knows you must give according to your means, not give all your income!'

'I've tried, so Lord help me, I've tried. But it's no good, she's gone off her head, to be sure. I've tried keeping some money back, but she accuses me of failing in my duty as a husband and demands the correct amount of housekeeping. I've always given her it, always, with never a quibble and no trouble till now. I mean, am I within my rights to withhold the housekeeping from her?'

'She must have something to spend on the family,' I said. 'But you could pay the grocery bills and so on.'

'She insists that I give her the money, but whatever I give her, she pushes into this box and says the Lord will provide! She has absolute faith in her religion, and cannot see doubt anywhere. She maintains that if we provide the church with money, the Lord will provide us with all we need. I can get no sense out of her.'

'I think a word with the Monsignor is called for,' I decided.

'He thinks she is wonderful, such a supporter of his church. I don't think he'll understand.'

'He will if he knows the truth. I think he'll listen to me,' I said with confidence. 'Come on, we'll both go.'

He followed me like a small dog, and I could well see him being dominated by his fanatical wife. We arrived at the presbytery, where the round and happy priest greeted us both, albeit with some surprise on his face due to memories of our recent and previous meeting, and my earlier suspicions of Hedda Flynn.

We had a cup of tea because it was Monsignor's teatime, and he listened to me while pursing his lips and looking solemnly at Hedda Flynn. When I'd finished, Monsignor addressed the worried Hedda.

'Is this all true then, Hedda my boy?'

'Yes, Monsignor,' he said. 'The constable thought it best if I came to you, although the Lord knows what we can do about her.'

'She's smitten with the faith, so she is,' smiled the priest. 'And terrible it is when folks get like that. Now, if we – or if I – tell her she's doing wrong, that she's sinning even or misbehaving in the sight of God, she might go all to pieces, eh? We might lose her all together. She won't understand at all. If she's so smitten, we'd be playing with dangerous emotions, so I think we'll leave her to her own devices – but we'll be cunning with it,' he added with a smile.

'But Monsignor,' I protested on behalf of Hedda Flynn. 'You can't let her go on giving *all* the family income to the church . . .'

His eyes flashed, albeit with understanding. 'I can, constable, I can, and I will. But I can give it all back to Hedda, not to Teresa.'

He stood up and went to a safe behind a painting on the wall, unlocked it and handed a roll of notes to Hedda.

'Here you are, Hedda Flynn. I'd been wondering where these huge amounts were coming from, and one day I saw Teresa stuffing the money into the box. I didn't think she could afford all this but didn't like to offend her or you by questioning your generosity. Now I know the truth, and it's your money. So take it. And now, you must continue to let her think she's doing the right thing – it'll keep the peace at home, eh? Let her put the money into the box, and then, every Friday, you come around at tea-time, and I'll give it back to you. How's that?'

'Oh, thank you, Father. Thank you,' beamed the happy fellow. 'Now I can pay all my bills . . . yes, I'll do what you say. But isn't that being deceitful? Isn't it unfair to Teresa to deceive her in this way?'

'I think the constable will agree I'm committing no crime by breaking into my own offertory box to give you your own money back. So just tell Teresa that the Lord is providing as she believes He will, and let it rest there,' suggested the Monsignor. 'Don't try to explain. Let this thing work itself out.'

And I agreed. I was pleased Hedda wasn't the thief, and later I saw Teresa walking with a saintly air about her, believing the Lord was providing all her family needs.

We never did catch the other person who was raiding the offertory boxes. I can only hope it was someone whose need was as genuine and as great as that of Hedda Flynn.

Another man with a theft problem was Rugby-player Ted Donaldson, a strapping local butcher who stood six foot six inches tall and who weighed seventeen stone. His worry caused my mind to return to my training school lectures and to problems of criminal intent, or *mens rea* as legal men prefer to call it.

'Gotta minute, officer?' He approached me as I stood beside the telephone kiosk in Strensford's bustling fishmarket.

'Yes,' I said, wondering why this massive fellow wore such a worried look.

'You might have to arrest me,' he said, and I must admit it was a thought that did not appeal to me, even if he was currently very docile and submissive.

'Why, have you done something wrong?' I asked.

'Dunno,' he said, and with that he produced a brown leather wallet from his jacket pocket. It was the type many men carried, the sort which could be bought at most chain stores. Then he produced another identical one and showed me them both, weighing one in each of his massive hands.

'Identical, aren't they?' he said, and I nodded.

'So, what's the problem?' I put to him.

'You've not had a report of a robbery with violence, have you?' he asked. 'You chaps are not looking for a bloke like me?'

'No,' I said. 'Should we be looking for somebody like you?'

'Bloody funny,' he said. 'Well, I'd better tell the story.'

He reminded me that the summer season in Strensford could attract some unsavoury characters, and in recent summers there had been a spate of hit-and-run pickpockets, handbag snatches and portable radio thefts. Teams of thieves would operate together, preying on wandering folks when they least expected it. Their technique was simple. In the crowds of a busy holiday resort, they would jostle a holiday-maker, and in the ensuing bustle and uncertainty they would relieve a man of his wallet, a woman of her handbag or a youngster of anything he or she carried – portable radios and cameras were popular targets. It was with such crimes in mind that uniformed police officers patrolled the crowded areas.

'Well,' said Ted. 'I'm a big bloke but two or three of 'em could have a go at me. Anyway, yesterday, I had some money to pay a bill for my father. Cash it was. I had £150 in my wallet and was aware of those villains. I reckoned they wouldn't really have a go at me . . . but, well . . .' He paused.

'They did?' I prompted.

'I thought they did,' he said, licking his lips.

'Thought? What do you mean?'

'Well, there was I, minding my own business and walking through the crowds along by the Amusements, when these two slobs knocked into me and nearly bowled me over. Running like hell, they were, Well, I nearly fell or tripped or something. Anyway, the minute I got my balance, I felt my pocket – and my wallet had gone.'

'And you're a Rugby player of some note in this town?' I could visualize the following sequence of events.

'Yeh, well, I'm not one for letting things like that go unchallenged, in a manner of speaking. So I set off after them and caught the one who'd knocked me.'

'And?'

'Well, there was a lot of hassle and shouting when I brought him down – with a good tackle, mind – and I shouted something like "My wallet!" I shouted a lot more besides I might add, so he might not have heard everything clearly . . . Well, he stuttered and stammered and gave me this.' He showed me one of the brown wallets. 'Then, like a bloody snake, he wriggled free and was off. Like lightning, he was. He vanished into the crowd.'

'But you'd got your wallet back?'

'No,' he said. 'That's the problem. When I opened this one, I found it had no money inside and thought they'd cleaned me out. They'd been quick, I thought, but when I got home my own wallet was on my dressing-table.'

'Full of money?'

'Full of money,' he said, licking his lips again. 'So this one wasn't mine. It looks like mine, but well, I didn't look at it closely at that time, what with all the hassle. So those lads hadn't robbed me. They'd just been a bit rough and careless as they ran through the crowd.'

'So you've robbed that youth of his wallet?' I said.

'Yes, I have, haven't I?' and he passed the slim, empty wallet over to me.

My mind was now racing over those training lectures, struggling with the intricacies of *mens rea* and wondering whether this qualified as a confession to a crime.

But was it a crime?

I opened the wallet and looked through its meagre contents. There was no name or address inside, although I did find a £1 note tucked deep into one of its folds, and some small, square snapshots of a pretty teenaged girl. But nothing else.

I took Ted's full name and address and thanked him for his honesty, saying I'd have to report the matter to my sergeant for advice. I informed him that I believed there were no grounds for prosecuting him for robbery, but did stress that I could not be sure.

The duty sergeant, who was not Sergeant Blaketon that day, could not decide the issue either, so he sought advice from the inspector. I told the story as Ted had given it to me, and the inspector said:

'Enter the wallet in the Found Property Register, Rhea. We've had no complaint from anyone about being robbed, so that means there's no crime. If we record it as found property, it'll go into our records.'

'And if it's not claimed within three months, sir, it'll go back to Ted Donaldson?'

But we did not let it rest there. We told the local paper, who printed the pictures of the girl, and it transpired that a youth in Scarborough had been robbed of his wallet by two men a week earlier . . .

Ted had simply recovered the wallet from the thief.

But, I often mused, suppose Ted's victim had been innocent and had complained that he had been robbed. Was there a criminal intent in Ted's mind at that moment?

4

A lost thing I could never find.
Hilaire Belloc, 1870-1953

The bewildering variety and massive quantity of objects which are recorded in the Found Property Register of any seaside police station is matched only by the variety and number which are recorded in the Lost Property Register. The snag is that the two registers seldom tally, for what is lost is seldom found, and what is found is seldom claimed.

This phenomenon is one of life's great mysteries, and it is one with which seaside police officers are especially familiar. By the end of every summer season, all corners of the police office are crammed with objects which no one has claimed or is likely to claim, and the range of property is truly amazing. How could anyone lose a wedding cake and never claim it? Or a pair of trousers or a brassière? Or their wallet, handbag, purse or shoes? One man even lost a bus and forty-two passengers, because he'd forgotten where he'd left it – we located it in a nearby car-park.

So far as normal lost and found objects are concerned, it might be wise to briefly explain some of the police procedures. These are followed meticulously because police officers have found themselves accused of stealing found goods when in fact the owner was more than careless when he or she lost it, or the finder less than truthful. To deal carelessly with found property can cost a police officer his or her career.

A good example of the risks can be shown when a wallet is reported found. Suppose a man lost a wallet which contained his personal papers and £100 or so in cash. Another person finds it, steals the cash and throws away the empty wallet. A third person then finds it and hands it to the police. If the policeman does not immediately, and in the presence of the finder, check the contents down to the last piece of dust, either he or the honest finder could be accused of stealing that missing cash. It is difficult to prove otherwise.

Due to the wide range of immense temptations which surround this curious aspect of police work, the handling of found property is very tightly controlled by printed orders, internal regulations and a mass of paperwork which involves meticulous records and the careful issue of receipts.

Police involvement in this social problem probably arose through well-meaning people bringing objects into the police station which they had found and which they believed to be the proceeds of crime. For this reason, every item of found property is checked against lists of stolen goods. In my time at Strensford, this was a manual task; now it is done by computer on a far wider scale.

Property which is reported lost is entered into a Lost Property Register, which is compared with the Found Property Register, and it is very gratifying, through this system, to restore some precious thing to a loser.

One reason for people reporting so much lost property is, I am sure, because they believe their goods have been stolen, rather than lost. Sadly, there is often no proof that a crime has been committed when something has gone missing, and so the object is recorded as 'lost' rather than stolen. One simple example is when a woman goes shopping with a purse sitting on top of her basket – when she wants to pay her bill, she finds it has gone. Has it been stolen or has she merely lost it? Who can tell? Without clear evidence of a theft, the object will be recorded as 'lost'.

It goes without saying that there is a tremendous amount of administrative work involved with both found and lost property, and most police forces operate very similar systems.

When an object is reported found and the owner of that object is not traceable, or the object is not likely to produce a risk of any sort, like a bomb, a gun, a small boy, a kitten or a box of apples going rotten, the police will ask the finder to retain it for up to three months. A report of the finding will be made, and the finder will be told that if the thing is not claimed within three months, he can keep it.

'Finder retains' is a lovely entry in the Found Property Register because it provides the solution to a lot of problems. For one thing, admin. problems are reduced, and space in the found property cupboard is saved.

Some finders, however, are determined not to retain the objects they find, which means they must be stored in the police station for three months in case the owner turns up. If he does turn up to claim his treasure, the problem is solved; if he doesn't, the property must be disposed of. The finder will be offered it, and if he does not want it, it will be disposed of in a manner appropriate to the object in question.

This well-tried system was truly tested when Mr Roderick Holroyd, a businessman from Halifax in the then West Riding of Yorkshire, found a set of false teeth. It was a full set in very good condition, and at first he thought he had annoyed a crab.

Roderick, a large and jolly gentleman, had taken time off during a business trip to Strensford so that he could roll up his trousers and for a few minutes paddle at the edge of the North Sea, just below Strensford Pier, where the sea was shallow enough for him to keep his smart grey suit dry. So he had pottered into the water and had allowed it to soothe his size 10s. He had enjoyed the caresses of the slimy seaweed, the feel of the shifting sands under his soles and the coolness of the water about his ankles. Then something had clamped itself around his toes.

I can well imagine his terror, but when he lifted his foot from its shifting base, he found a set of false teeth lying there, awash with sea-water and sand.

Recognizing them as high-quality masticators, he retrieved them from their briny resting place, put them in his pocket and, during his return to normal business routine, managed to locate me on patrol.

'Ah, constable,' he beamed as he came to rest before me. 'I've some found property to report,' and he produced the clean set of dentures from his pocket. As he told me the circumstances of his discovery, I cringed. I guessed the reaction I'd get from the station! But knowing the rules which surrounded this delicate topic, I could hardly advise him to forget them or to throw them into the harbour, and so I had to produce my pocketbook and make a full report of the occurrence.

I took the teeth from him and examined them. I hoped they might bear some kind of dentist's or manufacturer's identifying mark, but I found nothing.

I'm sure their maker could have identified them, but the expense and time involved in scouring the nation for their birthplace could hardly be justified in this instance. It was not as if we were engaged in a murder enquiry or the identification of a dead body.

'You keep them,' I said when I had recorded all the necessary information. 'And if they are not claimed within three months, they are yours.'

He backed off rapidly, leaving me holding the teeth.

'Oh, no, constable. I don't want them. I just thought some poor devil would be wandering around Strensford unable to chew his whelks. They'll surely be reported lost at your office, won't they? And you can restore them to the loser . . . Goodbye . . .'

And thus I was lumbered with this unattractive item of found property. I shuddered to think of the reaction from the duty sergeant when I presented the teeth to him for official documentation and for issue of a receipt to Mr Holroyd. But it was not my task to question official procedures.

'Rhea!' Sergeant Blaketon was duty sergeant this afternoon. 'You blithering idiot. Who in their right mind would accept these from a finder? You realize what this means? It means records, receipts, these teeth occupying valuable space in the found property cupboard for three months, then letters to the finder to ask if he wants to have them back . . .'

'I was just following Standing Orders, sergeant.' I shrank beneath his onslaught, for I knew he could not argue against this. Rules were his forte, he lived by rules and regulations, and so there was no way out of this dilemma.

He had to accept the teeth and he had to initiate the necessary procedures. I left him to it.

No one came to report losing them or to claim ownership, and during my three months at Strensford they remained on the front of a shelf in the cupboard, grinning at all who placed further items there. Shortly before I completed my tour, the three necessary 'finders' months were complete, and no one had claimed the teeth.

'Rhea,' said Sergeant Blaketon one morning. 'I've got a job for you.'

'Yes, sergeant?' I stood before him in the office.

'You can send an official form to your Mr Holroyd to inform him that three months have expired since he reported finding those false teeth and that, as no one has claimed them, they now officially belong to him. Ask him to come and collect them. Then we can get the things written off.'

And so I completed the necessary forms and posted them to the finder. Mr Holroyd rang the office next day just after 10 a.m., and by chance Sergeant Blaketon and I were both there, working an early shift.

Blaketon took the call and listened carefully. I heard him trying to persuade Mr Holroyd to collect the teeth next time he was in town, but he declined. He wanted nothing more to do with them. And then I heard Oscar Blaketon ask, 'In that case, have we your authority to dispose of them?'

The answer was clearly in the affirmative because Sergeant Blaketon endorsed the register 'Finder declines to accept after three-month period, and authorized police to dispose of this item of property.'

'There, Rhea,' he said. 'This little seaside saga is almost over. Now, here's your teeth!'

'They're not mine, sergeant!'

'You will dispose of them,' he said to me ominously. 'That's an order. We have the official owner's permission. It's all in the books. So there you are, take them and get rid of them.'

And he pressed them into the palm of my hand, now wrapped neatly in some tissue paper.

'Yes, sergeant,' I had to agree. I stuffed them into my uniform pocket and made a mental note to dispose of them in the station dustbin. But by the time he had finished instructing me about car-parking problems, bus-parking problems, youngsters in pubs and illicit dropping of litter,

I had forgotten about the teeth. I walked to my beat and passed the station dustbin *en route*.

A few minutes later, I found myself patrolling along the harbourside. It was when I arrived at the very place where I had been handed those teeth three months ago that I remembered them and became very aware of them sitting in my pocket. I removed the tissue package and simultaneously smelt the briny harbour water. A brisk breeze wafted the scents of the sea towards me, and I recalled that the teeth had been rescued from a watery grave. Quite impulsively, I felt that a return to the ocean would be eminently suitable for these teeth. It was far better than a dustbin, I felt, far more permanent and almost symbolic.

I moved into the shelter of a herring shed and then, making sure I was not observed, flung the teeth far across the harbour. With immense satisfaction, I saw them plop into the water and sink out of sight. The file was closed.

I resumed my patrol, glad it was all over.

Five minutes later, a small gentleman hailed me.

'Oh, er, excuse me, officer,' he began. 'Can I mention something to you?'

'Yes, of course.'

'Well, it's a bit funny, I suppose, but, well, three months ago I was on holiday here, a short break you know. And well, I went for a swim, just below the pier. I'm not much of a swimmer really and swallowed a lot of water, a huge gulp it was. Well, I coughed and spluttered and lost my false teeth in the sea, you understand. They just shot out, a new set.

'I looked all over but didn't find them, and, well, friends said I should have reported it to the police, just in case they'd been found. But you see I live a long way off and had to rush for my bus, and then, well, this is the first time I've been back to Strensford, so when I saw you, I thought I'd mention it. I don't suppose they have been found, have they? I mean, it would be odd, wouldn't it? A chance in thousands, really, but, well, I thought it might be worth asking . . . You never know, do you?'

'No, you never can tell,' I agreed, taking out my pocketbook to make a note of the matter.

Much found property is of little cash value, and it has more of a sentimental meaning to its loser. But there are times when the situation changes. I am reminded of an incident which occurred as I was patrolling the harbourside one fine August afternoon on my first spell of duty in Strensford, some years before this visit.

I spotted a roadsweeper moving steadily towards me. He was a small, chubby fellow with a flat cap and a dark-blue shirt with the sleeves rolled up. He was manoeuvring a barrow which was really a dustbin on wheels. This was the tool of his trade, and it contained a space for his brush and shovel. With the stiff-bristled brush, he was sweeping litter from the gutters and footpaths. It was a thankless task but he was obviously anxious to make Strensford as smart and as clean as possible, in spite of visitors' efforts to frustrate him.

I don't think he was aware of my presence barely a few yards ahead of him as he slowly moved about his careful work. With his head down, he kept his eyes on the road and the gutters, and his mind upon his solitary task. He swept all before him until it formed a medium-sized pile, and then, after removing his shovel from its resting-place on his barrow, he collected the debris and dropped it into his bin. His work was slow and methodical.

As I carelessly observed him, not really watching him but merely being aware of his presence, he scooped up a shovelful of waste and placed it inside his bin. Then he halted his routine and delved deep inside the bin; this change of action and routine caused me to take a little more interest. I saw him lift out a bundle of paper. From a distance, it looked like a screwed-up mass of newspaper or other white paper with printing upon it, but he was making a very careful study of it. Then he glanced around, noticed me and began to walk quickly in my direction, holding the bundle as if it was hot.

'Look,' he said. 'It's money. Fivers. Ah've just fun 'em in t'gutter.'

I took the bundle from him, and sure enough, they were £5 notes of the large, white variety, now obsolete but then very much in vogue. One of them represented something approaching a week's wages for some workers. With the little fellow watching, I expressed my amazement and then carefully counted them before his eyes.

There was a total of sixty notes, £300 in all, very close to a year's wages for the roadman, and not far off a year's wages for me either!

'Phew!' I breathed. 'You found all this money, down there in the gutter?'

'Aye,' he grinned a weak smile, a nervous one almost and showed thick, brown teeth. 'Just there, sweeping up. Noticed 'em on my shovel, just in time.'

'We'll have to report the find,' I informed him. 'Can you come with me now, to the station? I think you ought to be present when I record this.'

'Ah've all this length to finish before knocking-off time,' he said.

'I think that can wait, under the circumstances.'

I wanted him to come to the station for two reasons. First, in view of the amount involved, I felt he ought to be there when the official procedures were set in motion, and secondly, it was more than likely that someone had already reported the loss of such an amount. If so, the money could be very quickly restored to its rightful owner, and there might be a reward for the sweeper. He agreed to come along with me, albeit with some reluctance, and so we proceeded through the streets, with the little fellow in firm control of his barrow and with me hiding the wadge of notes in my uniform pocket.

At the station, a Sergeant Moreton was on duty and looked in amazement as I entered with the roadman.

'An arrest is it?' he asked as I entered the office.

'No, sergeant, it's found property,' I said.

I told my story, after which I plonked the £300 on the counter before him. His eyebrows rose in surprise and he looked at the roadman with admiration.

'Enter it in the register, son. Now, in view of the amount involved, we cannot let the finder retain this. But, strange though it may seem, we've had no report of a loss. Not yet. I suppose there's time for that. And, if there is no report of a loss, it will go to the finder, and that'll make you a rich man, eh?'

The roadman smiled briefly. I went through the formalities, recording that his name was Lawrence Briggs who was employed by the council as a roadsweeper and who was sixty-four years old. He had an address on the council estate across the river. I explained the formalities to him and told him that if the money was not claimed within three months, it would be his.

'It'll be a nice retirement present,' he said quietly.

'You're retiring soon, are you?' I asked.

'November,' he said. 'When I'm sixty-five.'

'If this isn't claimed, it could give you a holiday,' I suggested.

'New furniture more like,' he said. 'Me and the missus

has never had much, not on my wage. I'd love a television and some good furniture, a nice settee . . .'

'It was very honest of you to report that money,' I commented. 'I'd bet some wouldn't have.'

'Aye, well, mebbe so. But I'm honest, officer. Somebody'll have lost that and it'll mean more to them than me. No, I wouldn't dream of keeping it.'

'OK, well, it's in safe hands now. So if it's not claimed within three months, we'll be in touch with you and you can come and collect it.'

He smiled and left the office, and I saw him trundling his barrow down the cobbled hill and back into the busy streets. With luck, he'd get his length finished by knocking-off time, but I did find myself marvelling at his honesty.

'You know, son,' said Sergeant Moreton two hours later. 'This is very odd. No one's reported losing that cash, not a whisper. It's a fortune, you know; I mean, what sort of person carries that amount with him, let alone loses it and doesn't say anything?'

Like Sergeant Moreton, I could only marvel at the story but knew we dare not publicize the finding, otherwise all kinds of dishonest folks would suddenly 'remember' losing the money.

But in time someone did report its loss. The call came later that evening.

'It's Bridlington Police,' announced the caller. 'Sergeant Youngman speaking. Now, have you had a report of any cash being found in Strensford? A lot of cash. In notes. Fivers. I don't expect you to say you have, because if anyone found it, they'd say nowt.'

'Yes, sergeant,' I said. 'We have had some found.'

'£300 in fivers, was it?'

'Yes, it was found close to the harbourside.'

'Then I've got a very relieved loser here right now. He

lost £300 in fivers today. He's a Mr George Kenton from Surrey. He came to Strensford on the SS *Princess* from Bridlington today and, when he got back on the boat for the return trip, realized he had lost his holiday cash. He couldn't report it until the boat returned to harbour here, and well, he came straight to our office to tell us. I'll ask him to come over to Strensford as soon as possible to collect the money. Now, who's the honest character who found it?'

I explained how the roadsweeper had found the cash and provided his name and address. Sergeant Youngman said he would inform the loser of those details. Mr Kenton would come tonight, I was told, so after thanking Sergeant Youngman for his call, I made a note in the Occurrence Book so that the next shift would be aware of the situation.

I went off duty before the money was handed over to its rightful owner, and it seems he arrived late that evening to claim his cash. It was handed over against his signature and the matter was closed.

But he did not leave even a shilling reward for the roadsweeper. There was not a penny and not even a letter of thanks for his honesty. We all knew that he would not wish any thanks or a reward but would gain satisfaction from knowing that his honesty had been ratified by the money going to its rightful owner.

We waited a few days, but nothing came, and so Sergeant Moreton, who was friendly with the local reporter on the *Strensford Gazette*, decided to tell the tale to the papers. If Kenton was not going to give some reward, the story of the roadman's honesty was strong enough for the local and even the national papers. And so it won headlines in some papers and more than a few column inches in others, and we made sure a copy was sent to Kenton at his home address. But not even that prompted a response.

Happily, although the publicity did not prompt a response from Kenton, there was a small but touching flood of postal orders, cash and cheques for the roadman from readers all over England. If the loser did not appreciate his remarkable honesty, the public did. All the police officers at Strensford had a whip-round for him too, and he was able to buy himself a new settee with those generous donations.

Another odd use of the Found Property Register occurred late one night when I was working a night shift during that three-month spell of duty. I was sitting in the office around 2.15 a.m. having my break when a rather rough-looking, brusquely spoken character presented himself at the enquiry desk.

His name was Brian Stockfield, a taxi-driver in his early forties who was renowned in the town for his bad temper, his loud voice and awful, critical treatment of his fellow men. No one had a good word for Stockfield; he complained incessantly about everything, criticizing the council because of the rates, the police for letting holiday-makers park all over the town, the holiday-makers for crowding the streets, the children for their noise, dogs for barking . . . Every facet of Strensford's society was criticized by this chap, and the outcome was that those who knew him kept out of his way. He had not been in Strensford during my initial spell, so I had never come across him until now.

Stockfield earned his living by running a one-vehicle taxi business, and his premises were a small wooden garage close to the harbourside. He criticized other taxi-drivers for taking business from him, he wrote to the newspaper about their activities and claimed that some had not taken out the correct insurance for their vehicles, or that their hackney carriage licences were not in order. He was a regular caller at the police station, where his growing list of complaints was logged. In short, he was nothing but a confounded nuisance to everyone.

It was through chats with the local police that I discovered one of his unpleasant traits – perhaps, though, he had just cause for this particular behaviour.

When the police in Strensford came across a drunk who was not troublesome or a danger either to himself or to anyone else, they hailed a local taxi and persuaded the driver to take the drunk home. This system was very sensible, because it kept the cells empty, it saved the drunk from the trauma of a prosecution, it saved the police a lot of work and the courts a lot of time dealing with simple drunks. Furthermore, it helped to retain the friendly relationship between the residents and the police, for the people would resent any heavy-handed treatment of local merrymakers. It made a lot of sense to deal with them in this gentle way. Another aspect was that it kept all the taxi-drivers in business too, because they made useful, honest sums from their merry fares.

The system had a lot to commend it, but Brian Stockfield would not partake in it. He complained about the drunks, about their noise, their singing and their general conduct. He would not have anything at all to do with them. But this did not unduly worry the other taxi-drivers, who were happy to accommodate our discarded drunks. His financial loss was their gain.

On this night, as he arrived at the police station counter, I learned, he had answered such a call, and that was the reason for his presence. He had another complaint to make.

PC Joe Tapley, a local constable of considerable experience, was the office duty man that night, and he went to the counter to deal with Stockfield. I and three colleagues sat near the fireside, enjoying our meal, and we were just beyond the vision of the visitor. But we could hear every word.

'Ah, Mr Stockfield,' greeted PC Tapley. 'What brings you to us at this late hour?'

'I have a complaint to make,' he said. 'About a clever sod who's been to a dance at the Imperial Hotel.'

'Not paid his fare?' suggested Joe Tapley.

'Paid? Yes, he's paid. It's bloody awful, Mr Tapley, terrible really, what folks do to your taxis.'

'Oh, like that, is it? So what's he done?'

Joe had a pad of notepaper handy and was preparing to record the problem.

'Look, Mr Tapley, you know what I'm like with drunks, don't you? You and the lads. I go for class clients, not drunks. My vehicle is the cleanest taxi in town, even though I say so myself. None of my fares can complain about me running a mucky vehicle.'

'Go on, Mr Stockfield.' I noticed the formal exchange of names between these two, indicative of some past conflict.

'I got this call, right? From a chap attending the Imperial Hunt Ball, it is. He had a nice accent, and it is a class dance, as you know. Even though he sounded a bit fuzzy, a bit slurred when he spoke, I went for him. I picked him up at 1.30 a.m., on the dot, and took him to the Grand Hotel, where he's staying.'

'And he paid?'

'Yes, he paid. Charming he was, all done up in an evening-dress suit, a right toff.'

'Your ideal client, eh?'

'You would think so, wouldn't you?'

'So what is your complaint, Mr Stockfield?' asked PC Tapley.

'Well, I find this very embarrassing. I'm a clean-living,

clean-speaking man, Mr Tapley, but, well, he's used the back seat of my taxi as a toilet.'

'You mean he's peed on it?' I could discern the merest flicker of a smile on Joe Tapley's face, and he was doing his best to suppress it.

'No, the other. Two massive great brown turds, like a dog's, on the back seat. You come and see for yourself, and don't stick your nose in either. The smell is bloody awful.'

Joe followed him outside, and so we all trooped out as well, for this would be a sight to treasure. Sure enough, as Stockfield switched on the interior light, the centre of the back seat was graced by two shining examples of man's slavery to the urgent needs of nature. They were a pair of thick, brown turds.

We were all creasing ourselves with laughter, and happily the darkness of the night concealed most of our efforts to keep straight faces, but Joe achieved it with aplomb. He led us all back inside, and we seated ourselves at the fireside again, leaving Joe to finalize the matter.

'Well,' demanded Stockfield. 'What are you going to do about it?'

'Do you know the man's name? The chap who left it?'

'No, he's a visitor. I doubt if I would recognize him again. He was just a bloke who wanted a lift home from a dance.'

'Hmm,' said Joe, writing on the scrap pad. 'Name and description unknown.' When he had finished writing, he said, 'Well, thank you, Mr Stockfield. I have made a note of all the relevant details. Thank you for calling.'

'But what are you going to do about it?' demanded the taxi-driver, whose voice was beginning to grow louder.

'Do?' smiled Joe calmly. 'Nothing else. I've done all that I can. I have made a record of the event in our Found Property Register. If the owner cannot be traced, and if the property is not claimed within three months, you may keep it. As things are, you may now take it home and await any likely claim of ownership. We will keep the matter on file for three months too.'

'Found property?' cried Stockfield. 'You can't call this found property!'

'Then what else is it?' smiled Joe, as calm as ever. 'No crime has been committed, no byelaw broken, no traffic regulation breached, no street nuisance committed, no indecent public exhibition. It's simply a case of someone unknown leaving something rather personal in your taxi. And thank you for reporting it. Goodnight, Mr Stockfield.'

He left without a word, and we waited until the sound of his revving engine faded before collapsing into bouts of laughter. There is a lot to be learned from an experienced police officer.

5

Animals are such agreeable friends,
They ask no questions, they pass no criticism.
George Eliot, 1819-80

Night duty can be very lonely. After the pubs have closed, the restaurants have cleared their tables and the clubs have bolted their doors, the streets rapidly empty and there is little companionship for the patrolling constable. His solitary work, which in my case began at 10 p.m. and finished at 6 a.m., comprised the checking of lock-up premises and empty houses and a general watching brief on the sleeping town. I kept my ears open for those who prowled at night, for burglars and shop-breakers, for vagrants and other ne'er-do-wells whose illegal activities were conducted under the cover of darkness.

More often than not, nothing of this kind ever happened. There were few burglars and nocturnal villains to arrest or deter, and the resultant boredom was often relieved only by the appearance of the night duty sergeant or sometimes an inspector, with, very occasionally, the eminence of the superintendent himself. In the momentary absence of those supervisory officers, the constables would gather at some suitable place for a chat, flashing coded messages to one another by torch and making use of reflections from shop windows to pass our morse-like messages along streets and around corners.

There were times, however, when the exigencies of the service and the wanderings of supervisory officers meant that such meetings could not be arranged. This inevitably meant that the long hours after midnight became very, very lonely and excruciatingly boring, so that a companion of some kind, any kind, was most welcome.

At 1 a.m. on such a morning, I stood forlornly outside the GPO in the town centre of Strensford. I was making a point at the telephone kiosk and was feeling very melancholy as I longed for my meal break which was scheduled for 2.15 a.m. Then I'd be able to have a few minutes' chat and banter with my colleagues, all of which would be washed down with hot coffee from my flask and fortified with some of my landlady's sandwiches.

As I waited in the chill of that summer night, I became aware of a dog trotting along the street towards me. He was a stocky animal, a mature yellow labrador, and he was completely alone. I said nothing as I watched, and then he noticed me in the dim glow of the kiosk and headed in my direction. Without any hint of indecision, he came and sat at my side, his tail thumping the pavement in greeting.

'Hello, boy,' I acknowledged him. 'Who are you then?'

I fingered his collar, but it bore no name or address of his owner, nor his own name. But he was a solid-looking, well-fed dog in excellent condition and, I guessed, about five or six years old. He made a small fuss when I patted him but sat at my side almost as if he had been trained to do so. I spoke to him and used words like 'go home', but he did not shift his position until it was time for me to leave.

I now had twenty-five minutes of further patrolling before my next point at the New Quay telephone kiosk, and this would be occupied by checking the shops, back and front, and inspecting all the dark corners of the myriad of quaint passages which were such a feature of Strensford's ancient town centre. They were called yards, and the police nightly examined them for sleeping tramps, drunks, people who might be ill or lost, or villains who might be lurking there hoping to break into a shop or hotel through the back windows or doors.

When my five minutes' wait at the GPO was over, I said, 'Well, boy, I must go. I've a lot to do. Goodbye.'

But as I walked away, he followed. He walked at my heels on the right-hand side, his tail gently wagging with the swaying movement of his thick-set body. He was just like a trained police dog, and yet I had no idea where he had come from.

I decided to see just how carefully trained he really was. To carry out my little test, I stopped at the entrance to one of these dark and almost sinister yards and listened. He stopped at my side and sat down, ears alert. I had not given him any command.

Now I had to enter that dark and narrow tunnel-like passage to check dozens of shop premises, pubs and warehouses whose rear doors or windows were accessible from there, and consequently very accessible for an attack. It was a nightly task; armed only with a torch I had to check every pane of glass, and every cranny for lurking crooks. Without a personal radio set, I was alone and vulnerable. If I was attacked by burglars or layabouts, there was no way I could call my colleagues for help, other than by blowing my whistle, if I had time, or just shouting loudly in the hope that someone somewhere would respond. But now it seemed that I had some welcome assistance.

'Seek, boy,' I said to the dog, and off he went. Tail wagging and ears alert, he went ahead of me into the long, dark passage, and I waited at the entrance. The seconds ticked away and there was no sound, not even a reassuring bark or a cat scuttling for safety, so I allowed a full two minutes. Still with no sound or sign of him, I shone my torch into the dark void and, seeing nothing, decided that my companion of but a few moments ago had left me and that he'd gone home. Once more I was alone, so I entered the passage aided by the light of my torch, and there he was, trotting towards me in fine spirits. He wagged his tail in welcome, turned around and led me through the dank darkness.

As I checked all the premises along my route, he remained with me. He spent his time sniffing at doors, dustbins and windows and entering dark corners, outhouses, external toilets and similar dark structures well ahead of me. If there had been anyone hiding in those secret places, the labrador would have flushed them out or certainly located them.

For the next hour, he remained with me, always walking at heel without being commanded when I was patrolling the streets and open spaces but going ahead to search the alleys, yards and dark recesses of the town whenever I said, 'Seek, boy.'

He was a remarkable dog, and I wondered what he would do when I went into the police station for my break. As the long-awaited hour of 2.15 a.m. approached, I made my way across Station Square to the welcoming lights of the old police station, and the dog followed, always at heel and never straying. But when I approached the side-street door which always stood half-open at night, he rushed ahead of me, pushed open the door and hurried inside. I followed down the steps into the depths of this Victorian pile and was in time to see him curling up beneath the counter, settling down for a snooze close to the fireside of the cosy office.

When I joined my colleagues for my break, Joe Tapley asked, 'Has Rusty been with you tonight, Nick?'

'Rusty?' For the briefest of moments, I thought he was referring to one of the local officers.

'The dog, that labrador. We call him Rusty.'

'Oh,' I smiled. 'Yes, he picked me up at one o'clock and has been with me ever since. Is he yours?'

'No,' he laughed. 'No, although sometimes I wish he was. He's a wonderful chap, aren't you, Rusty?'

The dog lifted his head and acknowledged the compliment by flapping his tail several times on the floor.

'Where does he come from?' I asked, opening my sandwiches and flask.

'Dunno,' said Joe, shrugging his shoulders. 'None of us knows. He just turns up from time to time, selects one of us for his patrol and then walks the beat until six o'clock. Then he goes home. The trouble is, we don't know who he belongs to or where he goes. We call him Rusty, and he responds. He'll search all your awkward spots for you, you know. Just say "Seek, Rusty" and off he'll go. He could be the official Strensford Police Dog.'

'Don't his owners ever miss him?'

'No, I don't suppose they know he comes out at night. I imagine they shut him in some outbuilding for the night, and by the time they open up next morning he'll be back in residence. It's almost as if he has this secret life helping us, being a Special Constable really. He's great, a marvellous companion on nights.'

'Doesn't he show up in the day-time then?' I asked.

'No, never. He'll come to town several nights during a month, not every night, mind. He'll select one of the lads to be his companion during his night patrol and will stick with him all night. Then he'll wander off home. He's obviously from a good home because he's so well fed, and he won't eat with us either. He wouldn't touch our sandwiches, although sometimes he'll take a drink of water.'

'Has anyone tried to follow him home?'

'Not really. By six o'clock we're all shattered and ready for bed, besides we're all on foot anyway. He lives out of town, we know that, so we think he's from one of the nearby villages or farms. But beyond that we don't know where he hails from.'

At 3 a.m. I was due to commence the second half of my shift, and as I moved from my chair to pack away my things and rinse out my flask, Rusty opened his eyes, thumped his tail and joined me. I gave him a saucer of water, which he lapped happily, and then we resumed our joint patrol.

He remained with me until a few minutes before 6 a.m.; as before, he checked all the yards and passages ahead of me and helped me enormously during that shift. Then, as I made my final slow, tired walk across the town to book off duty, he suddenly veered away from me and began to trot away.

'Goodnight, Rusty,' I called after him, and he turned his head, wagged his tail and departed. Two minutes later, he was out of sight.

During my short spell of duty in Strensford, I was accompanied by Rusty on four or five occasions. He came more often, of course, and seemed to share himself between the other patrolling constables.

Of the happy memories which I shall always associate with him, two stand out. On one occasion, about 1.30 a.m., I despatched him down an alley to carry out his customary search, and this time he barked. It was a warning bark, and it was followed by a shout of alarm following which a youth bustled out of the darkness, dragging a girl with him.

He was one of the local small-time crooks, whom I recognized, and although I checked all the nearby premises and found them secure, I guessed Rusty had prevented a 'breaking' job that night. No doubt the girl was being used as a form of cover by the youth, and her (probably innocent) presence with him was designed to make the police believe he was merely courting. But I recorded the fact and his name in my notebook and left a detailed account for the CID, should any subsequent premises be entered.

Soon after that little episode, I was on day-time patrol and was asked by another local crook whether police dogs were operating in Strensford. Word of Rusty's presence had obviously got around.

I said, 'Yes, but they're not Alsatians. They don't look like ordinary police dogs; they're CID – canines in disguise.'

I don't know what he made of that information but I guessed it would circulate among the small-time crooked fraternity of Strensford.

The other memorable incident with Rusty occurred during the early hours of a chill morning, around 3 a.m. It was, in fact, the last time we patrolled together, and he had selected me for his companion during that night shift. I was finding the long, second half very tiring and was almost asleep on my feet as, with his help, I was checking shops and yards in another part of town.

I arrived at the entrance to Sharpe's Yard, which led off Shunnergate, and sent Rusty about his usual mission. He came back without barking, which I interpreted as the all-clear signal. I knew that no villains lurked down there. Nonetheless, I had to make my own search in case there were broken windows or signs of illicit entry to the rear of the shops.

With my torch lighting the windows above me, I began my journey, but after only a dozen strides, Rusty was before me, growling and barking. His noise filled the air and jerked me into wakefulness. I stopped immediately.

Was someone waiting down here? Something had alarmed him.

The hairs on the nape of my neck stood erect as the light of my torch searched the corners and ledges before me and above me. I could see nothing to cause me concern.

'It's all right, Rusty,' I said. 'There's nothing.'

I started to walk again, but once more he barked. I stopped and this time shone my torch upon him.

He was standing near the front edge of a gaping hole, his voice warning me not to walk into it. Someone had lifted an inspection cover to a draining system and had left it propped against the wall. A hole some seven or eight feet deep, with iron steps leading down, lay before me.

'Rusty!' I crouched on my haunches and hugged him, and he seemed to understand my gratitude. I replaced the cover and, feeling rather shaken at what might have occurred, concluded my night's patrol.

As always, just before six o'clock, Rusty trotted away. I shouted, 'Thanks, Rusty,' as he moved rapidly out of my sight, but he never looked back, and that was the last time we patrolled together.

I never saw him again. I did puzzle over the kind of formal training he had undergone because it had clearly been very thorough, and the incident with the missing inspection cover did make me wonder if he'd ever been trained as a guide dog for a blind person.

Even to this day, I do not know where he came from or who owned him, and perhaps I never will. But he was a lovely companion, a sincere friend, a super dog and a very good police officer.

I shall never forget him.

During that short sojourn to the coast, I had several memorable experiences with animals, most of which occurred during my night patrols.

It was a regular occurrence, for example, for animals to escape from their compounds at the slaughterhouse. It was almost as if they were aware of their impending fate and were making a last, desperate effort to escape and, hopefully, survive.

It frequently happened that night-duty policemen were the first to know of these escapes, and it became their responsibility to arrange for the capture of the fleeing animals. In my short time there, a pig got loose, a sheep escaped, a young bullock absconded and a cow managed to free itself.

The pig and the sheep caused no real problems because they were easily rounded up, although their moments of blissful freedom did entail wild and noisy gallops through the streets with posse-like constables in hot pursuit on foot or cycle. I do know that one such chase, with a very noisy pig as the target, aroused several streets of slumbering residents and many bewildered holiday-makers, some of whom thought that Count Dracula had come to the town. A screeching pig can produce a most unholy noise.

In spite of the noise, the general idea was simply to corner the animal, secure it and return it protesting to its death chamber.

The cow was rather different. She was bigger for a start, and when a cow takes fright and blunders about the streets at night, she can demolish shop windows, damage cars, leap into sitting-rooms and do all manner of wild and irresponsible acts which amount to genuine vandalism. So a rampaging cow has to be quickly halted, and sadly the solution is often a powerful rifle.

This particular cow, a hornless Red Poll of a delightful chestnut colour, was such an animal. In the thrill of the chase, she turned into a galloping powerhouse of beef, and we sensed tragedy if she wasn't halted in her tracks.

To cut a long story short, we knocked out of bed a member of the local Rifle Club, a Territorial Army firearms instructor, who joined the hunt with a .303 rifle. We drove the terrified beast into the coal yard, where she was put out of her misery by one well-aimed shot to the head.

The bullock was a similar problem, but he, being a lively young lad, took a good deal more catching than the cow of previous weeks. He was smaller for one thing, faster for another and very cunning too.

He was spotted in a shopping arcade by one of the patrolling constables, and seemed docile enough. He was not galloping aimlessly about the place, so the constable rang the office and alerted the sergeant, who in turn recruited the rest of us as reluctant matadors. We all set off in pursuit of the bullock, a handsome Hereford. His large, flat white face was like a beacon in the darkness, and it caught the light from the few street lamps as he moved casually about the town with us in close attendance. This had not yet developed into a chase, it was more like easy cattle-droving, for we were endeavouring to persuade him to walk into some enclosed space.

The snag is that town centres are not rich with enclosed spaces of the kind that will accommodate a frisky young bullock, and as he moved about the streets, we racked our brains as we sought a suitable paddock. Then the sergeant recalled Cragdale Hall, a large, deserted mansion close to the town centre. It had large iron gates and a high surrounding wall which provided a total enclosure, and the house was empty too. It was surrounded by overgrown lawns and gardens and was an ideal place to contain a bullock. He sent one of the constables ahead to open the gates in preparation, and the rest of us were briefed to guide the bullock in that general direction.

Things went very well until the bullock turned into one
of the dark yards which riddle the town centre. These are
long and narrow and link one street with another which
runs parallel to it. As the bullock turned into the narrow
entrance, the sergeant yelled.

'Two of you, get to the other end. Hold him in. We've
got him.'

Two young constables ran ahead and disappeared down
one of the adjoining yards, and we could hear them
thudding along its echoing sandstone base. Then we heard
the galloping of hooves followed by a shout of alarm, and it
seems that as those two policemen emerged at the distant
end of their yard, a shop-breaker, complete with his illicit
haul, with a young bull hard on his heels, emerged with
some speed and anxiety from the adjoining yard.

He had just climbed out of a rear ground-floor window
of the Co-Op as the bullock arrived at that point; I did
wonder if he thought the police had recruited bulls as well
as dogs for such duties, although I imagine he never gave it
a thought, at least not just then. However, his shout of
alarm had frightened our quarry; it caused the bullock to
begin a fast gallop hard behind the worried shop-breaker,
who immediately ran for his life. The pair of them sped
from the end of that yard like two peas exploding from a
peashooter, the crook maintaining the slenderest of leads.

And the shop-breaker had the wit not to release his
haul, which comprised a large carton of cigarettes, the
result being that he was caught red-handed. Happily, the
constables who emerged from the adjoining yard at about
the same moment were quick enough to appreciate the
situation and grabbed the villain, while the bullock did its
best to avoid the drama and vanished towards the
harbourside.

As the two happy arresters escorted their man to the

police station, the remaining matadors pursued their quarry at a sedate pace, not wishing to panic him into a burst of sudden activity. Their droving skills directed him along the edge of the harbour, and we were delighted when he entered one of the herring sheds. We reckoned we could contain him there while the owner of the slaughterhouse was contacted; and so we did. The man arrived shortly afterwards with a cattle-truck and two of his own men. With remarkable ease, they persuaded the bullock to enter it.

And that was that. The excitement was over, except that I wonder how many shop-breakers have been arrested by a bullock on night duty.

Another interesting hunt was started by a drunk who rang the police station about half-past eleven one warm summer night to say that he had seen a ferocious unidentified beast on the harbour wall and that it had washed its supper in the harbour water before vanishing below deck on one of the fishing cobles.

Unlikely as it seemed, it was a good enough yarn to be relayed to the policeman who was patrolling the harbourside, and he promised to keep his eyes open. Half an hour later, he rang the office to confirm the sighting. There *was* a peculiar animal upon the boats, and he had no idea what it was. He said it was about as big as a badger and of a nondescript colour so far as he could see; but it wasn't a badger, and it was jumping from one boat to the next. It certainly looked dangerous.

All the night-duty constables, including myself, were told to volunteer to help catch the fearsome thing before it spread rabies or did some other irreparable harm to the town. To help in this task, we recruited the fire brigade, the fishermen themselves and anyone else who could be

found at that time of night. This resulted in all the drunks
from the harbourside pubs volunteering, along with many
strolling holiday-makers and several motorists who shone
their car lights across the resting boats which bobbed and
swayed on the water.

Some of the fishermen had the bright idea of driving it
towards a wall of fishing nets which they would hold up,
and so the trap was set. At this point, we weren't really sure
where it was, and we certainly didn't know what it was,
which meant we didn't know what it might do. Nonetheless,
we all boarded the boats and began to beat upon their
wooden decks, hoping to flush out the beast.

Under lights beaming down from the boats' masts and
in the glow of car headlamps, we set about our mission,
and it is fair to say that there was a good deal of nervousness
which was hidden among the noise and laughter. None of
us knew whether he was going to be savaged by some
ghastly creature from another country as the noisy, bawdy
hunt continued.

Suddenly, the large furry thing bolted from below deck
and scurried across one of the boats. Accompanied by
shouting and banging on buckets and dustbin lids, it sped
from deck to deck, crossing the fleet of fishing cobles with
remarkable dexterity and avoiding the outstretched fishing
nets until it was able to leap onto the side of the harbour
wall. Then, remarkably, it clung to the seaweed and stones
of the wall and somehow scuttled along the side of the wall
until we saw it disappear beneath the wooden flooring of
the pier extension.

'What is it?' asked someone when that minor panic was
over.

'Dunno, but it looks like a giant bloody rat!' said one
man.

'I've not seen owt like yon, never. And it has a bushy

tail. Rats haven't bushy tails, leastways not ships' rats.'

The police officers present gathered to discuss the next phase of the operation, and Sergeant White, on duty that night, asked:

'Right, you all saw it. What was it?'

Our answers ranged from a giant mouse to a giant cat, by way of a monster mongoose or a massive squirrel. It was about the size of a badger, that was not in dispute, but the darkness of the night and the animal's rapid movements made it impossible to get a clear view of it. We all agreed that it seemed to be a brownish grey colour, although the darkness made it difficult to make a proper assessment. Someone said its tail was bushy, and black and white, and we all felt it wasn't either a dog or a fox, nor even a badger. Such animals could never cling to the side of the harbour wall in the remarkable manner it had shown.

Now, however, it was somewhere under the pier extension, probably clambering over the mass of steel supports and girders. At least it was isolated to a degree, and if it emerged from there, we would be able to see it.

Sergeant White spoke. 'PC Rhea, go to a telephone kiosk and ring Gerard Bright,' he announced. 'He's got the pet shop. His home number will be in the directory. Tell him what's happened – he might know what it is and what to do. Then report back to me. I'll remain here and supervise.'

I rang Mr Bright from the fishmarket kiosk, and he asked me to explain all that I knew. I relayed a tale of the chase and a varied descriptions of the animal which was based on all the garbled accounts I'd heard.

'Bloody hell!' I heard him exclaim. 'Hang on a minute, officer.'

He left the telephone and returned saying, 'I'll be down there right away. Don't chase it any more – leave it to me.'

I relayed this advice to Sergeant White, who called for all the hunters to keep back, to remain at a distance and under no circumstances to approach the animal. An expert was on the way, he announced with all the seriousness he could muster.

I tried to tell him that Mr Bright had not indicated the thing was dangerous, his advice being simply to leave it alone, but White was not taking any risks. He moved everyone back from the pier extension and waited. Somehow he managed to generate all the tension of a man-eating tiger hunt.

Mr Bright arrived on a pedal cycle and from the saddlebag lifted a vacuum flask of water, a dog's dish and two hard-boiled eggs.

'Right,' he said. 'Everyone keep back. I'm going for it.'

He walked to the end of the wooden pier extension, filled the bowl with water, put it on the ground and placed the eggs close to it. Then he shouted: 'Rocky, Rocky, Rocky.'

We all watched, breathless, and heard a scratching noise from beneath and then the head of a sharp-eared animal appeared. Then the rest of its body scrambled onto the surface of the extension and scuttled across to the eggs. It seized one, washed it in the water and settled down to eat it.

Mr Bright picked the creature up, and it snuggled against him as he carried it towards us.

'It's my pet racoon,' he said. 'He's escaped somehow. He's completely harmless, but very nervous when there is a lot of noise and shouting. Thank you for finding him.'

'It's a pleasure,' said Sergeant White. 'A real pleasure. Now, can we get the town back to normal?'

Of all the animals that have befriended mankind, the

seaside donkey is surely one of the most lovable. Stubborn at times, their overall patience with tiny children is renowned, and a donkey ride remains one of the highlights of a day on the beach. Grouped together in small numbers, seaside donkeys spend their working lives plodding a well-worn path along the sands to the gleeful shouts of youngsters and the tinkling of bells on their harnesses. And then, in the winter, they are split into singles or perhaps pairs and despatched to inland farms, there to enjoy a few months' relaxation. Lots of moorland farms are hosts to a donkey or two during the winter, and I recall a friend of mine riding two miles or so to primary school on a donkey which was boarded out at his father's farm.

The Strensford donkeys were no exception. There would be about fifteen of them, small patient beasts whose working day was like that of seaside donkeys everywhere.

They lived high on the cliff near the Abbey, and each morning during the summer they were driven down the donkey path which dropped steeply from the Abbey and followed a tortuous route into the town. From there, they made their colourful way through the narrow streets, their ever-tinkling bells marking their journey. They were an attraction among the cars and holiday-makers with their doleful faces, decorated harnesses and their names emblazoned across their foreheads. Their steady progress accompanied by the clip-clop of their dainty hooves brought the town's traffic to a slow grind behind them as they were cheered along their route, usually with a procession of happy children prancing around them. Children would sometimes run ahead to their pitch on the yellow sands and make their bids for the first ride on Blossom, Snowdrop, Daffodil or whichever donkey attracted them.

Throughout the long summer days on the beach, the donkeys would stand in an orderly and silent group, regularly carrying happy children or sometimes a giggling adult along the beach and back again for 3d a ride. And then, as evening fell, the tired little troupe would make its return journey through the busy streets for a night's rest.

The lady in charge of them, a dour woman in her sixties, seldom spoke as she ushered them along their daily route through the town; sometimes her grandchildren would accompany her and sometimes her husband, but the donkeys were hers. She owned them, she paid for their upkeep, and she took their earnings as her living.

Within the purple moors which surrounded the town, and indeed within the town itself, there was, and still is, a good deal of folklore surrounding the donkey. For example, there is a legend that suggests no one has ever seen a dead donkey. This is one of those enduring folk beliefs, just as the dark cross on a donkey's back is a reminder that this humble beast carried Christ into Jerusalem on Palm Sunday. And deep in the moors there lingered, until comparatively recent times, a belief that by riding a donkey many cures could be effected, and that the hairs from the cross on its back possessed curative powers. If those hairs were carried in a little bag around the neck of an ailing person, they would prevent toothache, whooping cough and other diseases.

I thought that such superstitions had long disappeared until early one morning, about five o'clock, when I was completing the final hour of a night shift. I was making a last check of lock-up properties along the harbourside when I became aware of an elderly lady walking towards the beach.

She was leading a donkey by its bridle. Seated on the donkey was a girl about nine or ten years of age.

The lady, thick-set with grey hair and a rather handsome, albeit swarthy face, walked with what can be described as a grim determination while the donkey plodded at her heels. This was not the usual donkey lady, although I was sure the animal was one of hers. The colourful harness and tinkling bell suggested that. I watched from the recesses of a yard as the little group moved along the deserted streets towards the sands, and I must admit I was puzzled.

There seemed to be no obvious reason for this, and so, acting on my suspicions, I decided the lady might have stolen the donkey, or removed it from its enclosure for spite or to donate it to the child or for some underhand reason. Clearly it was my duty to clarify the matter, so I stepped out of the darkness of the yard and began to walk along the street as lady and donkey drew alongside me.

'Morning,' I said.

'Now then.' It was evident she did not want company, for her pace increased.

'You're out early?' I began to probe in what I hoped was not an aggressive manner.

'Aye,' she said, tugging at the reins.

'Your donkey, is it?'

'No,' she said, then after a pause, added: 'But Ah've not pinched it, if that's what you're thinking. Ah've got it on a loan, just for this morning.'

'Is it a riding lesson then?' I smiled at the child who sat on board in what did not look to be a very comfortable position.

'No,' she gave another of her short answers.

We walked in silence for a few yards, and I began to wonder about this mission. Her demeanour and her personality assured me that she was not doing anything illegal. I cogitated on how next to question her without appearing too nosy or obnoxious, for there was clearly something curious afoot.

Now that I could look more closely at the lady, I recalled

seeing her about the Fish Market from time to time and felt sure she was the wife of one of the fishermen.

'I've seen you about the Fish Market, haven't I?' I added. 'Gutting herrings and things? Packing ice-boxes?'

'Aye,' she said.

Then the little girl piped up. 'We're off to t'sands. Grandma's going to get me cured,' she said. 'Ah might catch t'mezzles.'

'Oh?' I knew this was the local dialect word for measles and became more interested now. 'And how are you getting cured?'

The lady spoke again. 'In t'way that's been used hereabouts for years,' she said gruffly. 'Wi' donkey rides and donkey hairs.'

It was then that I recalled the ancient beliefs and was amazed that they should still be regarded as efficacious. I decided not to press the matter any more, and said, 'Well, I hope it works,' and veered away from them.

Ten minutes later, I was walking along the cliff top above the spa buildings and could see the deserted beach, the stretch near the water being as smooth as a plate due to the action of the ebbing tide. And there, approaching the water's edge, was the donkey as it went about its curious mission.

I saw the lady halt it and help the child dismount, and then she executed a rapid action which I knew to be the pulling of three hairs from the donkey's back. She took them from the dark markings of the cross, then took a small bag on a string from her pocket. She placed the hairs inside and fastened the bag around the child's neck. The little girl was replaced in the saddle but facing the donkey's tail, and then the donkey was led up and down the beach on a set route, its feet making deep indentations in the wet sand.

I counted nine trips along the little route, and then the girl was replaced in the more acceptable position, and the donkey was led away. They vanished out of my sight under the cliff.

As I booked off at six o'clock, I asked one of the married officers, 'Is there measles about in the town?'

'Yes,' he acknowledged. 'Why do you ask?'

'Oh, just something I heard,' I said.

It would be three weeks later when I was patrolling in the vicinity of the Fish Market and spotted the lady among a group of women who were gutting fish.

'Hello,' I said, and she nodded in recognition. I watched her deft hands work with the knife she was wielding among the plethora of fish, fish scales and innards, and then asked, 'Did your little girl get the measles?'

'Course not!' she said.

6

A second Adam to the fight,
And to the rescue came.
John Henry, Cardinal Newman, 1801-90

The coastal constable requires an ability to remain calm when all around are flapping, and to effect dramatic rescues at a moment's notice. Holiday-makers and indeed local residents possess a remarkable ability to get themselves into some dreadful and highly unlikely situations, and the successful resolution of those situations often requires the expertise of many people with bags of common sense, and some with formal training.

In the short time I was at Strensford, I was staggered by the frequency of incidents which required a rescue team. People of all ages would be cut off by the tide, which meant they had to be hauled up the cliffs on ropes – there were no available helicopters in those days. This occurred time and time again in spite of warnings in the papers and on noticeboards at regular points along the beach. Others would allow themselves to be swept out to sea on dinghies or rubber rafts, some would get lost on the moors behind the town, which meant a fully equipped moorland search party had to range across the hills, and little children would inevitably become separated from their mothers, which meant another type of search party. This one usually consisted of a distraught mother and a solitary constable on tour among the town's ice-cream kiosks and bucket-and-spade shops.

Some visitors put themselves beyond the stage of a rescue attempt. It was sobering to learn of the number of suicides along the coast, so often those of people from afar who came to the rugged Strensford coastline especially to throw themselves off the picturesque cliffs. It provided a spectacular finale to an otherwise boring and miserable life, but as a means of solving life's problems it was thoughtless, because it meant someone else had to clear up the mess. It was usually the police who found themselves with that job, although even they would admit it was a highly effective ending for those who took the plunge.

Very few survived those lofty crashes onto jagged rocks; even if they did survive the fall, the raging sea was often on hand to finish the job. Any rescue attempt here usually ended with a dead body rather than a living person. Some determined individuals drove off the cliffs in their cars, and shot themselves in the driving seat as the rolling car trundled towards the edge of the precipice and oblivion.

Over the course of an average summer, therefore, the local police often reached the stage where rescues became so commonplace that they rarely justified comment over a cup of tea. But some were different: some were worth repeating in the pubs and clubs, and in police canteens.

Such was the one which involved County Councillor James L. Whitburn JP, a man of business in the town. An important man, in other words, and particularly so in his own estimation.

Only some five feet two inches tall, Whitburn was a round, fat little man with no hair and not a very handsome face. He had piggy little eyes and a painful high-pitched voice which utterly failed to generate any warmth no matter how hard he tried. He was quite generous to the town, however, although cynical policemen did wonder if he was trying to buy friendship and favour with a view to earning an honour from the Queen. So far as I know, he never got one.

In spite of his unfriendly appearance, he was a successful businessman with a string of shops and businesses in and around Strensford. He proved himself to be a very able councillor too, fighting for the benefit of Strensford. His opinions and strategy were undoubtedly beneficial for the town, but as a magistrate he was disliked by the police.

Fortunately, he was not chairman of the Strensford Bench. This effectively curtailed most of his anti-police activities, although he always managed to make the police feel uncomfortable while giving their evidence. He would question and question the police officers until they were sick and tired of answering his probing, high-pitched voice, which invariably seemed to doubt the quality and veracity of their evidence or the value of the notes they had taken, the language they had used, the formalities they might not have observed, the motives behind their arrest and so on. He never let up, and his unspoken criticisms gained regular Press coverage. His insinuations were clear.

For this reason, no policeman liked to appear before Mr Whitburn, and some said they would rather let a petty villain go free than endure the veiled remarks of this spiteful JP. No one knew why he was so vindictive, but it almost reached the stage where the whole police station decided to test his Jaguar every day or check his insurance or find his car in a position where it created an unnecessary obstruction. They would have dearly liked him to appear before his own court to sample the atmosphere before the Bench rather than sit majestically upon it to utter his pontifications.

But we did nothing of the sort. We grumbled a good deal

about him, and most of us steadfastly tried to avoid any sitting of the court when he was on the Bench. That was the only action we took – we tolerated him, but only just.

I think the other magistrates even got a trifle fed up with his persistent and niggling comments, and on more than one occasion the chairman openly cut him short during his spirited inquisitions.

But we cured him, or rather Joe Tapley cured him.

I was patrolling the West Cliff area of Strensford on a shift known as half-nights, that is from 6 p.m. until 2 a.m., and the time had ticked away until it was almost 1 a.m. PC Joe Tapley, probably the most experienced constable in town, was on the adjoining beat, and I saw his torch flashing from a shop doorway. I left my own beat and walked the length of the street to chat with him.

'Would you like to see something interesting?' he asked as I reached him.

'Of course,' I said, not knowing what he had in mind.

He led me to the edge of the cliff, where we sheltered in the shadows of a fancy-goods and ice-cream kiosk and from where we could peer out across the sea and view almost the full length of the long, curving beach. The moon was full and it was a beautiful night, which meant our visibility was excellent.

'Look down there,' said Joe pointing towards the beach, his finger indicating an area below us and slightly to my right.

I could make out the distinctive shape of a dark-coloured Jaguar car which was parked on the beach not far from the foot of a slipway. The lights were out and there was no sign of activity.

'Councillor Whitburn's car.' Joe almost whispered the words as he spoke in a conspiratorial way. 'Do you notice anything else?'

I peered into the moonlit distance but could not see anything worthy of special interest.

'No,' I had to admit. 'Why? What's happening?'

'The tide,' he said in his soft voice. 'It's coming in, and it comes in very fast where he's parked. In less than half an hour, he'll be up to his hubcaps in salt water.'

'Hadn't we better tell him?' I said, thinking this was what Joe had planned.

'No-o-o,' he grinned. 'At least, not just yet. Let's wait a while. He'll be at it right now with someone's wife. His own wife – a lovely woman by the way – will be sitting at home thinking he's out on business. And there's his attitude to our lads in court, eh? I think he needs a little lesson, Nick, and right now you and I are in a perfect position to see that he gets one.'

Joe advised me to keep off the skyline so that our silhouettes would not be visible from the beach, and we made our way down the cliffside paths until we gained an unobstructed view of the dark car. Even now the creeping water was lapping around the front wheels, but the goings-on inside were still a secret, except that we did discern the occasional movement and gentle creak of top-quality leather upholstery. Whatever they were doing was of sufficient interest to render them unaware that the tide was rising so quickly around them.

'He'll never get that car off the beach!' I hissed at Joe as the water rose to cover the tyres at the bottom of the. wheels.

'No,' said Joe.

'It'll get inside, won't it?' I persisted, a few minutes later.

'Mebbe,' he said. 'I'm not sure how water-tight those doors are. But if he's busy on the back seat, he'll never notice, will he? Not for a long time, anyway, not until it swishes around his fat body. See, it's touching the bottom of the hubcaps now.'

'When are we going to tell him?' I asked, somewhat worried by the rapid increase in the depth of the water. It was almost possible to see it rising.

'In a minute or two,' he said, to my relief. 'When the moment's right. I've got it all worked out.'

I reasoned that he knew exactly what he was doing, and we waited for a few more minutes, perhaps ten or so, and by then the water was lapping around the centre of the hubcaps and had reached the lower edges of the doors. The sills were now covered.

'We'll give it two more inches,' he said.

When the water was about two inches above the base of the doors, Joe said, 'Right, now we'll raise the alarm.'

With me following tight behind, Joe hurried down the final yards of the path from where we had been waiting, and we came to a halt on the concrete slope of the slipway, right on the edge of the incoming tide. We could go no further because the water was lapping the foot of the slipway. From that point, Joe began to shine his torch on the windows of the silent car, simultaneously shouting and waving the torch about. I did likewise. We made a useful noise and created something of an illuminated commotion.

Our shouts and light-waving precipitated a great deal of action within the car; the wandering beams of our powerful torches touched upon startled eyes, white faces and many flabby lumps of bare flesh as the car rocked with their frantic attempts to adjust or replace their clothing. During that burst of instant action, the expensive leather groaned even more, and the car rocked in its large puddle.

Then the rear door burst open and Councillor Whitburn's piggy little face appeared; he opened his mouth to bawl his displeasure at us but almost immediately found himself standing knee-deep in cold sea-water. This effectively halted his outburst.

'It's the police!' shouted Joe as if we had just arrived in the nick of time. 'You're up to the axles in water . . .'

'Help!' screamed a woman's voice from inside. 'Jim, you'll have to do something . . . Get this car moving, for God's sake . . .'

'You'll never drive it out!' bellowed Joe as the Councillor paddled about in the water, hurrying around to the driving seat. 'Leave it, and come up here.'

'I can't leave it here!' came the squeaky reply. 'I'll drive it out, I'll move it.'

'I'm going!' said the woman. 'This is too bloody embarrassing for words. I'll have you for this, Jim Whitburn!' she cried at him as she disembarked. 'I'll never let you forget this . . . How bloody silly can you get . . .'

She paddled through the swirling water, holding her shoes and stockings high above her head and her skirts almost as high as she struck out for dry land. Joe reached out a hand and hauled her up the slipway.

'Hello, Mrs Beckett,' he greeted her. 'Nice night for a bit of courting, eh?'

'He'll never get me down there again, not ever!' she snapped. 'I'm going home.'

Pausing only to slip on her shoes, the lady stomped away up the slope and vanished towards the town.

'Mrs Beckett,' smiled Joe. 'She's a teacher at one of the schools in town. Nice chap, her husband. She's on the council, too, you see; she's doing her bit for the town tonight, in a manner of speaking.'

Meanwhile, Whitburn had managed to start his engine, and the twin exhausts were making the sea bubble behind the marooned Jaguar; it seemed the water had not reached the interior of the engine, and so long as he could keep it running, the power of the exhausts would keep the water at bay, at least temporarily and at least from that part of the vehicle.

But Whitburn's attempts to drive out of the sea were futile. The wheels utterly refused to grip the sandy surface, and as they turned, the car sank deeper into the holes they produced. Accompanied by deep gurgling sounds, the engine spluttered to a halt, and Whitburn came splodging ashore.

'Oh, it's Mr Whitburn!' Joe sounded very surprised. 'Won't it budge, sir?'

'It'll be swamped,' cried the distraught man. 'My car, my new bloody car! It'll be covered – it'll be ruined!'

'I'll drag it out for you,' offered Joe. 'Come on, Nick. Quickly, before the car's completely covered up.'

Parked only yards away, close to the lifeboat house, was the tractor which was always on stand-by to winch the lifeboat, or other boats from the sea. Its winching gear was in position on the rear, and Joe had no trouble starting the engine.

'Grab that cable and hook, Nick, and lead it out to Mr Whitburn as I unwind it. He'll take it. There's no need for you to get wet. Ask him to link it around the back axle of his Jag, and we'll haul it out.'

And so we did. In minutes, the car was back on dry land, a little wet on the outside but very wet on the inside. It was a very relieved Mr Whitburn who began to splutter his thanks, as the water sloshed about the floor of his car. The carpets would be ruined.

'Forget it,' said Joe amiably. 'It's all in the course of duty. There's no harm done, is there?'

'You're both very kind,' he managed to say. 'We might have been drowned . . .'

'I trust the newspapers won't get hold of the tale, Mr

Whitburn,' smiled Joe, adopting that amiable smile once
again. 'You know the sort of thing they'd print – "Local
Magistrate in High Tide Love Drama" . . .'

'You won't tell them, will you?' There was a sudden
flash of concern across that podgy face. 'I mean, you are
not allowed to talk to the Press, are you?' There was more
than a hint of menace in that squeaky voice, even in these
circumstances.

'Some things are forbidden, Mr Whitburn, things like
internal police matters, the secrets of criminal investigations,
a person's criminal record, that sort of thing. But, well,
brave rescues by policemen always make a good story.
But,' and now Joe spoke very slowly, 'I'm sure that if you
adopt a more sympathetic approach to our men in court,
that you bury whatever grievance you are nursing against
my colleagues, then we'll say nowt about this unfortunate
little episode. There's only us know about it, and Mrs
Beckett, but I reckon she'll not say much.'

It seemed to take a long time for the import of this
statement to filter through to his anxious brain, but in time
it did and Whitburn said, 'Well, I'm only after the truth,
you know, for the sake of justice. We must have the truth in
court.'

'Precisely,' agreed Joe.

'I'll try to listen more carefully,' promised the unhappy
Whitburn as he thanked us again and then went to examine
his dripping Jaguar. We left him to his worries and together
strolled contentedly back to the police station.

'I think we should have got him out earlier,' I said with
a twinge of conscience. 'We could have saved his car from
damage.'

'Nick, young man,' said Joe. 'That old bastard could
have ruined a good marriage, that teacher I mean, Mrs
Beckett. She's a good woman, but silly to get tangled up

with him. I reckon I've saved that marriage tonight. I might even have saved Whitburn's own marriage too. I've certainly done something to uphold the good name of the magistracy by keeping a scandal out of the papers – imagine what would have been said if they had drowned, and both of them in the nude too! And I've done our lads a little service as well. And the cost? Well, there's some embarrassment to Whitburn and Mrs Beckett, and a spot of sea-water damage to an expensive car. It'll always have a salt-water tide-mark round it from now on, as a small reminder of his experience. In all, I'd say he's learned a lesson, and for everyone it was a bargain, well worth the price.'

We arrived back at the station at 2 a.m. Sergeant Blaketon was the duty sergeant and asked, 'Well, Rhea? Tapley? Is everything correct on your beats?'

'All correct, sergeant,' we assured him.

Oddly enough, Joe Tapley and I were involved in another, more dramatic rescue from the sea, and it occurred within yards of the place where Whitburn's car had floundered. On this second occasion, some three weeks after the car incident, I was patrolling a night shift and had taken a long stroll along the pier. It was a peaceful, quiet night with a warm August breeze blowing off the land; an ideal night for long walks in peaceful contemplation. Indeed, it was pleasant on such a night to be a patrolling policeman; anyone out on a night like this owned the world. There was nothing to interrupt that peace and tranquillity; it was a blessed state which was there to be enjoyed.

Making use of a spare twenty minutes or so just after midnight, I had circumnavigated the lighthouse and had regained the streets of the town. I was waiting near the circular bandstand about half-past midnight because I knew Joe would pass this way *en route* to his next point. We made use of such meetings for brief chats, always a welcome respite during a lonely night patrol, and so I stood beside the bandstand, waiting in the warm night air.

I could see Joe's distinctive, rather ambling figure moving steadily towards me down the winding slopes of Captain's Pass, and as I watched him, I became aware of a young couple, a man and woman in their early twenties, racing towards me with their arms waving and shouting with enough fervour to rouse the whole town.

Joe had obviously heard them too, because he started to run towards them at the same time as I, and we all arrived together at the top of one of the concrete slipways. The couple were panting heavily, and I saw that their feet were bare, wet and sandy – obviously they'd just raced up from the beach. It was some time before they could pant out their news.

'Take it calmly,' said Joe, always a sobering influence. 'Easy now. Get your breath back.'

The man was pointing to the sea; we could hear the regular slap of the waves in the darkness beside the pier, just down the slipway behind us.

'Man, down there. Drowning . . . we tried to get him . . .'

'Right!' and with that Joe darted off with me in hot pursuit. He didn't wait for anything further but took immediate action. We raced onto the wet sands, and as we left the streets and houses of the town, the darkness hit us. We used our torches but the movement of the sea and our own rushing footsteps made it difficult to see anything in the bobbing lights. The couple had caught up to us, and the man was pointing.

'About here,' he said. 'In the sea. He waded in, fully dressed. I tried to stop him, but he hit me and said he was going to end it all.'

'When?' asked Joe.

'Just now, minutes before I found you. We could make nothing of him . . .'

'Jerry tried to drag him out,' panted the girl.

'Is he a local chap, then?' asked Joe.

'Dunno,' said the man called Jerry. 'I'm not. We're on holiday.'

As we talked, we ranged the circular glow of our torches across the sea, and then the beach, and then the sea again, but saw nothing. I began to wonder if we were too late, if the fellow, whoever he was, had gone under the surface for ever. The sea was well out; the tide was turning and would soon sweep in across those bare sands.

I lifted my own torch and searched the waves further out. Only a matter of yards from the shoreline, they rolled in majestically before breaking and roared up the beach. And there, suddenly, I caught sight of him. My beam reflected upon his wet clothing and hair, creating a momentary burst of brilliance out there in the wet darkness, and so I shouted and held my light on him. He was attempting to wade out in the face of the incoming waves; they were making his progress difficult as he breasted each new wave, the strength of it lifting him onto his toes as he fought to make progress.

There were no boats here, save the lifeboat tucked away in its shed, and there was no time to raise its crew; thinking as one person, Joe and I threw off our jackets and caps and waded in. We passed our torches to the young couple, asking them to keep the twin beams on the figure ahead of us. They would have to be our guides in the darkness.

'Don't shout,' said Joe. 'Just wade like hell.'

But it was easier said than done. When the sea was higher than our knees, we found the going very tough, but we forged ahead; sometimes the fellow would stop as if contemplating his fate, and this allowed us to gain a few precious feet, but in no time the water was up to our waists.

'We can't hang about too long,' said Joe. 'The tide's coming in. Come on, he's not far off now.'

The man, with the sea up to his chest, was finding the going more difficult than we did, but as it rose to our chests we had the same trouble. Then, with a terrible cry, he fell headlong into the water, arms outstretched; the torch beams shone into the unseen distance, and for a moment or two we lost him.

'Keep them shining near us!' bellowed Joe, and so we began to hunt for him among the rise and fall of the incoming tide.

'There!' I had seen him, floating face down apparently determined to drown himself, even if his clothing and the air in his lungs kept him afloat. He wore a fawn mackintosh which floated around him, making him fairly visible in the dark water.

The action of the incoming tide carried him closer to us as we waded out, and this helped us to reach him. The light of the torches was bobbing about close to us and helped a little. Without speaking, Joe and I separated as we closed in, and each of us seized an arm and lifted the man out of the water. He struggled in our grasp, coughing and spluttering, but we knew how to contain a person and in no time had our arms tight under his so that we could walk out of the sea, with him trailing behind and moving backwards towards dry land.

We carried him high onto the beach and laid him gently down. He was now silent. The couple came closer and shone torches on him. He was a very thin person, a man about forty with a head of lank, black hair and a very white face. He wore a suit under his old raincoat, and a white shirt and black tie.

Joe slapped his face.

'Leave me alone. I want to die,' he said. 'I just want to die . . .'

'That's not allowed,' said Joe. 'At least, not while we're about. So, you're not dead yet, which means we'll take you to hospital. Come on, on your feet.'

The man just lay there, so we turned to the couple to obtain their names and address, for we'd probably need a statement from them about the affair. Then we went off to locate our hats and jackets.

But in those few seconds, the man had leapt to his feet and was running back into the waves.

'Bloody hell, you can't turn your backs for a minute!' shouted Joe. 'Come on, Nick, here we go again.'

In those few moments the determined self-destructor had gained ten or twenty yards on us, and by the time we had thrown our belongings back to the ground and shouted for the couple to shine their torches upon him once again, he had reached the water. By the time we caught him, he was up to his waist in strong sea-water, thrashing ahead with enormous splashes as if he intended wading across the entire North Sea.

This time we caught him before he had time to lie down in the water, and we executed the same move as previously. But this time it didn't work. He began to thrash his arms and simultaneously kicked, shouted and struggled; he became like a human dynamo and windmill combined as he created a huge maelstrom in the water. In spite of this, we did manage to haul him to the shore, although both Joe and I got several knocks to our faces and bruises about our wet bodies. It was exhausting work.

As we arrived on the beach, he fell to the ground rather like a child who does not want to go for a walk, so we drew him along the sand and laid him down once more. He lay like a saturated rag doll.

'Let me die,' he was sobbing now. 'I just want to die. Why can't I die if I want to?'

Joe addressed the young man who was still hovering about with Joe's police torch shining upon the saturated fellow.

'Jerry,' Joe remembered the man's name. 'Be a good chap and call an ambulance, will you? There's a kiosk near the bandstand, where you found us, and the hospital's number is 2277. Tell them to come to the West Pier, and you wait there until they do, then call us.'

Jerry ran off to perform this useful task, while we and the girl stood around as the would-be suicide lay on the beach, weeping and covering his face with his sandy hands. We stood close enough to prevent him from another spring into the waves. The girl, now shivering violently, stood at a discreet distance with her teeth chattering.

'What will happen to him?' she asked, with obvious concern in her voice.

'We'll get him to hospital,' said Joe. 'They'll see to him. I would imagine he'll come back to his senses after a day or so.'

'I'm pleased you rescued him,' she smiled, holding a cardigan tight about her slender body.

'He owes his life to you,' I said. 'You noticed him and did something about it – promptly too.'

The man was struggling to get to his feet, and we were very wary of his next move. Already, I could feel the beginning of a black eye from his earlier thrash, and as I helped him to his feet I was very aware that he might attempt a new trick. But he didn't. He stood beside us, dripping wet with his head hung low.

'What's your name?' Joe asked him.

'I'm not saying. I'm not saying anything,' was his reply.

'Suit yourself,' said Joe. And so we waited in silence and

then, after about five long minutes, Jerry returned, waving the torch once again.

'It's come,' he called. 'The ambulance, it's waiting at the top of the slipway.'

'Come on.' Joe took the man's arm, but in a flash he had shaken free and was once more sprinting like a gazelle across the beach, heading for the crashing waves.

'This joker does not give up!' and with a cry, Joe and I set off in hot pursuit.

This time we reached him before he gained the water, and although I do not claim to be a Rugby football player, I did launch myself at him in what could be described as a flying tackle. I brought him down among cascades of sand only feet from the water's edge, and he promptly began another fierce and powerful struggle, with Joe and me battling for control. This time, it was a fierce and vicious fight. I got a bloody nose from a flailing fist, Joe had a tooth loosened, but it seemed impossible to subdue this man whose insane strength appeared to grow greater as ours weakened.

It was like fighting with a whirlwind; his crazy mind seemed to have driven him berserk, and as we fought on that beach, he was just as determined to drown himself as we were to stop him.

It was Joe who subdued him. With a mighty blow to the man's stomach, Joe winded him, and as he doubled up in breathless agony, Joe delivered a punch which would have delighted any boxer. It caught the man on the chin, and it felled him.

'Sorry, old son,' said Joe to the unconscious man at his feet. 'But we can't mess about all night.'

We carried him up to the ambulance, thanked the young couple and walked back to the station to obtain some dry clothing.

The following day, as we paraded for duty, the inspector was waiting for us at 10 p.m.

'Rhea and Tapley,' he said. 'Report to my office before you go to your beats.'

We went through and stood before his desk, and he joined us soon afterwards. He looked us up and down, then said, 'Would either of you describe yourself as violent?'

Joe and I shook our heads and denied such a possibility.

'Well,' said the inspector. 'We have received, via the hospital, a complaint against two of my constables. It seems that a patient alleges he was swimming in the sea last night, and was assaulted by two uniformed police officers. Now I know this occurred in the area which formed part of your beat, both your beats, in fact. I need not say that I regard this as a very serious allegation, and I want you both to think very carefully before making any response . . .'

'No comment,' said Joe.

And I concurred.

'Well done, the pair of you,' he smiled.

7

Husbands, love your wives
Be not bitter against them.
St Paul (to the Colossians)

If there is one aspect of human behaviour which stands out more than any other in police work, it is the multitude of ways in which husbands and wives manage to deceive one another. With the broad range of their miscellaneous duties, observant police officers see and learn much about the way that life is actually lived, rather than the way it appears to be lived, and this marital quirk is constantly observed.

In the area of supposed domestic bliss, therefore, the police are guardians of many secrets. They keep their eyes and ears open but their mouths firmly shut, for they know, often to their cost, that strife between man and wife causes more serious trouble than anything else.

Domestic rows in varying degrees of ferocity are a nightly feature of police work; one spouse engages in noisy and violent battle against the other, often over some trivial matter, and when the neighbours call the police in an attempt to restore order, the warring pair band together to assault the unfortunate peace-keeping constable. So police officers everywhere learn to cope with these outbursts.

Most 'domestics', as we call them, are concluded as rapidly as they arise, although some do spill into the streets as the whole neighbourhood joins the mayhem. Quite often, a good time is had by all.

Problems that arise through a man or wife misbehaving sexually, however, call for a different technique. The fact is noted, possibly for future use, but a discreet silence is maintained, even if the people in question are prominent in local public life. Discretion is an essential quality of police officers. The Yorkshire motto of "Hear all, see all and say nowt" was probably coined by a policeman with a long experience of others' illicit affairs. Every police officer has, at some stage of his or her service, had to cope with a domestic problem of some kind.

It is not often that real love or genuine respect by one spouse for another causes those kind of problems. Usually, it is lack of those virtues which creates the agonies. Yet on two occasions at Strensford, love or respect, or possibly a combination of both, did cause domestic problems in which the police were involved.

The first concerned Mr and Mrs Furnell, Edward and Caroline to their friends. They owned and ran a splendid private hotel on the cliff top; it was a veritable treasure house of style and culture, the sort of place frequented by very discerning visitors with money enough to pay for their expensive and exclusive pleasures. The sheer cost of staying there kept at bay those of lesser quality, and there is no doubt that the genteel luxury of "Furnells", as it was simply known, did establish standards which set it apart from the average seaside hotel.

Edward was a charming man. In his late forties, he was tall and slender, with a head of good, thick black hair which was greying with distinction around the temples. He was always smart in a dark grey suit or a blazer and flannels, and his turn-out was positively immaculate. He was handsome too, with a lean, tanned face and a sensuous walk which attracted many women. But in spite of the opportunities which must have presented themselves, he was never unfaithful to Caroline. Indeed, he was a pillar of the Anglican Church, a very active member of the Parochial Church Council and a sidesman who never missed the Sunday service. He was almost too good to be true as he ran his hotel with scrupulous honesty. Everyone thought he was a perfect specimen of manhood, an example to all. There is no doubt that many people regarded Edward as an example of the ideal husband and businessman, and that many husbands found themselves openly compared with him.

Caroline was similarly well endowed with good looks and charm. If a little inclined to be plump, she did her best to appear smart on every occasion, when her blonde hair would be set in the latest style, her make-up impeccable, her clothing beautiful and her treatment of others charming and welcoming. A little younger than Edward, she would be in her mid-thirties. Although she lived in a world of expensive tastes enjoyed by expensive people, she was neither aloof nor snobbish. At times she was a real bundle of good humour and warmth, especially on those rare occasions when she was not in the austere company of her proud husband.

There were times when I did wonder if Caroline would be more relaxed and 'ordinary' if Edward was not around. In my view, it did seem that his presence sometimes overawed or even suppressed her, and occasionally I wondered if she was trying desperately to live up to his lifestyle. I felt he set standards which were not normal for her. Marriage to Edward had perhaps forced her to adopt his particular way of life, but she coped admirably and everyone liked her.

The Furnells were always happy, always good company and always an example to others. Patrolling policemen were welcome to pop into their hotel kitchen for a cup of tea and a warm-up on ice-cold mornings. That's how we got to know the couple so well. Our presence served a dual purpose, because if there was any doubt about a guest, we would be told and we would carry out discreet enquiries in case he or she absconded without paying the bill. We had physical descriptions and car numbers well in advance, just in case.

This enviable state of bliss continued until Caroline started driving-lessons. Edward, perfectionist that he was, insisted on teaching his wife, because he felt he could do it so much better than anyone else. This practice is never recommended for normal husbands and wives, for there is no finer way to generate marital problems than to teach one's wife to drive. For some reason, a woman behind a steering wheel will steadfastly refuse to learn anything she is taught by her husband, and she will likewise blame him for all that goes wrong. How many lady drivers, when they have had a minor driving upset, have said to their husbands, 'You made me do that!'

But Edward was not a normal man. He was Mr Perfect, and so he guided his wife around the town's maze of quaint narrow streets, pedestrian crossings, junctions, lanes, bridges and corners and through columns of gawping tourists and dizzy townspeople until she was a very proficient driver. Sometimes they went out very early in the morning and sometimes very late at night for Caroline's lessons, although he did take her into the thick of the daytime traffic whenever his hotel duties permitted.

And Edward, being so particular about things, sent her to a driving school for the finishing touches before she took her test – even he admitted the experts did have a role to play. And then, one day in late August, Caroline was due to take her driving test.

An hour later, she returned to the hotel, where Edward was waiting.

'Well, darling?' he asked.

'Isn't it wonderful?' she breathed. 'I passed, Edward, I passed. First time! Me, a driver!'

'I knew you would, darling. I just knew. Now, here's a little present for you,' and he handed her an ignition key. Outside, on the car-park of their hotel, stood a brand new Morris 1000 in pale blue.

'It's for you,' he said. 'A present from me.'

And so the citizens, and indeed the police, became accustomed to seeing Caroline chugging around in her lovely little car, sometimes shopping, sometimes going about hotel business or merely visiting friends.

Then, one busy morning in early September, something went wrong. No one is quite sure what happened, but the little car ran out of control down Captain's Pass with a panicking Caroline at the wheel. She collided with some iron railings outside a café which acted like a spring, for she bounced off and slewed across the road like a shot from a gun. Having been catapulted across the road in this manner, miraculously missing other cars and wandering pedestrians on its terrifying journey, her little car mounted the opposite footpath and careered across an ornamental garden. It concluded its short but impressive journey among a jumble of rocks, cotoneasters and geraniums. The Council's Parks Department were not very pleased about it.

Fortunately, Caroline was not hurt, although she was rather embarrassed, and the immaculate little car suffered some plants in its radiator grill, a badly dented door panel, buckled wings and other minor abrasions. As a result, the machinery of law began to move, the police were informed and I arrived at the scene.

It was a 'damage only' accident involving just one

vehicle, with no personal injuries, so there were few problems. Willing helpers manhandled the car out of the flowerbed, and it was still driveable; meanwhile, the shaken Caroline was muttering something about a black dog running over the road and causing her to lose control.

Having ensured she was not hurt, I had to ask for her driving licence and insurance; she did not have them with her and therefore opted to produce them at Strensford Police Station within the legally stipulated five days. This was standard procedure in such a case. I did not expect any further proceedings, although I had to chant the words of a 'Notice of Intended Prosecution' at her, this being a statutory formality at that time in case there followed a prosecution for careless driving or some other more serious driving offence.

I asked if I should take her home and she declined. She insisted she was fit to drive, and in any case she would like to break the news to Edward herself. So off she went.

I was not at the police station when she arrived to produce her documents but shortly afterwards was summoned to see Sergeant Blaketon.

'Rhea,' he stood before me at his full majestic height. 'This Mrs Furnell of yours, the accident on Captain's Pass. She's been to produce her documents. You'll have to go and see her – her driving licence is not valid, and this being so, neither is the insurance on that car. It's your case, so you'll have to follow it up.'

When I looked at the details of her licence in the Production of Documents Book, they were for her provisional one, which had expired, albeit only a week earlier.

'She's probably brought the wrong one in,' said Sergeant Blaketon. 'Go and sort it out.'

When I arrived at "Furnells", Caroline was not her

normal, immaculate self. She was alone in the office as Edward attended to some business at the bank, and she gave me a coffee. But she was paler than usual, her lovely eyes looked dark and sad, her hair much less tidy than normal and her general demeanour much less confident.

'I know why you're here,' she looked steadily into my eyes. 'I'm sorry.'

'You produced an out-of-date licence,' I said, probably unnecessarily. 'It was your old provisional one. I need the new one, the one that was valid on the date of your accident. If it was a provisional one too, I'll need the driving examiner's slip to confirm that you passed your test, or, of course, I'll need a full licence.'

She hung her head.

'I didn't. I failed,' she said slowly. 'I failed that bloody driving test, officer. And I daren't tell that perfect bloody husband of mine! I daren't tell him I was a failure! He does not recognize anything that's second rate, he can't tolerate anything that's a failure, so I told him I'd passed. And when I said I'd passed, he gave me that car – it was all ready and waiting for me. He never thought I'd fail, you see. Never. So what could I do? I daren't tell him, not after all that.' She was weeping now. 'So I got myself into a trap . . . a snobby, awfully stupid trap. I don't know what he'll say when I tell him.'

She wiped her eyes, and her make-up began to run down her cheeks. She looked anything but elegant and self-assured.

'He doesn't know? Not even about the accident?' I was incredulous.

'No. I got the car fixed – it wasn't damaged much . . . but this will get my name in the papers, won't it? He'll have to know now, won't he?'

'It depends. You see, if you've no provisional licence in

force, it could mean your insurance is automatically invalid too. And you were driving unaccompanied by a qualified driver. And you had no "L" plates on. There's a lot of offences, Mrs Furnell. I've got to report you for them all.'

I had to go through the formalities of notifying her of an impending prosecution for those offences and possibly a 'careless driving', but the decision about a prosecution was not mine. Ultimately, it rested with the superintendent, who would study my report and make up his mind from the facts which I presented.

A few days later, I did see her driving around town again, with 'L' plates up and with a driving instructor at her side. She waved as she passed me. But I had finished my tour of duty at Strensford before she appeared at court.

I do not know what fate she suffered before the magistrates, although it would probably involve a fine of some kind with endorsement of her new licence for the insurance offence. I do not know how Edward accepted this blemish to his reputation, but I like to think that he, being a perfect gentleman, had treated his unhappy wife like a perfect lady.

The other case was very similar. It happened because Nathan Fleming loved his wife so much that he kept a guilty secret from her.

I had frequently seen Nathan about town because he was one of those characters that everyone knows, likes and respects. He seemed to be everywhere, a truly ubiquitous character. He was a member of one of Strensford's oldest fishing families and owned several fishing boats which plied from the town's picturesque harbour. In addition, he had a couple of wet fish-shops, a whelk stall and a little van which toured the outer regions of the town on Tuesdays, Thursdays and Saturdays.

I was never sure of his age. He was one of those men who could have been anything between forty-five and sixty, a stocky, powerful man with the swarthy, dark features of the indigenous fisherfolk. More often than not, he had a few days' growth of whiskers on his chin, and when about town he invariably wore a dark-blue ganser with a high neck, even in the height of summer, along with blue overalls and heavy rubber seaboots. The ganser's name is a corruption of guernsey, the name for a thick, dark-blue woollen jumper which originated in Guernsey on the Channel Islands. A jersey comes from Jersey too. Those boots came up to his thighs when on the boat, but he rolled them down when not on the boat, so that when he walked he looked like a tiny man in a pair of giant seven-league boots.

A distinctive aura surrounds a Strensford fisherman. It is difficult to define but doubtless comes from centuries of extremely tough work in appalling conditions on the North Sea. His clothes are sensible and ideal for the task, if almost a uniform; his language is also hard and liberally spiced with a dialect all of his own, a dialect that even his colleagues from Scandinavia can understand.

These fishermen live in a closed community, their families having lived and worked here since Viking times. It is rare, indeed very rare, for them to marry outside their own kind.

That is why Nathan's wife was so different. She was not from a Strensford fishing family but hailed from the Midlands. It seems she and Nathan had met as young people when she came to Strensford for a holiday, and much to everyone's surprise they married. She became the brains behind his various business enterprises, but she was not like the wives of the other fishermen.

Those other wives had emerged from days, fairly recent days, when the women virtually lived on the fish quays, drying the fish in the open in summer, gutting crans of herring and stones of cod, packing them in large ice-boxes, mending nets and baiting lines in spite of the weather and in spite of the hour. Being a fisherman's wife was hard, very hard.

Laura Fleming had had none of those experiences. She'd been reared near the Trent, the daughter of a shopkeeper in Stoke, and she had no intention of sitting all day among stinking fish and their bloody innards. So, by her own conduct, she was a woman apart, but a thoroughly decent woman who became a loved and respected member of Strensford society. She was President of the Townswomen's Guild, a strong Methodist and sincere chapel-goer as well as a tireless worker for charity.

I'd seen her once or twice. I'd noticed her supervising the assistants in their shops or at the summer-time whelk stall. She was a smart woman in middle age who enjoyed the light, peachy complexion which was such a contrast against the dark ruggedness of the other fisherfolk. Her features alone marked her out as a stranger among the local people, and her uncharacteristic mode of speech was another difference. Her mousy hair, just turning grey when I knew her, was always tightly tied in a bun, and she always wore sensible shoes, thick stockings and clothes which concealed her figure. Like Nathan, she was always busy with something, either running the shops, raising money for worthwhile causes, such as the Royal National Lifeboat Institution or various other maritime charities, or going about chapel business.

Being a policeman means that it is possible to acquire a knowledge of people without even realizing it; as citizens like Laura go about their daily routine, and as the policeman does likewise, their paths cross, they chat and they begin to discover more and more about one another, albeit unintentionally. Gossip, parade-room chat and frequent talks with my Strensford colleagues all provided little snippets about Nathan and Laura which I stored in my memory, usually subconsciously. It was all part of local knowledge, such an asset in police work.

The other fishermen's wives accepted Laura; there was no antagonism, and this may have had something to do with the fact that she was the wife of the respected Nathan Fleming, or it could have been due to Laura's own personality and quiet charm. Or a combination of both.

But it was Nathan I saw more than his wife. When he was not on his boat or seeing to his whelk stall, he was driving his van around the outskirts, pulling up in the streets as his customers flocked to buy what he described as the freshest fish in town. Whenever he stopped near me, I would gaze in admiration as he wielded his knife to provide every customer with a choice piece of the right weight, and he always found a morsel for the cats which rubbed their chins against his van wheels during these sales.

There were times when I wondered when he slept or took a break from his fishing and the business it generated. He was always busy, always to be seen around town, always happy and pleasant with people, always making a pound or two here and a shilling or two there. He did not run a car, so I pondered how he spent his hard-earned cash, although his home was beautiful. It was a large, old house which his wife, with her tasteful talents, had decorated and renovated. It was a mystery when he found the time to enjoy it.

He did employ others though; sometimes a young man would serve at the whelk stall, or wheel barrow-loads of fresh fish from the quay to the shops, or drive the van because Nathan was at sea. But the moment he returned, he did those tasks himself, apparently tirelessly.

As policemen are prone to do simply by keeping their ears and eyes open, I did learn what Nathan had secretly done with some of his hard-earned money. He did a lot of cash dealing, and over the years he had managed to siphon off a considerable amount of money. This had accumulated to such an extent that he had difficulty knowing what to do with it. To spend it on new equipment or a new business venture might exercise the curiosity of HM Inland Revenue who could begin to ask awkward questions. Worse still, I learned, was that he had managed to accumulate this nest-egg without the knowledge of his dear Laura. That alone suggested cunning of a very high standard.

According to tales which were circulating in the police station, through Joe Tapley's intimate knowledge of the fisherfolk, Nathan had kept his growing wad of cash on his boat. It had been concealed from everyone behind a clever piece of panelling, but the time had come, several months before my arrival in Strensford, for Nathan to do something about it. There was too much even for the place of concealment so he had either to confess to its presence and spend it on the business or bank it, every action being likely to arouse official scrutiny of his income.

The other alternative was to buy something expensive, such as an oil painting or piece of furniture, but that would cause Laura to ask too many questions. Besides, he wasn't one for admiring paintings or acquiring furnishings of excess quality.

So he bought a racehorse.

Very few people knew about this acquisition; it was a very odd thing to do because Nathan had never shown any interest in either horses or racing. We did wonder if it was done upon the advice of another businessman, the logic being that horse-racing, especially betting on the outcome, is one of the finest and speediest ways of getting rid of money.

Joe Tapley was one of the few people who knew of Nathan's purchase, and I know he did not spread the news indiscriminately. Nonetheless, he did tell me during one of our lone patrols, and he provided me with the history of Nathan which I have just related. This revelation and life history were prompted when we saw Nathan hurrying to his boat at 3.30 one morning.

Joe told me the horse was called Beggar's Bridge because it had nothing to do with fish.

'Has it won much?' I asked, not being a racing fan and therefore not knowing the reputation of this animal.

'It hasn't raced yet,' he said. 'It's due for its first outing later this year.'

'There'll be a lot of local interest in it,' I said almost as an aside. 'The whole town will be backing it, surely?'

'They won't!' said Joe. 'No one knows it's Nathan's, not even his wife. He hasn't told her.'

'You're joking!' I cried. 'Surely he's told his wife? I mean, it'll cost a bomb to train and keep . . .'

'He can't tell her, can he? She'll ask where he got the money to buy it and train it. Besides, she's a big chapel lady and doesn't hold with gambling. God knows what she'd do if she discovered Nathan owned a racehorse! Nathan will never tell her, Nick. So the fewer folks know about it, the better, then she's not likely to find out, is she?'

I knew that the code among Nathan's men friends would never allow Laura to learn of her husband's investment, but it seemed inevitable that one day she would find out from someone else about Nathan's secret racehorse.

I thought no more about it until one Sunday in late July. It was a warm, bright day with dark clouds scudding across the sky, interspersed with periods of intense sunshine, so typical of the month. I was working a beat just out of the town centre where I had to supervise the indiscriminate parking of cars by visitors and day trippers. My job was to ensure that all the coaches were left in the official parks provided by the Urban District Council.

This was before the days of yellow 'No Parking' lines and traffic wardens, and one major problem was that thoughtless drivers would park all day in the side streets and so block entrances to the homes of the local people. Even shops and other business premises found themselves blocked in with parked cars. We tried to solve the problem by positioning 'No Parking' signs at frequent intervals, but some motorists would move the signs so they could park their cars! We hit back by booking them for 'Unnecessary obstruction of the highway', but often they had dumped their cars and departed before we could catch them. In those days we did not tow cars away to compounds, and so the poor townspeople often had to tolerate this gross inconvenience. It was a constant battle – the motorists thought we were harassing them, and the locals thought we were doing too little about them.

Over my lunch of salad sandwiches and coffee in the muster room of Strensford's ancient police station that Saturday, Joe Tapley was chattering as usual, and I was listening to his fund of local yarns.

'Well,' he said eventually. 'Who's having five bob on Beggar's Bridge today? It's in the 3.15 at Thirsk.'

I pricked up my ears. This was Nathan's horse, but how many of the men knew that? I kept quiet but said to Joe, 'I wouldn't mind having a crack at it. What's the price?'

'I can get seven to one,' he said. 'I've a friend who can place any bets for us.'

I passed over my two half-crowns and made a silent

wish that Beggar's Bridge would carry them safely home at a profit. And having done that, I left the station and returned to the chore of instructing irate motorists to move their cars.

I had no doubt that when I returned to my beat after lunch, there would be several illegally and stupidly parked vehicles, and that I would spend hours hopelessly trying to find the drivers. We had a pad of tickets for such cases, so I could always stick one of them in each offending windscreen, asking the driver to call at the police station to explain why he had parked in a 'No Parking' street.

It was while patrolling one of the Georgian crescents on the West Cliff that I found a car very badly parked outside a boarding house. I decided to locate the driver by asking inside one or more of those boarding houses. After only two attempts, I entered one called Sea Vista and found the landlady in her little kitchen. She was watching television and, as I put my request about the badly parked car, I automatically looked at my watch. It was ten past three – I needed a note of the time if I was to book an offender.

The man, it seemed, was staying at Sea Vista and had just registered; he was upstairs now, having lugged suitcases and bags up several flights, and so I asked her to request him to move it the moment he had unloaded. I went outside and he appeared within seconds, flustered and full of apologies, so I directed him to a convenient car-park and decided not to report him for prosecution. I had no intention of spoiling his holiday, for he was clearly a genuine fellow doing his best for a growing family.

The moment he'd vacated the space, Nathan's fish van raced into the crescent and halted in the very same spot. Out he leapt and, instead of opening his van doors, he hurried to the door of Sea Vista, knocked and rushed inside. I wondered if there was an emergency, and so, thinking the car-parking episode would give me an excuse for going back, I followed.

'Mrs Parkin,' I heard Nathan say. 'Can I see your telly? Tyne-Tees? Sports?'

'Well, Nathan, I was waiting to get my order, but . . .'

The set was already on and tuned into the sports programme, and when she saw me hovering she said, 'Dunno what he wants, but it must be interesting. Your man moved his car, has he?'

'Thanks, yes,' I said, and then it dawned on me! The 3.15 at Thirsk.

'Can I watch as well?' I asked her. 'I've a little bet on Beggar's Bridge. It's running now, 3.15.'

'So have I. One of my guests said it was a good bet. Come in both of you. It's due to start.'

As the horses went to the start, she offered us a cup of tea from the ever-singing kettle, and by the time they reached the start we were all settled in silence before her TV set, the parking regulations forgotten.

Beggar's Bridge was No 8, which showed up clearly on the black-and-white screen, and we all sat in total silence as the starter's flag went up. Then they were off. Nathan started shouting, 'Come on, come on,' and I found myself watching him as much as I was watching the race.

In seconds it was all over. Nathan's horse had won by three lengths. It was a good, substantial win. As Beggar's Bridge crossed the line, Nathan leapt out of his chair, hugged Mrs Parkin and gave her a huge, smacking kiss, then rushed outside and came back with her order.

'Mrs Parkin,' he said with tears of joy streaming down his weathered cheeks. 'You've made me a very happy man today. Take this fish as a gift, a memento of today. I love everybody!'

She was lost for words and looked at me in total amazement.

'What's got into him?' she gasped.

'I don't know,' I smiled, and after thanking her too, I followed him down the steps and out to his van. He had closed the doors and was walking round to the driving seat as I arrived.

'Well done,' I said.

He studied me for a few moments and then smiled a long, slow smile.

'You had something on him, then?'

'Five bob,' I said.

'Good,' and he prepared to drive away.

'You didn't go to Thirsk to watch it run?' I put to him.

'How could I?' He shrugged his shoulders. 'What could I tell Laura?'

'What can you tell her now?' I countered.

'Search me,' he said.

'You've another problem looming as well, you know,' I whispered to him, man to man.

'What's that?' There was a genuine look of curiosity on his happy face.

'Mrs Parkin,' I said, indicating her bow window with a sideways nod of my head. She was gazing out at him, and there was the fire of love and longing in her eyes. 'How are you going to cope with her next week?'

8

The man's desire is for the woman.
Samuel Taylor Coleridge, 1772-1834

A heady summer-time mixture of sunshine, sea, fresh air and freedom invariably gives rise to nature's desires among healthy young people. That summer at Strensford also affected healthy older people. Perhaps it was the sight of bikini-clad beauties reclining on the sands that provided the necessary stimulus for the older chaps. But whatever the cause, it certainly brought more than a sparkle to their eyes because their wives seemed to spend all their time cooling down their husbands' obvious ardour instead of nurturing it for their own enjoyment.

Perhaps they knew that any nurtured love would not be channelled in their direction? The sexual adventures of the mature British male are fairly well documented in books, magazines, the *News of the World* and the divorce courts, so it is perhaps wise for middle-aged wives to keep a tight rein on their holidaying middle-aged husbands. Memories of a rampant youthfulness can be dangerous in advancing years. St Matthew summed it up succinctly when he said, 'The spirit is indeed willing, but the flesh is weak.'

During my early constabulary years, it was not considered seemly for young ladies to make overtures to young men, at least not in a way they would be noticed, although it must be stressed that, so far as cleverness and cunning are concerned in the eternal search for love (even if it is for a mere five minutes rather than something earth-shattering and eternal), the female sex leaves the masculine far behind.

For all, therefore, whether young or old, male or female, a holiday at the seaside is like a second spring. There, a young man's fancy lightly turns to thoughts of young women, and an older man's fancy heavily turns to thoughts of older women, middle-aged women and younger women. In those days, it was not considered normal for a young man's fancy lightly to turn to thoughts of other young men; consequently, when such thoughts developed into positive action, it was very illegal.

For ladies to fancy other ladies, however, and then to take practical steps to achieve their desires, was not unlawful. This was due not to the efforts of early feminists but to Queen Victoria. I have been assured that when a statute, which would have outlawed lesbianism, was presented to Her Majesty for the necessary royal signature, she refused to believe that such disgraceful things happened and promptly crossed out the relative sections of the Act. Thus lesbians won some kind of privilege – which to this day they still enjoy in spite of apparent sexual equality.

When faced with a seaside resort full of randy young men and available young women, the coastal constable had to be very aware of the provisions of the Sexual Offences Act of 1956 which legislated for many curious facets of human behaviour. We learned to recognize prostitutes (purely for future action which might have to be taken in the course of our duty!) and to know what constituted indecent behaviour or exhibitions.

There were the mysteriously named 'unnatural crimes' which our instructors failed to describe adequately, and a curious set of laws about indecent exposure of what is euphemistically called 'the person'. There were many legal discussions which tried to define precisely what our Victorian legislators meant when they made it illegal for a man indecently to expose his 'person'; we noted there was nothing in that Act which made it illegal for a woman indecently to expose *her* person, whatever that would have meant. Such were the privileges of our ladies. But we never did find out what a 'person' was, and the name 'flasher' was given to those pathetic fellows who performed this curious public display.

There were 'peepers' too, sometimes called 'pimpers'. These were seedy men of all ages who spied on ladies undressing, either on the beach or in their homes, hotels or boarding house bedrooms. It is amazing how many women insist on undressing before a lighted window without curtains, and this attracts many men with binoculars. They are attracted to the light as moths to a candle flame. This activity also brought complaints from the neighbours, which was how we became involved. As a result, we frequently offered 'suitable advice' to the ladies in question – we told them to close their curtains properly when undressing.

It is men of that propensity who hang around car-parks, beauty spots and picnic areas, there to observe the events of nature which occur when courting couples are engrossed in their overtures to one another. Because this behaviour terrifies ordinary folk, we had to patrol in an attempt to deter these nuisances.

Armed with this knowledge, therefore, the constabulary set about keeping order among the frisky holiday-makers. It is true to say that this aspect of our duty did keep us busy. We received many complaints about men indecently touching women on buses and in queues, of men using the pay-telescope on the clifftop to watch women struggling to undress decently behind deckchairs on the beach, of pimpers galore and flashers by the dozen.

It was with the purity of the town in mind that the superintendent was alarmed to learn that a newly formed local Working Men's Club had hired a belly dancer as the finale for the entertainment scheduled for its opening night. He was rather worried about the town's image in case this turned out to be a stripper, but he was also worried that the police could be criticized if they failed to take any action to stem this flow of overt sensuality.

Because such clubs had rather tight membership rules, he and his advisers considered it was impossible to smuggle a local police officer into the club as an undercover agent to observe the proceedings. This meant that subterfuge was called for. As the club was a new one, the superintendent decided that I and another young constable called Dave Carter would join the club, with the sole purpose of infiltrating that entertainment. We had to observe the proceedings in detail and report back to the superintendent through our immediate superiors.

Both Dave and I were unknown to the committee, so we applied for membership, giving our lodgings as our addresses and stating we were employed by the Ministry of Agriculture as Contagious Diseases of Animals Inspectors. We were accepted without question and provided with membership cards. The superintendent was delighted, and on the evening of the big event we dressed in civilian clothes and he took us aside to outline our final brief.

We were not to reveal our identities; we merely had to sit through the rumoured 'indecent performance' and take copious notes about the bodily actions, general behaviour and suggestive words or actions used by the belly dancer. We had not to arrest anyone or report anyone for summons – that possibility would be left for a decision by senior officers when they had carefully studied our report. We were there simply to report the facts. We said we knew what to do, and we were looking forward to this duty.

We were admitted without a second glance from the doorman and went to the bar, where we each purchased a pint of beer with our official expenses. Then, after half an hour, we were asked to take our seats in the big room for the evening's entertainment. We found a discreet table close to one of the exits, just in case we had to make a hurried departure. I noted that the audience comprised men and women.

There were speeches of welcome from officials, who outlined the club's future policies and who listed some forthcoming attractions later in the year. These included noted northern comedians, singers and entertainers. After the announcements, there followed a bawdy comedian who had us falling about with laughter. Very efficiently, he warmed up the audience. A male singer did a spot, then a trumpet player, who was followed by a group of singer-musicians with guitars. Finally, it was the turn of the belly dancer. She was top of the bill and had two spots; the audience, suitably mellow after the earlier acts, eagerly awaited her turn.

Our moment had come, but we daren't take out our notebooks. That would be too obvious – we decided to observe events and then jointly compile our report by relying upon our memories and powers of observation for the details.

A grand piano was pushed onto the side of the stage, and to resounding cheers the dancer's pianist emerged. He was a young man in evening dress, and he took his seat with elegance and style. A hush descended as he began to play. To my surprise, it was a piece of classical music, and everyone sat in a hushed silence, awaiting the delights which were to follow. There was a ripple in the curtains at the side of the stage, and as they parted, a tall, lithe young woman emerged. She was as thin as a bean pole, and she was dancing divinely – but she was performing a sequence from the Nutcracker Suite.

There was a momentary buzz of curious anticipation from the audience, but they settled down and watched her. She was graceful and beautiful, and she completed her first spot with charm and undoubted skill. But everyone was waiting for her suddenly to switch into a dramatic and sensuous belly-dancing routine.

After her first spot, which comprised several well-known ballet routines, she went off to polite applause, following which there were some urgent movements behind the curtains. They parted and the club secretary hurried onto the stage. We felt he looked rather sheepish and embarrassed as he caught us before we dispersed for a five-minute break.

'Lads,' he said. 'There's been a mistake. Sorry about it. I rang t'agency in London to book a belly dancer, but they don't understand English down there. They've sent us this slip of a lass, she's a ballet dancer . . .'

'Bring t'lass back on!' shouted somebody from the audience. 'She's worth watching.'

And this was followed spontaneously by a loud cheer. So after we'd replenished our glasses, she came back to complete a dazzling ballet routine. She was cheered to an encore and won more affection from that audience than any of the other turns.

She was given a right good Yorkshire welcome, and I was proud of my fellow club members. She would remember her visit to Strensford, just as I would remember my first spell of covert police work.

Flashers are probably the most harmless and ineffective of

men and yet, by their peculiar behaviour, they are regarded as ogres, sexual maniacs or dangerous, evil monsters. These unfortunates are likely to be sexually inadequate so far as mature women are concerned and would probably flee home to the safety of mother if a woman responded to their weird form of romantic advance.

To go about their performance, they frequently conform to their cartoon image by dressing in dirty, loose-fitting raincoats and little else, for this device enables them to fling open the raincoat at an opportune moment and so compel some embarrassed woman or girl to view their impressive, naked pride and joy, i.e. the male appendage known to the Victorian legislators as 'the person'.

It is not the task of the police to understand why they behave in this curious manner. Their job is to deal with them in accordance with the rule of law, and there are three provisions by which this can be effected, all of which operate on the basis that such behaviour constitutes a nuisance.

The first of those provisions is Common Law. This is the ancient code of practice from which most of our legislation has descended, and this decided centuries ago that exposure of the naked person was a public nuisance. This means that men or women may be guilty of an offence if the incident occurs in public, but few men ever complained if they noticed a naked woman in a public place.

Then in 1824, a few years before Victoria came to the throne, our legislators produced their famous Vagrancy Act. This made it an offence for a man 'wilfully, openly, lewdly and obscenely to expose his person with intent to insult a female', and this offence could occur either in private or in public. However, it was necessary to show that the flasher intended to insult a female. 'Insult' is the word, not 'impress', and it was this Act which appears to infer that only men may be guilty of exposing 'the person'.

A few years later, in 1847, the Town Police Clauses Act, which was, and perhaps still is, in force only in certain urban areas, created another form of this offence. It said that it was unlawful 'wilfully and indecently to expose the person in any street in any urban district where the Act is in force, to the annoyance of residents or passengers'.

We had to learn the subtle differences between all three provisions. The Vagrancy Act appears to apply only to men, while Common Law and the Town Police Clauses Act do seem to cater for female flashers who misbehave in public, although the Town Police Clauses Act does specify that someone must be annoyed. The three variations of this offence do differ in various ways.

Suppose a female flasher operates in private, or on the top deck of a bus, or on a pleasure steamer? Or suppose that, even though she did flash in public, no one complained that they were annoyed? Is the law then broken or not?

In an attempt to understand these statutes, we would dream up situations which were designed to test the precise meaning of these three provisions, because every word is important. For an offence to be committed, every word counts. And then, in the present century, we encountered streakers, naked people of either sex who dashed through busy places for a laugh. Did they offend against any of these provisions? Was anyone insulted or annoyed, or was it just a laugh? The law is so precise in the use of its words that policemen must think carefully before they act or make an arrest.

If the academic side of these three laws exercised our minds and gave us lots of laughs, the practical aspects also provided a good deal of amusement during that summer in Strensford.

The first occasion came from a middle-aged spinster

living in a flat on the West Cliff. Her complaint was that a
neighbour, a man in his late twenties, regularly indecently
exposed himself to her, and so I was despatched to interview
her about it. I listened to her tale of woe and asked her to
show me from where the man operated. She took me to
her bedroom and made me stand on a chair so that I could
look into his bedroom . . .

We took no action in that case, except to tell the fellow
that he was the centre of some attention from a lady
pimper who had to stand on a chair in order to view him in
his naked splendour.

The other occasion was more serious and baffling
because we came to appreciate that we had a cunning and
persistent flasher on our patch. Even though he never
physically touched his victims, he fitted the traditional
image because he did wear an old raincoat and he did
confront lone women on the streets, whereupon he would
fling open his raincoat to display his impressive wares.

He operated both in daylight and in the darkness, and
his behaviour became very frightening for two reasons –
first, he wore a woollen balaclava mask over his face, and
secondly, he always operated in thick fog. After making his
victim scream with shock, he would vanish, leaving her
with the terrifying task of making her solitary way home in
that same, dense, clinging fog.

In all cases, he used the streets, and in all cases the state
of his rampant 'person' provided ample evidence of his
intention to insult a female. This meant that, when we
caught him, he would be proceeded against under the
provisions of the Vagrancy Act 1824. This gave the police
the power to arrest him, and the magistrates' court the
power to declare him a Rogue and Vagabond!

The link with the fog rapidly dawned upon us because
whenever there descended one of those dense coastal sea

frets, known locally as roaks, he would emerge. Dawn, noon or night made no difference, but he did seem to know precisely where to locate women who were either working alone or walking alone in the town. Examples included a cinema usherette walking home after work, two girls from a small factory walking home at lunchtime, a shop assistant locking up her premises, a visitor walking down the pier, a fish-and-chip-shop lady tidying up after closing time . . .

In all cases, it had been foggy, and the fog horn had been wailing in the dense white blanket which suppressed most of the other sounds. We did wonder if the sombre blasting of the fog horn affected his horn in this odd way, but his activities reached a stage where something positive had to be done, and done efficiently. We had to hunt him down, rather than wait until we discovered him in action.

But in a large area of a town, with all its streets, shops, houses, factories and other premises, and with twenty-four hours at one's disposal, how could we begin to trace him? Other than the fog links, there were no indications that he operated to a system. It seemed he simply roamed in the fog and selected his victims at random.

We missed him three times. One night we were positioned at several strategic locations in town, places where women would be alone. I was concealed near a local pub whose barmaid cycled home alone at closing time, but he did not strike that night. Instead he went into the suburbs and flashed himself at a woman walking her dog in the fog.

In spite of the nature of his operations, we never publicized them in the Press; if we had, we might have stopped him for a time, but we would never have caught him. That discreet silence probably meant he was unaware of our growing dossier on him, and it would, we hoped, encourage him to be careless. We were sure that one day he would make an error.

Another aspect of this patience was that, by our silence, we did not unduly terrify the ladies of the town. It was true that the victims did talk about it to their friends, and that some very localized rumours did spread – rumours that suggested a sexual maniac was lurking in every shadowy side street with intent to ravish every female in the town – but the lack of general publicity was to our advantage, and it prevented widespread alarm in the town.

But due to the growing list of complaints, the superintendent decided that a decoy must be used. A policeman was clearly of no value because our flasher would never operate if there was a man in the vicinity, so the superintendent sought the co-operation of Scarborough Police. The superintendent at Scarborough agreed his policewoman should help.

The outcome was that, whenever a sea fog descended upon Strensford, we had to ring Scarborough Police and they would immediately send an available policewoman to Strensford, a matter of thirty minutes' drive. She would patrol in plain clothes in an attempt to tempt and then trap 'The Strensford Flasher'. It was all we could do – there was no resident policewoman at Strensford, and we felt it was not a job we dared entrust to the keenest of civilian volunteers, however well backed up she might be with our own reinforcements.

The problem was that the Scarborough policewoman was with us only for about six hours out of the twenty-four and only on the days when she could come to Strensford. It was a forlorn hope that she would ever be in the right place at the right time. The chances of a policewoman being his victim were remote to say the least. There were tens of thousands of vulnerable women in the town.

Sure enough, at eleven o'clock one night, an hour after she had left to return to her own station, he flashed at a waitress as she was leaving a restaurant. On another occasion, our policewoman was patrolling the area near the laundry. She had been told to patrol there, in civilian clothes and in the fog, because the laundry workers were due to depart at the end of their shift. He had never been reported in action at that location, and it was thought highly likely that sooner or later he would turn up there. But he didn't, at least not on that occasion. He performed outside a fancy-goods shop whose manageress was quick enough to throw a cheap plaster ornament at him. But she missed. The ornament smashed on the pavement, and he vanished into the all-embracing mist.

We could not give up now. Sooner or later someone from the town council or from the Townwomen's Guild or some other formal organization would be making an official complaint about our lack of success. The resultant publicity would frighten him into lying low for a long time, and he'd emerge later to continue a new series of flashings. While it was true that a halt to his activities could be beneficial in the short term, we needed to catch him and arraign him before the magistrates because of all his stupidity and the terror he was creating. And we were still confident he did not know that we were aware of all his previous behaviour.

Then one summer afternoon, soon after lunch, a thick fog descended. It completely enveloped the town for it was a chilling sea roak of very dense proportions. It saturated everything with its droplets of clinging cold moisture. People came in from the beach, and others evacuated the town centre to go to their hotels, boarding houses or homes. Some sought shelter in the shops and amusement arcades, while the cafés did a roaring trade in hot drinks.

As the people moved about the place, their heads were covered with the droplets, their clothes were saturated and their flesh was chilled to the proverbial bone. It was a thorough pea-souper of a fog, a fog to end all fogs, and the fog horn high on the cliff was bellowing its sombre warning to ships off shore.

But this weather was ideal for the Strensford Flasher; it was his kind of afternoon, if a little cold for long exposures, and so we urgently requested a policewoman from Scarborough. She came by train because of the fog-bound condition of the coastal road, and she arrived just before four o'clock.

This was Monica Wilson, a nice-looking and very capable girl of about twenty-eight. In her civilian clothes she was highly attractive and she knew the town fairly well as she had been with us on some previous Flashing assignments.

I was on duty that afternoon, and during a small conference in the muster room we discussed the Flasher's previous venues and the action we would take if Monica called for assistance. For urgent communication we had to rely on shouts or whistles; Monica was capable of fully utilizing both.

One thing of some importance did emerge from that conference. We learned that the Flasher had never used a venue more than once. He had zoomed in, flashed and left, never to return to the same place. This helped a great deal because it meant we could eliminate a lot of possible venues.

Monica listened and made notes, and then suggested she patrol near the railway station. Her logic was that many office workers would be making their way to the station for the 5.35 p.m. train to Middlesborough, and so would many miserable holiday-makers whose day out had been curtailed by the chilling fog. It seemed a good idea, and everyone agreed.

She was backed by six uniformed constables, one plain-clothes detective, two sergeants and the inspector, and we all had had our orders in the event of a call from Monica.

We had a feeling he would arrive; there was that tingling air of expectancy as we vanished into yards, alleys, shops; we lurked behind the portals of the railway station and the bus station, and we realized that today we did have a possible timetable for what we hoped would be his last great flash.

We were all in position by five o'clock. The train left at 5.35 p.m. and so provided Monica with a period of thirty-five minutes in which to make a name for herself by capturing the Strensford Flasher.

It was an eerie sensation, waiting in the silence of that great cold roak, with visibility only a very few feet, but this time we were successful. Or rather, Monica was.

We heard her shout; we rushed to her aid, and there in the fog she had arrested the Flasher. Of all the people he could have selected, he had flashed before Monica, who, unimpressed by his credentials, had rushed at him and now had him in a strong, firm grip. She was proudly marching him towards the police station.

With her free hand, she had removed his balaclava, but I did not recognize him, and so, before a growing crowd of well-wishers and sightseers, she towed him toward the police station.

But it was her mode of seizure which impressed everyone, because Monica, thinking fast and acting as quickly, had seized him by that collection of male equipment the Victorians had christened 'the person'.

He had tears in his eyes as we allowed her to steer him to his just rewards. The Strensford Flasher had flashed his last.

Another recurring problem of a similar type was that of pimpers, those who peep secretly at courting couples or peer through gaping curtains at night, hoping to catch a glimpse of bare flesh or ladies' underwear.

One such man received swift punishment when he was peering into a ground-floor flat. He was intent on watching a woman undress for bed and became so excited at what he saw that he wished to share his experience with passers-by. He broke cover and beckoned a man who was walking his dog along the adjacent street, and the man, who showed some interest in this event, padded across the lawn to have a look. Having looked and understood, he promptly felled the pimper with one swift blow of a very powerful fist. The pimper had been observing that man's rather luscious wife.

Because there was no law which expressly forbade this obnoxious conduct, the police (if they caught a pimper) had to rely on the six-hundred-year-old Justice of the Peace Act of 1361 (34 Edw. III cl. 1360-1). This gave the magistrates a wonderfully flexible power to bind over those who were guilty of conduct which was likely to cause a breach of the peace. Many would argue that peeping through curtained windows at night was conduct which was very likely to cause a breach of the peace, as was illustrated by the judicial flattening of the pimper I've mentioned above. And so, if and when we caught anyone behaving in this way, we took him to court, where we presented all the salacious facts for the benefit of the magistrates, the Press and ultimately the public. And we smiled as the court publicly bound over the pimper to be of good behaviour. This usually did the trick, the resultant publicity being more than an adequate deterrent to others.

We all reckoned Edward III was a very wise man when he made this highly flexible preventative law. It is still widely used to bind over silly people to be of good behaviour, or to keep the peace, sometimes with a penalty if they fail or refuse to abide by the court's ruling.

In many ways, 34 Edw. III Cl. 1360-l was tailor-made for dealing with pimpers, but there was one little snag – we had to catch the pimpers in the act.

The one place which gave us more problems than any other, because of its compulsive attraction to pimpers, was the Nurses' Home. Situated just behind the police station, it was a new brick-built construction designed to be the home of forty-eight single nurses who worked at Strensford Memorial Hospital. But the truth was that only a dozen or so required this kind of accommodation, and so the Home was greatly under-used.

Owing to their long shifts, only some six or eight nurses were present in the building at any one time, and the authorities had closed off the top two storeys.

It was argued that eventually, when the hospital expanded to its full potential, the whole of the building would be utilized, but when I was at Strensford, there was no likelihood of this. So the upper floors were closed, and left undecorated, unheated and far from welcoming. This meant that the small band of resident nurses used the ground floor, which boasted such facilities as the kitchen, lounge, laundry and other offices.

Because they slept at ground level, and because women are notoriously poor at properly closing their bedroom curtains, the narrow slits of light which emanated therefrom, were just too much for the town's army of pimpers. Like moths being drawn to a flame, they crossed the lawns and pushed through shrubs in the hope they would see something more thrilling than last time. Quite often they did catch glimpses of female flesh which thrilled them, and the word got around. At any one time, several pimpers might be concealed in the shrubbery, all breathing heavily as the nurses went about their personal and private tasks.

The police station, therefore, received regular panic calls from the matron, as a result of which patrols were organized from time to time. The girls were advised how to close their curtains and why to close their curtains, and for a short time afterwards the pimpers turned their attentions elsewhere. But, within a week or so, they were back because some curtains had been left an inch or so open, so the whole circus started anew.

We never did catch a pimper at the Nurses' Home, for the simple reason that its hilltop site meant that the lurking lechers could observe the approach of any constable well in advance of his arrival, and so vanish until another time. This being so, there was always the possibility that a nurse would peer out just in time to observe the timely arrival of a policeman, and so come to believe that the town's constables were pimping. Such are the risks of police duty.

But we did have the last laugh.

During one weekend that summer, the whole of the county constabulary was ordered to take part in a joint military and police exercise. It was called Exercise Viking, the idea that army volunteers would attempt to enter several unspecified police stations throughout the county. It was being done so that the security procedures at all police stations would be thoroughly tested. Forty-five soldiers were to act as infiltrators and they were to begin their subversive mission at 6 a.m. one Sunday. For reasons which we failed to understand, they were to operate from a base at Strensford, a factor which meant that our police station was not a target.

The CO came to the superintendent to ask if there were any premises which would provide primitive accommodation for his men during that Saturday night. A church hall would be ideal, as they'd bring sleeping-bags. But the superintendent, being a man of imagination, had a brainwave which was due somewhat to another call from the matron of the Memorial Hospital. She had a further complaint about pimpers.

'Matron,' he oozed, 'I know that beneath that starched front of yours, there is a heart of gold. Now, I need help – can you accommodate forty-five young men next Saturday night? I need beds for them between about 11 p.m. and 6 a.m. They'll be out by six the next morning at the latest. They're soldiers, and they'll bring sleeping-bags.'

'Soldiers? In the hospital? You must be joking! They're not ill, are they?'

'I wasn't thinking of the hospital, matron. I was thinking of your Nurses' Home, all that empty space. That would be ideal. Haven't you a large number of empty beds?'

'But I can't mix soldiers with my nurses, in the same building!'

'I thought each floor was self-contained,' he continued.

'Well, up to a point, but there are common areas, such as the lounge, kitchen and so on, and there are internal linking staircases.'

'I thought these men might help us catch those pimpers,' he added shrewdly. 'I can imagine a pimper finding a soldier there instead of a nurse . . .'

'You could make use of the rooms, I'm sure, Superintendent, if they were not being used by my girls. With the consent of the hospital authorities, of course, but . . .'

'I've accommodation for ten people in the police station, matron. We've good, warm, cosy beds. They used to be the single men's quarters, so they're very well appointed. We keep them in case of emergencies . . . ten men could sleep here, and thirty-five could come to your spacious home and use the upper floors.'

'I cannot have mixed sexes under one roof,

superintendent! That is final. But I have had a thought. I might persuade those girls who are here on that Saturday to come down to the police station, under supervision, of course . . .'

'I would arrange for a woman police officer to be on duty,' he said, craftily smiling to himself.

'And if I had an emergency at the hospital, your men would run any nurse to the wards, to be in attendance just as if she had been in the Home?'

'Of course,' he beamed. 'And then all the soldiers could make use of your premises, just for one night. There is no question of feeding them, or supplying bed linen. They just need a bed to support their sleeping-bags, nothing more.'

'I'll have to put it to the nurses in question,' she said.

They thought it was a marvellous idea. The prospect of all those men so near was a thrill too, so the nurses, only eight of them, agreed to use the single men's quarters at the police station for just one night while their own beds, on all floors, were utilized by the soldiers.

The officer in charge, a young captain, was asked to visit the superintendent, who sought assurance that there would be decorum from all ranks. The matron must not be upset.

'Oh, and Captain,' said the superintendent. 'There is one other matter. Over recent months we have had bother from pimpers around that Nurses' Home. Ask your fellows to close their curtains, eh? Especially those on the ground floor. We don't want pimpers spying upon a lot of hairy soldiers, do we?'

'I'll acquaint them, sir,' said the Captain.

He did, and some promptly left their curtains open and kept watch, hoping to teach the said pimper(s) a lesson. It should provide an evening's sport.

It was midnight when there was a scuffle in the entrance

to the police station, and I was on night duty. I left the security of the office and saw two soldiers dragging a youth into the interior. He was crying, and they were dressed in pyjama tops with army uniform trousers.

'We've got your pimper, mate,' said one, throwing the hapless youth to the floor. 'The lads got him, mind, and gave him what-for.'

'What was he doing?' I asked as I gripped the collar of the youth and dragged him to his feet. He was small and limp and weeping softly.

'Pimping through the curtains,' said one of them. 'A few minutes ago, as the lads were undressing.'

'Right,' I said to the youth. 'Get in there. So you're the one who's been bothering those nurses, eh?'

'No, sir,' he simpered, his wrists hanging limp and his body wriggling like a worm. 'I haven't been to see the nurses. I just like looking at soldiers . . .'

9

Our deeds still travel with us from afar,
And what we have been makes us what we are.

George Eliot, 1819–80

When I was patrolling the sea front at Strensford, there were times when I wondered how the holiday-makers acquired the amount of money they spent so freely. Young people, some with tiny children, appeared to have limitless amounts of cash which they spent on their endless fun.

My police income was so small that it allowed me to feed and clothe my growing family, who were at home while I enjoyed this spell of seaside duty, but there was nothing left for holidays or luxuries. I knew it was wrong to be envious of others because, after all, I had chosen this career and had known the salary structure before I joined. If I wanted their kind of riches and a life of holidays and fun, the remedy was in my own hands. I would have to leave the Force and do something else. But what could I do? Besides, what other job offered such a variety of work, with such a lot of contact with the public and so many interesting and varied occurrences?

Nonetheless, I must admit that I did wonder what other people did for a living; I wondered how they could afford so much time off with so much spending money.

Those musings reached their pinnacle one Saturday night as I patrolled Strensford's West Cliff area. It was here that the best hotels could be found, and in the summer months they were always busy. One or two of them organized Saturday-night dances, or even dinner-dances, and whilst these were chiefly for the benefit of guests and their friends, some were open to the public – at a cost. It was the high price which kept at bay the riff-raff who frequented other Saturday-night hops and who caused trouble of various kinds.

There were few major problems at those hotel dances although we did patrol the streets outside, partly as a deterrent to passing or possible trouble-makers, and partly to ensure that visiting cars were correctly parked and lit. A small number of streets remained illuminated throughout the night but an unlit parked car on a dark street could be a hazard.

Such cars provided one of our minor worries. In those days, all cars which were parked on the streets overnight were supposed to leave their sidelights burning, and although the police did occasionally turn a blind eye to some, such as those in cul-de-sacs or quiet side streets, we did insist that those on the main roads, thoroughfares and busy streets should conform to the law, if only for reasons of safety. Many visitors were caught out by this because in some larger towns the local councils had made byelaws which allowed overnight street parking without lights in designated areas. Visitors from those areas wrongly believed that their system applied throughout the country, and they got a ticket.

But we seldom took the offenders to court. We put a ticket on the offending car, and eventually the owner received a 'caution' – a warning letter from the superintendent stressing that he must not in that way offend again.

One surprising aspect of these vehicles was that many

visitors left their car doors unlocked all night, and it is fair
to say that thieving was not the problem it is today. It was
very seldom we received a report of a theft from an
unlocked car, but this act of trust (or carelessness) did
enable us to switch on the lights of many cars which were
left parked on the main roads. That small act was our good
turn for the driver, even if it did flatten the battery.

One Saturday night, somewhere around 11.15 p.m., I
was making my slow way around my beat. I was moving
along a wide main street which boasted several hotels, and
the largest, the King's Head, was having one of its dances.
A row of expensive cars was parked outside.

I noticed that the one at the front was not displaying any
lights, and so I approached it to see if the driver was still
there. He wasn't, but I strolled around to examine and
admire it. It was a gleaming Jaguar in dark blue. Because of
its colour, it would be difficult to see by an approaching
motorist, and for safety's sake it needed lights. I tried the
driver's door, and it was unlocked. I reached inside, and as
I did so, the strong scent of leather upholstery and rich
carpets met me. The car reeked of quality. After a few
moments searching, I found the light switch. I switched on
the sidelights, but while my head was inside the vehicle and
the interior lights were on, I took the opportunity to
admire the interior – the intricate dashboard, the walnut
fascia, the dials, the plush seats, the position of the interior
lights . . .

It was then that I noticed a briefcase. It was lying on the
back seat and was like a small, black suitcase; furthermore,
it was open, and astonishingly it was full of money. There
were notes galore, £5 notes and £1 notes. I had never seen
so much cash, not even on a bank counter.

This placed me in an immediate dilemma. If I left it as it
was, so easily visible from the pavement, someone might

steal it. I could not secure the car – there weren't internal locks on all doors as there are in modern vehicles. I could, I suppose, close the case lid to conceal its contents, and then push it out of sight under one of the seats. Or I could take the case down to the police station for safe custody.

In those days, without personal radio sets or the help of the Police National Computer, immediate assistance and advice were not available. For one thing, I could not trace the name of the owner of the car. That would have to wait until the Local Registration Office opened on Monday morning.

The boot was locked, so I closed the lid of the briefcase and removed it to the driver's seat, where I placed it on the floor, partly under the seat. It would not fit completely beneath, so I placed a rubber floor-mat on top of it, hoping at least it would be safe from prying eyes and therefore less open to temptation. I could lock the rear doors by depressing the internal handles and likewise the front passenger's door. But I had to leave the driver's door unlocked, for without a key I could not secure it.

I now decided to search for the driver. He was surely at the dance in the King's Head, so, having made a note of the car number, I went in. At the reception desk, I checked to see if the owner was a resident, for the hotel register contained the resident's car numbers, but it was not there. I asked the receptionist if she would use the tannoy system to ask the driver to come to the front foyer, where I would meet him. I explained it was an urgent matter.

I heard the Jaguar's registration number being relayed throughout the hotel and its dance floor, but after five minutes and two repeats of my message, no one appeared. I thanked the girl and requested that if the driver did come to her desk, she ask him to check his car thoroughly. I thought a vague sort of message would not draw too much unwelcome attention to it.

An hour later, I met Sergeant White, our supervisory officer for that shift, and told him of my discovery and my actions.

'Oh, bloody hell! Is he in town?'

'You know him?'

'Know him? Everybody knows him. Wasn't he at that dance?'

'If he was, he never emerged when I called him. Who is this man, sarge?'

'Leo Farrand. A real character, once seen, never forgotten. Forget about the money – he's so bloody careless, he wouldn't know, or even care, if it did get nicked.'

'You're joking!' I cried. 'There must have been thousands of pounds in that case.'

'He always carries about five thousand pounds around with him, in cash. And when he gets drunk, he gives it all away. Seriously! I'm not joking.'

I learned from Sergeant White that Leo Farrand lived, at least some of the time, at Keldholme Hall, which lay in a fold in the valley about five miles out of Strensford. When he was not in residence there, he lived in London, and the sergeant said that Farrand's antics had caused the local police to believe he was involved in big-time crime in London, or that his money was forged. Accordingly, they had contacted Scotland Yard for discreet enquiries to be made into his background, but he was no criminal, nor was he ever suspected by them of being one. In fact, he was a Harley Street specialist, a very clever man whose specialization was dental matters.

'Because of our suspicions,' continued Sergeant White as we patrolled the streets, 'we got hold of some of his notes, but they were genuine. It seems he is honest, if somewhat stupid. Now, whether he comes up north just to get away from the pressures of the city, we don't know, but when he does come, he certainly makes his presence felt. He does so by getting drunk and throwing money away. He throws it about like confetti. Literally, I mean.'

I asked the sergeant to describe him so that I would know him, and he told me that Farrand was very tall, probably about six feet two or three inches, and on the thin side. He had a mop of thick black hair and wore a black moustache and a small black, neatly trimmed goatee beard. He was about forty-five years old, and he always dressed in a flamboyant fashion, often wearing a black cloak with a purple silk lining. I could imagine this character dressed in a top hat and tails, being a magician on stage or an actor in a Gothic drama of some kind. I could visualize him in a horror film or acting as a handsome lover in manorial surroundings. He sounded fascinating, and so I thereupon decided to do my best to catch sight of him.

But I did not see him that Saturday night. My beat took me away from the vicinity of the King's Head, and when I returned in the early hours, the car had gone. There was no report of his cash being stolen, so I guessed he'd gone quietly home.

Within two weeks I did see him. I was despatched upon a spell of duty at Glenesk Mart, a busy cattlemarket two miles into the valley of Strensbeck. Because the local constable was sick, I had to deputize for him by issuing licences at the market.

I positioned myself in the little wooden hut for the afternoon and set about issuing dozens of licences which authorized pigs to be removed from the mart to various destinations. This was really a form of record in case swine fever or foot-and-mouth disease broke out. Through these licences, the police or the Ministry of Agriculture could trace the movements of any suspect animal. It wasn't a difficult job, but some market traders and attenders were merry because the pubs were open all day. This was known as a General Order of Exemption, and it locally extended normal licensing hours so that the pubs were open all day for the refreshment of those who were attending the market.

It seemed that Leo Farrand had decided to attend that market and that he had also availed himself of the abundance of liquor. I learned of this when there was a good deal of shouting at a disturbance near the pub, so I had to temporarily abandon my pig licences to find out what was happening.

From Sergeant White's description, and the actions of the central character of that fracas, it was easy to recognize Leo. I walked to the scene of the bother – we always walked slowly to any centre of bother, the reason being that we had time to determine our course of action before arrival. It also allowed some of the aggravation to evaporate before it was our turn to join in. This simple strategy invariably paid dividends. By the time we arrived, the protagonists had knocked themselves silly, and we simply swept up the pieces.

As I approached, I could see Leo's tall, dramatic figure. He was violently waving his arms as he showered money around the front door of the pub. Even as I approached, the air was full of paper money which fluttered to earth as a crowd gathered around him.

To my surprise, none of the crowd seemed to be keeping the money. As Leo delved into his briefcase and hurled untold numbers of notes into the sky, the crowd were rushing around and collecting them, then stuffing them back into his case. And he simply threw them sky-high again. He was laughing as he did so, and it seemed more like a very expensive game than something which could develop into a fight.

I began to wonder if this could be considered 'conduct likely to cause a breach of the peace', for among greedy people such behaviour could certainly intensify into a mad scramble for the cash, with fists and feet flying as everyone tried to acquire Leo's free riches. But I could imagine the comments in court and in the Press, if I arrested a man for throwing away his own money.

Leo saw me as I approached.

'Why, hello,' he boomed, his loud, strong voice matching his personality. 'It's the law. Now, constable, are you coming to join the scramble for gold?'

'No,' I said. 'And I think you'd better stop too.'

The crowd began to grumble – I was spoiling their fun, so I had to think fast.

'These notes are all fakes,' I shouted at the crowd. 'We've been after this chap for a long time. Anyone caught with a fake note in his possession could be sent to prison. So, come on, put them all back and let's settle down.'

My subterfuge worked. Several people threw notes onto the ground, and Leo and I spent time packing them into his case.

'They're not fakes, constable,' he said with a slight slur to his words as we rammed the notes into the case. 'It's real money, every single note of it.'

'I know, but you can't go throwing your money about like that!' I said. 'It's just not done.'

'Why not?' He stood to his full, majestic height. 'Why can I not throw money away? It is mine. I can do as I please with it, surely?'

He could, of course. There was no law to prevent him, and yet, somehow, this did not make me happy. Perhaps it was because policemen earn their cash by such a long,

hard and thankless struggle that there seemed to be
something morally wrong, rather than legally wrong, in
doing as he was.

'You were obstructing the footpath,' I said, thinking
fast. 'And I think you've had too much to drink. Where's
your car?'

'I came by train,' he said. 'It's market day, and I knew
I'd be getting too much liquor, so I came by train. I won't
drive my car home when I'm drunk, constable. That *would*
be asking for trouble, wouldn't it?'

'So what will you do now?'

He was fastening the lid of his briefcase. 'I will make my
way home,' he said. 'And I will have some tea, and then
tonight I might go out for a meal.'

'With all this money?'

'I might find someone who welcomes my generosity,' he
said. 'Those farmers were handing it all back.'

'They're honest men, Mr Farrand. They deal in cash all
day and every day, and they know the value of money.
They'll score points over each other quite happily in a deal,
but they won't *steal* another's cash. You were lucky it was
them, and not a crowd of villains. They were just enjoying
the game.'

'But I wanted them to have my money,' he said. 'Why
don't people want my money?'

'Dunno,' I said. 'But look, if you want to give it away,
why not send it to a charity, something like the Red Cross
or the lifeboats or the church, somewhere it will do a lot of
good?'

'I do,' his voice was definitely slurred. 'And when I've
a lot left over, I give more away. Now, what's wrong in
that, constable? Tell me why I cannot give away my own
money.'

There was no reason, of course. I could not think of

anything logical to say, so I merely shrugged my shoulders then added, 'Well, when you do give it away, don't let it hurt people, eh? Don't let it cause fights and greed or trouble of any kind, Mr Farrand.'

'If you say so, constable,' and he wandered off, heading for the railway station with his case of notes clutched in his hand.

Later I heard he'd been to a village pub high in Strensbeck Valley where he'd given away hundreds of pounds to everyone in the place, and had bought drinks all night. On another occasion he'd gone to an agricultural show in the valley and done the same.

I saw him once more before my tour of duty was over. Dressed in his flowing cape and with a Robin Hood type of hat on his head, he was standing at the west end of the bridge which split the town as it spanned the harbour. He had what appeared to be a cinema usherette's tray held before his tall figure by a cord slung around his neck, and he was offering pound notes to everyone who crossed the bridge.

But no one took his money.

He noticed my interest and beckoned to me. I strolled across and greeted him.

'Hello, again, Mr Farrand. How's business?'

'Would you believe no one wants my money?' he said. 'I've heard about this sort of thing happening – I did it on Westminster Bridge, you know, right in the heart of London, and no one would accept my money. Now the same's happening here in Yorkshire. I find life is very odd.'

'It is very odd,' I agreed. 'You just can't understand people.'

Another fascinating Strensford character was a policeman, a grizzled old constable who was almost at the end of his service. I saw little of him because his shifts and mine seldom corresponded, but like many officers in the North Riding I had heard of his exploits, and his name was something of a byword in local police folklore.

He was Max Cooper, a heavily built and very jovial character who had seen his fortieth birthday some years ago. He was what we termed an old-stager, a man totally satisfied with life. He was utterly content with his lot and had never even attempted his exams; for Max, promotion was regarded as greasing up to one's superiors.

He had the chubby, pink face of a countryman with a strikingly clear complexion, although his hair had thinned almost to the point of extinction. His hobbies were fishing, which absorbed him almost totally, and drinking, which he undertook with gusto. Overall, Max had an infectiously carefree attitude to work and to life in general. In other words, he did as he liked, and he was one of those men with whom 'nowt could be done'.

No one, not even the sternest superintendent, could dictate to this stolid Yorkshireman. It was possible to persuade him to adopt a certain path but never to drive him. When he executed his night-shifts, for example, he took with him some extra comforts, which included a small alarm clock, an inflatable rubber cushion and a flask of coffee. The rest of us left our flasks at the station, but Max didn't. He carried his around his beat and claimed it kept him awake as he patrolled throughout the night hours.

Max's propensity was to fall asleep in strange places, and I did learn that, over the years, the locals had come to know him and his odd trait. Most of them therefore refrained from calling out the ambulance or the police when they found a hefty policeman apparently dead or drunk or possibly asleep in their greenhouse or coalshed.

Strensford's seasonal visitors were not to know this, of course, and so it was not uncommon to receive reports of dead policemen in fishing cobles, touring buses, back alleys and telephone kiosks. In all cases, the 'corpse' was Max. It was this incurable habit which compelled him to carry the alarm clock and the cushion.

When making a point at a telephone kiosk, Max would go inside, inflate his cushion, place it on the floor and sit on it. As he waited in that comfortable position, he would set the alarm clock to rouse him just in time to walk to his next point, timed for half an hour later. Unfortunately, he regularly forgot to set his alarm, which meant he forgot to wake up as he sat curled up in his telephone kiosks. His absence from sundry appointed places meant that a search was made by his colleagues, just in case he had been assaulted or attacked or had even died.

It followed that Max was a problem to his supervisory officers, but somehow he avoided disciplinary charges for sleeping on, or for being absent from, his place of duty. Most of the time his colleagues covered up for him, for in the daylight hours he was a fine fellow, a very good policeman and a jolly asset to the town.

Now that I've left Strensford, two memories of him stand out in my mind.

One bright July morning, I paraded for duty at 5.50 a.m., in readiness for my early turn shift which ran from 6 a.m. until 2 p.m. We always reported ten minutes before the official start of any shift so we could be briefed about our forthcoming duties. By six, therefore, we were all ready to patrol the town, when the outgoing shift sergeant, a thin fellow with poor teeth, came into the Muster Room. He spoke to our sergeant, Sergeant White.

'Chalky,' he said so we could all hear. 'Max has done it again. He hasn't come in to book off duty. He'll be asleep somewhere. I'm sending two of my lads around all the likely places on his beat, but I thought your lot might keep their eyes open as well. I'll skin that bloody man alive, so I will. Why can't he come home to sleep like the rest of us, instead of kipping in kiosks and keeping us all out of bed?'

With no personal radio sets, we had to maintain contact with the police station through the network of telephone kiosks about the town and were told to ring in the moment we found him. Then the search would be called off. But no one found him. I patrolled my town centre patch and checked pub toilets, cottage outhouses, garages, waste land, telephone kiosks, shop doorways, buses, cars – everything and everywhere that might have provided a bed for the slumbering Max

The office duty constable rang us all to keep us informed of the nil result, and I rang the office in my turn to report a nil response. This lack of a result began to generate some concern. Even though we had searched all Max's regular nodding-off places, no one had found him – and he wasn't easily overlooked.

By 8.30 that same morning, there was increasing concern which amounted almost to panic. Because no one had found Max, it was genuinely feared that he had come to some harm – perhaps he'd fallen into the harbour, or been attacked by villains, or become ill and collapsed somewhere. So at 8.45 we were all summoned back to the station for a briefing. There we were told that a full-scale search would be mounted, with police dogs and more men being drafted in.

A last-minute check was made at his home, just in case he had wandered back, but he was not there. His wife, a big lady called Polly, was not in the least worried – she said he often went on fishing trips and didn't come home on time, because he had fallen asleep on a river bank somewhere. She was virtually unflappable – she knew him so well!

But the Force, in its official capacity, was worried, hence the preparations for a major search. The inspector and the superintendent had been called from their beds at the god-forsaken hour of 7.30 a.m., and we all assembled for this vital briefing.

The clock was striking nine as the superintendent walked in to allocate to each one of us an area for intense search and thorough enquiry.

'You all know PC Cooper,' he said. 'Even those who are with us for temporary coastal duties are familiar with his appearance, so I need not bother with a physical description. Now, last night, he was patrolling No. 3 Beat . . .'

At that stage the constable on office duty gingerly opened the door of the Muster Room and poked his head around the corner.

'Sorry to interrupt, sir, but it is important. It's Max . . . er . . . PC Cooper, sir. He's all right, he's on his way home, sir . . . I just got a call . . .'

There was a long silence followed by murmurings of relief as the superintendent, valiantly suppressing his anger, vanished upon his mission of discovery of the truth, while those who had remained on duty since six were dismissed and sent home for their overdue rest. I and the other early-turn men all returned to our normal duties, not daring at that stage, or in that tense official atmosphere, to attempt to discover what Max had done. We'd find out in due course.

Later that day I did find out where he had been.

We learned about 3 a.m. he had gone into the deserted railway station, as indeed we all did, and had entered a carriage for a sit-down. He had fallen asleep in a corner without setting his faithful alarm clock, and at 5.30 the empty coaches had been taken up the line to Middlesbrough. The sleeping Max had gone with them.

Strensford Station in those days closed after the last train at night, which was at 5.35 p.m., and opened next morning around 6.45 a.m. The 7 a.m. train steamed up the valley to Middlesbrough and returned with a load of passengers, but on this occasion the empty coaches which had been left overnight in Strensford were required for an additional summer train from Middlesbrough. When they had arrived, they had been shunted into a siding, and so had Max. He had woken at 8.30 and, thinking the sun was higher than normal for the time of day, had emerged to find he was not in Strensford but in Middlesbrough, some thirty miles away. We were assured that this surprised him somewhat.

He was fined three days' pay for that lapse, because several disciplinary offences were heaped upon his shining head.

But it was an ensuing, albeit similar performance, which caught the public's eye, because on that occasion the Press found out.

The preliminaries were very similar to Max's unintentional train journey because he had been working another night shift, complete with clock, cushion and coffee, and at six o'clock had failed, yet again, to appear when it was time to book off duty. Once again, the customary search was launched, and this time we included all the coaches at the railway station but without result. Every one of Max's known sleeping spaces was checked plus a few unknown ones, but he had vanished completely.

The panic and concern this time were at a level considerably lower than upon his railway trip, but there *was* concern and there was worry. This time he had vanished without a trace.

As worry increased, tension mounted and a larger search was authorized. The police dogs were called out, and radio-equipped vehicles brought in from other divisions. There was a total complement of about twenty men, so that a complete search of the town could be effected. It is fair to say that by 11.30 that morning everyone was worried, and even the stolid Polly was beginning to show some concern. He was now 5½ hours overdue. Her concern, however, arose because today was his day off, and he had arranged for her to knock him up at ten o'clock, after only some three hours sleep, so he could go fishing on the River Swale. That, she said, would have made him come off duty on time, and for that reason she was worried. She showed her anxiety by coming into town to join the search.

The sudden influx of police officers, vehicles and dogs, and their urgent enquiries around the town, soon came to the notice of the local reporter, who flashed the news to his friends on the national papers. The rapid arrival of several reporters from the nationals with their photographers, happened to coincide with Polly's decision to join the search. She was pictured with a worried frown as she made a token inspection of a boilerhouse – a lovely human-interest photograph.

By noon, the regional and national programmes were pumping out the story of Strensford's missing constable, and there is little doubt that the whole town, resident and visitor alike, knew of our very genuine concern. This time we were very worried, and the public joined the hunt. The locals knew where to look for Max, but failed to find him, while the visitors searched the most unlikely places, such as caves on the beach and deserted woodland glades.

Eventually the time had arrived for the harbour to be dragged. There had grown a nagging fear that the large constable, weighted down by his heavy uniform, might have slipped into the tidal waters and been drowned as the powerful undercurrents dragged him below. A few tentative searches of the waterline had been made, but there was nothing that resembled the soggy mess of a waterlogged Max.

To the delight of the newsmen, the superintendent made the decision to drag the harbour. This would provide a marvellous seaside angle to the hunt and would produce some suitably dramatic pictures. As we had no marine section of the Force, he sought the help of the local fishermen. But they were not available either, because they were out of the harbour, fishing steadfastly somewhere on the grey North Sea. This meant we had to seek the assistance of some men who manned the pleasure boats. These were small cobles with a motor engine; they could carry a dozen folks out to sea, around the buoy and back again for a few shillings each.

Several of them offered to cruise up and down the harbour dragging the fearsome-looking grappling irons; we kept those at the station for such occasions. And so the search gathered momentum. As it did, so our concern, both official and private, steadily increased.

By two, I was due to book off duty, but every one of us volunteered to remain at work until Max was found, however long it took. By chance, I was parading an area at the top of Captain's Pass where the hotels had underground cellars. I had to check every one of them, and as I made my methodic searches I was worrying about Max's awful fate. I could see the harbour, and the little boats dragging their grappling irons. This made me think of the fishermen . . . suppose they netted his corpse or found him floating out to sea . . . The fishing boats, British and foreign, had gone out of the harbour this morning at high tide, some time before 5.30 a.m.

And those boats had very comfortable cabins . . . and those cabins were open at night . . .

As my mind followed those thoughts, I guessed where Max could be. It was the only answer. I walked along the clifftop to the coin-operated telescope which stands for the use of visitors but, before using it, looked out to sea with my naked eyes. I had no idea how far those boats travelled before dropping their nets, but if they were within sight of the shore, they could be seen with the telescope. Together, they would look like an armada or a small floating town, but I couldn't see them with my unaided vision.

As I was about to press a 3d bit into the telescope's coin box, I noticed Sergeant White walking briskly up Captain's Pass. He had not seen me, so I put my fingers to my mouth and produced a piercing whistle which he heard. I beckoned for him to join me.

'Now, young Rhea, what's up?' he asked when he joined me, slightly breathless after his steep climb up the cliff-face steps.

I explained my theory, and he smiled with quick understanding.

'The daft bugger!' he said, smiling at the thought. 'You'll be right, lad. He'll have gone below deck for a kip; he'll be somewhere near Dogger Bank now . . .'

'I wondered if we could check with this telescope?' I said. 'I was about to look when I saw you.'

'Go on, then.'

I pressed my 3d bit into the slot, put my eye to the eyepiece and waited for the internal shield to move aside.

When the view cleared and I began my 3d worth of sight-seeing, I could make out a clutch of fishing vessels some distance off shore. I had no idea how far out to sea they were, but the quality of this telescope was insufficient to identify anything clearly. I could not even decide whether the boats in view were those from Strensford or the visiting foreign fleet.

'Hang on,' said Chalky White when I told him. 'I'll go across to the Imperial and ring the coastguard.'

I continued to watch until my money expired, and when I removed my eye from the telescope, I was surprised to find that a party of people had assembled around me.

'Is he out there?' someone asked, coming forward with his money. 'On those boats?'

'We're just checking,' I said. 'But feel free,' and I indicated the vacant telescope. Now we had a new tourist attraction in town – spot the constable. I stood aside as a longer queue formed; based on the theory that the British can't resist queuing, everyone wanted to see what I'd been looking at. Such is human curiosity.

From regular visits to the Coastguard Station, I knew that the coastguards in their look-out high on the cliff at the opposite side of the harbour had a remarkably powerful set of binoculars; they were supported by a strong pillar and were more like a powerful telescope. Sergeant White would be asking the duty coastguard to examine those ships or even to make contact with them, to see if Max was on board.

It took a few minutes, by which time a growing crowd had gathered around my telescope as word passed among them. I wondered what they all expected to see, but when they saw Sergeant White returning with a smile, they all looked at him with expectancy.

'He's there,' he said, with a mixture of anger and relief. 'The silly . . . er . . .' He hesitated as he realized the crowd was hanging onto every word. 'Er . . . the silly fellow's there. He's on a Polish ship, the *Piaski*, and they've got him working. They don't like policemen in Poland, you see, and thought he was a spy. And they make stowaways work!

So he's swilling the decks . . .' and he burst out laughing. 'They have refused to come all this way back with him. The coastguard's been in touch. So he'll have to stay there until the fleet comes home. The Poles knew nothing of the search, of course. Serve him right . . . Well, folks,' he addressed the crowd. 'There he is, see if you can find him. It makes good viewing.'

And we left the growing crowd as we went into the Imperial Hotel to use their phone to ring the police station.

Mrs Cooper was very philosophical. 'Mebbe that'll put him off fishing,' was her only comment, as she awaited the headlines in tomorrow's papers.

Max was fined seven days' pay for that escapade, but he also became something of a folk hero. The town still talks about the night sleepy Max Cooper dreamt he was fishing – and woke up on the North Sea to find that he was.

10

And young and old come forth to play
On a sunshine holiday
John Milton, 1608-74

Because our brief spell of duty at Strensford was specifically
to cope with the seasonal influx of holiday-makers, it was
probable that we saw more of those than we did of the local
people. There was very little time to form personal
relationships or to get to know the residents.

This might have given us a false image of the town and
its population, but we did find that the visitors, whether
they were there only for the day or for longer periods, were
a friendly bunch of folks. The only regular trouble came
from youths who grew rather boisterous after drinking too
much, and from a few confidence tricksters who left their
hotels and boarding houses without paying. And thoughtless
motorists were a constant irritation.

Generally, those who took the trouble to journey to this
corner of north-east England were a colourful, happy and
fun-loving people, and as I walked that summer beat
among them, I did experience several twinges of regret.
That regret was my own wife and four tiny children could
not be here too, that they could not enjoy the sands, the
sea and the sunshine. I'd bring them later, I promised
myself; it was such a charming place. Olde-worlde in many
respects, it had a powerful character of its very own, a

character moulded by generations who had earned a tough living from the sea. That Strensford is picturesquely situated is never in doubt, for it is supported by some of England's finest and most dramatic countryside.

But if circumstances forced me to concentrate upon the visitors, they did not prevent me from noticing Edwin Dowson, a local man. Edwin was a man of routine, a life-long Strensford resident who was now well into his seventies, a gnomelike figure with a mop of iron-grey hair over his sharp little face.

Edwin's daily routine comprised a walk into the town centre and a visit to the Lobster Inn. He'd been a groomsman in his younger days and had worked for one of the Strensford major shipping families. Now that he was retired, Edwin followed his routine every weekday, beginning at 10.30 a.m. He concluded his first session at 2.30 p.m. This allowed him time to get his breakfast, tidy his cottage and walk into town. In town, he went to the bar of the Lobster and sat on his own chair in his own corner where he remained until closing time. He drank very little but he did enjoy the companionship of locals and visitors alike who drank in the same bar. Every weekday Edwin lunched at that pub. And then at night he performed a similar exercise. He left home at 7 p.m., walked down to the Lobster and left at 10.30 p.m., when it was closing time. On the way home, he bought fish and chips.

He did his own shopping during the afternoons when the pub was shut, and on Sunday his routine varied slightly to accommodate the change in the licensing hours. But he never missed a day at the Lobster, and his routine never altered, day in, day out, year in, year out.

That is, until one day that summer.

It was a Saturday morning, and I was making my point at a telephone kiosk on the New Quay, just around the corner from the Lobster Inn. I knew that Edwin would be walking past at that time, for he left home prompt at 10.30 a.m. and arrived at the pub at 10.40 a.m. That was his weekday routine and it never varied.

When he failed to walk past, I grew a little worried. After all, he was well into his seventies and he did live alone, and so I wondered if he might have suffered some illness during the night. I walked to the door of the bar, which always stood open during the summer months, and peeped in. Edwin was not in his usual corner, and so I decided I should visit his little cottage, just to check on his welfare.

I climbed through the town via the steep steps which riddled the knots of red-roofed cottages as they clung so precariously to the cliffs which overlooked the harbour. High among the cluster of houses, I found his pretty little home. It was a one-up and one-down cottage and it was sandwiched between others of similar style. I knocked, but there was no reply and so I peered inside. Its very neat and tidy appearance suggested it was unoccupied. I hammered again, in case he was in bed, and then a door opened at the adjoining house.

'Yes?' said a lady in a flowered apron. 'Is it him you're after?'

'Yes. I'm just checking. I haven't seen Edwin this morning,' I explained. 'I wondered if he was all right.'

'Aye, he's fine,' she said, wiping her hands on the apron. 'He's gone on his holidays. Took a taxi at half eight this morning, loaded down with two suitcases, he was. He's gone for a fortnight.'

'Well, that's a relief. Where's he gone?'

'Dunno,' she said. 'He just went off with all his stuff.'

I thanked her for her help and returned to my beat. I must admit I was very relieved, and I thought no more about Edwin for some five or six days.

It was a hot Friday night, the town was very busy, and I was performing a half-night shift, that is from 5 p.m. until 1 a.m. I was working a harbourside beat, and the place was thronged with people enjoying the balmy air. Some time after nine o'clock, a group of youngsters in one of the pubs started a fight in which several glasses were broken, and I managed to quell that; then two other fights started at another pub, and it was evident it was going to be one of those nights. It threatened to be a duty interspersed with many minor scuffles. This sort of thing wasn't regarded as serious trouble, it was just a nuisance, and I coped. A lot of credit must go to the good humour of all concerned, including the local people. We, and the landlords, knew that the heavy hand of the law, or swift, hard retaliation from the locals, could stir up real bother. We humoured our visitors, we jollied them along, and nothing serious broke out.

Then Sergeant Blaketon met me at half-past ten. I was patrolling the quayside when I noticed his impressive figure in the light of a street lamp.

'Now, Rhea, anything doing?' he asked.

I told him about the scuffles in the various pubs and said that things were now under control.

'Right,' he said. 'Then we'll do a few pub visits.' He checked his watch. 'It's closing time now, so we'll clear them quickly and show our uniforms at the same time, just to prevent any bother later on.'

Together we patrolled all the quayside inns, checked a few youngsters' ages and cleared the bars of late drinkers. In most cases the landlords were pleased to see us, and we did get all the drinkers out. One or two continued to sing in the streets, and most of them wended their way home in an alcoholic haze. For them, life was wonderful – until morning!

The last inn on our tour was the Lobster. By that time it

was almost eleven o'clock, and obviously word of our presence had got around because, when we entered, the bar was empty – except for one man. He was sitting there with a large pint in his fist.

I looked, and looked again. It was Edwin.

But Sergeant Blaketon spoke first.

'You!' he almost shouted at the little fellow. 'It's closing time, and you are drinking after hours! Give me that drink. Landlord!'

The surprised landlord emerged from the back of the bar, wiping a glass as he came towards us.

'Landlord, it is half-an-hour past closing time, and this man is still drinking. That is an offence.' Sergeant Blaketon began to lay down the law. 'It is an offence to serve after time, an offence to drink after time, and an offence . . .'

'No, it isn't, sergeant.' The landlord spoke softly, not flinching an inch before the might of Oscar Blaketon. 'Not in this case. Edwin is a resident. The licensing hours do not apply to residents.'

'What's your name?' barked Sergeant Blaketon to Edwin.

Edwin told him.

'Address?'

And Edwin gave his address, a matter of ten minutes from the pub.

'No, he's not, landlord,' said Blaketon in triumph upon learning Edwin's home address. 'That is the oldest trick in the world – you can't trick old-stagers like me, you know. Oh no! Getting late drinkers to sign in as residents and put their names in the register. You ought to know better.'

'I *am* staying here,' piped up Edwin. 'I've booked in for two weeks.'

And he had. Blaketon insisted on seeing his room, but Edwin was right. This was his holiday. Because all his friends were here and because he liked the food, Edwin had simply come down to his favourite inn for two weeks holiday, when his food and bed would be provided, his washing-up and cleaning done for him, and his bed made every day. For Edwin, this was bliss.

'There's no point in going somewhere that's strange, is there, constable?' He looked up at me. 'I mean, what's the good of going on holiday where you don't know anybody? Besides,' he added, with a twinkle in his eye, 'I can drink late, can't I?'

It would be only two weeks later when a party from a Working Men's Club at Sunderland descended on the town. They came in two coach-loads, which meant there was around eighty of them, and they had consumed several crates of beer on the way to Strensford. Their mission in Strensford that Saturday evening appeared to be to consume as much local ale as they could, and this was to be achieved by visiting as many pubs as possible. Afterwards, they would catch their coach home. Those who could not walk to the coach would be carried by their pals. They would not see much of Strensford's quaint beauty and historic features, but that did not appear to bother them. They poured out of their buses at seven o'clock and marched purposefully towards the nearest pub. And so their mammoth binge began.

We were alerted and all the duty constables kept a discreet eye on their activities, knowing that after closing time we would have to act rather like sheepdogs as we shepherded them all safely to their waiting coaches.

And so we did. By the end of their marathon boozing session, they had split into little groups, and so by closing time all the pubs were evicting specimens of the working men of Sunderland. They were in various stages of intoxication, ranging from the merry to the legless, but they were no trouble. They were a happy, cheerful lot who couldn't remember where their buses had been parked, and so we, as expected, guided them to the coach-park.

I was one of the constables who had been allocated this task, and it was a laugh a minute getting them all into their seats.

When almost all were on board, I saw two men, both exceedingly merry, wending their way towards us.

'Howway, Jack, Eddie, man. We're waiting – get a move on!' called someone from one of the buses.

The one called Eddie was legless, speechless and clueless and was being stoutly supported by his pal.

'Eddie was on the other bus!' said his pal Jack with difficulty as he approached the open door.

'Never mind which bus he came on, man, get him on this yan, and you. It's time we were moving – an' we've ten crates of ale to finish afore we get yam.'

I stepped forward to help the near-unconscious Eddie on board. He was a huge man with a loud-checked jacket which was obviously new. We had difficulty getting him up the stairs and along the narrow aisle, but we succeeded, and he flopped onto a seat, where he promptly fell asleep.

It was with considerable relief that we watched those coaches depart from our area.

When I went into the police station to book off duty at a few minutes before one o'clock, Sergeant Blaketon was at the counter dealing with a distraught woman. I did not hear what she was saying, but as I walked in, he hailed me.

'Ah, PC Rhea,' he addressed me by my rank in the presence of a member of the public. 'You've been on the quayside and thereabouts all evening, haven't you?'

'Yes, sergeant,' I said.

'Well, this is Mrs Turnbull, and her husband has gone missing. She tells me they arrived at Strensford only this afternoon for a week's holiday, and this evening her husband went out for a drink. She didn't go with him because she was tired, and so she stayed behind at her lodgings . . .'

'He likes his drink, ye see, officer, but he canna swim a stroke,' she said in her strong Geordie accent. 'Man, he's so daft, ye knaw. Ah've never got him away on holiday before. Not the once. Ah had neea end of bother getting him doon here, he disna like leaving his mates, you knaw. And I bought him a lovely new jacket for the trip . . .'

'Where are you from, Mrs Turnbull?' I asked.

'Whey, Sunderland, man.'

'And your husband's name and description?'

'It's Eddie, and he's a big man, bigger than any of youse polis.'

'Is he a member of the Working Men's Club in Sunderland?' I asked.

'Whey, aye, man. They're all his pals. How is it you knaw all this then?'

'He's gone back to Sunderland,' I said. I tried to explain that the men wouldn't realize Eddie was here with his wife; when they encountered him in one of the pubs, they'd naturally think he was on their outing and, being mates, they'd made sure he got home safely.

'Ah canna win wi' that feller, can Ah?' She was in tears. 'When Ah think of all the bother Ah had to get him here, and now he's forgotten he was here with me! By, lad, Ah'll knock the living daylights out of him when Ah get back . . .'

'He is safe,' I said gingerly. 'At least he's not come to any harm.'

'Not for this week!' she growled as she stalked out of the station. 'He can stew at home. I'll stay here and enjoy myself without that silly bugger. Ah'll deal with him when Ah get back!'

'You know, Rhea,' said Sergeant Blaketon when she'd

gone, 'maybe that Eddie wasn't so drunk after all.'

Thinking about it later, I tended to agree. He would probably have a very happy holiday in Sunderland.

My most enduring memory of those weeks involved the most traditional of seaside sights – a small child playing with a bucket and spade on the sands.

It began when I was working a 9 a.m. to 5 p.m. shift in the town centre, a rare treat for any policeman because it meant he did not have to rise at the crack of dawn, neither did he have to work until late at night. It was a pleasure to be on duty. I walked slowly from the police station, savouring the warmth of the sunny day and the pleasing sight of casually dressed holiday-makers, especially the lovely girls.

As I passed the railway station, I noticed that one of the seaside-special trains had just pulled in. It was disgorging its complement of passengers into the town, and they were spilling out across the roads and pavements. I stood and watched, not for any particular reason, although it was nice to see their happy faces and relaxed behaviour. I was not studying the crowd, nor indeed observing them in the police sense, but I did notice a tiny girl with her blonde hair neatly plaited in two long tails. At the time, I did not know why she caught my attention, but she did. Maybe it was her demeanour or her long plaits? There was no reason to observe her. Nonetheless, I watched her walking beside several other people, and she was clutching a red bucket and a tiny spade with a blue blade. Together with the others, she crossed the road outside the railway station and followed the crowd towards the beach, a good ten minutes' walk away.

Having seen the dispersal of that train-load, I went about my daily task of keeping traffic on the move, acting as unofficial guide and instant information service and generally attending to the multiplicity of minor tasks that came my way. My beat took me down to the harbourside, where I enjoyed the sunshine, the scent of the sea air and the eternal cry of wheeling gulls. If all police duty was like this, I could be very content.

Then a pretty, tanned woman in a suntop and shorts hailed me.

'Oh, thank goodness I've found you,' she said. 'I've found a little girl. I think she's lost.'

'Where is she?' I asked, for the woman was alone.

'I left her in the souvenir shop just around the corner.'

'I'll see to her,' I promised and hurried along to the shop in question.

We operated a well-oiled routine for dealing with lost children – dozens became separated from their parents during the season, and we never failed to re-unite any of them. More often than not, the child would be placed in the beach superintendent's hut, and in time an anxious parent would arrive to claim him or her. Those found wandering nearer the town centre were usually taken to the police station, where we kept a store of toys and games to amuse them until the worried parents turned up. So a lost child was not a real problem; some were a positive delight.

With the tanned woman at my side, I went into the shop and found the child seated on a high stool. She was sucking an iced lolly and I recognized her as the little girl I'd noticed leaving the railway station.

'Hello,' I said. 'And who are you?'

'Janice,' she said, sucking the lolly without any show of concern.

'And where do you live?'

'Number 42 Tayforth Street.'

'Which town is that?' I continued.

'Don't know,' she told me disarmingly.

'And where did you lose your mummy and daddy?' I said.

'I didn't lose them,' she sucked happily. 'I didn't have them.'

'You didn't have them?' I puzzled. 'What do you mean, Janice?'

'They never came. I came by myself.'

I halted in my questioning and now realized why she had been so prominent during my initial sighting of her. She had been walking alone; she had not been with anyone, not holding hands or being bustled along by anxious parents. She'd simply attached herself to some adults and children and had followed them . . . I could see it all now. It had meant nothing to me at that first sighting; now it meant everything.

'Janice, where do your mummy and daddy live?'

'With me, at home,' she said.

'No, I mean which town. You must know which town you live in.'

She merely shrugged her shoulders. At this the woman at my side attempted to gain this information.

'Janice, how old are you?'

'6¾,' she said.

'And which school do you go to?'

'Roseberry Road Infants,' she said without hesitation.

'That's in Middlesbrough,' the woman told me. 'I'm from Middlesbrough, but I've never heard of Tayforth Street. I wonder if it's on that new council estate?'

'What's your other name, Janice?' I asked.

'Massey,' she said. 'Janice Massey.'

'And you came to Strensford all by yourself?'

'Yes,' she said. 'I want to see the sands and the sea and dig sand castles.'

'Do your mummy and daddy know you've come?'

She shook her head. 'They couldn't bring me, so I came by myself. I'm all right.'

My heart sank.

'What about your money?' I put to her. 'How did you pay the man for coming on the train?'

'No, he never asked. I walked near other children.'

'And you walked near other children when you got here?' I asked.

She nodded. 'Then I got lost. I'm looking for the sands, so I can dig my castles.'

'You nearly got there,' I smiled. 'But look, I'll have to take you to the police station, and we'll have to tell your mummy and daddy where you are. They'll be very worried. Then I'm sure they will come and take you to see the sea and to dig castles on the sands.'

'All right,' and I helped her off the high stool. She was so light and fragile; she looked almost undernourished, but she was a pretty child with blue eyes and that long blonde hair. But at close quarters she needed a good bath; her hair was full of dirt and needed a thorough washing. Her pale skin was grimy too. Her cheap, thin little dress was crumpled and poor, and on her feet were a pair of sandals which were almost worn out. I began to wonder about her background.

I thanked the shopkeeper for taking care of her and also the woman who'd found her, and told them both that I'd take her to the police station. There she would be fed, and there were those games we kept for such occasions, and while she was there, we would ask Middlesbrough Police to locate the parents and ensure they collected her.

Janice held my hand tightly as we walked through the town, and she kept asking me where the sea was and which way she would have to go to find it. I told her but said that first we had to tell her parents. As a small consolation, I took her along the harbourside and showed her the fishing boats and pleasure cruisers, and she loved the gulls which settled on the pavements and roads, seeking titbits from visitors.

She would not say a lot about herself, except that she had no brothers or sisters, and Dad and Mum were out all day. She did not know what her dad did for a living, or whether her mum earned any money, but it seemed they were both out of the house when she left home that morning. But Middlesbrough Police would find them – the neighbours would know their whereabouts. I felt very confident about that.

I took her into the dark depths of Strensford Police Station where Sergeant Blaketon was the duty sergeant.

'Hello, what's this, Rhea? A new girl-friend?'

'Yes, sergeant,' I smiled, still holding Janice's hand. 'This is Janice. She's come all the way from Middlesbrough without her mummy and daddy.'

'Has she, by jove? And why has she done that?'

'I want to see the sea,' piped Janice. 'And dig sand castles.'

'Hmm, well, what about your mummy and daddy then?'

I explained the circumstances and he rubbed his chin.

'All right, well, Rhea, you've done your bit. Now it's down to us. You go back to your beat and we'll find something for Janice to do while we locate her mum and dad.'

I bade farewell to the child, and she smiled at me as Sergeant Blaketon took her into the office. There he would leave her in the capable charge of the office constable who would ring Middlesbrough Police to set in motion the search for her parents and her eventual collection.

If they'd arrived home and found her missing, they'd be frantic with worry, but from what she'd told me, they would have no idea she'd undertaken this journey.

I returned to my beat and patrolled the town until it was lunch-time.

I booked off at one o'clock and saw that Janice was having a meal supplied by a nearby café; she was on a tall stool in the main office with her plate on the counter, and she seemed quite content. At least there were no tears, and she seemed to be enjoying the food.

Three-quarters of an hour later, I returned to report that I was resuming my patrol – our lunch breaks were of forty-five minutes duration precisely. But Sergeant Blaketon called me to one side for a chat before I left for the town.

'Nicholas,' he said, and his use of my Christian name made me wonder what was coming next. 'That little girl, Janice. We've traced her parents – as we thought, they had no idea she'd come on that train. Now, her dad is at work until six tonight and he hasn't got a car. He's a warehouseman in Middlesbrough. Mum's a part-time voluntary worker in an old folks' home – she gets nothing for it, and it seems the family is not well off. Anyway, they'd arranged for young Janice to go to her granny's today – but she hadn't. Granny wasn't unduly worried when she didn't turn up because Mrs Massey sometimes changes her mind about going to the old folks' place, and the parents thought the child was at Granny's.'

I listened to his long story, and wondered what he was coming to.

'Well,' he said. 'The outcome of all this is that her father will have to borrow a friend's car tonight, after work, to come here for her. There are no trains or buses into Strensford from Middlesbrough after six.'

'I'm pleased we've found them, anyway. So she'll have to hang about here until, well, nearly eight o'clock tonight?' I said. 'That's a hell of a long time for the child.'

'Exactly,' he confirmed. 'Which is the point of this conversation. Now, she likes you, so she tells me, she thinks you are kind. And young Rhea, you are a family man.'

I waited for his next suggestion.

'That little bairn has come all this way all by herself just to see the sea and build sand castles; she's even got her bucket and spade ready, but she's been sat in our office for hours already, waiting. Just waiting as good as gold. And with never a sniff of the sea or a sight of the beach.'

And I do believe I caught a tremor of emotion in his voice, and just a hint of moisture in his dark eyes. I had never seen him like this before.

'Yes, sergeant,' I agreed with him, for I did feel sorry for the little girl.

'So, go back to your digs, get changed into something light, the sort of stuff you'd wear on the beach if you took your own kids, and then come back here and take young Janice for a holiday on the sands.' The words tumbled from him; it was almost as if he didn't believe he was uttering them.

'As part of my duty, you mean?' I was amazed that he, of all the supervisory officers, would take me away from uniform duties for a joyful task of this kind.

'Of course, Rhea. But be back no later than eight tonight – that's when her parents are due, and it'll be too late for them to take her onto the sands. We can't let her go home without making a sand castle, can we?'

I had some holiday clothes with me, and I did as he suggested. With little Janice carrying her precious bucket and spade and clutching my hand, I took her down to the seaside.

As I would have done with my own children, I helped her build castles, dams and holes in the smooth, warm sand; I gave her rides on the donkeys and we hunted for jellyfish, starfish and crabs in the rockpools. We found seaweed, shells and rounded stones which she loved, and there was a Punch and Judy show which she thoroughly enjoyed. I took her into an ice-cream parlour for a treat and showed her the lighthouse, the lifeboat and even the machines in the amusement arcades. But the sea and the sands were her great love – we went back and she paddled at the water's edge and allowed me to dry her feet on a towel I'd brought. Not once did she complain or misbehave. She was a lovely child, and by six o'clock both she and I were shattered.

We sat and let the hot sand run through our toes, and then she filled her little bucket with her collection of shells and rounded stones.

Shortly afterwards, from a kiosk close to the beach, I telephoned my landlady to ask if I could bring a lady-friend in for high tea and she agreed. When she met Janice and heard the story, she treated the little girl just like an important guest.

By eight the child was almost asleep on her feet. I gave her a piggy-back to the police station, and when we arrived, her parents were already there. Sergeant Blaketon was there too, having returned to make sure they did come for their child. I was more than delighted that they welcomed her with kisses and open arms, rather than subject her to an angry telling-off. I suspect Sergeant Blaketon had something to do with that, and she went happily to her parents. It was clear that they loved her, and that she loved them.

From her father's arms, she flung her thin hands around Sergeant Blaketon's neck and kissed him, and then she did the same to me.

'Thank you for taking me to the sands,' she said. 'I love you.'

And then she was gone.

She must be getting on for thirty now. She is very probably a very beautiful woman. I often wonder if she remembers that day with a constable by the sea.

Constable
along the Lane

1

How shines your tower, the only one
Of that special site and stone!
Edmund Charles Blunden, 1896-1974

Among the unpaid benefits in the life of a village policeman
is that of leisurely patrolling the beautiful lanes which
pattern and serve our countryside. Every season has its
delights and my patrols took many forms. Sometimes I
toured the villages and hamlets in the section car, at other
times I depended upon my official-issue small, noisy but
reliable Francis Barnett motor cycle. But by far the most
pleasant and rewarding way of performing my duty was to
meander among the cottages and along the lanes on foot.
The seasons did not matter – every day had its own charm,
but this allowed precious time to see the sights, smell the
perfumes and hear the sounds of England's living and
ever-changing countryside. There were times when my
slow pace made me feel part of the surrounding landscape.

By comparison, the car and motor cycle were speedy
and functional as they presented the image of a busy
police-officer going about his vital work with the aid of
modern technology. The latter was in the form of an
official radio fitted to both the car and the motor cycle.
The crackle of that radio, the zooming off into the unknown
to go about some urgent mission, plus the polished livery
of the police vehicles with the occasional flash of blue light

or sound of a multi-tone horn, served to nurture an essential aura of efficiency and style.

Early morning patrols by car or motor cycle were generally spent in the eternal search for cups of tea, people to talk to and the occasional evidence of criminal activity of the rural kind. If I am to be honest, our missions were seldom urgent, unless executed in response to a traffic accident; the truth is that those pastoral wanderings enabled us to see a great deal of the changing landscape and the people who lived and worked there. The car, but more often the motor cycle, carried me through the hills and valleys, across the moors and dales, past ruined abbeys and crumbling castles and along the highways and byways, invariably on a route which had been pre-arranged by a nameless senior officer.

In fixing our routes, he would try to incorporate several villages and hamlets within, say, a three or four hour patrol, where we halted hourly in nominated villages. There we had to stand beside the telephone kiosk in case we were required. Someone in the office would ring us on those telephones if necessary. The fact that we were equipped with radios did not change that ancient routine because hourly points at telephone kiosks had been a feature of rural patrolling for generations. The system could not be abandoned simply because we now had radios! Senior police officers do tend to be belt-and-braces types, especially where their patrolling subordinates are concerned.

In my rural bobbying days, they liked to know what their village constables were doing at every moment of their working lives. It was an admirable method of stifling initiative but it also revealed their lack of confidence in themselves and a corresponding lack of trust in us. Nonetheless, the system did ensure that every tiny hamlet, as well as the more populated areas, received a regular visit from a uniformed officer, particularly at odd hours of day and night. As a piece of positive policing, they were valueless but they did keep our supervisory officers content in the belief that they had us just where they wanted us. And the public did see us going about our endless missions and probably wondered why we were passing at such peculiar times when nothing had happened.

But from my point of view, I did enjoy the early morning routes, as we called them, especially in the spring and summer, even if I had to drag myself out of bed at 5 a.m. at least once a week. But when the sun was shining, the birds were singing and the air was redolent with the scents of new blossom, it provided experiences I would not have missed for the world. I saw nature and the countryside at its beautiful best and the freshness of the morning made me glad to be alive and to be working in such amenable surroundings. To patrol with an accompaniment of the fabulous dawn chorus; to see young animals and birds enjoying their first taste of life and to hear the season's first cuckoo never ceased to thrill.

But even in such bucolic circumstances, it's nice to dodge the official system. As I started those routes from my hilltop police house at Aidensfield, I did so in the happy knowledge that there were several calling places on my patch. There I could enjoy a break from the routine or a spot of refreshment and human companionship. Farms and bakeries provided early morning buns and cups of tea which were most welcome during a tour of duty. In addition, the tiny police station at Ashfordly also provided sanctuary.

So far as Ashfordly Police Station was concerned, I had to be very careful; like all my rural colleagues, I had to enter without the resident sergeant hearing me, because if

Sergeant Blaketon was woken by one of his tea-seeking constables, he would rapidly and effectively make his displeasure known and we would thereafter be denied that calling place.

For an erring constable, life would be hell for a short time thereafter, and so we all adopted a simple technique. We would park our motor bikes some distance away and walk to the police station. This silent approach was most effective. After 6.30 a.m. however, the doors were open because that's when Polly, the station cleaner, arrived. Approaching sixty-five, she was iron-haired with grey eyes and the clean, fresh complexion of a countrywoman. She fussed over our little station as if it was her own immaculate home; she polished the furniture and brasswork; she cleaned out the fireplace; emptied waste-paper baskets and, if the cells had been occupied, she cleaned them and aired the blankets. And if Alwyn's chrysanthemums were in the cells, she would make sure they were tended.

Polly's strength lay in the fact that when one of the rural constables was performing an early morning route, she knew he was abroad because she could decipher the contents of the duty sheet. Knowing he'd love a cup of tea, she always had the kettle ready.

This little ritual meant that at some stage between 6.30 a.m. and 7.30 a.m. (when Sergeant Blaketon usually left his bed), Polly would put the kettle on and brew a pot of hot tea, as a result of which the early patrolling constable would pay a visit to the police station. There he would enjoy tea, biscuits and a chat with Polly. If Sergeant Blaketon happened to wake early to try and catch us, Polly would hear him moving upstairs and would stand her mop in the front porch as a warning that Blaketon was likely to appear. This was the signal for us to head into the lanes of Ryedale and to the next kiosk on our agenda, thirsty but devoid of any slanderous criticism from our supervisory officer.

Sometimes, though, Sergeant Blaketon would surprise everyone by creeping downstairs in his slippers. To cope with that eventuality, we always carried some reports or papers which provided us with an excuse for being indoors. 'I've just popped in with these papers, Sergeant,' would be our excuse, at which he would retort, 'Well, don't hang about here, stopping Polly from working and don't loiter when on duty!'

But by and large, those many little subterfuges worked to our advantage. The police office at Ashfordly became a regular haven of refuge, one which was particularly welcome during winter patrols. During those dark and chilly mornings, when our fingers, toes and ears were frozen, Polly always had a blazing fire and her splendid cups of tea to warm us. Through every spring, summer, autumn and winter for years, Polly had been there with her fire, her cups of tea, her awareness of the sergeant's movements and, in times of need, her warning mop at the door.

Then a crisis came to Ashfordly Police Station.

Polly retired.

We made a fuss over her departure and had a farewell party in one of the local pubs. Sergeant Blaketon made a nice speech and presented her with a portable radio we had bought for her.

That we missed Polly was never in doubt, but for a few idyllic days afterwards, we did honestly believe we could encourage any new cleaner to be as thoughtful and accommodating as Polly. But Sergeant Blaketon had quietly made his own decision about the kind of person who would be suitable for the appointment, and we were to learn to our sorrow that his ideas did not correspond with ours.

My first encounter with the new cleaner came that April. The appointment had been made only days before, and upon my first tour of duty afterwards, I was performing one of those early morning routes. I had started at 5.30 a.m. from my police house at Aidensfield, and had made my first point at Elsinby at 6.05 a.m. with my second at Briggsby at 6.35 a.m. As Ashfordly lay only a five-minute ride from Briggsby, there was time for a quick visit to the police station before my 7.05 a.m. liaison with another in my allotted chain of telephone kiosks.

If my colleagues had done their work efficiently, the new cleaner would have lit the fire; the kettle would be boiling and it would be known that a lonely, patrolling constable was in need of tea, warmth and amiable companionship.

As I made my lonely vigil outside Briggsby's kiosk, I wallowed in anticipation of a hot cup of tea. The early spring morning was, in Yorkshire terms, 'nobbut a fresh 'un', the real meaning of that description being that the morning was extremely cold. Indeed it was, for April can produce some very chilly northern mornings; it can also produce some memorable April showers, and in both achievements it excelled itself that morning.

As I stood shivering beside my motor cycle with the cheerful singing birds for companionship, I wondered momentarily whether I was in the right job. After all, other folks were still in bed or had warm cars to carry them about their work. As I pondered upon the unfairness of a constable's life, the heavens opened.

In a matter of minutes, the beautiful blue morning sky had been obliterated by a mass of swiftly moving black clouds, some with delightful silvery edges. As they succeeded in shutting out the rising sun, they opened their taps. Huge dollops of heavy rain lashed the earth from that sombre

ceiling and in seconds, the roads and fields were awash
with urgently rushing water and dancing raindrops. In no
time, brown rivulets were gushing from the fields and
roaring along the lanes.

In my heavy motor-cycling gear, I was reasonably
prepared for most kinds of weather, but on this occasion,
water ran down my neck and into my boots as the pounding
rain bounced off my helmet and battered my face, which
was already sore from the effects of a chill morning breeze.
The downpour persisted for several minutes, then the
monstrous black clouds moved to a new venue upon their
journey of misery and the sun came out.

Brilliant and warm, it caused the roads to dry a little and
the birds to resume their singing. As I climbed aboard my
motor bike little clouds of steam began to rise from the
tarmac, but as I kicked the bike into life, I wondered if the
rain had waterlogged the electrical essentials. But it started
without any trouble and I chugged over the hills to enjoy
the dramatic vista as I dropped into Ashfordly. As I
motored sedately into view, I could see the beautiful
effects of that awesome shower – the glistening pools in the
fields as they reflected the morning sun; the patches of
rising mist as the water evaporated in the bright coolness of
that day; the sheer greenery of the panorama before me
and the freshness of the new spring colours. It was as if the
landscape had had its morning bath.

But I was cold as the pervading dampness soaked into
my clothes beneath my motor-cycle suit. The one salvation
was that a few minutes' drying out before the lovely fire in
Ashfordly Police Station would cure that problem. On the
final run-in, I drove through some running rivulets, some
lingering pools of muddy residue which the downpour had
produced. Very soon, my boots, legs and machine were
spattered with mud.

When I arrived at the police station, therefore, I was soaked externally with the mud and residue of the roads, and internally with rain that had flowed down my neck. I coasted the final few yards to avoid arousing Sergeant Blaketon and having parked the little motor bike, I switched off the radio. With visions of hot tea before me, I prepared to enter the warm office.

I was surprised when a powerful voice bellowed 'Out!' It was a voice I did not recognize.

I stood for a moment in the porch, stamping my feet on the doormat and I must admit that I did not immediately connect the voice with my arrival. I continued to stamp in an effort to shake off the surplus water and then the inner door opened.

I was confronted by a short, thick-set fellow with a bull-like neck and cropped hair. It was still black but shaven so close that it looked like a well-worn black-lead brush. Two piercing grey eyes stared at me from the depths of the heavy, pale features of a man dressed in a long, brown dust-coat. He'd be in his middle fifties, I guessed, and was only some 5 feet 5 inches tall. But he looked and behaved like a bulldog.

'Out!' he ordered. 'Get out of here!'

I stood my ground, still shaking off the after-effects of that shower. 'Who are you?' I demanded. 'You can't tell me to get out. I'm not even in yet!'

'And you're not coming in, not like that. I've cleaned the floor, I'm not having muck dropped and paddled all over. Taken me hours to get it something like, it has, so clear off.'

'Who are you?' I asked again, having stopped shaking off the water as he stood in the centre of the doorway to effectively block my entry. It would require a strong physical action to shift him, I reckoned.

'Forster. Jack Forster, I'm the new caretaker.'

'Caretaker? Cleaner, you mean.'

'Caretaker,' he affirmed. 'I takes care of this police station, so I'm a caretaker. Now, if you want to come in, you'll have to go into the garage and get rid of that mucky suit. Leave it there to dry off and make sure your feet are clean. I'm not having you lot messing up my floors. So you and your mates can all get that into your heads right from the start. I don't clean floors so that folks can muck 'em up again.'

'I'm soaked, I want to dry myself in front of the fire,' I said. I wanted to see if there was any compassion in that squat, powerful frame.

There wasn't.

'Not here,' he continued to block the doorway. 'Yon fire's not lit. I'm not lighting that fire while I'm working, it makes me too hot when I'm polishing. It's laid, but I'm not lighting it today. So you've no need to come in, have you?'

'I've got some official business to conduct,' I said. 'Telephone calls to make, reports to read. I'm on duty,' and I stepped up towards the door, but he stood his ground, determined.

'Then take them mucky clothes off,' he said. 'Otherwise, I'll get Sergeant Blaketon to issue an order saying no motor-bike suits allowed in here. I'm not having my floors messed up, no way. Look at you! Mud, water, muck everywhere!'

I was in a momentary dilemma. He had no right to bar an officer from his own police station, but I was acutely aware that if I physically moved him aside, he might lodge a complaint. He seemed the kind of person who might claim he'd been assaulted by a policeman. Time and time again in police circles, we met cleaners and similar operatives who used their mundane tasks as a source of petty power over others; cooks, cleaners, domestics, car washers. There was always one who lusted after power and who liked to exercise his or her own brand of dominion over others. This man was of that breed, and the fellow was here, in Ashfordly, blocking my route into the office.

If I ignored his demands, he would, without any shadow of doubt, run to Sergeant Blaketon. He would then take great delight in banning us from using the office as a refuge and tea-room. This meant that I had the future welfare of myself and my colleagues to rapidly consider as I stood dripping before this little Hitler. The options flashed through my mind as I watered the floor of the outer porch. Already, I had created a distinctive pool of mud.

But as I swiftly considered the alternatives, I concluded that, under no circumstances, must a trumped-up cleaner be allowed to succeed in banning me or my colleagues from the station. That fact must be established immediately.

I was tempted to use bad language to express my views, but realized this could also be used as ammunition when this fellow made his inevitable complaint to Sergeant Blaketon.

'Mr Forster, by standing there, you are obstructing a police-officer in the execution of his duty,' I said with as much pomposity as I could muster, and thrust him aside as I pushed into the office. I don't think that accusation would have convinced a court, but my action took him by surprise. Any threat of greater authority, I knew, would compel him to retreat. He did, but he was not finished.

'You'll regret this, you'll be disciplined!' he began to shout as he backed into the office. 'I'll have Sergeant Blaketon informed of this, so help me!'

Once inside, I made a great show of ringing up Divisional Headquarters, reading circulars, checking my in-tray, reading notices and generally doing all the routine chores which were expected during a formal visit of this kind. And all the time I dripped mud and water along my circuitous route across Forster's floor. I felt some guilt but justified my conduct because of his uncompromising attitude. He followed me around, red-faced and angry, fuming at the mess I was leaving in my wake, and threatening all manner of actions from my superior officers. I decided not to stay for tea. The atmosphere was not conducive to a relaxing visit, and the fire was unlit anyway. It was laid out with regimental accuracy with the fire-irons arranged in sequence upon the hearth and the coal heaped neatly upon the paper and sticks. Those portions of the clean floor gleamed like polished silver. I was reminded of my days in the RAF, doing National Service, when we polished the floors of our billets to such a standard that no one dared walk on them. We moved around by sliding on little mats made from old blankets, one to each foot.

That ensured the floor was always polished and saved us lots of time on Bull Night. Now, this floor was heading that way. But, having messed it severely, I left. I found a welcoming bakery where I warmed myself as I enjoyed a nice bun and a mug of hot tea, and soon I was glowing amid the scents of newly-baked bread and cakes.

Later, I discovered that Forster had complained to Sergeant Blaketon. To give the sergeant some credit, he had not spoken to me about the affair of the muddy visit which perhaps revealed something of his disdain for the nature of the grumble, but he did resort to his normal tactic – he displayed a typed instruction on the police station notice-board. Each of us had to read and initial it.

Sergeant Blaketon was prone to issuing typed instructions through the medium of the station notice-board. We learned that the degree of his anger was reflected in the method of typing – a notice produced in black lower case type was routine. This might embrace matters like holiday dates, special duty commitments and so on. A black notice in upper case type was more important – that could include warnings not to use the office telephone for private calls or to make sure our monthly returns were submitted on time.

A notice typed in red was rather more serious. If it was in lower case red type, it was of considerable import – such as 'Members will refrain from revving up their motor cycles outside the station at 2 a.m.' or 'Members *will* repeat *will* study all Force Orders and *will* repeat *will* initial each copy when it has been perused.'

We were never instructed to 'read' papers and documents – always, we had to *peruse* them, and we were always classified as 'members' in Sergeant Blaketon's vocabulary. I never did find out of what we were members.

But a very important notice was always typed in red upper case letters. For example, 'MEMBERS WILL STUDY THE ACCOMPANYING PHOTOGRAPH OF THE CHIEF CONSTABLE AND WILL ACKNOWLEDGE HIM IN THE STREET BY SALUTING' or 'MEMBERS WILL *NOT* REPEAT *NOT* USE OFFICIAL VEHICLES FOR COLLECT- ING GROCERIES OR FISH AND CHIPS.'

After my first meeting with Jack Forster, therefore, an instruction did appear on the station notice-board. In lower case red type, it said, 'Members will take every care to keep the police office clean and tidy at all times and should not enter in soiled motor-cycle protective clothing unless unavoidable owing to the exigencies of duty.'

The 'exigencies of duty' was a marvellous phrase for making exceptions to most rules, and when this notice appeared, the story of my meeting with Forster became widely known. So did the reason for the appearance of this order, and from that time forward, we discovered more of his tactics. He objected to smokers putting cigarette-ends in ashtrays; he disliked tea or coffee cups being left unwashed; he objected to paper containing crumbs of food being placed in the waste-bins; he wanted all lights switched off when the office was empty; he objected to out-of-date posters being left on the notice-board and apple cores on the mantelshelf.

In fact, he objected to everything and everyone. He seemed to have a passion for cutting official expenditure, which probably explained his unwillingness to light the fire, his passion for switching off lights and his theory that much of the paperwork in the office was not necessary. I think he based this judgement upon the amount of waste paper which accumulated in the waste-bins. The outcome of his arrival was that the office *did* remain clean and tidy, chiefly because we rarely went in. There was no longer any pleasure in visiting our little section headquarters and the result was that the lanes around Ashfordly were very regularly patrolled. We made very frequent visits to establishments like hotels and bakeries which offered warmth and occasional refreshment, and we also made use of each other's homes.

In one sense, the social life of our happy little section was enhanced because we saw more of each other and of each other's families, but it was clear that Sergeant Blaketon was growing concerned about our unwillingness to make regular visits to the office. To circulate our paperwork, we tended to rely upon his visits to us, rather than our visits to him. To counter this, he compiled an instruction, in red lower case type, about the matter.

It read, 'Rural members *will* repeat *will* visit the Sectional Office at Ashfordly at least once during each tour of duty. It is essential that all members keep up to date with correspondence, local procedures, new legislation, Force orders and internal instructions. This instruction is effective immediately.'

And we all had to initial it and comply. Thereafter, we made these token visits to collect our mail and to obey Sergeant Blaketon's order, although most of us managed to make our visits when Jack Forster, whom we nicknamed Jack Frost because of his chilly nature, had completed his daily stint. He worked from 6.30 a.m. until 9.30 a.m. each morning consequently avoidance was not difficult, except when working an early route.

But overall, the effect of his presence could not be ignored. We moved around the clean, tidy office as if it was a showroom of some kind, hardly daring to touch the furniture or leave footprints on the floor. We cursed Jack for his cussedness, and we cursed Sergeant Blaketon for engaging him. I must admit that I often wondered whether poor old Blaketon had really foreseen what the outcome of Forster's appointment would be.

Some of us did try discreetly to frustrate or annoy Jack. We did paddle upon his floors; we did leave waste paper lying about; we did spill tea or coffee from our flasks and we did make the office look as if it was a place of work and not a disused museum.

But the real punishment for Jack arrived late one night; it was something that could never have been planned and it was doubly pleasing because it could be logged under that wonderful heading 'Exigencies of duty'. I was pleased too, because I was the officer involved. I felt that some kind of poetic justice had descended upon Jack Frost.

It so happened that I was not working one of those motor-cycle routes, but was performing a full tour of night duty in Ashfordly. A complete week of night duty came around every six months or so, when we worked from

10 p.m. until 6 a.m. the following morning.

I was patrolling on foot in the outskirts of Ashfordly. It was 1.30 a.m. and I was looking forward to my meal break which was scheduled for 2 a.m. I would take that break in Ashfordly Police Station, careful not to dirty the place because of Jack's ferocious responses.

During patrols of that nature, we kept our eyes open for villains and villainy of every kind, from drunken drivers to car thieves, from burglars to cattle thieves, from runaways to tearaways. So when I saw a small, rusty Morris pick-up inching slowly along Brantsford Back Lane without any lights, my suspicions were immediately roused. It was moving jerkily and rather noisily towards me, and so I decided to investigate.

My first job was to halt it so I stepped into the lane and flashed my powerful torch at the vehicle, waving it up and down in the manner then used to halt motor vehicles.

Always wary that vehicles of this condition might not have brakes, it was unwise to stand right in front of them. The procedure was to keep clear as they came to a halt, and then move in to continue the investigation. But there were no problems as the slow-moving pick-up came to a halt with my torch shining into the driving-seat.

The driver, a thin-faced individual with thick, dirty hair, looked pale and ill and he awaited me with a suggestion of resignation on his face. I opened the driver's door, removed the keys from the ignition switch and said, as all policemen do, 'Now then, what's going on here?'

'Summat's gone wrong wi' t'electrics,' he said in a hoarse whisper. 'Sorry, Officer. Ah know Ah shouldn't have drove, but Ah had ti git 'ome . . .'

At that point, there was a tremendous rumpus in the rear and some heavy object caused the pick-up to rock and sway, so I hurried to the back. A massive pig, a Large

White sow, was struggling to climb over the tailboard, and as I reached the back, she half-tumbled, half-climbed from the vehicle into the road. Fortunately, she did not gallop off; judging by her massive size she would have difficulty even in walking, so she stood close to the vehicle, snuffling around the rear wheels. I saw that she had a rope attached to one leg but there was no way I could get her back into that vehicle. He must have had a ramp of some kind for her to climb up.

It was then that the contents of a crime circular of some weeks ago echoed in the recesses of my mind. There'd been regular thefts of livestock in the area over a period of months and some livestock owners had reported seeing a small, darkened vehicle leaving the scene late at night . . .

I grabbed the end of the rope and clung to it, then said, 'This pig. Is it yours?'

The fellow in the pick-up made a non-committal response. I followed with a request for his name and address, and asked where he had obtained the pig. He produced more non-committal and indecipherable replies.

'Come along, out you get,' I said. 'Leave the van here. We'll talk about this at the police station.'

'No, Officer, Ah can explain . . .'

'In the police station!' I had made up my mind to question this fellow in the security of the station. The van was in a quiet lane, and was parked on the verge where it was not a danger to other traffic. After noting its make, size, colour and registration number, I discovered it was not taxed either. There'd be a catalogue of traffic offences here, so I seized the driver's arm with one hand and kept the pig's rope in the other. 'Police station!' I said as I guided man and pig towards Jack Forster's shining palace.

The fellow shuffled along, sometimes groaning and sometimes uttering words which I did not understand. I jollied the huge sow along the road by slapping her ample back from time to time as she waddled contentedly through the streets. She was clearly domesticated and seemed unflustered by this turn of events.

Sometimes, she would stop for a snuffle in the hedge bottoms but she was no real trouble. Her companion was no trouble either as he walked, with some support from me, towards the station.

Sergeant Blaketon was having a day off, so I knew I must not arouse him. I told my captive to hang on to the pig's rope, which he did, as I unlocked the door of the office. As I switched on the light, the big sow hurried inside, dragging the man with her, and I followed, closing and locking the door for security.

'Has thoo arrested me?' was the man's first question as the lock went home.

'Yes,' I said, for I did not want him to leave. Had I said, 'No, you are just helping with enquiries,' he might have decided not to assist with the many enquiries I must make.

'What for?' he asked.

'Suspicion of stealing that pig,' I said. 'So where did you get it?'

He sighed. 'Aye, all right, Ah took it. From a sty over Brantsford way. Don't know whose. If that truck o' mine hadn't brokken . . .'

I cautioned him and wrote his admission in my notebook, then obtained his name and address, age and occupation. He was Cecil Matthews of 56 Roselands Road, Ashfordly, forty-three years old and a general dealer. Having checked this, I said, 'Right, I'll have to get a sergeant to see you. So it's the cells for you and for that animal!'

I searched him, listed his belongings and placed him in Cell No 1, and then, by putting on the light of Cell No 2, persuaded the waddling, grunting sow to go in there. She seemed to like places that were well-illuminated because she went straight in. It was the Female Cell anyway, which I felt was appropriate, although it was very bare now that it did not house Alwyn Foxton's chrysanthemums. He was replenishing his stock, I think. Having locked up my two prisoners, I rang Eltering Police to contact the duty sergeant.

It was now after 2 a.m. I told my story and he said he'd come immediately. I made a cup of tea and took some in for my prisoner, then settled down for my break. I had sandwiches, a piece of cake, an apple and a cup of tea, then Sergeant Bairstow arrived.

'Now, Nicholas old son. Where's the prisoner?'

'In the cells,' I said. 'He's admitted pinching the pig. I got a voluntary out of him. He can't remember whose it is, but it's from somewhere near Brantsford.'

'Ah! A nice easy cough then? Good for you. Right, I'll have words with him, then I'll charge him and bail him out from six o'clock. You stay here in the office until six, and then send him home. I'll bail him to Eltering Court for next Friday.'

'Right, sergeant.'

'And the pig? Where is it?'

'In No 2 cell, sergeant,' I said. 'There was nowhere else . . .'

'The van! Why not leave it where it was?' he cried.

'It got out,' I explained. 'And there's no way to get it back in. It's docile enough . . .'

'Right, the minute somebody comes on duty at Brantsford, get them to find out whose it is, and have the bloody thing collected. We can't keep pigs in the cells . . .'

'Yes, sergeant.'

And so the official procedures for prosecuting Cecil Matthews were put into action. Sergeant Bairstow dealt with him kindly but firmly, and then we placed him back in the cell until six o'clock. Sergeant Bairstow departed about three o'clock, leaving me in the office until my relief came on duty at six.

Each half-hour I peeped into the prisoner's cell to check that he was safe, but around four-thirty, he started to produce some ghastly noises. He began calling for help. I went in, wary that it might be a trick of some kind, but it was clear that the man was ill. Beads of perspiration stood out on his forehead and his face was a dull, pasty green colour; he was holding his stomach and was doubled up with pain.

I rushed to the telephone and dialled for Doctor Williams for I had no wish to have a man die while in my custody. After explaining the problem, he said he would come immediately, in spite of the hour. When he arrived only minutes later, a dour, heavy man, I showed him into the cell; he recognized Cecil and after a brief examination, said in his lilting Welsh voice, 'Stomach trouble, constable, it is.'

'Is it serious?' I was genuinely worried.

'Not so that it will kill him, you know, but he'll be very ill for a while. Gastric troubles, of long standing they are. Now, I have something in my bag which might be of help . . . leave him to me . . .'

I left the cell, glad to be away from the suffering man, but I then became aware of more awful noises, this time from the adjoining cell. Screeching, heavy snufflings and gruntings, painful cries. I hurried to the door, but was unable to open it. When I slid back the inspection hatch, I could see that the huge sow was lying against the door, holding it shut as she uttered the most pained and piercing cries. It sounded like many pigs in distress.

I was in two minds whether to ask the doctor for advice, but felt he might be offended; even so her cries were agonizing and so I decided to call the vet. Not giving me time to explain the somewhat unusual story, he said he would come immediately.

When he arrived, he made an initial examination through the inspection hatch and smiled.

'She's farrowing, giving birth,' he said. 'Soon, the place will be full of little pigs . . .'

I groaned. 'How many?' was all I could ask.

'Ten or twelve perhaps. She's a Large White, so she'll have a lot. Large Whites always do, Constable. Some achieve twenty a farrow. Yours, is she?'

I explained in detail how she came to be here, and he laughed. 'Well, there's a bonus for the loser. He's lost one and will gain many. Now, if you don't mind, I'll hang on until she's produced them all, just in case there are complications. She'll roll clear of that door sooner or later, maybe to have a drink from that loo in the corner of the cell.'

'Will you have a cup of tea?' I offered him.

'Love one,' he said. 'Three sugars.'

I went off to make a cup of tea, and when I returned, I found Doctor Williams having a hearty laugh with the vet, a man called Harvey. We sat and discussed the patients, Doctor Williams saying that Cecil's stomach would result in him being sick all over the cell along with some uncontrollable diarrhoea, and the condition would persist until his gastric trouble had eased. Mr Harvey said the pig would make a mess too, what with giving birth and exercising her bowels . . .

And as I sat there, I wondered what Jack Forster would make of it all when he arrived at half past six. But I was off duty at six. I decided not to wash the cups either.

2

When I was at home, I was in a better place
But travellers must be content.
William Shakespeare, 1564-1616

Having been compelled to spend more time patrolling the
lanes around Aidensfield and Ashfordly, it was inevitable
that I should become more deeply acquainted with Arnold
Merryweather's rattling old buses. In their faded purple
and cream livery, the pair of them were a familiar sight in
Ryedale. They provided a vital means of transport and an
equally valuable method of communication for many of
the villagers. Those without cars relied upon Arnold's
buses to carry them to work or to the shops or merely on
visits to relatives and friends; it was impossible to envisage
a contented rural life without the service that Arnold
provided.

His buses were never off the road, a fact which meant
that on several occasions, I had to speak to Arnold about
the condition of his vehicles. In his rustic and carefree way,
he managed to ignore the laws which governed the operation
of passenger vehicles. He seemed to think that the laws
which applied to large companies and city transport did
not apply to his little business.

He would use the aged buses as delivery vehicles and
would carry parcels, goods and even livestock to market;
I've even known him use a bus as a breakdown vehicle.

Because they were always in use, their maintenance became somewhat suspect. In addition, his willingness to help others often led to him flouting or even breaking the law. Never did I prosecute him, although I found it necessary to constantly remind him of his statutory responsibilities. And, in his own way, he did try.

'Aye, Mr Rhea, Ah'll see to it,' he would say. 'One o' these days, Ah'll get it fixed' or 'Ah'll get Hannah to make sure it doesn't happen again.'

But he seldom did get it fixed, whatever it was, and he relied on Hannah, his huge conductress, to exercise her own judgement over the events which occurred on board the service bus.

Miss Hannah Pybus, with her loud voice, masculine appearance and authoritative manner, kept order and, in her own way, helped Arnold's business to thrive. Unattractive though she was, there was always a hint of romance between Hannah and her boss. Thick-set Arnold, with his mop of ginger hair now greying slightly as he progressed towards his sixties, seemed an ideal partner for the tall and equally thick-set Hannah. Her heavily-freckled face and mop of sandy hair complemented his features and even if she did walk along his aisles with the swaying gait of a sailor, we all knew there was some attraction between them.

But their romance never blossomed. I think this was because Arnold spent all his working days either behind the wheel or in the depot in Ashfordly effecting repairs. In addition, his limited leisure time was spent in the Brewer's Arms telling Irish bus jokes and drinking Guinness.

His only contact with Hannah was on board his bus. After work, she would mount her trusty cycle to ride home to Thackerston. Occasionally if the weather was bad, Arnold would place her cycle in the bus and take her

home, but he never went in. He never took her to a
restaurant, the theatre or cinema, or even to the local pubs.
One reason was that his only mode of transport was his
bus! Hannah would say, 'If you think you're taking me to
the pictures in that, you've another think coming!' The
result was that not once, to my knowledge, did Arnold
enjoy a social outing with the formidable Hannah.

For those who have not been introduced to Arnold's
bus service through my *Constable around the Village*, he
operated along the picturesque lanes and through the
pretty villages between Ashfordly and York. Each day, one
of his groaning coaches, furnished with wooden seats
bolted on iron frames, would leave at 7.30 a.m. and weave
its slow way through Briggsby, Aidensfield, Elsinby and
beyond until it arrived in York.

It made a return journey, and then a second trip from
Ashfordly to York, making a final return trip at 5.15 p.m.
On Fridays, Arnold's other bus made a special run to
Galtreford because it was market day and lots of rural folks
regarded that as a day out.

During these runs, Arnold carried the village workers
into the city where he did bits of shopping and ran errands
for those who could not make the journey. He collected
eggs *en route*, delivered laundry, and performed a whole
series of useful deeds, many of which probably infringed
the various laws which governed the use of public service
vehicles.

Arnold's helpfulness is illustrated in an incident in
which he came to the aid of the constabulary. The same
incident also highlights the importance of a village
policeman's knowledge of his patch and the things that
occur on it. In this case, that knowledge involved the route,
timing, halting places and general *modus operandi* of
Arnold's bus service.

Just after eight o'clock one Wednesday morning, I received a frantic telephone call from Abraham Godwin, an animal feeds salesman who lived in Aidensfield.

'Mr Rhea,' he panted into the mouthpiece, 'my car's been stolen, just now. Less than a minute ago . . .'

The urgency of his voice propelled me into action, although I had just got out of bed, having worked until two o'clock that same morning. I was not feeling on top of the world. In less urgent circumstances, I would have adopted the well-proven procedures of having details of the car immediately circulated to all our patrols. I'd have then recorded the details in a statement before filing the event in the criminal records and stats. files. It would rest upon some other distant police officer to locate the vehicle when eventually it was abandoned.

But as the thief had just struck, it didn't make sense to follow the normal procedures. With only a minute's start, it might be possible to catch the villain.

I'm sure that thought was also in Godwin's mind.

'Which way did it go?' I asked.

'Towards Elsinby. The thief's dumped another in my drive, Mr Rhea, an old Ford,' he panted.

'Right, what's your car number?' I asked.

'DVN 656C,' he said, 'A red Hillman . . . you know it.'

'I do, but my colleagues don't. So,' I said, 'I'll come to see you soon, but I've work to do right now if we're to catch him.'

And I slammed down the telephone. I knew it was utterly futile dressing in my motor-cycle gear to give chase. That would take several minutes. In the meantime, the stolen car, especially if driven by a thief, would be racing away and I would never catch it. It was time for immediate, albeit unorthodox, action.

I looked at my watch. It was five minutes past eight and

I knew that Arnold's bus would be trundling towards York. If I was right about the habits of an opportunist car thief, he would also be heading for the city, either to vanish there or to steal another car to continue his journey. The fact he'd dumped one in Godwin's drive suggested he was hitching lifts through the countryside by stealing a succession of available cars.

I looked at my map. I tried to recall the day I'd once used Arnold's bus on its circuitous journey into York and reckoned his bus would, at any moment, be calling at Hollin Heights Farm.

He called regularly to collect a load of eggs and actually took the bus into the farmyard to do so. I rang Jim Harker, the farmer, and he answered.

'It's PC Rhea,' I said. 'Has Arnold's bus got to your stop yet?'

'Just coming down oor lane, Mr Rhea.'

'It's urgent that I speak to him.' I tried to stress the urgency of this call, but I knew old Jim Harker could not rush. That was something he found impossible.

'Ah'll tell him,' said Jim, and I heard the handset being placed on a hard surface. I could only wait. But surprisingly, only a minute or so passed before someone picked it up.

'Merryweather,' said the voice.

'Arnold,' the relief must have been evident in my voice. 'It's PC Rhea. I need help.'

'Fire away, Mr Rhea. Ah've time to listen while they're loading t'eggs.'

Once before, I'd advised Arnold not to carry loads of eggs on his bus because it was illegal but there was no time to worry about that. I explained that Godwin had just had his car stolen and that it seemed to be heading towards York. I began to describe it, but Arnold said, 'I know it, Mr Rhea, that red Hillman.'

'I wondered if you could halt it, Arnold,' I said. 'I know there might be a risk, but if . . .'

'If that car comes up behind me, Mr Rhea, Ah'll stop him. Then Ah'll call you,' and the phone was replaced.

It was a long shot, but it might work. I now made the necessary formal circulation of the stolen car's particulars by ringing our Control Room and Divisional Headquarters. I arranged for the CID to visit Godwin's home to examine and fingerprint the dumped vehicle and executed all the formalities that were associated with a reported crime.

Having done this, I hurried down to Godwin's house, explaining to Mary that if Arnold rang, she should contact me there. To save time, I drove down in my own private car. Godwin, extremely upset at the audacity of the thief, was still in a state of anxiety, but I suggested he take me into the kitchen where I asked his wife to brew some coffee. The performance of a mundane domestic chore often removes a good deal of tension; besides, I hadn't had my breakfast.

Godwin explained that after starting his car, he had driven it on to his forecourt where he had left the engine running to warm thoroughly. After locking the garage, he'd gone into the house to collect his briefcase and papers. While doing that, a strange car had entered in his drive and driven on to the lawn. A slim youth in his early twenties and dressed in a pale green sweater and jeans, had then jumped out and had got straight into the waiting Hillman. Then he'd driven off at speed towards Elsinby and York. For sheer cheek and opportunism, this theft was almost unique.

It took me a while to complete the necessary crime report forms. I required the engine and chassis numbers in addition to the more obvious details, and explained it was necessary if the car was altered or broken up; parts of it might still be identifiable and for that reason, our C.10 Branch, the stolen car experts, would need those kind of details.

I made a rapid examination of the dumped and ancient Ford, noted its number, and on Godwin's phone, rang the details to Control Room. Efforts would be made to trace its owner and the source of the theft, if indeed it had been stolen. All this took about three-quarters of an hour, and then the telephone rang. It was Mary, slightly breathless.

'Arnold's stopped that car,' she said. 'He rang from Woodland Hall, that's about a mile the other side of Craydale. He's got your thief; he's at the entrance to the Hall. He says can you go straight away, so he isn't too late into York?'

Godwin beamed with pleasure at the news, but I was worried about the state of his car. Thieves have no respect for the vehicles they use so carelessly, and so it was with some apprehension that I asked Godwin if he would come with me and drive his own car home. He agreed.

Twenty minutes later we arrived, to be confronted by the results of Arnold's remarkable bus-driving skill. The thief had been trapped too, so my arrest was easy.

Afterwards, I learned how Arnold had contrived this. While driving his bus and its assortment of passengers out of Craydale, he'd noticed the red Hillman approaching from behind. When the speeding car was level with the rear of his bus and overtaking it, Arnold had eased over to his offside, keeping pace with the car. The car, now with a very anxious driver at the wheel, had been forced to move over and as the vehicles sped along, Arnold's mighty bus had moved still further to its wrongside. In that way, it had literally forced the stolen Hillman off the road and into a shallow ditch.

It had been trapped on one side by the high dry-stone

walls of Woodland Hall and on the other by the bus. The driver had become a prisoner, and the Hillman had suffered some minor damage to the offside front mudguard.

Afterwards, I discovered that Arnold had given his passengers a running commentary to explain his odd behaviour, but as his bus had drawn to a halt beside the trapped car, a young passenger had leapt out. Quickly, he had placed two large stones from the Hall's wall behind the wheels of the car, very effectively preventing it from reversing to freedom.

The bus's position across the road meant that traffic could pass by, although some did stop to enquire if they could be of assistance at the 'accident' but Arnold had declined. And so, thanks to Arnold, we caught a car thief.

I submitted a report to the Chief Constable about Arnold's actions. In gratitude Arnold was presented with a 'thank you' letter and a helmet badge mounted on an oak plaque. The Press publicized the tale too, which gave him and his coach service some useful publicity, but this was minor praise in comparison with the hero status he was awarded by the local people and regular customers.

On another occasion, Arnold used his bus as an ambulance. I happened to be using the bus at the time. It was a Tuesday.

Arnold had eased his groaning old coach to a halt outside the gate of Ridding Farm on the moors above Elsinby, where Aud Mrs Owens boarded it for her weekly trip to York Market. Inevitably, Arnold and his passengers had to wait as the diminutive figure of Mrs Owens pottered up the long track laden with baskets.

That Tuesday, however, we noticed two figures making their slow and painful progress towards the bus. One was Mrs Owens and the other was her husband, Kenneth, who seldom appeared in public. His life was spent almost entirely on the farm; he had no car and no wish to see what lay beyond the boundaries of his spread. He led a life of self-sufficiency and seclusion.

As the couple approached Arnold's bus, it was evident that Kenneth was hobbling painfully.

I saw he was using a home-made crutch. It was simply a broom upturned, the head tucked under his right armpit and the shaft supporting his limping progress. His right leg, which wore a wellington boot, was held awkwardly aloft in a kind of sling which had been created by tying a length of rope about the sole and ankle of the wellington, then up and around his neck and shoulder. It kept his foot off the ground.

Kenneth's age was a matter of debate. He would be well over fifty, probably nicely into his sixties. Today, he wore some soiled corduroy trousers which bore evidence of many years of work and milking cows, and a rough, grey denim jacket, hereabouts called a kytle. A battered, flat cap decorated with a patch of cow hairs sat low upon his head and concealed most of his thin, weary face. The cow hairs were from his habit of resting his head on the flanks of the cows as he milked them.

His wife gave little support as poor old Kenneth made his slow, difficult way towards the bus. I was about to offer my help, but Mrs Owens anticipated this by calling, 'Leave him be! He'll manage best on his own.' Kenneth had a very difficult job manoeuvring himself up the steps into the coach, but with some help from Arnold and Hannah, and some cursing from his little wife, he made it and hopped into a seat. There he sank onto the wooden framework with an audible sigh of relief.

'And what's up wi' thoo, Kenneth?' asked Arnold as he slammed the bus into gear and began to guide it away.

''E fell off an haystack,' said Mrs Owens. ''E reckons 'e's

brokken 'is leg. 'E should 'ave been watching what 'e was doing, that's what Ah say.'

'Where are you taking him then?' It was Hannah's turn now as she hovered with her ticket-machine.

''Ospital,' was the reply.

'He can't walk from the bus station . . .' said Hannah.

'Nay, so you can tak 'im, it's only down a few side streets,' she said. 'Tak him on t'way in,' she shouted at Arnold. 'Leave 'im there. Ah'll see to t'milking and t'hens tonight.'

Hannah looked at Arnold who was now in the driving-seat with his back to this little drama, but he simply said, 'Aye, right-ho.'

'So that'll be one return to York and back, and one to York only, for 'im,' Mrs Owens ordered her tickets.

'Are you leaving him?' Hannah asked.

'Might as well,' said Mrs Owens. ''E's nobbut a nuisance about the spot like this, suffing and sighing from morning 'til night, and Ah shall 'ave his hens ti feed and eggs to collect, then there's t'cows to muck out and milk . . . 'e's as well off in 'ospital oot o' my road.'

The subject of this discussion sat and said nothing as he gazed out of the window of Arnold's coach, his injured leg sticking into the aisle and his broom standing like a sentinel as he clung to it.

'Do you think he's broken his leg?' Hannah asked as she spun the handle of her ticket-machine.

'Aye, Ah reckons so,' said Mrs Owens. 'There was a mighty crack when 'e landed and his foot wobbled a bit. So Ah made 'im keep 'is welly on, and then 'e couldn't walk on it 'cos his foot end went all sloppy. After a day or two like that, we reckoned it was brokken. So Ah thowt we'd better get him seen to.'

'When did it happen?' asked Hannah aghast.

'Thursday or Friday last week it would be. Ah've not 'ad a day's work out of him since, so Ah thowt Ah'd better tak 'im to 'ospital.'

We overhead this curious exchange, but the placid Arnold simply drove on and collected more people along the route. In York, he diverted his bus from its journey and drove through some side streets until his bus full of people arrived at the Casualty Department of York City Hospital.

There, a repeat performance occurred as Mrs Owens, with help from several passengers, including Arnold, Hannah and myself, manipulated Kenneth and his brush off the bus. Once he was established on his feet outside, Mrs Owens pointed to a sign which announced, 'Casualty Department'.

'In there,' she ordered Kenneth and got back on to the bus.

'Aren't you staying?' asked Hannah.

'Ah am not!' said the redoubtable lady. ''E's old enough to fend for 'imself and Ah've no time to fuss over a thing like that. Ah've got work to do in town. So come on Arnold, let's be off,' and she made her way to a seat.

Arnold hesitated for a few moments to make sure poor old Kenneth completed the short journey, but a nurse discovered him and eased his final yards into the building. Arnold then continued his journey.

On his first return trip, with Mrs Owens still somewhere in York, Arnold did make a second detour and personally called at the hospital to enquire about poor old Kenneth. He learned he had suffered a broken leg and that he would be allowed home when the doctor was satisfied the bone was healing and that the plaster cast was performing its function.

When Mrs Owens caught the bus on its second return run, she said, 'Ah'll write 'em a note, Arnold, to see 'ow 'e's getting on, and when 'e's fit to come 'ome, mebbe you'll call and pick 'im up?'

'Right,' said Arnold, not wishing to cause a flutter in the Owens' household by saying an ambulance would bring home the injured farmer.

Kenneth was brought home in due course and I found him hobbling about the premises with his pot leg as he fed the pigs and mucked out the cows.

He seemed quite content and said very little about his sojourn into city life. I realized that country folk like Kenneth and his wife were so self-reliant that they rarely ever asked anyone for help. If they wanted something doing, they did it themselves; their method of coping with Kenneth's broken leg was an example of that independence.

Arnold's bus service, however, called at another market once a week; this time on Fridays at the small market town of Galtreford. Arnold's second coach was utilized, with a relief driver as a rule.

I heard that when this bus travelled via Galtreford, there was a good deal of wheeling, dealing, buying and selling on board before the bus actually arrived. By studying the Public Service Vehicles (Conduct of Drivers, Conductors and Passengers) Regulations 1936, I learned it was illegal to beg, sell or offer for sale any article in the vehicle . . .

But, in rural areas, one closes one's eyes to a great deal, and really, I felt, this problem was not really mine. It could be argued that the enforcement of such rules was really the responsibility of the Traffic Commissioners, not the police.

So the minor infringements continued and they helped everyone aboard to feel content and happy. In fact, a trip to Galtreford Market on Arnold's bus seemed to be a very jovial and happy affair.

Judging by the accounts which came to my notice, it was more of a party than a domestic outing or a bus trip. Songs were sung, for example, and drinks were handed around, albeit never to the driver when he was behind the wheel.

My very discreet enquiries led me to believe that a trip to market was a very sociable occasion which included community singing. This was led by two Aidensfield characters nicknamed Bill and Ben. In their late forties, they were inseparable and had been pals since their schooldays. They went everywhere together. Bachelors with no regular means of financial support, they went to Galtreford Market every Friday.

Their real names were Arthur Grieves and Bernard Kingston; Arthur was 'Bill' and Bernard was 'Ben'. Each lived in a small rented cottage and undertook casual work in the area. They found employment on farms at potato picking time, harvest time and hay time; they took jobs on building sites, or washed windows – in fact, they would do anything anywhere for a small fee. They always worked together and it was their unhampered life-style that allowed them the freedom to go to market each Friday.

Arthur (Bill) was the elder by a few months and had lived in Aidensfield since birth. His mother, widowed in her twenties, had reared him but had died before I was posted to this beat. He was a dour character who said very little, and whose main interests appeared to be darts and dominoes at the Brewer's Arms.

A stocky man, he had a square, weathered face with skin as tough as leather and thinning hair which encircled a tanned bald patch. In his mode of dress, he always appeared smart because he constantly wore a dark suit, a white shirt, a dark tie and black shoes, but closer examination would show that the suit was a little threadbare, the shirt could have done with washing and ironing while the tie bore evidence of several pub snacks and spilled beer. But from a distance, he looked fine.

Ben was more casual; taller than his friend by perhaps three inches, he was lean and angular, with a good head of dark, curly hair and a loping gait. Always untidy, his clothes generally seemed too wide or too long; sometimes he wore a grey suit, sometimes a pleasing sports jacket and flannels and occasionally, he would appear in casual wear such as jeans or a bright-squared shirt which made him look like a Canadian timberjack.

Ben was rarely seen without a smile on his face; he always appeared to be happy with the world, and as he lived with his aged parents, he never had to worry about cooking his own meals or washing his own clothes.

All that kind of chore was done for him, and it was perhaps the influence of his mother which explained the size of his clothes. Maybe she still treated him as a growing boy who required clothes just a fraction too large so he would grow into them. I think she failed to realize he had matured. Like Bill, he spent a lot of his time in the Brewer's Arms playing darts and dominoes.

Close as their bachelor friendship was, there was never a suggestion there was anything sinister or unsavoury in their behaviour, and no one even considered theirs was a homosexual relationship. It wasn't; they were two heterosexual men who loved a good time and who, in reality, had never grown up. Theirs was a life of casual ease with no responsibilities.

This eternally juvenile aspect of their existence had led to their outings at Galtreford Market; ever since leaving school, they had made the weekly trip on Arnold's bus. Their mission was to wander around the market and then adjourn to one or other of the local pubs to sample the ale, play darts or dominoes and meet some of their acquaintances, especially those of the female sex.

When Bill and Ben got among the women, there would

be banter and chatter, but nothing else; certainly no dates and no real courtships arose from these carefree meetings.

On the return journey these lads, as everyone called them in spite of their age, would lead the community singing on Arnold's bus. The more I heard about this outing, the more I thought I'd like to experience a trip to Galtreford Market. I did not want to catch Arnold by identifying possible breaches of the many bus laws, but felt I'd like to experience the in-bus entertainment which seemed to cheer all those who travelled that route. I knew that singing on a bus was only illegal if it annoyed the passengers, and was sure this did not – how could it annoy if everyone joined in?

My opportunity came one Friday when I was having a day off duty. It was my long weekend. I had Friday, Saturday and Sunday off duty, a welcome sequence which came around once every seven weeks. On this date, it coincided with Mary's turn to have the local children's play-group at our house.

Several mums with tiny tots took turns in hosting a playgroup; it allowed some of these harassed young ladies to take time off from their children, to enjoy a short shopping spree or to have their hair done and relax in other ways. Even though our four youngsters, aged between one and five, would make a class of their own, we both knew it was beneficial for them to mix with others of their age before starting primary school. So we joined that lively group.

On that Friday, it was made plain that if I remained at home, I'd be in the way. Because Mary might need the car to ferry home some of the visiting children, I felt the occasion presented me with an ideal opportunity to disappear by jumping onto Arnold's bus and experiencing the delights of Galtreford Market.

And so, as I stood at Aidensfield bus stop at half past nine that morning, I was joined by Bill and Ben. As we waited, no one said a word and eventually others joined the little queue, including a large brown and white spaniel.

Eventually, Ben looked at me, his curiosity getting the better of him. He asked, 'Gahin ti market then, Mr Rhea?'

'Yes,' I said. 'I've heard a lot about this outing, so I thought I'd come along.'

'Then stick wiv us, Mr Rhea, we'll show you what's what, me and my mate. Do you play dominoes? We could do with a third hand.'

'You're on,' I said as Arnold's bus came into view.

The little queue clambered aboard and from the outset, it was evident that Bill and Ben had their own seat. The spaniel pushed its way through the queue and slid beneath one of the other seats from where it eyed everyone, almost as if it expected to be ejected. But it wasn't.

Bill and Ben's seat was the first one inside the door, a prime position because it allowed Ben to pass comments about everyone who entered and, if necessary, to lend a helping hand to any aged person. As there was no conductress on this bus (Hannah had travelled into York on the other one), their help was appreciated, even when spiced with bawdy remarks.

Ben's running commentary included remarks like 'Howway, Mrs Preston, we can't hang about all day just 'cos thoo's gitten arthritis' or 'If thoo taks onny longer gittin in, Elsie, this bus'll run oot o' petrol,' or 'Now then, Phyllis, leaving t'old man again, are we? Ah'll bet 'e's chuffed about that. 'E'll have that little milkmaid in ti make 'is coffee this morning, mark my words!'

It was all part of the on-going entertainment and Ben held forth with his chatty line of banter at each stop. The driver was one of Arnold's pool of part-timers and he bore the chatter in silence as he accepted the fares and guided the old bus towards Galtreford. It pulled into the market-place, halted with a groan of brakes, and everyone, including the spaniel, spilled out on to the cobbles to go their separate ways. It was just ten-thirty.

'Now then, Mr Rhea,' said Ben, as I waited for their next move. 'What's thy plans for today?'

'I have no set plans,' I said. 'I think I'll just have a look around, and then think about something to eat.'

'Right,' said Ben, who appeared to be spokesman for both. 'Then thoo'll have a game o' dominoes with us, eh? In t'King's Head. We allus 'ave a mooch about till twelvish, and then settle for t'day with dominoes. There's sandwiches, pork pies, pickled eggs and crisps in t'King's Head. We need a third hand, today. Thoo'll be there, eh?'

'Right,' I said, and off they went, with the spaniel trailing behind.

I wandered around the colourful open-air stalls, listening to the banter of the traders and looking at second-hand books, antiques, furniture, crockery and all the other regular offerings of this busy little market. I enjoyed a coffee in one of the pubs which turned its bar into a coffee shop on market day mornings, and in no time, the town hall clock was striking twelve.

Somewhat apprehensively, I entered the King's Head, a fine-looking coaching inn just off the market-place, and spotted Bill and Ben seated at a table with the domino box already before them. Four pints stood beside it, and the spaniel lay beneath the table, apparently asleep.

'Yan o' them's yours.' At my approach, Ben indicated the beers with a wave of his hand. 'Flossie'll be here in a minute.'

'Play this game much, then, Mr Rhea?' asked Bill, eyeing the box of dominoes as he spoke.

I shook my head. 'Not a lot. Used to play at our training-school, or during break-times when we were on nights.'

'Then you do know a bit about it. We play fives and threes, threepence a knock,' Ben informed me.

'Fine,' I said.

'And it's Nick, isn't it?' Then he leaned across and whispered, 'We shan't let on thoo's a bobby, so thoo's among friends!'

'Thanks,' I said, with genuine appreciation. It would be nice, being away from my own patch and being anonymous for a while, but I did wonder who Flossie would be. Then a heavily made-up woman arrived and sat down, sipped from one of the pints, and said, 'Who's your friend, lads?'

'Nick,' said Ben. 'Pal of ours.'

'Hello Nick,' she said, and took a heavy draught. 'Right, highest for off.'

Bill upturned the box and spread the dominoes face down upon the table and he selected a six four. He had to play first. I was still wondering about Flossie who could have been any age between thirty and forty-five.

She was a brassy woman with a husky voice and very heavy make-up which was adorned with rich, red lipstick and nail varnish. But to this day, I don't know who she was or where she came from, or what she did for a living. But she could drink pints of beer with the best of the men, and I was to learn that she could play dominoes too.

As the game progressed, each of us bought at least one round of pints, and then we had a kitty to take us up to bus time. In between, we had sandwiches, pickled eggs and a pork pie each, which we shared with the spaniel, and the afternoon vanished in a haze of clicking dominoes and coins, shouts of delights, lots of spots totalling five or three or multiples thereof, and several pints of strong Yorkshire ale. Because, on market days, the pubs are open all day, we drank quite a lot.

I think I lost about six shillings and ninepence in all, but it was a very entertaining and relaxing way of spending a day. We all said farewell to Flossie, and at five-thirty returned to the bus stop, with the spaniel at our heels.

'We enjoyed that, Mr Rhea, thoo'll etti come again,' said Ben.

'It'll be a long time before I get another Friday off,' I managed to say. 'But when I do, I'll come along. Thanks for inviting me to join your game.'

'Flossie'd die if she knew you were a bobby,' laughed Ben. 'But she's good fun.'

'Where's she from?' I asked.

'No idea,' he said. 'No idea.'

And then the bus pulled in.

'If thoo hadn't bought all them taties and carrots, Mrs Baxter, thoo'd git onto this bus a bit faster,' once more Ben launched into his commentary. 'By, Mrs Harrison, Ah'll bet thoo's spent all this week's wages on that there kettle, and I happen to know there's nowt wrang wi' that awd 'un o' yours. Ah'll bet thoo reckons yon's a bargain. But what's your Fred gahin ti say? He nivver likes spending a penny . . . he's as tight as a duck's . . .'

Bill and Ben settled on their special seat, the spaniel slid beneath another and I occupied one mid-way along the aisle. Then, as the old bus creaked away from the market, the singing started.

Led by Ben and a woman whom I did not know, it seemed that the entire complement of passengers joined in a happy programme of real sing-along songs like 'Mother Kelly's Doorstep', 'Ilkley Moor Bah't 'At', 'Maybe It's Because I'm a Londoner', 'Blaydon Races', 'Shine on Harvest Moon' and many more of that popular range. Bill and Ben produced bottles of beer from their pockets and so did several of the other passengers, women included, and a party atmosphere was rapidly generated.

The spaniel joined in by howling as some of the notes reached a high pitch, and I reckoned my own awful voice would not be condemned. So I joined in the noise too.

We would be around half-way home, when the bus eased to a halt in Pattington. As it began to brake, Bill stood up and Ben clambered down the steps.

He jumped out as the bus halted, and so did Bill; the spaniel followed and so, because I now considered myself a member of their party, I did likewise. Others followed and said their cheery goodbyes, and the bus pulled away. We watched it leave as it echoed to the sound of happy singing; by now, the Merryweather Coaches Mobile Choir were well into 'Home, Home on the Range'. As it vanished around the corner *en route* to Aidensfield and Ashfordly, Bill, Ben, myself and the dog stood on the side of the road in silence. No one said a word. I have no idea how long we remained there in our little group, but I wondered if this was part of their market day ritual.

At length, I said, 'Well, what now?'

Ben looked at Bill.

'Thoo got off,' he said. 'Why?'

'Ah didn't,' countered Bill. 'Ah just stood up to find my handkerchief. Thoo was t'one ti get off. Ah just followed.'

'Ah thought thoo was getting off!'

'And Ah thought thoo was getting off.'

'And I thought you were both getting off,' I added.

The dog wagged its tail.

'Thoo was getting ready to get off!' snapped Ben.

'Nowt o' t'sooart,' retorted Bill. 'Ah just stood up to dig deep for my handkerchief, then thoo jumped off.'

'Ah just jumped off because Ah thought thoo was gahin ti jump off . . .'

And so we stood there like three stupid charlies, the bus now weaving its ponderous way through the distant lanes as the spaniel looked at us for guidance.

'It's a long walk back to Aidensfield, Mr Rhea,' said Bill slowly, reverting to the formal mode of address now that our day was drawing to a close.

The walk home was about six miles, many furlongs of which were steep rising hills, but there was no alternative. How on earth we came to be here still seemed something of a mystery, but we started our long walk. The spaniel seemed to be enjoying this part of the day, for it frolicked in the hedgerows and along the floral verges of the long, winding lane.

'At least your dog's happy about it,' I said to Ben as we got into our stride.

'It's not my dog, Mr Rhea,' said Ben.

'Nor mine,' added Bill.

'Well, it isn't mine,' I felt I had to clarify that point. 'Whose is it?'

Ben shrugged his shoulders. 'No idea,' he said. 'But he's a grand little chap, reet good company. He comes wiv us ivvery Friday on that bus, follows us aroond t'market and then 'as a pork pie in t'pub. He likes yon pie and comes home on t'bus as well. He nivver pays a fare, 'cos nobody claims him, but Aud Arnold doesn't mind.'

I could have inspected the spaniel's collar to determine the identity of the owner, but he was some distance ahead of us now, sniffing and fussing about the roadside vegetation. To be honest, there seemed no point in worrying about his owner – clearly, the dog was his own master, just like Bill and Ben, and he would go home in his own good time. They were three of a kind, carefree and content, with no responsibilities and no one to answer to. They went where they pleased; they did as they liked, and thoroughly enjoyed their method of existence.

I began to wonder whether I was envious of them as we strode out of Pattington. But once away from the cottages, Bill, Ben and I were subjected to the effects of the beer and desperately found ourselves having to attend to the needs of nature. We found a tall and sheltering hawthorn hedge, climbed over a five-bar into a field and stood behind that hedge like three sentinels as we watered the undergrowth to the accompanying sounds of intense relief. The spaniel joined us by cocking his leg against the gatepost.

Thus satisfied, we renewed our walk home, and had walked about a mile when it started to rain. Instead of complaining or attempting to shelter, the happy pair began to sing 'April Showers' in the style of Al Jolson. The dog howled as they reached the higher notes and the rain intensified with every passing minute.

I was pleased no one knew me, for we must have seemed a strange quartet of men and beast. But I enjoyed walking along with this strange, happy-go-lucky trio of market-attenders; perhaps I did feel just a hint of jealousy over their carefree way of life.

As I contemplated their mode of existence, and as the increasingly heavy rain saturated my clothes and hair, I began to wonder what Mary would think when she realized I hadn't come home on the bus. A meal would be ready and she would be tired after hosting all those children, so I pondered upon her reaction when eventually I did walk into the house, weary, beery and wet.

Explanations would not be easy but I was pleased I didn't have to make my excuses to Sergeant Blaketon. I was reminded of an old piece of Yorkshire wisdom which goes, 'Being late home from t'market often spoils a good bargain.'

I lengthened my stride and joined the singing of 'April Showers'.

3

When other lips and other hearts
Their tales of love shall tell.
Alfred Bunn, 1796-1860

To those who have never been there, North Yorkshire's image is seldom that of a land of sylvan beauty. They don't think of it as being graced by charming villages full of thatched cottages and peaceful ponds. But North Yorkshire's Ryedale, reclining on the southern edge of the North York Moors, can shatter those illusions, if indeed they lurk in the mind. For Ryedale is a valley of thatched cottages, peaceful inns and village ponds. There are charming woodland glades, ruined castles and abbeys, quiet streams and a countryside so gentle that it would be more in keeping with the south or the west of England.

One of the most photographed of England's thatched cottages is to be found here; it graces many a box of chocolates and country calendar. There are thatched inns too and many of the villages boast interesting collections of thatched homes. Some are remote and some are positioned at the side of our main roads. Some have been modernized and some have had their thatch removed, while several are the old-fashioned cruck houses.

Most are single-storied and contain oak beams which are dark with age. They derive from the early long-houses of the dales, being built with little architectural skill, but with the essentials of rural life in mind. Quite often, the family lived at one end and their livestock at the other, but those lowly homes were functional and cheap both to construct and maintain.

Cruck houses, many of which still stand, were constructed from early in medieval times until late in the seventeenth century. Pairs of oak trees were used, each pair being shorn of their branches until a tall, straight trunk remained. These were positioned with the thick portion on the ground, and the tips were then drawn together and linked with a 'ridge tree' to form a letter A. When standing upright, one or two spars were fixed to them so that the 'A' shape had two or even three crosspieces.

Several of these 'A' shapes were used, each erected some five yards from the other, and they formed the framework of the cottage. They were linked lengthwise to one another by more beams and spars. Stone walls, a flagstone floor and a thatched roof completed the building, and many of these stand today.

When I arrived in Aidensfield to occupy the hilltop police house with its lovely views of the valley, I found great delight in locating these delightful cottages. At one time, I considered making a register of them, purely for my own interest, but somehow, never found the time. Perhaps this interest in old houses coincided with a sudden interest in buying and renovating ancient country cottages. People everywhere wanted to buy them and occupy them, and there was a ready market for all kinds of ancient piles.

Wealthy people from the cities bought all manner of hovels and spent much time and lots of money 'doing them up'. Some of the results were horrific, but it is fair to say that many were tastefully restored and brought back to life when, without this surge of interest, they might have been left to fall into total ruin.

Perhaps rural folk did not appreciate the architectural or historic significance of these little homes. They allowed them to be sold off, seldom making a bid to buy them. For them, the houses were often 'That awd spot up t'rooad that's tummling doon and leeaks like a coo shed'.

As I toured the lanes of Ryedale, therefore, I became aware of all the thatched cottages in their various locations and in their various stages of repair or disrepair. From time to time, I saw our local thatcher at work – we called him a theeaker – and marvelled at his casual skills. Sometimes the cottages would be completely gutted and rebuilt, with all their ancient oak interior woodwork and flooring being removed and replaced with modern fittings.

But occasionally, someone would come along and buy a remote thatched cottage, then proceed to restore it in its original form, albeit with modern benefits such as damp-proofing, up-to-date plumbing, central heating and electricity. When done properly, such a house could be a delight, a real gem.

It was during my patrols along the lesser known byways around Aidensfield that I discovered Coltsfoot Cottage, a pretty country home if ever there was one. Tucked behind a tall, unkempt hawthorn hedge and almost hidden among a paddock thick with tall rose bay willow herbs, it had a thatched roof, whitewashed walls and tiny Yorkshire sliding windows. These were, and indeed still are, a feature of some moorland and Ryedale cottages.

Owned by one of the local estates, it had for years been occupied by an elderly man who paid the tiniest of rents and who therefore lived in a rather primitive manner. His toilet was an earth closet; he had no hot water and no electricity and the floors were sandstone flags. The estate had offered to implement a full modernization scheme but old Cedric had declined.

Having lived in the house since birth, he had no wish to change either it or his way of life. Dark, damp and neglected, it was a tumbledown old house and was known to date to the seventeenth century. But the interior was lovely; dark oak beams, an inglenook, tiny cosy rooms and a position of almost total seclusion gave it the status of a dream cottage. It was the kind of house that the country cottage-seekers of that time were desperately hunting for, and was probably more attractive because it was so very ripe for modernization.

From the quiet lane which passed the front gate, it appeared to be unoccupied and derelict, although there was a patch of garden which produced hollyhocks, delphiniums and several varieties of rose. Some of those climbed the walls and smothered the thatched porch with colour in the summer, mingling so beautifully with the honeysuckle.

When Cedric died, the estate decided that it would be too expensive to bring the cottage up to contemporary standards. The subsequent rents would never justify the expense and so it was placed on the market. And even as the estate agent's 'For Sale' signs were being erected, a wealthy insurance broker from London chanced to be passing.

With commendable speed and decisiveness he bought it; the price being very low due to its lamentable condition. But, like so many townspeople of the time, his great wish was to own a picturesque and isolated cottage wherein he could live a life of rural bliss far from the pressures of his high-flying career. It was a place he could 'do up'; it needed thousands of pounds and many man-hours spending upon it, but the new owner of Coltsfoot Cottage was prepared to do all that. He wanted the perfect hideaway and he had found it.

In my role as the village policeman, I had to be aware of

events on my patch, and so I kept a discreet eye on the empty cottage.

I did not want it to be vandalized or occupied by unauthorized visitors such as squatters who might come across it and establish a commune there. But within weeks of the purchase, the new owner began to make his impact. He came every weekend and sometimes during the week; he did a lot of the work himself, although he did employ contractors for the specialized tasks. The theeaker came to re-thatch the roof; a plumber came to install hot and cold water, a bathroom, shower and central heating while the electrician wired the house for lights and power.

A damp-course was installed; the garden was cleared; the walls were re-pointed and whitewashed and the woodwork was either varnished or painted. The exterior rubbish was cleared with the assistance of a JCB, and a drive and parking area constructed to accommodate his Rover and her MGB. This was laid with gravel which crunched when anyone walked across it, and then a small conservatory was added at the rear, partly as a draught-proofing scheme and partly to grow flowers and cacti.

Within a year, Coltsfoot Cottage had been transformed. Happily, roses still climbed up the white walls and trailed across the porch; but now, with its new roof of clean thatch and sparkling exterior, it was the ideal dream cottage. Modern, clean but incredibly beautiful, I would have loved to have been the owner, but such things were not for constables. This man had money, and he knew how to use it.

During his weekend visits, I learned his name was James Patrington; once or twice as I patrolled past his gate on my little Francis Barnett, I would stop for a chat, ostensibly to pass the time of day and to make him aware that I was keeping an eye on his premises. Frequently, I found him in the garden dressed in a pair of old grey trousers, a holey brown sweater and wellingtons. Sometimes, his wife was there too and one day they invited me in for a coffee.

They were a handsome, friendly couple; he was in his mid-forties and a shade less than six feet tall. Stockily built, he was balding and had once had a head of thick, black curly hair, evidence of which lingered about his neck and curled over his collar. Round-faced with dark, intelligent eyes, he smoked a heavy pipe which never seemed to leave him, and told me he was a partner in a firm of City insurance brokers.

His wife, Lucy, would be in her late thirties and was almost as tall as her husband; slim and elegant, she had dark hair too, and this was showing signs of premature greying, something she did not try to hide and which therefore made her most attractive. She had very slender hands, I noticed, the kind one would expect in a piano player and her peach-complexioned face always bore a pleasant smile.

I was to learn that she ran a fashion shop in Chelsea and that its demands did not permit her to come to Coltsfoot Cottage every weekend. James, however, always seemed to be there from late on a Friday evening until late on a Sunday evening. I knew that he worshipped the cottage and he asked me to keep an eye upon it during his absence. This I was happy to do. I was supplied with both his business and home address, and his telephone number at both places in case of problems.

'Come and see my cacti,' he invited one Saturday afternoon when I called. He was alone and led me into the conservatory at the rear where I saw hundreds of tiny plant pots. All were neatly labelled with obscure names and some plants bore incredibly beautiful flowers. 'I grow these for fun, I suppose,' he said. 'I sell some, but I reckon that I've every known variety here and at my other home . . .'

And so I became on good terms with the Patringtons. I cannot claim friendship, however; the relationship was that of the village bobby and those who lived on his patch, a friendly albeit business-like acquaintanceship. But both of them always made me welcome and sometimes, I felt, when James was alone, he was glad of someone to talk to. Gradually, he did make his own friends in the area, people of the same professional class to which he belonged, and I would see him *en route* to the local inns or restaurants, or perhaps heading for a cocktail party or drinks gathering at one of the homes in the area.

Lucy, when she came, did not often leave the cottage. Sometimes, she drove up from London with James and sometimes, if she had to return early, she would drive up in her red MGB. Clearly, her own commercial interests kept her very busy and when she did come to Coltsfoot Cottage, she wished for nothing more than a quiet weekend before the blazing log fire in its oak-beamed inglenook, and perhaps a pleasant dinner with James at one of our splendid local inns or restaurants.

They came and they went, not interfering in the village activities, but simply enjoying the unhurried pace and solitude offered by Coltsfoot Cottage. Incomers though they were, they had rescued the old house from destruction and decay, and I'm sure that no local person could or would have raised the capital necessary to buy and renovate it.

Once the Patringtons were established, I saw less of them; every so often, though, I would receive a telephone call from James advising me that he would not be at Coltsfoot that coming weekend and asking if I would keep an eye on the cottage during my patrols. It would be about two years after he had bought the cottage, that their pretty little home hit the headlines of the national newspapers. It happened like this.

High on the hills behind Aidensfield lies the Yorkshire and North of England Sailplane Club, one of the busy gliding clubs of this area. Gliding is very popular from here because the lofty moors provide ideal conditions for launching these engineless aircraft. The thermals created by the ranging hills and dales give the light aircraft a tremendous uplift on rising currents of air, while the views from aloft are staggering in their range and beauty, and the peace they signify.

Since the war, gliding in these elegant sailplanes has become more and more popular and the thriving Club now has its own landing strip, runway and control tower, along with administrative and social buildings. There is also a caravan site for its members. By the time I arrived at Aidensfield, the prestige of this Club had become such that it hosted events which were of considerable importance in the gliding world – these included both local and national championships, as well as Club gliding events and social functions.

During the long, lazy summer which marked the Patringtons' second anniversary in Coltsfoot Cottage, the Club hosted the British Long Distance Sailplane Championships. This attracted a host of enthusiasts to the area who were accommodated at local hotels, inns, boarding-houses and cottages. They swamped the nearby caravan sites and their presence brought wealth to the area. These people had money and cheerfully spent it.

Many of them were from the world of business and commerce and I wondered if James Patrington had joined the Club. As I patrolled my beat during the two weeks of the Championships, I could imagine him soaring aloft in a glider as he enjoyed the solitude and silence of the skies above the North York Moors. Perhaps he was involved, perhaps he wasn't. I did not know.

But, like all previous sailplane championships, there were problems. The more regular of these problems involved a glider coming to earth in an unexpected place. With so many competitors and so many engineless aircraft in the sky, I suppose it is inevitable that some of them fail aloft or cannot make the return journey back to base. The result was that over the two weeks of this event, some six or seven gliders crash-landed around the Club premises. Fortunately, none of these resulted in serious injury to the pilot or anyone else.

I witnessed one of these crash landings. I was patrolling my patch on Saturday afternoon and had parked my Francis Barnett in Crampton. I was performing a short foot patrol around that village and had just emerged from the village shop when my attention was drawn to a whistling sound overhead. And there, floating dangerously low over the village, was a gleaming white glider. It didn't need an expert to realize that it had lost its necessary height, and that it was coming rapidly to earth. To be honest, it was the sort of thing the local people had come to expect and Ryedale does possess many suitable places upon which to safely land.

With the wind hissing about its framework, it came frighteningly low over the chimneys and pantile roofs and it was banking as it circled in a desperate search for a safe landing site. Beyond the village there were flat fields and indeed, there is a disused wartime airfield – I felt sure the pilot was urging his downward floating craft towards that.

As I hurried between the cottages to watch the pilot's frantic efforts to both save the village from danger and to safely bring down his aircraft, I lost sight of the glider. It disappeared behind a row of cottages as I realized it could never regain the air. It was far too low; it had lost all its altitude.

I hurried to my motor cycle, activated the radio and called my Control Room.

'Delta Alpha Two-Nine,' I radioed. 'Location Crampton. It appears that a glider has crash-landed in the vicinity of Crampton – am investigating. Over.'

'Received Two-Nine. Please provide sit-rep as soon as possible. Control out.'

With several villagers watching with interest, I motor cycled out of Crampton towards Brantsford, for that road led into a bewildering array of narrow lanes and tiny hamlets. The glider was last seen heading in that direction; I was sure it had come down somewhere in that maze of lanes and fields, or even on the disused airfield. It could not have flown far and there was no sign of it in the air.

As I drove along the lane which ran through the old disused airfield, there was no sign of the glider, so I turned left and chugged along, sometimes standing on the footrests so that I could peer over the hedges into the large fields at either side. I was now heading for Seavham.

I drove through the hamlet and remained alert for any signs or news that the glider had landed nearby. But there was no one in the street and the Post Office was closed. At least ten minutes had elapsed since my sighting, so I continued through the village and turned left at the end, passing the oval pond which was overlooked by two pretty thatched cottages.

This lane took me on a circular route back to Crampton and I felt that the aircraft couldn't have travelled much further. It hadn't.

As I crested a gentle rise in the lane, I could see its tail sticking into the air like that of a diving whale and I could distinguish one crooked wing behind a copse of sycamore trees. I accelerated now, anxious to save life if that proved necessary, and within a minute was drawing up at the scene of the crash.

I was horrified.

The glider had come down squarely on the top of Coltsfoot Cottage. The nose had penetrated the newly-thatched roof and had thrust piles of straw on to the earth around the house.

Both the nose and fuselage were hidden deep inside the walls, while one wing had cracked off completely and was lying in the garden. The other was sticking out of the cottage, its fuselage-end deep inside the walls and the slender tip rising awkwardly to the sky like a huge broken feather. And the tail stuck up too, like a sentinel.

For one fleeting moment, I thought it looked like a giant white seagull sitting on a nest, but this was serious. I parked my motor cycle on the road outside and ran into the grounds. My first contact was with a woman.

She was comforting James Patrington as he sat on the lawn.

She saw me approaching.

'Thank God,' she said.

'Anyone hurt?' was my first question.

'This gentleman's wife,' she said. 'We were driving past at the time . . . we saw it all . . . my husband's rushed her in his car to the hospital. Brantsford Cottage Hospital . . . she had a knock on the head . . .'

'And the pilot?'

'Him as well, he was bleeding from his face and leg . . . my husband's taken him as well. This gentleman isn't hurt. Just shocked, I think. No one's badly hurt.'

The first aid training I'd received told me that shock alone could be a severe medical problem, so I radioed

Control Room and provided a brief outline of the accident, then asked for an ambulance to take James to hospital as well, for a check-up. The good news was that no one was seriously hurt.

From this point, there would be all kinds of official bodies to inform; all that action would be undertaken by the Force Control Room who would operate from a pre-arranged set of instructions for dealing with crashed aircraft.

My priority now was to ensure that James received immediate medical attention, and that there was no imminent danger from the aircraft or the house. Happily, there was no aircraft fuel to worry about and there were no fires burning in the house. That reduced the fire risk enormously but it couldn't be ruled out. I decided to keep everyone away from the house and to preserve the scene against the sightseers who would inevitably arrive.

As I marshalled my thoughts I made sure that all the relevant services were notified and that attention was given to the people and the premises. But I could have wept at the sight of the cottage. Perhaps, because it was a thatched roof, it could be repaired fairly easily and likewise because it was a soft landing, there had been no serious injury. It looked a real mess.

Later from home, I rang Brantsford Cottage Hospital to learn that James had suffered severe shock and had been detained. The pilot, a man called Alastair Campbell from Edinburgh, had a broken leg and severe bruising. He had also been detained. I then asked about Mrs Patrington, but the hospital had no record of her. When I added that she was a victim of the glider crash, I was told she had been removed to Scarborough General Hospital for treatment.

As I looked up the telephone number of Scarborough Hospital, my own telephone rang. When I picked up the receiver, a woman's voice asked, 'Hello, is that PC Rhea?'

'Speaking,' I acknowledged. 'Who's that?'

'Lucy Patrington,' she responded. 'I've just heard the news on the radio. Is it true, that a glider's crashed into our cottage?'

I must admit that I was thrown completely off my stride by this call and for a moment, I did not reply. Was she really ringing me to ask this, or was she in hospital, dazed perhaps? I wondered if the shock of the event had caused her to lose all memories of the crash. Maybe she'd been unsettled by the trauma of the event?

'Hello?' she said anew.

'Oh sorry, Mrs Patrington,' I apologized, 'I was completing something . . . Er . . . yes, I'm afraid it is true. James is in the Cottage Hospital at Brantsford now, but he's not hurt. Just a check visit. I was about to call and ask after you,' I rabbited on. 'Now, are you fit to be released . . . I mean, should you be out of bed . . .?'

'Released, Mr Rhea?' she cried. 'What on earth are you talking about? I'm in my shop in London, and James has gone to Scotland for a weekend seminar . . .'

Then her voice trailed away and I knew I had let some sort of cat out of some sort of bag.

'James has not gone to Scotland, has he?' she put to me in no uncertain terms.

'All I know,' I told her, 'is that he was at the house when the glider came down. Maybe he stopped off *en route* to Scotland? I can confirm that a glider has landed on your roof, and no one is seriously hurt, although there is a good deal of damage . . .'

'The news said a woman had been taken to hospital, Mr Rhea,' she pressed me.

'She had gone before I arrived . . . I don't know who she was. I am, at this moment, trying to find out who she is and the extent of her injuries. Perhaps it was someone from the village, visiting the cottage . . .' Rather irrationally and without any real reason, I found myself defending James Patrington.

'Perhaps it was that bitch of a secretary of his,' she snapped. 'It serves them right!' and she slammed down the telephone.

So because something fell out of the sky, James Patrington's little secret had been revealed to the whole world and a few weeks later, the now deserted cottage, still in its damaged condition, was once again put on the market. I never saw James and Lucy again.

I often wonder if he had his cottage insured.

I was more directly involved in another story of love which came about because of a broken romance. This one was almost as unlikely as the Patrington saga.

At three o'clock one morning, my telephone rang. It was downstairs in the office attached to my house, and its continuous shrilling gradually penetrated my sleep. As I staggered downstairs, I rubbed my eyes and tried to shake myself into clarity of action before I lifted the noisy instrument. It was a call from a kiosk.

'PC Rhea, Aidensfield,' I announced, shivering as my feet grew cold upon the bare composition floor.

At the other end of the line, coins were inserted and the pipping ceased, then all I could hear was sobbing. I waited for a brief moment, hoping that the person would say something, but the sobbing continued.

'Hello?' I called into the phone. 'Hello, this is the police.'

It continued and I realized Mary had joined me; she stood at my side, wrapping her dressing-gown tightly around her slim body. She'd had the sense to put on her slippers.

'What is it?' she asked. With late calls of this nature, it was natural to think it was a personal family crisis of some kind.

'Somebody sobbing. Listen,' and I passed the handset to her. She listened and passed it back.

'Hello,' I tried again and increased the volume of my voice this time. 'Hello, this is PC Rhea speaking.'

'I want to come and see you,' said a faint voice, a female voice, through the sobbing.

'Who is it?' I asked, holding the handset so that Mary could hear both sides of the conversation.

'I must come,' continued the voice. 'Now, or I'll jump under the train . . .'

'What train? Look, who are you? I want to help you.' I had detected a note of real desperation in that voice and did not think it was a joke of any kind. 'Where are you?' I added.

'Newcastle Railway Station,' she sobbed, 'and if you don't say yes, I'm going to jump off the platform . . .'

Mary was hissing in my ear.

'For heaven's sake say yes,' she snapped. 'Don't string her along, don't make it appear you're not going to help . . .'

'But . . .' I began as my suspicious police mind began thinking all manner of thoughts.

'Do it,' said Mary.

'Look,' I said to the caller. 'I'll welcome you, we'll welcome you, my wife and I. You can come and see me. But how . . .'

'I can get the next train to York.' Even now, the sobbing sounded less dramatic.

'Yes, all right,' I said, 'I'll meet you there, at York Station.'

'Thank you, oh, thank you,' breathed the voice, sniffing

as the sobs subsided. 'Oh thank you . . .'

The pips sounded and the call was abruptly ended.

I stared at my handset and asked Mary, 'Well, what do you make of that?'

She shrugged her shoulders. 'One of your ex-girl-friends getting worked up about something? A blast from the past? Or have you been misbehaving when you've been away on your various courses? Maybe you've broken someone's little heart?' There was a trusting twinkle in Mary's eye, but I knew that this call could have been misconstrued in all kinds of ways.

'I don't know who she is or what she wants!' I began a weak protest . . .

'Then you'll have to go to York and find out. Bring her here,' said Mary. 'She sounds as if she needs help and friendship, whoever she is and whatever she's done.'

There are times when one is thankful for a marvellous, understanding wife who possesses oceans of common sense, and this was such a time. Policemen especially require wives who have all the qualities of angels coupled with a high measure of earthly common sense. So, in response to Mary's advice I nodded in agreement and said, 'OK, I'll have a cup of tea and get dressed. I'll drive to York to meet our mystery lady.'

It was then that I realized it was a Sunday and it should have been my day off. However, I checked the arrival times of trains from Newcastle and as I drove into York in my own car, I wondered whether this was classed as police duty. Was this a private matter or could I claim that I had used my car for emergency duty purposes?

If such thoughts seem petty, this is not so because if I had an accident on this trip, it would be vital to my future security as to whether or not it was a 'duty' commitment. But there was nothing I could do about the technicalities of the situation at this stage; I would worry about those kind of things after I had met my damsel in distress.

And so it was, that shortly after 4.40 a.m. that chill but sunny Sunday morning, I was standing on York Station awaiting the Newcastle train. I must admit that I wondered whether I was a fool or not, or whether this was some curious prank, but on reflection I knew I had no alternative but to turn out. I had to discover for myself the reality of the situation.

The train was about ten minutes late. A few minutes after its arrival, as I stood at the ticket-collector's barrier, I noticed a young woman heading my way. I did not recognize her. In her late teens or early twenties, she was pretty without being beautiful, and had mousy hair which straggled down to her shoulders. She was dressed in a rather crumpled, short tartan skirt, a dark green velvet top and white blouse. She wore no stockings or tights and was waif-like in many ways. As she drew closer, I could see that her pale face bore a hint of freckles, but other than some pale lipstick she wore no make-up. She had no luggage or topcoat but did carry a black handbag.

After passing through the barrier, she managed an embarrassed smile as she came nervously towards me. She was like a naughty child who was anticipating a telling-off by an angry parent.

'Hello.' Clearly she knew who I was. She stood before me like a lost kitten.

'Hello,' I returned, racking my brains in an attempt to recall her name or where we'd met. In those few brief moments, I failed. I had no idea who she was.

'I'm sorry . . . for all this . . .' she began in an accent which I did not recognize as either Yorkshire or Tyneside. 'I was silly . . . I'll go back. I'm all right now.' She turned to walk away from me.

'No,' I said, still baffled. 'Don't go. You need help, don't you? Look, my car's outside and my wife has got a cup of tea ready. The buffet's closed, I'm afraid, so we can't talk here.'

'No,' she said, 'I'm all right now, honest. I can go. I'll go back to Newcastle on the next train . . . I was silly . . . I'm confused . . . I'm a nuisance to you.'

'No,' I said, 'my wife wants to meet you and I want to know what all this is about. So, come along. No arguing! I'm here because I want to help you.'

She hesitated momentarily, then followed me to my waiting car. Without a word, she climbed into the passenger seat and settled down as I drove through York's deserted streets.

'Well,' I said as we cleared the town, 'so what's all this about? How about a name to start with?'

'Tessa,' she said. 'Teresa, really, but everybody calls me Tessa. Tessa Underwood.'

'I'm still baffled,' I admitted. 'I don't recall that name. Tell me about the phone call, Tessa. You wanted help, so why did you ring me? I don't know you.'

'It all sounds so silly now, Mr Rhea,' she used my name quite normally. 'It really does. After the train ride, I came to my senses. It was so silly . . . I feel a right fool, I do, bothering you like this, when you don't know me . . .'

'It wasn't silly at three o'clock this morning, Tessa. It was very serious then, and it could be serious again so let's hear about it.'

And so, during the half-hour trip from York to Aidensfield, I managed to drag the story from her. Brought up in Staffordshire, her parents had been killed in a road accident about four years ago, when she was seventeen. For a time, she'd lived with an aunt, but had fallen out with her. So eighteen months ago, she had moved to Newcastle-upon-Tyne where she now worked as a shorthand typist in a factory on a new industrial estate.

She lived alone in a little flat which she rented and, apart from Mark, her boy-friend, and some of the girls at work, she knew no one. Some of the girls at work had made fun of her because of her curious accent, but three days ago, her boy-friend had left her.

At this stage, the tears started again; I was tempted to halt the car and comfort her but felt it wiser to continue. I exhorted her to carry on. Through her sobs, she said Mark had left her for a married woman he'd met in a night club, a real old scrubber according to Tessa. All attempts at reconciliation had failed; Tessa, with no parents to turn to and no relations other than the awkward aunt, felt she could not confide in anyone. She was alone in the world; she'd felt unloved and unwanted.

In her own way, she provided me with a graphic account of how her misery and loneliness had turned into a suicidal determination. Burdened with her worries in the early hours of this very morning, she had gone down to Newcastle Central railway station with a determination to throw herself under one of the speeding expresses. Even now, as she re-told her story among floods of tears, she wondered how she could have contemplated such a thing.

'I wasn't thinking straight,' she said. 'It was horrid. I was . . . oh . . . so silly, so miserable and sad, lonely . . . it was Saturday night, you see, and everyone goes out with friends and I had none, only Mark, and he'd left me . . . I had no one, Mr Rhea. No one. If you hadn't said you'd see me . . .'

'But I did. I said you could come to see me and here you are. If that action has stopped you from doing something silly, then I'm delighted. Now, do you think you've got rid of those awful thoughts?'

She nodded and wiped her eyes. 'I'll be all right now.'

'But,' this was the point that still puzzled me, 'why ring me? Of all the people who would have helped – the local police, for example, the Salvation Army, the Church – and you rang me!'

She produced a thin smile and looked embarrassed. 'It was so good of you. I mean, you could have said no and . . .'

'And you might have jumped in front of a train?'

'You didn't ignore me, Mr Rhea . . . I'm . . . well . . .'

'I know. But, Tessa, I don't know you. I still can't understand why you rang me?'

She hesitated. We were now drawing close to Aidensfield and in the growing light of dawn, I could distinguish my police house on its lofty site which overlooked the ranging and beautiful countryside. By now, it was after five o'clock and the lights of some houses were showing as smoke rose from our chimney. Mary had prepared a welcome for this girl.

'Can you remember a car breaking down outside your house, about a year ago?' Tessa asked, smiling at the memory.

Vaguely, I did recall the incident.

'Me and . . . that boy . . . well, we'd had a day out on the moors in his car, and when we came along the road somewhere in this area, we found a small suitcase lying in the road. So we picked it up and thought we'd better report it to the police. Well, yours was the first police station we saw. So we stopped and Mark, that's him, made me bring it in.'

I was now recalling the incident with more clarity.

'He didn't want to bring it in, so I did. I handed it to you and you made a note of it in case the loser came asking.'

'She did, I remember,' I said. 'She was most grateful – it

had fallen off a roof-rack. So that was you, was it? You look
so different!'

'I've changed – I've lost my puppy fat for one thing, and
I've had my hair cut.'

'So you remembered me from that little incident?'

'Well, you remember Mark's car? When I went back to
the car after bringing in the suitcase it wouldn't start. Mark
tried and tried, so you ran him down to a garage in the
village and got a set of plugs or something for the engine.'

'Points,' I corrected her. 'A set of points. Yes, and we
put them in, me and your friend. I can recall it now.'

'Well,' she was still trying to reach the end of her story,
'I remembered how helpful you were . . .'

'It was nothing,' I said.

'But you see, I wasn't used to policemen helping me,
Mark neither. But, well, I kept the receipt you gave me for
that suitcase. It was in my handbag, it has been there ever
since. You know what women are for carrying stuff around
and well, last night when I was so unhappy and depressed,
I was rifling through my bag, getting rid of his letters and
things on the station. I was putting things in the rubbish
bin, you know, getting rid of everything, then I found that
receipt. It had your number on as well. So I rang – and here
I am.'

'I'm pleased you rang if it meant so much.' I was
sincere. 'Well, we're almost home.'

'I'll go straight back,' she said. 'I shouldn't have come.
I've been a silly, stupid nuisance and I've thought things
out on that train, sensibly I think. I had time . . .'

'At least come in and have some breakfast,' I offered.
'And you are welcome to stay until you get yourself
completely sorted out.'

And so she did. At Mary's invitation, she stayed three
days and Mary was marvellous with her. Tessa was lovely

with our children too, and that girl and our family are still good friends. She still calls, albeit now with a new husband and two lovely children of her own.

But her presence in our house did cause a flutter of interest and some speculation in the village. Mary and I decided we must not tell anyone of her real reason for being with us, and so we were faced with questions like, 'Is that the wife's sister then?' or 'Been arrested, has she?' or 'Is she a policewoman in disguise, watching summat in Aidensfield?'

In all cases, we simply said she was a friend who was staying for a day or two.

But I often wonder whether that event was part of my police duty or not. I think not, for I never mentioned it to any of my superiors.

4

Little deeds of kindness, little words of love
Help to make the earth happy, like the heaven above.

Julia Carney, 1823-1908

There was great excitement in Ashfordly one Friday morning in June. It arose because BBC radio had decided to broadcast its 'Good Morning' programme from a mobile studio in the market-place. It was to be a live broadcast from the North Region, and would be on the air from 7 a.m. until 9 a.m. At that time, the 'Good Morning' series visited a different town or village each week and the series had a dedicated following.

It was natural that the people of Ashfordly were excited and delighted that their charming market town had been selected and in due course, a list of candidates for interview was drawn up. Personalities from all walks of life were procured and the interviews would be interspersed with music and reports about a selection of the interesting places in the locality.

Late on the Thursday afternoon beforehand, the BBC's entourage arrived and the galaxy of technicians and production staff established themselves and their vehicles at the prearranged place. The little town awaited the honour of tomorrow's spell of publicity, while the participants grew more nervous as their hour of glory approached. The police, as always, had their role to play.

In addition to keeping a protective eye on the vehicles and their loads of expensive equipment during the preceding night, they had to maintain a discreet presence on the day itself. We had to be there just in case someone tried to gatecrash the proceedings or otherwise make a nuisance of themselves.

As an outdoor audience was anticipated in the vicinity of the mobile studio, there would be a degree of crowd control and some car-parking to supervise. Duties of this kind were undertaken in conjunction with every crowd-pulling event and the BBC's 'Good Morning from Ashfordly' was no exception. As our duty rota had been compiled some weeks in advance, I was delighted to find that I was to perform an early morning patrol that Friday. My duties were from 6 a.m. until 9 a.m. and I was therefore allocated a foot patrol in the town centre so that a uniformed police presence would be evident.

I looked forward to the work.

I left home at six o'clock on my Francis Barnett, arrived at Ashfordly Police Station at 6.15 a.m. and left my motor cycle there. I also left my motor-cycling weather-proof clothes and donned my uniform cap as I set about my patrol. Even at that early stage of the morning, a small crowd of onlookers had gathered but they stood at a respectful distance and appeared to be causing no bother. The technicians were hard at work setting up and checking their sophisticated equipment while the producer of the programme had gathered the programme participants in a separate caravan for a final briefing.

I did not intrude. I could see that things were moving apace so I kept in the background, watchful but discreet. The minutes ticked away and then, as seven o'clock approached, much of the crowd melted away.

I realized they would be going home to hear the broadcast

and I wondered if Sergeant Blaketon would be listening. He had not yet made an appearance and I did wonder if he was just a wee bit upset because he was not one of the selected personalities . . . But I reckoned he would be tuned in as he enjoyed his breakfast.

I knew that I could listen to parts of the broadcast in a friendly bakery just behind the market-place. Confident that my presence was not required, I sidled away and entered the bakery by a side door. I was assailed by the marvellous whiff of new bread as the manager noticed my entry. He pointed to the kettle and then to a radio perched on a shelf.

I got the message. They were listening as they worked, and I was invited to join them and to make myself a cup of tea; they were already drinking theirs. I asked if anyone required a refill, but they were content and made hand signals to inform me of the fact, so I made myself a cup and stood in silence beneath the radio. At seven, the broadcast started with the announcer sounding bright and breezy as he introduced the programme and gave a brief résumé of Ashfordly's topography and the delights in store.

Then he said, 'And here am I, in the middle of the market-place awaiting my guests. And in my rush to get everything ready this morning, I forgot to bring some sugar for my tea! We've no sugar in the studio, folks, but perhaps someone will fetch a spoonful along . . .'

No one in the bakery made a move, and so I decided to help out. After all, I reasoned, everyone else was glued to their radios at home, and would hate to move away in case they missed something. If everyone took this attitude, no one would provide the sugar! And so I thanked the bakery staff for the tea and left. The shops which stocked sugar would not yet be open, so I hurried to the police station, located the tin of sugar we used in our own tea-swindle, and poured some into a milk bottle.

Rather than carry it through the streets in my uniform I donned my crash helmet, popped the bottle of sugar into the pannier of my motor cycle and scooted the few yards back to the market-place. Lifting the machine on to its stand, I removed the bottle of sugar and walked across to the BBC's collection of vehicles. At the door of the studio, I found an assistant, handed over the sugar with my compliments and left.

I returned to my bike, placed the crash helmet upon the saddle and resumed a normal patrol. And that, I thought, was that. It was my good deed for the day. Twenty minutes later, I was in the local newsagent's shop, a courtesy visit during my patrol, and I heard the broadcast issuing from their radio.

Miss Phyllis Oakworth, a leading light in Ashfordly WI for fifty years, had just been interviewed, and the announcer was once again in full flow.

And to my horror, I heard him say, 'I am delighted that my plea for some sugar has been answered. I've now got enough for myself and my guests. For this, my thanks go to the local constabulary in Ashfordly who rushed a supply to our studio by police motor cycle. Now there's an example of co-operation between the police and the public – if you need help, just ask an Ashfordly policeman. Well done, Officer, whoever you were, you've saved the day. I think your policemen are wonderful, Ashfordly. And now to our next guest . . .'

'You?' asked Ken, the newsagent.

I nodded and grimaced at the unwarranted publicity, but he just laughed. 'Nice one,' he said and continued his work among the morning papers.

I left the shop and wondered who, among the dozens of my senior officers, had heard that; furthermore, I wondered what their reaction would be. Could my action be construed as too frivolous for a police officer? But as the morning passed and the local folks listened to their own town, its people and its attractions being so professionally scrutinized, my worries began to evaporate.

Then, at quarter to nine, I noticed the tall, smart but severe figure of Sergeant Blaketon as he moved towards me across the market square. Rigidly upright and with military bearing, he came towards me, an impressive man in his immaculate uniform. He was prominent among the crowd which had grown larger thanks to the arrival of some workers who were due to start their day's toil at nine o'clock.

They had paused for a moment before disappearing into their offices and places of work, and the broadcast was drawing to a close in those final minutes.

'All correct, Rhea?' he asked. I noticed the more-serious-than-usual expression on his face as he arrived at my side.

'All correct, sergeant,' I responded in the traditional manner.

'No problems? Trouble from the crowd? Parking?'

'No, sergeant.'

'No crimes, no pickpockets in the crowd, no thieves at work as everyone's attention was diverted by this affair?'

'No, sergeant,' I said, hoping that no one had taken the opportunity to steal a bike or to take someone's wallet. That sort of thing just did not happen in Ashfordly, I felt, and so I was confident in my bland assessment of the situation.

'No overnight break-ins? Car thefts? Broken windows not discovered?'

'No, sergeant,' and my answer must, by this time, have sounded quizzical. He was going on a bit, I felt, certainly more than usual. In normal circumstances, my 'All Correct' speech would have been sufficient, but he was probing now. I realized he was leading up to something; judging by the expression on his face, it was something serious. I began to wonder if a crime *had* been reported or if some incident had occurred. If so, I was not aware of it and that could infer that I had neglected my duty.

Somewhat worried by his attitude, we made a brief perambulation of the market square and I noticed that the crowd was now dwindling as the people finally went to their places of work.

'If you have been so vigilant, Rhea, and have had such a positive command of the situation, how is it that you have found the time to be entertained by a radio programme?'

'Sergeant?'

He came to a halt in a quiet recess near the town hall and we stood together as he mustered his speech. 'The sugar, Rhea. There I am, sitting at my breakfast-table, when I learn that one of my constables has heard of a plea for sugar from this lot here, these broadcasting people. That alone indicates that the constable in question must have been neglecting his duty, that he was failing to work his beat in accordance with instructions . . .'

'I . . .' I couldn't believe what I was hearing.

'And furthermore,' his voice rose to stifle any comment I might make, 'there is the question of the misuse of police vehicles, that is, the use of an official motor cycle and fuel, to say nothing of police time, to convey the sugar from the police office to these broadcasting people, and there is also the question of the ownership of the sugar, eh Rhea? Was it yours to give away? Was it your personal property? Or was it sugar which belonged to the Police Authority? Was it sugar from a fund of some kind?'

'But, sergeant . . .'

'And on top of all that, Rhea, how do you think the

public will react to this? Will those listeners, those thousands or even millions of them out there, think that Ashfordly Police have nothing better to do than to act as delivery men for the BBC? We will be a laughing-stock of police forces, Rhea, we will be the butt of jokes from our city counterparts who are coping with murders and mayhem. They will now believe that we occupy our duty time by running cupfuls of official sugar from police stations to broadcasting people who then announce it to the world . . .'

Sergeant Oscar Blaketon was on top form. All his prejudices and formal police attitudes were emerging as he stood there in the recess near the town hall, giving vent to his concern.

'But, sergeant . . .'

'And Rhea, let us now suppose that the superintendent or even the Chief Constable himself was listening to that programme! What are they to think about it all, Rhea? How am I to justify your actions; your highly unofficial and thoughtless actions; your neglect of duty in this very public manner; your misuse of police property . . .'

'Sergeant, I thought . . .'

'I don't care what you thought, Rhea. What I do care about is what you did. And what you did could amount to a breach of the Discipline Code with the severest of repercussions for you and for the force . . .'

I must admit I had not for one moment thought of that aspect. Anyone else, in any sort of job or profession, would have done the same, so why should the police be any different? But, according to Blaketon's interpretation of Police (Discipline) Regulations, it did seem that I had fallen foul of those rules, and I knew him well enough to realize that he would have checked the provisions of that code before coming to speak to me. He was not the man to leave such detail to chance.

As he continued his diatribe, I visualized the punishments that could be imposed for such breaches of the Discipline Regulations. There was dismissal from the force, with an alternative of a requirement to resign; there was reduction in rank (which didn't apply to me because, as a constable, I was at the bottom of the scale); a reduction in pay; a fine; a reprimand or a caution.

I began to feel pale and sick and started to worry about my future, both in the immediate and long term. I knew the Discipline Code was strict and that some supervisory officers reinforced it to the letter . . .

'So, Rhea,' said Blaketon as he concluded his lecture, 'you will submit a report about this incident. In triplicate. And it will be on my desk not later than twelve noon today.'

'Yes, sergeant,' I said, with evident meekness.

Having delivered his lecture, he strode away, grim-faced, awesome yet somehow majestic in his unassailable attitude. With my mind ranging across the problem I had now created for myself, I watched the BBC technicians begin to dismantle their equipment and decided I was no longer required. I went across to my motor cycle and mounted it.

A voice called to me from the assembled BBC personnel. 'Thanks for the sugar, Officer!'

'Cheers!' I responded with a wave of my hand and knew I dare not tell them of Blaketon's reaction or of my impending ordeal. Communication with journalists about internal police matters was another disciplinary offence, so I left it at that. Dejected and worried, I started the Francis Barnett and motored slowly back to Aidensfield.

Over breakfast, I told Mary all about it and she thought it was a ridiculous attitude, but at ten o'clock I settled in my office to type the report. I knew it must be totally factual and that I should not try to make excuses; I therefore decided on a plain, simple and honest account of my sugar mission. I would set it out in chronological order.

At twenty minutes past ten, my telephone rang.

'PC Rhea, Aidensfield,' I announced.

'Just a moment,' said a woman's voice at the other end of the line, 'I have the Chief Constable for you.'

I nearly fell off my chair. The Chief! I saw myself being summoned immediately to Police Headquarters to account for my actions. I saw myself writing out my resignation and looking for another job. My heart thumped as I waited for the great man to speak.

I tried to marshal my thoughts in an attempt to justify my actions. I clung to the telephone, nervous and worried, as his secretary connected me.

'Chief Constable,' I heard his crisp response.

'PC Rhea, Aidensfield, sir,' I answered.

'Ah, Rhea. I have been in touch with your Divisional Headquarters and they tell me that you were the constable on duty at Ashfordly this morning.'

'Yes, sir,' I admitted, quaking.

'And am I right in thinking that you were responsible for supplying some sugar to the BBC during that morning broadcast?'

I swallowed. So he had been listening, just as old Blaketon had feared.

'Yes, sir,' my voice must have sounded faint and weak as I croaked my reply.

'Bloody good show!' he said. 'That was an excellent piece of public relations, Rhea. It gave the police a sympathetic and human image, and I was delighted it was my force which had done it. Excellent, well done. I just wanted you to know that I was delighted, and so was the Government Inspector. He heard the broadcast too and was delighted. He has just called me.'

And so, in one single moment, all my worries and tensions evaporated.

'It's good of you to ring, sir . . .' I managed to splutter.

'Not at all. It's the least I could do. Keep up the good work, Rhea,' and he ended our conversation.

I sat in my chair as a feeling of release swept over me. Now, I had the perfect ending for my report to Sergeant Blaketon.

To conclude it, I added this sentence, 'At 10.20 a.m. today, I received a telephone call from the Chief Constable who had heard the broadcast in question. He congratulated me on my actions and stressed the public relations value of the publicity. The HMI also expressed his pleasure in similar terms and had conveyed his appreciation to the Chief Constable with a request that it be transmitted to me.'

At half past eleven, I signed my report and drove into Ashfordly with it. Sergeant Blaketon was on the telephone as I walked into the office, so I placed my report on his desk and walked out.

Never again did he refer to the matter.

On another occasion, it was the police who needed assistance and I found myself involved in that episode too. The ingredients were an ancient ruined abbey, a religious service, some severe car-parking problems and a stubborn Yorkshire farmer.

In the spring of the year, Ashfordly Police Station received a visit from Father Geoffrey Summerson, the Roman Catholic parish priest. Sergeant Bairstow was on duty at the time and warmly received his visitor.

Father Summerson was a small man who had passed his sixtieth birthday; he had been at Ashfordly for many years

and ran a happy, busy little parish. He was constantly
involved in events and happenings in the town and his
diminutive, but powerful personality made him popular
with all faiths and even with those who professed no
known religion.

His frail figure, with a somewhat gaunt and hungry
appearance, belied a bundle of energy which he used for
the good of both the town and his parishioners. At first
sight, he looked humourless and severe, with a sallow skin
drawn tight over thin, high cheekbones. Small, pale eyes
glinted from behind rimless spectacles and his hands were
never still. He was fond of gesticulations; constantly
emphasizing his words with sweeping gestures or meaningful
movements of his thin arms and surprisingly long and
slender hands. They were the hands of an artist or musician
but I do not know whether he possessed either of those
talents.

That day, however, he arrived at the police station on
foot, clad in his dark grey suit and dog collar. I was on the
telephone at the time, receiving a long, involved message
about warble fly. I saw the priest being invited into the
sergeant's office and guessed it indicated a matter of some
importance.

I concluded my call and at a wink from the sergeant, put
on the kettle for some coffee.

'Well, Father,' Sergeant Bairstow was always happy and
cheerful, 'what can we do for you this bright, spring
morning?'

'Good of you to see me, sergeant,' began the priest. 'It's
about Waindale Abbey. It is within your province, isn't it?'

'Yes,' said Bairstow. 'It's on our patch.'

Waindale Abbey is one of several beautiful ruins dotted
around the area. Wrecked by the Commissioners of Henry
VIII during the Reformation, it sits beside the gentle River

Wain where its impressive location and magnificent broken outline give testimony to its dramatic past. Today, it is a popular tourist attraction where its mellow stone and lofty columns give no hint of the role it once played in the economic life of the locality.

'The year marks the thirteenth centenary of the foundation of the Abbey,' began the priest. 'It is one of the oldest ruins in the land and dates to the earliest times of Christendom in this country. So,' he went on, 'we – that is the hierarchy of the Catholic Church, with the blessing of members of the Anglican faith I might add – have decided to mark the occasion. We are going to hold a Concelebrated Mass with the bishop and priests of this diocese. It will take place in the ruins and the proposed date is 24 August, that's the Feast of St Bartholomew, patron saint of the Abbey.'

'So that will mean a considerable influx of people and vehicles, Father?'

'Yes, I estimate there'll be well into tens of thousands. Bus loads, cars, foot and cycle pilgrims, priests, nuns and laity – they'll come from all the northern parishes and even further afield. That is why I am here, to give you due notice, so that you can make your own plans.'

I took them a cup of coffee each and settled down in the front office to enjoy one too. They continued their chat and I could hear every word. It was not a confidential meeting.

'We appreciate adequate warning, Father, then we can arrange our duties to cope. Will you want a police presence inside the Abbey grounds, do you think, or merely on the outside to cope with the traffic and crowds?'

'Certainly on the outside, sergeant. As for the interior, well, I imagine our pilgrims will behave, although a discreet police presence is never amiss.'

'I'll mark the date in our duty diary,' said Sergeant Bairstow. 'You'll not have the time of the service yet?'

'No, those matters are to be finalized, but it will be during the afternoon, probably beginning at 2.30 p.m. or 3.00 p.m. But some people will arrive much earlier; some will bring picnics, I know, and they will give the day a holiday atmosphere, a form of celebration.'

'Good, well, Father, thank you for this advance notice. You'll keep in touch please, about the timing and other details?'

'Of course, and don't hesitate to contact me if there's anything more you need to know.'

Father Summerson left and Sergeant Bairstow came into the front office. 'You heard all that, Nick?' he asked.

I nodded. 'It looks like being a busy day.'

'You're telling me! There'll be lost children to consider; wandering old ladies; lost and found property; toilet facilities to provide; car and coach parking . . . There'll be other traffic in the valley, trying to squeeze past the pilgrims on those narrow lanes, and the local residents will play hell about it all. We'll have to ensure access for any emergency vehicles and there'll be litter; first aid facilities to think about; possible crimes like pickpockets or other thefts . . .'

'It'll keep us busy for weeks!' I laughed.

'And for that remark, young Rhea, consider yourself involved right from the start! Right now, in fact. Come along, we'll go and inspect the scene, shall we?'

In the sergeant's official car, we drove the four miles or so across the hills and into the valley of Waindale. The lanes were peaceful, with the hedges just bursting into fresh green leaf, while the fields and woodlands were changing into their spring colours. Flowers like wild daffodils and celandines adorned the verges and birds sang in marvellous harmony as we dropped down the steep incline into the lovely valley. To give the monks due praise, they certainly knew how to select an ideal site.

The tiny village with its cluster of yellow stone cottages, some thatched and others with red pantile roofs, reclined beneath the shadow of the hillside, while the magnificent Abbey occupied a huge, flat site deep in the valley.

'You know, Nick,' breathed Sergeant Bairstow, 'this view never ceases to thrill me. It really is incredible, those woods, the fields, the river down there – see? And the Abbey, silent and just a little mysterious . . . I've seen it with a mist around it at dawn; I've seen it at night in the light of a full moon, and at sunset too . . .'

I knew what he was trying to say. There was a magic about the place, an indefinable atmosphere rich with the scents of history and drama and it was something I'd experienced on the occasions I'd come here.

We eased our little police car into the car-park and emerged to breathe the crisp, fresh air of Waindale.

'And to think we get paid for this!' smiled Sergeant Bairstow. 'Come along, let's have a critical look at the interior.'

After explaining our purpose to the lady in the little wooden hut at the entrance, we walked around as we tried to envisage how the huge congregation would be accommodated; where the altar should be sited both for safety and for vision. We wondered whether crowd-barriers were needed and which was the best place to site the portable toilets, the first aid centre, the lost children tent and other essentials.

We had to ensure that the village was free to go about its normal business, and we must be equally sure that ambulances could gain access to any possible casualties in the crowd. Thoughts of this kind were part of any exploratory visit and Sergeant Bairstow was sufficiently experienced to be aware of the requirements. We both knew that an Operation Order would be needed to cope with all the problems of the day, and as a plan formed in his mind, he decided it was an ideal opportunity to make use of our band of local, dedicated Special Constables.

My next contact with Father Summerson came through a telephone call. I was in Ashfordly at the time and accepted the call.

'It's Father Summerson,' he said. 'I'm ringing about the Abbey celebrations.'

'It's PC Rhea, Father. I am familiar with the event so far.'

'Good, well I thought you'd better know that we have received some intelligence from our parishes. At this stage, we believe that the congregation will be in excess of 20,000 – it might even rise to 30,000. I thought you had better be aware of these numbers.'

I found it difficult to visualize such a crowd in Waindale Abbey, and expressed that point.

'Oh, the Abbey will accommodate them,' he said with some assurance. 'There is plenty of space. It is the traffic that worries me, Constable. From what I hear, most will be coming by coach but there will be many cars.'

I realized that the volume of incoming traffic would be similar to that which arrives at a popular race meeting, but this was no race track and there was a distinct lack of parking space. There were none of the facilities necessary for coping with such numbers. In short, we, and the church organizers, were to be faced with a car-parking problem of some magnitude. It could not be left to chance or ignored.

I thanked him for this advance information and wrote the details on a note for the attention of Sergeant Bairstow. He contacted me a couple of days later and said, 'Nick, I'll pick you up at half past nine this morning. We'll have another look at Waindale Abbey – it's about the parking problems.'

We stood in the centre of the tiny official car-park and calculated that it would accommodate no more than twenty cars – and at an average of four persons per car, that was a mere eighty people.

'That'll just about cater for the official party,' Bairstow said. 'And there's nowhere else. They can't park in these lanes – they'd be blocked in no time. So young Nicholas, what are we to do?'

'We could organize parking elsewhere and bus them in here,' I suggested.

'Have you ever tried that? It causes chaos and delays. Besides, don't forget many of these folks will not be in organized parties. They'll drive to the dale in their own transport, and they'll come right here. We have no control over them.'

'There is a field about a hundred yards away,' I told him. 'Just beyond that cottage and small-holding.'

'Flat, is it? And dry?'

'I think so. We can inspect it now,' I suggested.

We walked along the lane towards an old stone cottage with smoke rising from its chimney. Hens clucked in the yard and there was a goat tethered among the apple trees in a small orchard. An elderly woman was sweeping the doorstep with a large stiff brush and Sergeant Bairstow addressed her.

'Excuse me,' he said. 'This field – do you know whose it is?'

'Aye,' she said. 'Awd Arthur Craggs. Up yonder,' and she pointed to a farmhouse almost hidden by trees. It overlooked the valley and the Abbey from its elevated site.

'Thanks.'

The field was ideal. There were two wide entrances, one at each end. Each was large enough to permit coaches and cars to turn off the lane as they entered the valley from both directions. It was a large, flat area of grass which had once been two fields, and the surface was solid. We tramped across it, testing the ground with our heels and trying to estimate how many vehicles it would contain.

'Even if it rains,' I said, 'this surface will be sound enough. They won't get bogged down – it's solid enough to take the buses, isn't it?'

'I reckon it is, Nick. It's just what we need. But it won't rain,' chuckled Bairstow. 'I have it on good authority! Father Summerson says he's praying for a fine day. He assures me it will be fine and that there will be no rain and no weather problems. He's not even thinking of a wet weather programme or an awning for the altar!'

'That's faith for you,' I said. 'But God works in mysterious ways!'

'Then let's hope He approves of this field as a car-park!'

We decided not to take the car up to Arthur Craggs' farm, but walked up the steep, unmade track and found ourselves in an expansive and rather untidy farmyard. Other than a few bantams pecking for scraps, there was no sign of life, so we went to the house. The door was open so we knocked and shouted, and a woman called, 'T'dooer's oppen.'

We knew it was an invitation and so we stepped in. A farmer and his wife were sitting at a large, scrubbed kitchen table, each with a mug of tea and a huge slice of cake before them.

'Sit down,' she said without waiting for any introductions and went across to the kettle which was boiling on the Aga. Being familiar with the customary hospitality of the local farmers, we settled on chairs at the table, and she produced a mug of hot tea and a massive chunk of fruit cake for each of us. We weren't given the luxury of plates.

'Is it about me stock register?' said the man.

'No,' said Sergeant Bairstow. 'Are you Arthur Craggs?'

'There's neearbody else of that name lives here,' he said, grinning widely and showing a mouthful of stained and rotten teeth. He would be in his late sixties, I reckoned, a ruddy-faced man with a few days' growth of beard around his jowls and chin. His eyes were light grey and clear and he wore rough working clothes, corduroy trousers with leather leggings and hob-nailed boots. We had arrived at ''lowance time', as they called their mid-morning break and even though this couple did not know us, we were expected to share their food. His wife, a plain and simple woman, now settled at the table but did not speak.

'Well,' said Sergeant Bairstow, 'this is lovely cake and a welcome cup of tea.'

'Thoo'll 'ave cum aboot summat else, though?' Those eyes flashed cheekily, playfully even. He knew we wanted some favour from him.

'Yes. You'll have heard that a service is planned in the Abbey, in August.'

'Aye,' he said, those sharp eyes watching us.

'Well,' said the sergeant, 'we are looking for somewhere to park the buses and cars. We understand that the field just this side of the Abbey belongs to you.'

'Aye,' he said, not volunteering anything.

'Well,' said Sergeant Bairstow, 'we wondered if you would permit the church authorities to use it as a car and coach-park, just for that one afternoon.'

'And dis thoo think they'd let me graze my cattle and sheep in yon Abbey, then? There's some nice grass in there. Or mebbe they might let me use yan o' their choches or chapils as a cattle shed, eh?' and he laughed at his own jokes. 'Christians share things, deearn't they?'

It was clear we were dealing with a difficult and stubborn old character, but Sergeant Bairstow plodded on.

'It would be needed all day, I reckon,' he said. 'On 24th August, it's a few months away yet, but we need to be finalizing our plans . . .'

'Well, sergeant,' he said, sipping from his mug. 'Ah might 'ave sheep in yon field by then, or coos, or even some beeasts Ah might be aiming o' buying. There again, Ah might decide to put some poultry 'uts in there . . . thoo sees, sergeant, Ah'm a busy farmer and my lands are needed all t'time, for summat or even for summat else. Ah's allus shifting things about . . . nivver stops . . .'

'It would be required only for that one day . . .'

'Yar day's t'same as onny other in my mind,' he said. 'It maks neea difference what day it is. Besides, sergeant, Ah's nut a Catholic, and it's them lot that wants to come, isn't it?'

'I expect there'll be pilgrims of all faiths on the day,' Sergeant Bairstow said truthfully.

'Well,' said Craggs, 'Ah's nut gahin to say they can 'ave yon field. It's a lang while off yit, and Ah just might want to use it mesell.'

And he got up from the table.

With that note of finality, we made a move towards the door, and Sergeant Bairstow added, 'Thanks for the 'lowance. But can we ask you to think about it? For the good of the village, really, to keep all the traffic off the roads?'

'Aye,' said Arthur Craggs, with those eyes twinkling and almost mocking us. 'Thoo can ask me ti think aboot it.'

We said nothing to each other until we were clear of his premises, and then Bairstow sighed. 'By, Nick, there's some stubborn old mules around these parts. We need a

decision from him – a "yes" decision I might add – before
we can go ahead with the planning of this. Do you know
him?'

I shook my head. I didn't. I'd never had cause to visit
this farm, and so Sergeant Bairstow decided to ask someone
else to make an approach to the farmer. Rather craftily, he
discovered that Craggs had married in the Waindale
Methodist Chapel and therefore asked the local Methodist
minister to plead with Craggs. But this failed too. The
cunning old farmer refused to commit himself one way or
the other.

His indecision created an enormous problem for the
organizers and for us. We began to look at several other
alternatives for car and coach-parking, all grossly
inconvenient but vitally necessary.

And then, in late June, Sergeant Bairstow received a
very unexpected telephone call.

'It's Craggs,' said the voice. 'That field. Ah sha'n't be
needing it on t'day of yon service. Thoo can 'ave it,
Sergeant. Mak sure t'gates is shut when you've finished
wiv it,' and he put down the telephone.

The relief was tremendous, and the arrangements went
ahead with a new impetus. And then the big day dawned.
It was fine and warm, a beautiful day as Father Summerson
had predicted. During the previous week, the church
authorities had fulfilled their role; the signs, toilets, first
aid, lost children and lost property – everything had been
fixed in readiness and the huge empty field bore enormous
signs proclaiming it as the 'Car and Coach-Park.'

Until lunch-time, things went very smoothly. Then, as
the time for the commencement of the service approached,
the traffic intensified. With an hour to go, the tiny valley
and its narrow lanes were congested with slow-moving
vehicles, all heading for the car-park. Special Constables

and regular officers were guiding them along and ensuring none parked on the verges or roadside, but the queue grew longer and longer. There was clearly a delay of some kind at the head of the queue.

'Nick,' Sergeant Bairstow had come to investigate the problem. 'Pop along and see what the hold-up is.'

When I arrived at the field, I soon discovered the reason. Farmer Craggs had positioned himself at one entrance, and his wife was at the other; each was equipped with a card-table and a money-box and they had erected crude hand-painted notices which said, 'Parking, Coaches £3; cars 10/-; motor cycles 5/-; pedal cycles 1 shilling' and they were taking a fortune.

The queues, which extended in both directions from the gates, were the result of motorists and coach drivers pausing while having to pay. I had no idea whether this was part of the deal which had been struck over the use of this field, and knew I could not intervene. It was private premises. But the queue was lengthening and the delayed people would interrupt the Mass by their late arrival. I suggested to the passengers in several cars and coaches that they disembark now, before parking, and so they did. Others copied them, and soon we had a steady stream of pilgrims entering the ruins of this hallowed place as the drivers waited to park.

When I returned to the entrance, I found Sergeant Bairstow talking to Father Summerson.

'Well, Nick?'

I explained the cause of the hold-up, and Father Summerson grimaced. 'The crafty old character!' he said. 'He demanded a fee from us too and now he's charging the drivers!'

I could see it all; the cunning old farmer had withheld his permission until he knew the church would be willing to pay almost any price to have access to his field. I did not ask what price he had demanded, but then to ask parking fees as well . . .

'It's all cash too!' said Sergeant Bairstow. 'He'll make a fortune today!'

'But he has saved us a lot of problems,' said Father Summerson generously. 'We must not be too harsh about him; after all, it is his field and I'm sure we must have inconvenienced him somewhat.'

And so the day was a success. Craggs' field did accommodate most of the traffic and, as so often happens on these occasions, most of the vehicles were somehow parked before the service began. I went into the Mass and so did Sergeant Bairstow; it was a moving experience to see those ancient walls filled with people at prayer after so many centuries.

It would be some three weeks later when I saw Farmer Craggs again. He was crossing the market-place in Ashfordly and I hailed him.

'Thanks for helping us out that Sunday,' I said.

'Ah's done meself a load of harm,' he said, 'lettin' yon field off like that.'

'Harm?' I asked. 'What sort of harm?'

'Somebody's told t'taxman about it, and now he's been through my money like a dose o' salts, checking this, checking that, counting egg money, taty money. Gahin back years, he is . . . Ah shall be worse off than ivver now . . .'

And he skulked away towards the bank.

I never did know who had informed the Inland Revenue about Mr Craggs, but it was not a very Christian thing to do.

5

Tenants of life's middle state
Securely plac'd between the small and great.
William Cowper, 1731-1800

While serving the rural community which comprised my beat at Aidensfield, it dawned upon me that Crampton rarely featured in my duty commitments. But I did not neglect the village. I paid regular visits to its telephone kiosk during my patrols and from time to time, performed traffic duty outside the gates of the Manor. Whenever His Lordship and Her Ladyship hosted one of their frequent and glittering social functions, my role was to prevent people in smart clothes and equally smart cars from interrupting the routine of Crampton by indiscriminate parking. A car thoughtlessly parked in a farm gateway can cause untold havoc and delay in a rural timetable. Afterwards, I was usually invited into the servants' quarters for a meal, an acceptable reward.

It was the ordinary people of Crampton who seldom featured in my work. Apart from the occasional firearms certificate to renew or motoring offender to interview, there was rarely anything of greater moment. No serious crimes were committed; there were no domestic rows or breaches of the peace of any kind. There was no council estate and no pub either; these facts might have been responsible for the happy absence of social problems, but this was not the entire answer. It appeared to me that the inhabitants of this peaceful place lived their quiet lives in an oasis of blissful contentment.

It was almost as if they lived on an island of ancient peace in the midst of a turbulent modern world. Without doubt, Crampton was different from many other villages, including those on my patch and elsewhere, but I could not immediately identify the subtle points of difference. By local standards, it was a medium-sized place of perhaps 300 inhabitants with a Methodist chapel and an Anglican parish church complete with a very scholarly vicar. There was a shop-cum-Post Office, a village school, several farms and many cottages, while prominent on the outskirts was the Manor.

These factors placed it squarely on the same basis as many local villages, while its pleasant situation overlooking the gentle and meandering River Rye gave it an added scenic dimension. It was a place of remarkable calm and beauty, one which was well off the proverbial beaten track and which therefore avoided the plague of tourism and the subsidiary diseases it left in its wake.

The entire village was constructed of mature local stone which grew more charming with the slow passage of time. The gentle tan shades of the stone; the careless patchwork of red pantile roofs interspaced by the occasional thatched cottage; the tiny well-kept gardens which glowed rich with colourful flowers from spring until autumn and the whispering trees in the surrounding parkland, all combined to provide Crampton with a serenity that was the envy of many. Its way of life echoed of centuries past.

The pace was so unhurried; the inhabitants were shy and retiring and even the schoolchildren went about their business in a quiet, well-ordered fashion. The handful of teenagers who lived in the village never caused me any concern and I often wondered how they spent their free time. They, and everyone else, seemed very content with their lot, but I felt they were not subdued in any way. As time went by, Crampton became an object of some fascination and even curiosity; I wondered what made it so different and why it existed in such a quiet but distinctive way.

The first clue came one Sunday.

It was 10.15 a.m. on a bright, sunny morning in April and I was standing outside the village telephone kiosk, making one of my points. I had hoisted my motor cycle on to its stand and it was leaning at an awkward angle with my crash helmet perched on the fuel tank. Its radio burbled incomprehensibly in the peace of Crampton, but none of its messages was for me. This was the quiet scene as I waited in case the duty sergeant came to visit me, or in case someone from the office rang me on this public telephone.

All around, the birds were singing with the joys of spring and the village presented an idyllic picture of rustic calm. Its neat cottages nestled along each side of a trio of short streets; each of those streets clung to rising slopes of the valley as the morning sun glinted from their polished windows and fresh paintwork. Then I heard the sound of an expensive car engine.

Instinctively glancing in the direction of the noise, I saw a vintage Rolls-Royce emerge from the gates of Crampton Manor. It crawled sedately along the gravel road with a uniformed chauffeur at the wheel, and I could see His Lordship and Her Ladyship in the rear seat. They were on their way to church. The splendid car, with every part shining after years of devoted care and constant polishing, cruised into the first street and stopped. The immaculately dressed Lord Crampton, a tall, slender man who oozed with the aristocratic breeding of his kind, climbed out and rapped on the door of a cottage with his silver-knobbed cane. Without waiting for a response, he moved to the adjoining cottage and repeated this action, then moved on to more cottages.

As he rapped successively on a sequence of doors, the car inched forward and then disappeared into Moor Street. I left my place near the kiosk and hurried in that direction, ostensibly upon a short patrol but in reality fascinated by this behaviour. I was in time to see His Lordship rap on a further four doors, then he climbed into his car which cruised up the street, turned right at the top and vanished from view.

But now, Moor Street was alive with people dressed in their Sunday finery. From all the houses visited by His Lordship, there emerged families in their Sunday best, and as they trooped up the street towards the parish church on the hilltop, they in turn knocked on all the doors they passed. More people emerged and in seconds, More Street was filled with smart people of every age, all heading towards their parish church.

Now the Rolls-Royce was cruising down Dale Street and it halted at the top where a repeat performance was commenced. After His Lordship had rapped on four doors, the villagers emerged and knocked on others, and soon the populace of Dale Street was heading towards the church. As they walked and chattered happily, the Rolls turned into Middle Street which was where I happened to be. I had now returned to my kiosk and as the splendid vehicle turned towards me, Her Ladyship waved graciously and I responded with a police salute, hatless though I was. I wondered if my action appeared to be the submissive touching of a forelock, but it was really a courteous acknowledgement.

The magnificent vehicle now stopped in this street. His

Lordship, silver-topped cane in hand, thwacked more
doors before ordering the car to continue. Off it went and
by the time it halted at the lych-gate at the top of Middle
Street, the entire Anglican population of Crampton, men,
women and children, was marching towards the church.
I've no idea how the Methodists, Catholics and other
faiths fitted into this pattern and I did wonder, for just a
fleeting moment, whether I was expected to attend. But I
didn't make the gesture. I saw that His Lordship and Her
Ladyship were first to enter the church, and noted that the
early worshippers stood outside until the VIPs took their
seats. Then everyone filed in. Only when the congregation
was seated and the church full, did I hear the organist
strike up the first hymn. It was precisely ten-thirty.

As I observed this quaint church-going arrangement, I
realized I had witnessed a custom which had probably
endured for centuries. I could imagine many past Lord
Cramptons doing this self-same task from their ponies-
and-traps, or from their coach-and-fours, and I now knew
that I was working in a village whose ways had changed
little since feudal times. The Rolls had replaced the horses;
that was one visible sign of these modern times.

Few outsiders would be aware of this system of calling
the faithful to church and I wondered whether the presence
of individuals was monitored or checked in any way. Did
His Lordship know when anyone had missed the service?
And if so, what did he do? It was by pure chance that I had
been in the village as this ritual was being executed, and it
did give me a vital insight into the regulated mode of life in
this charming, if somewhat old-fashioned village.

That Crampton continued to function along ancient
feudal lines became more evident when I realized that the
entire village was owned by Crampton Estate. It owned all
the farms, the cottages and the shop; furthermore, most of

the inhabitants worked on the estate. Some, however, were retired and continued to live in estate cottages for a meagre rent. I did learn, however, that one or two of the homes were now rented to younger village people who did not work for Crampton Estate, having secured work elsewhere. As time progressed, the number of estate workers was dwindling, but nonetheless, the estate had employed the parents and grandparents of these younger people, so the link remained.

From that time, as I toured the village on my periodic patrols, I did notice that several of the smaller cottages were unoccupied and sadly noted that some were falling into dereliction. Even if Crampton was clinging to its ancient ways, the estate's power was being reduced simply because people were no longer working for it and occupying its cottages. Sooner or later, these would be sold, I guessed, perhaps to be revived as second homes for wealthy outsiders, or even to be turned into holiday cottages by the estate.

One such cottage was occupied by eighty-two-year-old Emily Finley, widow of the late Archie Finley who had been one of the estate's carpenters. After Archie's death six years ago, Emily had continued to live in their beautiful little home for the tiniest of rents. She was well looked after by the estate from both the financial and welfare point of view, a fact which made her old age and widowhood as happy as possible. Then Emily died, and I received a telephone call from the Estate Manager, Alan Ridley.

'It's Ridley at the Estate Office,' said the voice one lunchtime. 'You've probably heard that old Mrs Finley's died?'

'Yes.' Word had reached me via the rural grapevine. 'I had heard. There's no problem, is there?'

I was thinking in terms of the coroner and whether the death was in any way mysterious or suspicious; if so, I'd

have to arrange a postmortem, with all the resultant
enquiries and maybe an inquest. A Sudden Death, as we
termed this kind of happening, entailed a lot of police
work.

'No, nothing like that, Mr Rhea. She died naturally, of
old age I'd imagine. Her doctor's seen her and has issued
the certificate. But it's her funeral on Wednesday in
Crampton Parish Church. Eleven in the morning. The
estate is acting as undertaker. We do this for most of our
employees and past employees and their spouses, free of
charge, of course. There'll be a lot of cars and people
about and we wondered if you would come along and keep
an eye on things.'

'Of course.' I was only too pleased to oblige.

'I'd like to meet you on site to discuss the parking
arrangements for the cortège, and of course, His Lordship's
vehicle and those of the chief mourners.'

And so I agreed. We fixed a date and time, and this
aspect presented no real problems. We could utilize the
village street for parking the cars of any incomers, while the
church had adequate space to accommodate and park the
funeral procession including the vehicles used by His
Lordship and the official party. Most of the mourners,
being residents of Crampton, would be on foot anyway, for
it seemed that Emily had no close family – no children,
brothers or sisters.

The body would remain in the cottage until the day of
the funeral, unlike some villages where it would be taken
into the church the previous night. It was scheduled to
depart from Holly Cottage at ten minutes to eleven and to
arrive at the church in time for the eleven o'clock
commencement of the service. I decided to arrive at
Crampton, in my best uniform and white gloves, by no
later than ten-thirty.

Before embarking on this duty, I consulted Force Standing Orders to see if there was anything I should know about my conduct at a funeral. I learned that the only specific instruction said, 'When passing a funeral cortège, members of the Force, of whatever rank, will salute the coffin.'

Just before ten-thirty that Wednesday, therefore, I presented myself outside Emily Finley's cottage in full knowledge that there would be little to do. But I did know that the presence of a uniformed police officer at a village funeral meant a great deal to the relatives of the deceased – for one thing, it added a touch of local stature to the final journey of the dear departed.

As I approached, I discovered that the entire population of the village had arrived outside Holly Cottage. Old and young alike were there, and I learned that the estate had given all its workers the morning off so that they could attend the funeral. Dressed in their dark mourning clothes, the villagers congregated around the tiny house, spilling onto the road and across the smooth grass which fronted these pretty little homes. Due to the numbers, I did find myself having to keep them in some sort of order as several pressed forward and obstructed the route the coffin would take. It did mean, of course, that Mrs Finley was assured of a fine send-off. I felt she would have been surprised at the turn-out, but on reflection accepted that this response was normal in this village.

Then the hearse arrived. But it wasn't a motor hearse, nor was it a horse-drawn vehicle. Some villages, I know, did make use of a black horse-drawn hearse with a smartly groomed black horse to draw it, but this was something entirely different. Between the ranks of assembled people, there appeared six young men smartly dressed in black suits, white shirts, black ties and bowler hats. I blinked as

I saw them; they were all so like one another that they were difficult to tell apart. They resembled sextuplets, I thought, for they were like peas in the proverbial pod and they even moved in unison. In sombre silence, they were guiding something towards the cottage. It was a small four-wheeled trolley constructed of smart oak, with metal springs, spoked wheels and pneumatic tyres. Planks of oak formed two platforms, one above the other, the top one being about waist height. This polished and well-oiled vehicle, reminiscent of a pram without its cradle, moved silently and smoothly at the hands of its attendants. I noticed that Alan Ridley followed, now acting in his capacity as Estate Undertaker. He was also clad in a black suit and bowler, and the little procession came to rest at the door of Mrs Finley's cottage.

Like everyone else, I stood in respectful silence to observe the proceedings and then the six men, preceded by Alan Ridley, moved indoors. They left the trolley outside. After a few minutes, the six emerged bearing the coffin on three strong slings which passed beneath it.

With obvious experience of similar small houses, they manoeuvred the coffin from the cramped space within and did so without dislodging the solitary wreath which lay on top. They hoisted the coffin on to the trolley, folded and stored the slings, then Alan Ridley approached with several more wreaths in his arms. These were carefully arranged on the lower level of the trolley hearse. When everything was in position, the funeral procession moved off. I walked ahead to halt any oncoming traffic that might arrive. To the sound of a tolling bell, the sombre procession filled the narrow confines of Middle Street as it climbed slowly towards the church; the six men did not have an easy task, guiding and pushing their precious load up the slope, but they succeeded.

They grew redder and redder in the face as the climb steepened and at the top, the vicar awaited beneath the lych-gate, the traditional resting place of corpses on their way to burial. His Lordship and Her Ladyship also waited at a discreet distance, standing close to the main door. Beneath the wooden cover of the lych-gate, the six bearers halted for just a moment to regain their breath and wipe the perspiration from their brows, and then the vicar began to recite the preliminary prayers. At this stage, the coffin, still on its wheels, was steered into the church. As it moved down the aisle, the accompanying mourners filed silently into their seats.

I saw Lord and Lady Crampton enter their pew as the coffin arrived at its position before the altar. I stayed at the back of the church.

At eleven o'clock prompt, the service began.

Even though I had never known Emily, I found both the service and the interment to be very moving. I gained the impression that the estate and its workers were like a large and happy family; a true community which was being eradicated through the progress of time. Had Emily been buried by her few relatives, the church would not have been so full, nor would her funeral have been such an important event for the village. As things were, she was given a fitting farewell by those who knew and respected her. Following the interment, there was the traditional funeral lunch of ham in the Tenants' Room at the Hall. Everyone was invited, including myself.

There, I was privately thanked by Alan Ridley for the small part I had played, and I learned that the six bearers were three brothers and their three cousins. They all worked on the estate as carpenters, stone masons, electricians and plumbers. Acting as bearers during estate funerals was one of their regular additional commitments.

As I motor cycled home afterwards, I realized why this village did not feature greatly in any of my crime returns or in the Divisional Offence Report Register. It was due, I felt, to the family atmosphere of Crampton and the close relationship between everyone who lived and worked there. That closeness affected both their working and private lives.

I had no doubt that if a small crime did occur, a theft for example, it would be dealt with locally and I would never know about it. Perhaps the threat of dismissal from employment by the estate caused everyone to be law-abiding, and I did know that the estate dealt with any local disputes between neighbours. There were no domestic disputes in Crampton of the kind that officially concerned me, but I knew that this feudal type of existence was drawing to a close. And with its decline would come social problems and community strife.

As the deserted cottages were sold and occupied by outsiders, so this enduring family atmosphere would be diluted and the problems and difficulties of the outside world would afflict the village. The estate would lose its paternal control for better or for worse, and I wondered if this would happen during my period as the village constable. After all, we were in the second half of the twentieth century, but it was pleasing to know that this kind of contented and untroubled life did continue in part of the English countryside.

But there was one occasion when I had to deal with a small outbreak of trouble in Crampton. Curiously, it arose as an indirect result of Emily Finley's death. Perhaps, to be more precise, it arose because of her empty cottage, but it did mean that I had to take out my notebook and begin the steps necessary to institute criminal proceedings.

To set the scene, it became the policy of Crampton

Estate to sell off those empty cottages for which they had no foreseeable use. This applied especially to those which required a lot of renovation and modernization. As cottages became vacant, in the way that Emily's did, the estate had to decide whether they were required for new workers, married staff, larger or smaller families or retiring employees. The work force was contracting; it was happening everywhere in the countryside and fewer cottages were needed. Nonetheless, Crampton Estate did occasionally take on new workers from outside.

Some of them required a house, and Emily's cottage had become vacant at the very time the estate was considering the appointment of a trained accountant. Its increasingly complicated book-keeping now required those kind of skills and so Emily's little house was earmarked as a possible home for this new member of staff. Over the weeks following her death, I noticed that the house was renovated. Scaffolding appeared outside and pointing of the stonework was undertaken. New tiles were fitted to the roof and piles of stones, bricks and cement appeared in the garden as internal structural changes were made. A new bath was fitted and the kitchen was brought up to the standards of the period; the house was re-wired too and a partial damp-course installed.

Around this time, one day in May, I had to visit the Estate Office about some cattle movement licences and was offered a coffee by Alan Ridley.

'I see Mrs Finley's cottage is nearly finished,' I said after we had concluded our official business.

'Give it another week,' he said. 'It looks nice now. I wish she could have seen it, the work was long overdue. But we can't do that kind of job with folks living in them. Besides, old folks don't like upheaval or changes to their homes.'

'You've appointed an accountant, I hear?' I put to him.

'Yes, a woman. A Miss Rogers. Jean Rogers. She starts a week on Monday.'

'And she'll occupy that little house?' I was updating my local knowledge of the village.

Alan laughed. 'In theory, yes. In practice, no. You know,' he added almost as an afterthought, 'I think you ought to be in Crampton a week on Monday, say from eight o'clock in the morning.'

'Really, why?' I asked, slightly puzzled.

'That's the day we hand over the keys to Mrs Finley's cottage,' he said, and I detected a distinct twinkle in his eye. 'But we give them to the Maintenance Foreman; he arranges the housing moves. Might I suggest you are outside Mrs Finley's house just before eight?'

'You won't be expecting trouble, will you?' I asked, wondering what lay behind his suggestion.

'No,' he said, 'but I think you'll find it an interesting experience.'

So I arranged my duties to accommodate this unusual suggestion and on that Monday morning, I decided to perform one of my rare foot patrols around Crampton. I began at seven-thirty, and enjoyed the morning stroll; the village was full of rich blossom and in places, the clean, crisp air was heavy with varied scents. Birds were singing and the morning was dewy and bright, with the sun gaining in strength as it rose in the sky. It was a moment from a corner of heaven.

Just before eight o'clock, I made my way around to Middle Street, towards Mrs Finley's cottage, as everyone called it. Few people referred to it as Holly Cottage. I was surprised to see that a small crowd had gathered. It comprised men, women and children and I must admit that this baffled me. The sight made me wonder what was about to happen and why I was really here.

Then Alan Ridley arrived on foot. He acknowledged my presence with a brief nod and stood before the front door of the cottage, awaiting eight o'clock. As the church clock struck the hour, the Maintenance Foreman, a dour Yorkshireman called Charlie Atkinson, came forward. He was dressed in his overalls and ready for work.

As the clock was striking, Alan handed over to him the two keys of Mrs Finley's cottage, one for the back door and one for the front.

Charlie then called, 'Sidney and Alice Brent!'

A man came forward and accepted the keys. At the same time, Sidney Brent handed some keys to Charlie who announced, 'George and Ann Clifton.'

The Cliftons came forward, accepted the Brent keys, and then passed up some of their own.

'Alex Cooper,' and an elderly man emerged from the crowd to accept the Cliftons' keys. He handed some back to Charlie, and so the process continued with about twelve families waiting to hand over their keys and accept others in return.

During this short ceremony, Alan Ridley moved to my side.

'Well?' he asked quizzically. 'Have you got it worked out?'

'No,' I admitted. 'What's going on?'

'We're re-housing,' he smiled. 'Or, to be exact, our tenants are rehousing themselves.'

'All these?'

He nodded; already, those who had been first in the queue, were disappearing hurriedly towards their homes.

'All of them,' he said. 'In a few minutes, all hell will break loose. The Brents will be coming here, to occupy Mrs Finley's cottage, and they'll want to be in right away. But that's Charlie's problem. Come along, let's go.'

He began to walk along the village towards his own office in the Hall and I fell into step at his side.

'So what's going on?' I asked as we distanced ourselves from the gathering.

'It's an old practice on this estate,' he adopted a serious voice. 'When we appoint someone to our staff, we offer to house them. It happens everywhere – tied cottages, you know. And so we select one of our empty houses and modernize it. We clean and decorate it, as we did with Mrs Finley's.'

'But all those people handing in keys . . .' I began.

'Yes,' he said. 'At some time in the past, long before my arrival here, this kind of thing caused an upset in the village. In appointing and housing newcomers in refurbished homes, we created the situation where workers of long standing were living in properties which were below the standard we offered to the newcomers. The newcomer's house was always refurbished and modernized, in the way you've just seen. So the tenants decided that whenever a house became vacant and was modernized, the longest serving tenant should move in, if he or she wanted to.'

I realized how things worked.

'So they all move up a notch?' I put to him.

'Yes, the whole village waits for an empty house like this. On the day, they're packed and ready, and so, in a few minutes, the Brents will move into Mrs Finley's nice cottage, and then the Cliftons will move into the Brents', old Alex Cooper will move into the Cliftons' . . .'

'And your new accountant? Where does she fit into all this?' I asked.

'It's not going to be easy, with her coming from outside the village. I'll have to explain things to her. To be honest, some of our manual workers, especially those born here, are quite happy to accept a cottage which is, to be truthful, at the bottom of our heap. In the past, they did so because they desperately needed accommodation, and the rents we charged were affordable to the poorest. But low rents meant we hadn't the funds to modernize the homes. For a peppercorn rent, those folks were happy to live in less-than-perfect accommodation. Their "carrot" was to wait for the kind of movement you've seen today. It enabled them to move up the scale and, let's face it, the estate benefits because it needs to modernize only one house every few years. It saves us money and keeps rent down. Eventually, everyone should get a chance to occupy such a place. But I fear our new lady worker will not tolerate a house which is the last of today's line – it's grotty, to say the least. We may sell it. She has hinted she might buy a house locally. If we appoint more people from outside, then our system of moving tenants is likely to die out, I feel.'

'A strange system,' I commented.

'Now, if you go back into the village, you'll see that there is a flurry of activity, with well over a dozen families moving house. They're all moving today and all before ten o'clock!'

'You impose a deadline?'

'We must. Officially, they're not supposed to do it, but we close our eyes and go along with the idea, up to a point. That's why Charlie handles all the keys – it keeps some sort of order, and it makes the tenants think it's got our formal blessing. So we give them time off between eight and ten to make their moves.'

When I walked back through Crampton, an amazing sight met my eyes. The village seemed full of carts, cars, lorries and anything that would transport furniture. Already, many items were on board – three-piece suites, wardrobes, beds and tea-chests full of crockery. The gardens and grassy areas outside the cottages were covered with household belongings and people were rushing in and out with arms full of objects. Helpers were flinging things on to the vehicles and it seemed there was a race to be first into another home. It was an amazing sight, a community house removal of the like I've never seen before nor since.

As I strolled about to observe this peculiar occurrence, I came across an argument, a rare event in Crampton. From a distance, I knew some kind of dispute was raging and that it involved a pile of furniture on a horse-drawn cart. The air was full of ripe language while angry arms were waving between the protagonists. Then one of them spotted me.

'Here's t'bobby,' I heard. 'Ask him!'

One of the men hailed me and I strode across.

'Yes?' I asked of anyone who might answer. There would be eight or nine people standing around the loaded cart. It was one of the old so-called market carts, a tipper with two wheels and a tailboard which lowered to facilitate loading and unloading. Already, it looked precariously overloaded with a tall wardrobe standing upright and a chest of drawers hanging over the tailboard. Every spare piece of space was filled with domestic odds and ends.

'Mr Rhea,' the man holding the horse's head addressed me. I knew him by sight, but did not know his name. 'Settle this for us, wilt thoo?'

They all began to shout at once, and I appealed for calm, then addressed the man with the horse.

'Ah'm t'owner of this cart,' he said, 'and Ah live out near t'bridge, on t'road to Brantsford. Hawkins is the name.'

'Go on,' I invited.

'This chap 'ere,' and he pointed to a young man close to the tail of the cart, 'well, 'e asked me to help him shift this stuff today. Hired me 'orse and cart to 'im, Ah did. Half a crown an hour.'

'Is this right?' I asked the man lurking at the tail.

He nodded, with a sly grin on his face, as the cart-owner continued.

'Two jobs to do,' he said, 'his mum and dad out of this house here, and into that 'un there,' and he pointed to a pair of houses almost opposite one another. 'Then, after that, Ah was asked to shift him and his missus and kids out of his spot and into that 'un what was occupied by his mum and dad.'

'Yes.' I followed it so far. Mum and Dad into a smaller house, and son and growing family into their old house, which was slightly larger. Very sensible.

'Well,' said the cart man, 'him and his mates, all his brothers and what-have-you loaded me up with his dad and mum's furniture for t'first job and got me unloaded, all in seven minutes. Seven minutes to move house! When Ah got loaded up for t'second trip, from his house to his mum's spot, he said they'd do t'same all over again, load and unload in another seven minutes.'

'So?' I had not yet discovered the cause of the dispute.

'Well, they're saying that because Ah charges half a crown an hour, and it hasn't taken an hour, then they don't have to pay!'

'Did you tell them that the half-crown was the minimum charge for an hour or part of an hour?' I asked him.

'Nay, Ah didn't! There's no need for that sort of carry-on, Mr Rhea. Damn it, Ah thought two house jobs would take all morning, not fourteen minutes . . .'

This was not a police matter. It was what we called a business dispute, and so I told him that. I said it was nothing to do with the police; it was purely a business disagreement which must be sorted out between themselves.

'Then Ah shall keep this stuff on t'cart until t'hour's up,' he said, 'then Ah'll be in my rights to ask for t'money.'

'We'll unload it,' said the young man to his brothers and family. 'Howway, lads, get cracking. We can beat our last record for unloading, I reckon . . .'

But Hawkins had a different idea.

'Nay!' he shouted. 'Thoo can't touch this stuff! Not yet,' and he rapped the horse's flanks with a rein. It moved off quickly, but everyone followed, trying to grab items and carry them indoors. Some of the smaller stuff was lifted off, but the larger items were impossible to move. As the horse broke into a trot, its intrepid owner ran alongside and then jumped on to the front edge of his cart where the shafts met the body, and he sat there, reins in hand, as he whipped the horse into a gallop.

The furniture bounced and jolted along the street as the horse and cart left the family behind and then Hawkins halted. In a flash, he jumped off his cart and loosened the primitive tipping mechanism. With a jangling of metal, the bolts fell free and he slapped the horse.

It moved a short distance and the cart, now unbalanced, tipped backwards as all the furniture slid off the back and spread across the road. In a long, untidy line, furniture, clothes, pots and pans, clip rugs and a motley collection of things rolled into the street.

'If you're not paying, then Ah'm not moving it,' said Hawkins, folding his arms to observe the mayhem. At the moment the family ran towards their scattered belongings, a service bus, followed by an oil tanker, turned into the street. And at that same moment, I knew I had before me a clear case of 'Obstruction of the Highway'. The bus driver started to shout at Hawkins, but he only laughed as he managed to secure his cart to its chassis during the fuss. All this was happening as I approached the scene in the ponderous strides of the constabulary in action. Hawkins, however, was quickly mobile and trotted away his horse, chortling at his own astuteness.

'You'll have to move this stuff!' I ordered the owners. 'It's obstructing the road.'

'Not us!' snapped the brothers. 'Hawkins dumped it, Hawkins can shift it!'

'You'll all get fined for obstructing this road,' I shouted above the din. 'And it'll be far more than the cost of hiring that cart!'

'Nope,' said the family. 'It stays.'

Hawkins was already some distance away, and I would have to report him too; I knew where he lived.

The tanker driver leaned out of his cab. 'Are they going to shift that rubbish or shall I drive over it?' he shouted above the noise.

A stout, middle-aged woman wielding a broom came running to the scene, crying and saying, 'Our Harry, you stupid oaf! Get it shifted, now,' and she started to belabour him with the broom handle. Confronted by such positive persuasion, Harry and the other men of the family soon cleared a road through for the bus and the tanker, and then, as the heat of the moment evaporated, they began to manhandle their stuff to the side of the road. It took much longer than seven minutes.

So far as I know Hawkins never received any payment for that task, but he did eventually receive a summons after I had reported both him and the key members of that large family for 'Obstruction of the Highway'. When the superintendent read my report, he laughed and formally cautioned each party, so there was no court case.

Never again was I involved in the house-moving customs of Crampton, and sometimes I wonder if they still continue. And I'm also curious as to whether anyone has broken the Crampton record of seven minutes for moving the contents of one house into another.

6

The love of money is the root of all evil.
St Paul, d. *circa* AD 67

One of the less publicized aspects of constabulary work is the quiet assistance that police-officers give to members of the public; it would be possible to fill a book with glowing examples. This help comes in many forms, such as assisting in the repair of a broken down car; catching stray budgies; helping with the formalities of bureaucracy or coaxing worried souls through the maze of complex problems that life throws at them.

I recall one example which involved a colleague of mine. He was performing night duty on a main trunk road and came upon a family car which had broken down. It was a major defect and there was no overnight garage in the area. He learned that the occupants were heading for London; driving through the night to catch a morning flight for a long-overdue visit to an aged relative in Australia. Marooned as they were in the middle of the North Riding of Yorkshire, the constable promptly ended his shift by taking some time off duty. He was able to do this because of some overtime previously worked, and with no thought of being paid or even thanked, he drove the stranded family to London in his own car. It was a distance of 250 miles each way and they caught their flight.

Countless minor tasks are completed during a police-officer's daily round, each in itself a small thing, albeit of great value to the person who is helped. One feature of this work is that it provides a vivid insight into the private lives of others.

One example which occurred on my patch at Aidensfield involved Awd Eustace, whose real name was Eustace Wakefield.

His problem was that he could not light his fire, a fact which came to my notice early one winter morning. The house next door to his was empty for three months while the owners were overseas, and I was keeping an eye on it. This meant regular visits to ensure it hadn't been broken into or vandalized, and it was while examining the rear of this house that I noticed Eustace. He was chopping sticks just over the separating fence, so I said, 'Good morning.'

'Morning.' He was a slight man with long, unkempt grey hair and was stooped with age. Ragged old clothes, over which he wore a tattered cardigan, attempted to protect him against the icy winds of winter and he wore woollen gloves without any fingers. He was hacking away at some small logs and chopping them into kindling sticks.

'That'll warm you up,' I said, mindful of the Yorkshire notion that the act of chopping sticks warms you twice – once when chopping them and again when blazing on a fire.

'It would if Ah could get that bloody fire o' mine going,' said the little fellow. 'Damned thing, it won't draw. Them sticks is wet, mebbe.'

'They look OK to me.' I peered across the fence to examine them.

'Ah've tried and tried this morning,' he said. 'Damn thing won't blaze so Ah can't even boil me kettle.'

'I'll come round,' I heard myself make an offer of help. There was no wonder his fire wouldn't ignite. It stood no chance. His grate was part of an old range of the Yorkist type. It had an oven at one side and a centrally positioned black-leaded grate some two feet above floor level. At the opposite side of the oven was a hot water tank; this was built into the fireplace and fitted with a brass tap to draw off the heated water. A small can with a wire handle hung from that tap, and a kettle of cold water waited on a swivel hob.

But the grate was overflowing with ash. It was inches deep within the grate itself, but the tall space below was also full. The ash spilled and spread for a distance of about a yard into the dusty room. Directly on top of all this, he had tried to light his pathetic fire; the evidence was there in the form of charred newspapers and sticks, with odd lumps of coal uselessly placed.

'It'll never go with all that muck underneath.' I kicked the accumulated ash with my boot. 'It needs cleaning out. You need a draught for a fire to blaze. You've choked it to death!'

'Oh,' he said, as if not fully understanding the elementary fact.

'Where's your shovel?' I asked and he produced a battered one from its place near the sink. I began to scoop shovelfuls from the huge pile of ash and soon had enough to fill his dustbin. After a few minutes of this dusty, hectic work, during which I removed my tunic and cap, I had his fireplace cleaned out and had added a layer of thick dust to that which coated all his belongings.

'Right,' I said. 'Paper and sticks next.'

He had a store of old newspapers in a wall cupboard and brought in some of the sticks he had been chopping.

'You ought to get some more chopped,' I suggested, 'and put them in this side oven to dry. But these aren't bad, they're dry enough.'

I laid his fire then went out to his coal-house. But it was almost bare. In one dark corner were a few lumps of coal, scarcely enough to last out this day. I managed to scrape sufficient for my task and laid it on the fire, applied a match and very soon it was blazing merrily.

'I'll tell the coalman to call,' I said to Eustace, taking his kettle and weighing it in my hands to see if it was full. It was, so I turned the swivel hob over the blaze so that the kettle would boil for his pot of tea. 'You're nearly out, you'll need some today.'

'Ah've no money,' he said. 'Ah've no money for coal . . .'

'Your pension's due on Thursday, isn't it?'

'Aye, well, t'coalman might wait a day or two then.'

As I stood before the welcoming blaze, I was well aware that this old man was poverty-stricken. The tiny back room, which served as lounge, living-room and kitchen, was dismal and virtually bare. The only furnishings were an old armchair with the stuffing protruding, a battered table and one old kitchen chair. There was a small, well-worn clip rug before the fire, but the stone floor was otherwise bare and in one corner there was a large brown earthenware sink with a cold water tap. The wooden draining-board contained all his crockery; it had been washed and stacked there until required. The bare walls had been distempered years ago and never cleaned or papered since.

The toilet, which was a WC, was outside next to the coal-shed and there was another room downstairs, but I did not go in, nor did I venture upstairs. It was plain to see that Awd Eustace lived in desperately poor accommodation with no money to spend on luxuries or even the basic necessities of life. I felt sorry for him and promised to look in from time to time.

When I left, he seemed happier and the kettle was

beginning to sing. Later in the day, I came across the coalman as he was making some deliveries in Elsinby and asked him to drop a few sacks into Awd Eustace's shed. This he promised to do. I explained about Eustace's pension and the coalman was quite happy to wait for his payment.

From that time onwards, I made a practice of popping in to see Awd Eustace, but he never improved his ways. He never cleaned out his grate and always had trouble getting a fire going, so I became his regular grate-cleaner. Sometimes, I would stay and sample a cup of weak tea but he seldom chatted about himself. I did learn, however, that he had no family, except for a brother who lived somewhere in the Birmingham area. They'd never communicated for years. To earn a living, Eustace had worked on local farms all his life, labouring and doing odd jobs. He'd retired about twelve years ago, and had come to spend his final years in this tiny house.

Then one day I called and there was no sign of him. A bottle of milk stood on the doorstep and immediately I feared the worst. I knocked several times, then forced my way in and found him dead in bed. It is unnecessary to dwell upon the formalities that followed, except to say that he died of natural causes. A few days later, a solicitor contacted me. He asked me to be present as he searched Eustace's home for personal effects and documents. And the result was astounding.

We found twelve Building Society passbooks, each containing the maximum deposit of £5,000; there were bags of bank notes under the bed and stuffed in his cupboards; a sack half-full of gold sovereigns, and share certificates galore filed neatly in a battered suitcase. For a police constable, whose salary was then about £650 per annum, this was a fortune. The wealth in this hovel was staggering.

Awd Eustace had left a fortune and I expected it would go to his brother. Eustace had always existed on the smallest amount of money; putting all his savings away in stocks and shares, and in the building societies. The house was his own too, and so he could have lived a very comfortable and happy life. Why he chose to live in such lowly conditions, I do not know but there were many like him.

One old character always sat and read by the light of a candle, and once when I called to see if he was all right, he welcomed me into his room, settled me in a chair, and then blew out the candle.

'Thoo dissn't need t'light of a candle just ti chat,' he said, as if in explanation. 'There's neea point in wasting good money.' And I learned later that the same old man, who'd been left a lot of valuables by his well-to-do father, was quite content to barter a silk tie in return for a cabbage, or an exquisite piece of china for a few eggs. It was rumoured he could be seen in the light of his candle as he counted his piles of money, but I never witnessed this.

There were many similar instances of Yorkshire canniness in the handling of money; it has often been said that if a coin fell over the side of a ship with a Scotsman and a Yorkshireman on board, the Yorkshireman would be first into the water to retrieve it. There is no doubt that some Yorkshire folk are very careful and this trait was noticeable among police-officers and their wives.

There were, and still are, some very tight-fisted policemen and some equally careful wives. It must be said that the policeman's wage at that time was very poor and those with growing families did find it difficult to manage, myself included. Many made skilful economies but some went to extreme odds. I knew one lady who bought an electric washing-machine after months of careful saving, and then, in order to use it, sat up until after midnight so she could take advantage of cheap electricity. The burning lights probably cost more than she saved – unless she worked in the dark.

Another had a similar line of thought. Her parents bought her a washing-up machine, a fine piece of equipment which washed all her pots. But the woman worried about the cost of running it; the thought of massive electricity bills so horrified her that she decided to run it during the night. In this way, the cheaper electricity could be utilized to the full and the machine would be used only when it was completely full of dirty pots.

The snag was that the family had only one set of crockery. When all the pieces were dirty, they were placed into the machine and the family had to wait until next morning before they could be re-used. The mother would not hear of the machine being used during the daytime, so she bought a second set of crockery. But as one set was used at breakfast, another at lunch and some pieces casually during the day, two sets were not enough. So she bought a third set, with a few spare mugs and plates . . .

The result was that during the night hours, her washing-up machine, filled with three full sets of crockery from breakfast, lunch and tea, rumbled along on its cheap power. I don't know what it cost her in spare crockery and I often wonder if she thought she was being economical.

Inevitably, with circulating tales of such tightfistedness (a state of mind which is very often regarded as common sense by its perpetrators) there are discussions as to which person, within our knowledge, is the meanest. All men know the fellow who will never buy his round in a pub; who coasts downhill in his car to save petrol or who always uses the office telephone to make his calls. Invariably, though, there is one person who becomes a legend in his own lifetime so far as tightfistedness is concerned. The police service is just as prone as any other profession and in our case, such a man was Police Constable Meredith Dryden.

Of middle service and approaching his forties, he sported a ruddy, moon-shaped face and a nice head of dark, curly hair. He'd been reared in a village on the Yorkshire Wolds, and was as careful as any man I know. He did free-wheel his private car down hills to save petrol, and did switch his house lights off each time he left a room, even for five minutes: what he saved on electricity was spent on replacing baffled bulbs. He grew his own vegetables which he sold to his wife at market prices; made all his family use the same bathwater to save on heating costs, and even cut his own hair.

When he first came to my notice, he was stationed on the coast, but was later transferred to Brantsford, just along the road from Aidensfield and Ashfordly. His reputation preceded him; long before Meredith arrived, we heard about his legendary meanness and wondered how he would get along with the happy-go-lucky members of Ashfordly section.

One of his habits quickly manifested itself. He got others to run errands for him on the grounds that it both saved his boot leather and obviated a lot of the aggravation that followed his miserly actions. I came across this one day when I was in the tiny police office of Brantsford. Meredith was sitting at the typewriter and a young probationer constable was at his side.

As I entered, midway through one of my motor-cycle patrols, Meredith said to the youngster, 'Paul, nip down to the newsagents, will you? Get me a copy of the *Yorkshire Post* – I can read it over my coffee break.'

Eager to please, the lad put on his cap and off he went;

I made some coffee as Meredith worked, and by the time the kettle had boiled, Paul had returned with the newspaper.

'Thanks,' said Meredith, not offering any payment to the youngster. We chatted over our coffee, and Meredith scanned the newspaper. Then, when we'd finished, he handed it back to the lad.

'Thanks, take it back to the shop. Tell 'em I'd gone when you got back.'

And so the young policeman was faced with the embarrassing choice of either taking back the paper, or keeping it himself. He kept it, but he learned not to run any more errands for Meredith the Miser, as we named him. In the office, he collected bits of string and old envelopes for use at home and on one occasion when a lady came collecting for the Red Cross, Meredith slipped a threepenny bit into her box, and then made an entry in his official notebook to the effect that he had done so. This was complete with the date, time and place of the transaction.

'You never know when folks are on the fiddle,' he said earnestly. 'I'll check that the money has gone to the right place, just to be sure.' And he did.

We had heard that Meredith used his tea-bags several times before throwing them out and that he made his wife wait until the shops were on the point of closing before entering to make her purchases of perishable goods. That way, she often got the tail-end bargains of the day, such as cheap fruit and vegetables, or damaged tins of stuff. On the topic of housekeeping, word had reached us that his wife, Ruth, had to make a weekly request for the precise amount of cash she needed, whereupon Meredith would draw the cash from the bank.

Just how precisely his mind operated was revealed to me one Friday morning. On another of my motor-cycle routes, I popped into Brantsford Police Station with some reports for signature, and Meredith was there.

I brewed some coffee and brought two cups into the front office. We sat and talked for a few minutes about our work, then I stood up and said, 'Well, Meredith, I must be off. I've work to do and people to see.'

'That'll be tuppence,' he said, 'for the coffee.'

'No,' I tried to correct him, 'we pay into a fund for the coffee, both here and at Ashfordly. Sergeant Bairstow collects it – I'm up to date with my payments.'

'I know, but we ran out of office coffee. This is my own – I brought it in for today, for myself. You owe me for one cup and some milk. Tuppence.'

For a moment, I thought he was joking, but the expression on that florid face told me he was serious. I handed over two pennies.

'Going far?' he asked, as I replaced my crash helmet, still smarting from his actions.

'Briggsby eventually,' I said, 'and then Thackerston.'

'You couldn't do a job for me, could you?' The request was pleasant enough. From an ordinary person, there would have been an instant and positive response, but as this was coming from Meredith the Miser, I had to consider all the likely consequences.

'What sort of a job?' I was wary of the things he had asked others to do.

'Cash a cheque for me at the bank before you leave town?'

After a moment's reflection, I agreed. I needed to cash one of my own for housekeeping, and so it would not be a hindrance. Meredith gave me a cheque for £6 13s 2d, and I said I would be happy to cash it.

It transpired that this was for his wife's housekeeping that week. I had no problem cashing it for him, but I now realized that it was true that Meredith did calculate the week's housekeeping allowance literally down to the last penny. Furthermore, he regularly went shopping with her when his duties permitted, his purpose being to ensure that she bought the cheapest goods without exceeding the tight budget he imposed. If possible, she had to save from her allowance. We began to feel sorry for poor Ruth Dryden.

Then Meredith had an apparent flush of generosity because he invited Alwyn Foxton and his wife for a day's outing on the moors. Alwyn had been at training-school with Meredith and was perhaps his closest companion.

'It's my birthday on Sunday,' Meredith had told him. 'I'm forty. Life begins at forty, so they say. I thought you and Betty, and me and Ruth, could have a day out on the moors to celebrate. I'm off duty that day. We'll use my car and we'll stop and have lunch at a pub, and then take things as they come.'

I do know that Alwyn was surprised by this invitation, as indeed everyone was, and he agreed to go on the outing. For the rest of us, as mere onlookers, it did seem that Meredith had mellowed and that the onset of forty had opened his mind and his wallet.

This historic outing was scheduled for the second Sunday in May and I recall that it was a beautiful day with clear skies and bright sunshine. The countryside was at its best, with fresh, new greenery along the hedgerows, colourful flowers in abundance both in the wild and in the rustic gardens, and a barrage of birdsong to complete the idyllic picture. The outing should be wonderful; I wished I was going (albeit not with Meredith), but I was performing a local duty that day.

It would be about a week afterwards when I next saw Alwyn, his grey hair perhaps a few shades whiter and his face drawn with anger. He had an envelope in his hand.

'Are you all right, Alwyn?' I asked. At that moment, I had forgotten all about the moorland outing and was concerned for his health. He did look pale and sick, and I had a feeling it was connected with the letter in his hand.

'No I am not!' he fumed. 'The bloody man!'

I did not know what to say or how to react, but he said, 'You know that bloody man Meredith the Miser?'

'Yes,' I said tentatively.

'You were there, weren't you? When he invited me and Betty to have a day out with him? It was his birthday.'

'Yes,' I acknowledged. 'How did it go?'

'It cost me a bloody fortune!' Alwyn snapped, sitting down at the desk. 'Meredith turned up in his car, as promised, and in we jumped. We went up to Rosedale and Hutton-le-Hole and after a walk we all went to a cafe for some morning coffee.'

'That was nice of him,' I commented for want of something better to say.

'Nothing of the sort!' snapped Alwyn. 'By the time the bill came, he managed to disappear into the toilet. I paid, and I was happy to do so at that time. At that point, there was nothing to grumble about.'

It was evident that Meredith had been on top form that day, and so I settled down to hear more from Alwyn.

'We drove all over, stopping in villages, pausing to look at views and that sort of thing. In fact, Nick, it was a lovely outing. The moors were splendid and there's some magnificent scenery off the beaten track. Then we stopped at a pub which served bar snacks for lunch. Well, I paid for the first round of drinks and when the time came for the second, he went to make a telephone call. I paid for that round as well. Then Meredith told the landlord it was his birthday and ordered wine, and we had a smashing meal. And would you believe it, when the landlord brought the bill, Meredith vanished into the toilet again.'

'He did you again!' I grinned.

'Yes, I paid. I thought he'd square up with me later, so I paid up. I didn't want to cause any embarrassment in the pub. I thought he'd go halves at least, but he never offered a penny. Not a bloody penny! He just jumped into his car and came home, and thanked me for a lovely day out. I hadn't the heart to demand half-shares from him, not on his birthday.'

'Alwyn, old son,' I said, 'you know what the fellow's like, we all know what he's like. You should have been wary of him – and now you've given him a birthday treat, haven't you. I reckon he spends hours planning these campaigns.'

'That's not all.' Alwyn held up the envelope which had so clearly upset him. 'Seen this?' and he passed it to me.

It was a bill from Meredith. He was asking Alwyn to pay for half the petrol used on that outing.

In spite of our knowledge of Meredith and his methods, he continued to score against us in our off-guarded moments. At one time or another, most of us found ourselves at the expensive end of Meredith's guile. He managed on one occasion to get me to buy two raffle tickets for him; as the seller waited for Meredith to finish a telephone call, I paid her, but he never paid me. I don't think he won a prize but nor did I.

Then it was time for duty at York Races. The May meeting is always so pleasant, for the course is at its floral best and every one of us wanted to be selected as additional strength to aid York City Police. Extra officers were drafted in from all the neighbouring forces for duty at this busy course on race days. Such duties came around only once in a while, and it was so nice to be nominated. When I looked at the names of colleagues who were to accompany me, I saw that Meredith was one of them. I made a vow to keep out of his way where money was involved.

In those days, we travelled by train and had to lodge overnight in York for the duration of the three-day meeting. Our digs were in some old terraced house which overlooked the racecourse and for each of the three days we paraded at 11 a.m. for our duties. They included car-parking; security of the track, the horses and the jockeys; plus a watch for pickpockets, car thieves and the other unsavoury characters who prey on their fellows at race meetings; with a general brief to ensure that things progressed smoothly. It was a hard, but pleasant three days and we usually finished duty around six o'clock following dispersal of traffic after the last race. During our two evenings in digs, we went either to the cinema or to the local pubs for a drink or two, but if we were broke, we stayed in and played cards or dominoes.

Although we were not allowed to place bets while in uniform, we did manage to persuade CID officers or other acquaintances to put money on our selections. We enjoyed race meetings; they were a real tonic and a break from our more mundane duties.

Throughout that May meeting, Meredith's miserly reputation caused him to be frozen out of many social events; if drinks were bought, he was ignored unless he could be forced into buying a round. And that was a rare event. He was not allowed to play darts, dominoes or cards unless he put his money on the table first and in this cruel way the men, all of us, kept him at bay. Our actions did not make him alter his attitude; he remained as tightfisted and miserly as ever, and after the final day, as we travelled home by train, this character-trait shone through more strongly than ever.

Our train journey took us to Eltering where an official

car would be waiting to take us home. The trip from York was through some delightful countryside but we were too tired and too broke to appreciate it; exhausted, broke and hungry, we were concerned only with getting home.

None of us had any money left; we'd either lost it on the horses or spent it on our enjoyment at the pubs or pictures, and so that long journey was pretty miserable. There were no refreshment cars on a trip of that kind – besides, none of us could have found the necessary cash to buy anything. There were eight of us in our carriage, all sitting quietly as we brooded over the past three days. Meredith was one and he was just as quiet as the others.

As the train chugged along, someone would say, 'By, I could just eat a round of fish and chips!' or 'I could do with a drink,' or 'I'm famished . . . oh, for summat to eat . . .' But no one had anything to offer. We were skint.

And then, on the final miles into Eltering, our train entered a tunnel; it was about half a mile long, and in those days, the trains did not have lights on for such short trips in the darkness. We all sat there in silence, and when we emerged, Meredith was eating a toffee.

'Meredith, you sneaking sod!' snapped one of the men.

'Well, I did pass them round,' he said, chewing contentedly.

He made no offer to pass them round again, and from that point, I believed the story that Meredith could and indeed would peel an orange one-handed while it was in his pocket.

But with tales of such behaviour circulating among a group of men like police-officers, it was inevitable that they would make some effort to teach Meredith a lesson.

I'm not sure how or where the notion originated, or indeed who was the instigator, but gradually there arose a group feeling that Meredith was due to receive some kind of comeuppance, preferably of a financial nature. He had to be forced to pay for all his past transgressions, and we knew that this would be one of our most difficult achievements. Getting Meredith to pay for anything was rather like trying to climb Everest in a swimsuit.

As this germ of an idea floated around, it produced some good suggestions and some improbable ones; and it was by coincidence that Sergeant Bairstow said there ought to be a get-together for all members of the section. He proposed dinner at a local inn, one to which we could take our wives and meet one another socially and at leisure over a meal and a drink. Getting policemen together like this was nigh impossible due to their varied shifts and periods off duty, and even a determined effort like this would mean that someone was left out. We decided that Special Constables would man the market towns that evening so that the maximum attendance was assured.

Basically, it was a good idea. As the notion began to gain substance, it dawned upon us that this was the ideal opportunity to get our revenge on Meredith. We counted the likely numbers who would attend, and included our two sergeants, Charlie Bairstow and Oscar Blaketon. It was important that we discreetly tempted Meredith to attend; getting him there at all would be a difficult task because it meant he must be willing to pay his share. So we decided to invite the inspector. Almost imperceptibly, the purpose of the occasion changed from a social function to a 'Get-Meredith-to-pay' event. We were well aware that he had promotion in mind and therefore regarded inspectors as God-like figures who might help him on his way to the top; Meredith liked to grease around those in authority.

We reckoned we could make good use of that character-trait and accordingly spread the news that the inspector was to attend. We also hinted that previous events had shown that promotion came to one of the officers who attended, sometimes within six months. That was enough for Meredith; he put his name down on the sheet.

By this time, Sergeant Bairstow was enjoying the situation and had entered the 'get-Meredith' field. Having achieved a suitable number of attenders, he rang the Boswell Arms at Brantsford and booked us in for a Friday night; then Bairstow stuck out his neck and told the landlord his name was Meredith Dryden and that he would be meeting the entire bill.

Word of this got around to everyone except Sergeant Blaketon, who lacked humour; we didn't inform the inspector either, in case he objected to the subterfuge. To further our aims, we contrived a situation so that when all twenty-four of us were seated, Meredith was seated next to the inspector's wife. We knew that would please him and that in such a position, he would be malleable.

Our plans made, we waited for the great night. True to form, Meredith scrounged a lift from a colleague at Brantsford and arrived to find a seating plan at the table. We enjoyed our preliminary drinks, during which Meredith's were paid for by someone who wished to ensure that he remained completely oblivious of our plans, and eventually we were asked to take our places at the table.

As it was a pre-arranged menu, there were no choices to be made, although the waitress did ask one of us which was Mr Dryden, whereupon she asked Meredith to choose the wines. He did this with pride, revealing a surprisingly good knowledge which impressed the inspector. The meal was excellent, the companionship good and the night a huge success. After the meal, as we sat around the table completely sated and very content with our liqueurs and coffee, finally, the landlady came to Sergeant Bairstow with the bill for twenty-four dinners and wine.

It was a discreet move, one which passed almost unobserved by the majority of the diners, but Charlie Bairstow pointed towards Meredith and said, 'That is Mr Dryden, he's paying.'

As she walked towards him bearing the bill on a silver tray, it dawned upon the assembled guests that a historic moment was nigh. The purpose of the night was about to be achieved. We observed the steady progression of the landlady's approach to Meredith's chair. He was engrossed in an animated conversation with the inspector's wife and failed to notice the impending arrival of the bill.

As the landlady halted at his shoulder, we all watched, hearts beating with anticipation at the arrival of the supreme moment. Meredith Dryden was about to pay for something, for none of us would settle this bill.

'The bill, Mr Dryden,' she eased the tray before him. His face said everything. His brain, so finely attuned to the avoidance of paying, especially for anything which was for the consumption of others, must have told him that this was a set-up. He must have instantly realized that everyone – well, almost everyone – at that table, knew what was happening.

Meredith was fully aware that no one would come to his aid; he was on his own in this crisis. He had been well and truly cornered. Sergeant Blaketon was at the far end of the room beyond his reach, and the only person of substance close at hand was the inspector. I'm sure Meredith realized that the inspector knew nothing of this plot and so the inspector was like an innocent babe as he faced the formidable financial skills of Meredith Dryden.

'Sir,' we heard Meredith say in a hoarse whisper, 'I've forgotten my cheque book – might I ask if you could pay the bill, and I will settle with you tomorrow when I come to the office?'

The inspector, a leader of men and a man of substance who suddenly found himself being observed by almost every member of Ashfordly and Brantsford sections, flushed a deep red, but he pulled out his wallet. It was he who had been skilfully cornered, and so he wrote a cheque for the full amount. To give the fellow credit, he even gave a £1 tip to the staff.

None of us knew what to make of this, except that it was abundantly clear that Meredith had scored yet again.

'We'll have to make it up to the inspector,' I heard Charlie Bairstow say later to Alwyn Foxton. 'We all know what it's about, so we'll have to have a whip-round. We'll have to pay our share. The bugger's beaten us again . . .'

'Meredith won't pay,' said Alwyn. 'The inspector will finish up paying his share anyway!'

And so it was. We all paid our due amounts into a kitty which was passed over to the inspector, but we knew that Meredith never paid his share. The inspector had paid for Meredith's meal – Meredith the Miser had won yet again and had enjoyed another free meal.

But his success was short-lived. Less than three weeks later, he was transferred to a distant station.

7

With secret course, which no loud storms annoy
Glides the smooth current of domestic joy.
Samuel Johnson, 1709-84

For a large number of British workers, whether male or female, there is a clear distinction between their work and their domestic life. The home, with its comforts and traumas, is left firmly behind when a living has to be earned and throughout the working day, the pressures of the office or the working environment supersede all but the most severe of domestic worries or the blissful contentment of home. It is right that the domestic life of an employee should rarely intrude into his or her business or work, and so all but the closest of workmates have no concept of a colleague's home life and circumstances.

But there are those who work either at home or from home; rural doctors and vicars are popular examples, as are the local postmasters or mistresses, or shopkeepers, farmers, sales representatives and many village businessfolk. To that incomplete list can be added the village policeman.

For many rural bobbies, the village police house is both home and office. And so it was with me. It was inevitable that there were times when aspects of my domestic life became inextricably intertwined, albeit in the most pleasant of ways, with my professional duties. Apart from being the police office of Aidensfield, my house was also my home to my wife and four tiny children, along with all our hobbies and domestic activities. Like all policemen in that situation, I did endeavour to keep work and leisure completely separate, but at times this was impossible.

There is no doubt that the police house at Aidensfield ranks among the most beautifully located in Yorkshire, and possibly in England. Built in the 1960s on a superb elevated site, it is stoutly constructed of local yellow stone with a red pantile roof. It boasts a lounge with panoramic views, a dining-room and tiny kitchen, with three bedrooms and a bathroom. The garage adjoins and there is a through-passage which separates the house from the garage; off that passage there is an outside toilet and a wash-room. These outbuildings, small as they are, did help to accommodate that awesome range of bulky objects that young families accumulate, such as tricycles, prams and pushchairs. At the other end of the house, the west end, is the office. This is a spacious room with a solid wooden counter and separate entrance. In my time, it was furnished with an official desk, chair and telephone.

The hilltop site, which isolated us from the village below, was enhanced by a steep, mature and well-stocked garden. To the back and front of the house were panoramic views across the North York Moors, the Wolds and the valleys below. In the summer, it was a delight; in the winter, it could be a nightmare because, at times, the winds were so powerful that the garage doors could not be opened, while the carpets and rugs rippled like snakes as powerful draughts invaded our home and rattled the windows. At times, we were very prone to being snowed in; a fact which created frequent notes of disbelief among senior officers who sat in warm offices in distant, low-lying towns.

I must admit there were times when I was sure they

thought I was inventing the snow to avoid a winter patrol on my motor cycle. On one occasion, it took me four hours to dig my way out of the garage, after which I was subjected to a telling-off for being late on patrol . . .

But, winter apart, it was a lovely place in which to live and to rear a family. By comparison with many other police houses, it was, and still is, a gem. At that time, of course, the privilege of having an officially-provided house was of immense value, especially on a constable's meagre salary with a growing family to support.

Perhaps, at this point, it would be of interest to learn how a young constable qualified for his very first police house. The Aidensfield house was not my first, but in order to progress through a range of police houses, one had to qualify for the first: once into the system, it was a simple matter of being transferred from one to another. The first hurdle was the most difficult.

In my own case, we had married some five years before we were posted to Aidensfield and we began our wedded bliss in a flat at Strensford. We rented this accommodation independently of the police but after three months in that second-floor flat I was summoned to the superintendent's office.

'Rhea,' he said with a glow of benevolence on his face, 'a police house has become vacant in the town; it's an end-terrace house with three bedrooms and is not therefore, one of our standard houses. It's a modern house, by the way. But as our most recently married member, you might qualify to occupy it. Now, are you in a position to furnish a house?'

Quick as a flash, in spite of our solitary bed, our dining-table, two fireside chairs and clip rug, I said, 'Yes, sir.'

He wasn't to know that my scant furnishings would barely fill the kitchen, let alone a complete house, but I did not want this opportunity to evaporate. A modern three-bedroomed house, rent free, was a godsend.

'And do you intend remaining in the force as a career?' was his next question.

'Yes, sir,' I said with as much conviction as I could muster.

'And what about a family, Rhea? You have none, have you?'

'No, sir, not yet.'

'And your wife is working, is she?'

'For the moment, sir, yes. She's a secretary at the council offices.'

He chatted about my future, and about the responsibilities of occupying a police house, and then he said it was mine. I could have the keys next week.

When I told Mary, she was delighted, for our new home was a modern, brick-built house with up-to-date kitchen fittings and beautiful décor. It had a small, pleasant garden and it overlooked the harbour at Strensford with magnificent views of the Abbey and old town. It ought to be said, however, that the railway station and some sidings did lie between us and that water. But that was a minor blemish.

When the tide was high, the views across the wide, upper reaches of Strensford Harbour were delightful, but when the water was low, it revealed a narrow channel among acres of shining black mud littered with junk which had been deposited over many years. But the house was lovely.

The fact that it was not a standard police house did not worry us. Standard houses were constructed so that when a police family moved from one to another (as they did with staggering frequency), their furnishings and carpets would fit. As a theory, it was fine, but some standard lounges were three inches shorter than others; some bedrooms were narrower or longer than others, and there were many minor variations which made nonsense of the system. Even in standard houses it was difficult to make the furniture fit, and another problem was that the décor which pleased some families was horrific and bizarre in the eyes of others. But it was nice to know that the authorities had our interests at heart.

Our house had been rented by the local police because of a shortage of standard houses in Strensford, but luxuries like fitted carpets or full bedroom suites did not concern us. We hadn't any. Happily, the decorations and exterior paintwork were in good repair.

At that early stage of marriage, we would have had difficulty filling a caravan with our belongings, let alone a semidetached mansion. Happy with our new home, we settled in and were very content. A few weeks later the superintendent met me during a patrol.

'Rhea,' he said, 'I intend carrying out my house inspections and will be starting next week. I shall be calling on you. What is a convenient time?'

I performed some rapid mental gymnastics because I wanted him to come when the tide was full. I knew the harbour view would impress him, so I said, 'Next Wednesday, sir? Would 3 p.m. be suitable?'

He checked his diary and agreed.

When I told Mary, she grew flustered. I had to explain that his visit was not to check upon our cleanliness or her housekeeping ability, but to ascertain whether any repairs or other work were required on the house, either externally or internally.

'If he looks in all the rooms, there's nothing . . . we've two empty bedrooms, nothing in the dining-room . . .' She began to worry about our lack of furniture, and whether we would be asked to vacate it.

I must admit that this did bother me too, particularly as I'd recently assured him I could furnish a home. To cut a long story short, we borrowed from friends a dining suite, a three-piece suite, two single beds, two wardrobes, rugs, carpets and some sundry furnishings. The result was that on the day of the house inspection, our little home looked almost luxurious. All the young constables did this; we regularly borrowed each other's stuff on such occasions.

Because Mary was at work at the appointed hour I stayed to show him around. When the superintendent arrived, I took him into the lounge, now fully furnished and smelling heavily of polish. A vase of flowers occupied the window ledge and pictures hung from the walls, but he was only interested in the lovely view. It was a fine sunny day and the full harbour glistened in the brilliant light. He rhapsodized over the scene which spread before him and chatted about the yachts and small boats on the water as he admired our superb maritime view.

Then he asked if any maintenance work was required and I said, 'No, sir, it's in good repair, inside and out.'

'Good, well, as you know, Rhea, we decorate internally every three years and externally every seven. That will be done automatically. If you need urgent work done, such as plumbing leaks, washers on taps and so on, submit Form 29.'

'Yes, sir.'

'Well, you keep a nice home, Rhea. Give my congratulations to your wife. It's nice to see things looking so well – and you've nice taste in three-piece suites. PC Radcliffe has that design on his suite too, you know.'

Then he smiled and left. The superintendent was very astute, I decided, and Mary was pleased that he did not venture any further than the lounge. Our impressive view had kept him in one room.

And so we started as occupants of several police houses. We bought more furniture when funds permitted and produced a brood of infants within surprisingly few years. By the time we arrived at Aidensfield, we had, of necessity, to furnish all the rooms to accommodate the six members of our family.

Once again, we were fortunate to be provided with a lovely house and a lounge with a view, even if it did mean regular house inspections. In addition, we had local government bureaucracy to contend with when maintenance or improvements were necessary. This led to several battles. My first concerned the outer passage and washing-room. The passage had a door at each end, and just off it was the room which housed the clothes-washing facilities and which also acted as a storeroom. It sounds most convenient, but that neither the passage nor the washing-room had windows or lights. In the passageway, an open door would provide light during the daytime, but the wash-room could have served better as a photographer's dark-room.

So I made application, on Form 29, for a light to be fitted in the windowless washing-room. Then we would be able to use it for that purpose. The superintendent rejected my request on the grounds that it was an 'improvement'; improvements to police authority houses needed special approval from on high, from bodies like the Standing Joint Committee and the County Architect. To reach them, my application would have to proceed via Headquarters' departments and the Chief Constable himself! For reasons he did not explain, the superintendent refused to forward my report to them; our local 'official channels' terminated upon his desk. There seemed no way to by-pass that blockage.

I did try by explaining that it was impossible to work in

that room and that, in its present form, it was useless for its intended purpose, or indeed any other. He continued to utter 'improvement' as his excuse for refusing to allow my report to reach other decision-makers. I grew more determined and renewed my campaign by tackling it from another angle.

My next Form 29 suggested that an outside light was necessary to eliminate possible danger to callers at the police house. I suggested that its best position would be above the passage's north-facing door. It would then shine along the passage at night (if the door was open), and would also shine along the entire frontage of the house. I thought it might even shine into the washing-room if two doors were left open!

That was rejected too, again by the superintendent. Now even more determined, I re-applied for a light to be fitted outside the office door. This time, my Form 29 pointed out the possible danger to the public who might stumble over the steps and who might then sue the Standing Joint Committee for damages or compensation . . .

This time, I got an external light fitted – but it was over the door of the police office and its welcome light did not shine into the passage or the wash-room. When eventually I left the police house at Aidensfield, that washing-room and passage were still without a light. We had to squeeze our washing-machine into the tiny kitchen, no mean feat when it daily washed mountains of nappies.

Also under the heading of 'improvement' was my suggestion that some radiators be run off the little domestic coke boiler.

This tiny furnace was installed in the kitchen and its fierce heat filled the room and heated the water; even in summer, we had to keep it stoked up to cope with masses of baths, nappies and kiddy clothes. We lost gallons of perspiration and I reckoned it would keep two or three central heating radiators well supplied. But because this was an 'improvement', it was not permitted. My Form 29 was rejected.

Then the pipes of this boiler began to make frightening noises. Narrow pipes connected the boiler to the mains water supply and to the hot water tank upstairs, and they began to rattle and vibrate as the heat intensified. In time, I grew very alarmed and rang the superintendent's office about it. He returned my call to say that such noises were normal in the plumbing world. He expressed the opinion without hearing the racket they made. I felt the noise was far from normal but realized that once again, I was battling against bureaucracy. I waited for a while and the noise grew worse; a friend said the pipes sounded as if they were blocked, a common occurrence in hot water pipes hereabouts because the lime deposits from the local water furred them.

Repeated requests via Form 29 met with nil response and this frustrated me. Being country born and bred, I was used to coping with my own domestic maintenance – we would never call in anyone to do jobs we could do ourselves such as painting, decorating, running repairs to machinery, tiling, pointing – in fact, anything and everything. But as occupants of a police house, we were instructed not to attempt any repairs or work, not even the replacement of a tap washer. I found these restrictions very frustrating.

The clattering grew worse. We reached the stage where we were frightened to light the fire because of the clamour coming from those pipes and this meant we had no hot water. Then came salvation. It came in the shape of a memo from the superintendent which announced that he was coming to conduct a house inspection.

I recognized the opportunity presented by his visit.

He was due at 11.30 a.m. one Friday, a busy day for nappies and infant washing, and so I arranged for the boiler to be well-stoked up and the flues opened wide to coincide with his visit. I was confident that the resultant noise from those pipes would terrify him. It didn't matter which part of the house he was visiting at the time, because I was sure the din could be heard throughout a building of castle proportions.

He came, inspected, had a coffee and asked about the pipes. After all, a succession of Forms 29 had made him aware of the problem. I said they were worse, upon which he ventured into the kitchen. It was now uncomfortably hot as the coke performed its heating role and he looked at the offending pipes. There was nothing to see – they were just two pipes running up the wall.

And then, almost as if they knew he was standing there, they performed on cue. It was just as if a giant with a big hammer was inside, banging and hammering to be let out and the whole house vibrated as the pipes visibly shuddered in their moment of triumph.

'My God!' he panted, rushing from the kitchen, white-faced and anxious . . .

Early next day, a plumber arrived. After an examination, he said the pipes were almost blocked; the hot water was trying to rise through the cold pipe and had we not called him, there could have been a shocking explosion . . .

My final Form 29 confirmed that the pipes were working normally.

In such minor ways, my work and domestic life overlapped, although there were other instances. For example, at 4 a.m. one morning, a lorry driver knocked me out of bed and roused the entire family, simply to ask directions to Home Farm. On another occasion, at 6.30 a.m. one day when I was on holiday, a farmer came to the door to seek a pig licence. When I said I was on holiday and that he should go to Ashfordly Police Station, he said, 'Well, you're t'bobby, aren't you?'

I issued his licence.

In many ways, it was my young family which further involved me in this curious mixture of duty and home. One day, when I was enjoying time off during the week, I decided to do some gardening. I claim no green-fingered skills, but felt that if I dug enough holes and cut enough grass, I could believe I had achieved something positive. During this enterprise, Mary asked if I would look after the children while she went to Ashfordly to do some shopping. I agreed, so she jumped into our car and cheerfully vanished towards the market town.

The day was fine and warm, and I was thoroughly enjoying myself. The children were playing in the garden behind the house and I had fixed up a plastic bath half full of water which they were using as a paddling pool. After about an hour, I broke from my chores to make myself and the children a cool drink.

'Where's Charles?' I asked.

'Gone to the toilet,' said Elizabeth.

He was only three and I accepted her answer. I put his drink on the step and settled down to await his return. He did not come. I went indoors and looked at both toilets; he wasn't there. I went into his room and looked in the bed, the wardrobe and under the bed. He wasn't there either.

Knowing that children love to play hide and seek, I searched the whole house as only a policeman can, but found no sign of him. Now more than a little worried, I checked my office, the garage, the passage and the washing-room with its darkness. There was no Charles. I re-checked all the beds by pulling back the covers and looking underneath, then I searched the pram and finally tackled the garden. There were shrubs, trees and plants, a cold frame and plenty of long grass to conceal a little boy, but my frantic hunt failed to locate him.

By now, my concern was becoming genuine alarm and I made several more sorties into the house, the garage and the garden. And then I wondered if he'd jumped into the car to accompany Mary?

That seemed the logical explanation, but the more I thought about it, the more I realized he hadn't. She'd have mentioned it, surely? She'd wanted a moment or two to herself . . . I'd seen her leave alone . . .

I stood in the middle of my garden, by this time a very worried man. Where on earth could he have gone? Even though the garden gates were shut, I went onto the main road and looked up and down. I was able to gaze along almost half a mile of highway, but there was no sign of the toddler. He'd vanished into thin air and I was in a dreadful dilemma. I could not leave the rest of them alone while I went to seek Charles, and I began to understand the problems of some parents. What could I do? Anyone else would have telephoned the police!

With this possibility rapidly gaining strength in my mind, I realized I couldn't remember what he was wearing. Of course, a three-year-old lad wandering about unaccompanied wouldn't be too difficult to locate . . .

I decided upon yet another thorough search of the premises. It drew a blank. Outside, the other children played happily, quite oblivious to my growing alarm, and at last I went into my office and dialled the Ashfordly Police Station number. It rang and rang; there was no reply. They're never there when they're wanted, I grumbled! I decided to ring the Divisional Police Station at Malton to ask if a car was patrolling in the Aidensfield area. That was quite possible because I was not on duty, and the area would not be left totally without a patrol. If there was a car nearby, it would be radio-equipped and the driver would keep his eyes open for any missing child.

I began to formulate my request; I would ask the driver to keep observations for a child aged three, with light brown hair, clothing unknown, who might be wandering . . .

As the phone began to ring, someone knocked on my office door. What a time to call! I was off duty anyway! Slamming down the phone, I opened the door. A lorry driver was standing there and he was holding Charles in his arms. His vehicle was parked outside.

'Found this kid,' he thrust the infant towards me. 'Wandering down t'hill . . . . biggest wonder he didn't get killed . . . some parents . . . thought you'd know who he belonged to . . .'

'Er, yes,' I didn't know how to respond. 'Er, come in . . . have a cup of tea . . .'

'No, got a schedule to keep. You know him then?'

'Yes,' I said, humbly.

'Good, thought you would. Give his mum a rocket, eh? For letting him get out like that . . . stupid bloody parents . . .'

And off he went.

I hugged Charles with relief, being unable to explain to the little fellow the problems he had created. I decided that my immediate priority was to fix child-proof locks on the garden gate, but also decided not to tell a soul about this. Not even Mary.

My latter plans went haywire too. A lady in the village had been present when the lorry driver collected the wandering child and had directed him to the police house. She told Mary . . .

The whole village knew too. I was suitably humbled, embarrassed and chastened. And little Charles never batted an eyelid, although I did fix child-proof locks to the gates. Ever since, I've had sympathy for parents whose children go wandering.

Another personal domestic crisis concerned Margaret, our two-year-old daughter. From the moment she could crawl, she could climb. She climbed the stairs and chairs, steps and trees, bookshelves and pantry shelves. She could climb on to the car bonnet, on to the motor cycle and on to the backs of settees and indeed upon almost any piece of domestic equipment or furniture. At times, I felt she had a wonderful future as a rock-climber or steeplejack and this was confirmed when she managed to climb out of her bedroom window on to the outer ledge.

She remained there as I pleaded with her not to move; with her safely indoors, I then secured the window, but soon she was climbing up the shelves of the wardrobe and sitting on top. On one occasion, she was marooned up an apple tree and on another managed to climb into a fireside chair and from there gain access to the mantelpiece. From these escapades, she was unscathed.

But, inevitably, an accident was bound to happen; one day she would fall and hurt herself.

One lunchtime, I returned from a motor-cycle patrol to find Mary holding little Margaret over the kitchen sink as blood poured from her tiny mouth. The accident had happened only seconds earlier. Without even removing my crash helmet, I took one look at the injury and found a gaping wound inside her mouth.

Without asking for an explanation, I rang the village doctor who, fortunately, was at home having his lunch. 'Bring her down,' he said. I packed some cotton wool over the wound to stem the flow and rushed Margaret to the doctor. Mary couldn't come – she had the other children to look after.

'No good,' the doctor said instantly. 'She needs hospital treatment, stitches. You take her there now, I'll ring to say you're on the way.'

With the tiny child sitting in the front seat of my car and holding her cheek against the wad of cotton wool, I furiously drove the seventeen miles into Malton to the hospital where a doctor met me. In moments, my little daughter was lying on an operating table, without anaesthetic, as the doctor examined the wound and prepared to stitch it.

'What happened to her?' he asked.

'I don't know,' I had to admit. 'I didn't ask . . .'

'It'll mend,' he said, producing a huge curved needle. I winced; I began to feel emotional at the thought of that tiny child suffering as I submitted her to this instant surgery. Margaret, God bless her, never cried and never complained. It was awful, watching her tiny frame being subjected to this treatment.

During this work, a nurse hovered around the theatre and as the doctor began to skilfully sew the wound, she came over to me.

'Some parents!' she said. 'Look at that poor child . . . and you'd think they'd bring her themselves . . . the police get all the rotten jobs to do . . . Fancy you having to do this . . .'

As she ranted, it became clear that she had no idea that this was *my* child; the fact that I was sitting there in full police motor-cycling uniform had obviously led her into thinking I was doing my duty by protecting some neglected youngster . . .

She continued her verbal onslaught against callous and thoughtless parents as the doctor continued his work on the mouth wound. Then she produced a sheet of paper.

'Child's name?' she asked.

'Margaret Rhea, aged two,' I said.

'Father's name?'

'Nicholas Rhea.' I watched her write down these details.

'Address?'

'The Police House Aidensfield,' I said.

'No,' she threw me one of those withering glances that one expects from matrons, not nurses, 'the child's address, not yours!'

'That is the child's address,' I said. 'She's my child.'

'Oh,' she said. 'I had no idea . . . I thought . . .'

'She'll be fine now.' The doctor had finished. 'I've put three stitches in, they'll wither away in time and there'll be no mark. It's young, clean flesh, so it will quickly mend. There's no other injury.'

'Thanks, Doctor,' and I carried little Margaret out to my waiting car and drove home. Other than a puffy cheek, she seemed no worse and never once complained. When she arrived home, she sat in her high chair and ate her dinner. She behaved as if nothing had happened and the wound did not appear to give her pain.

I ate my lunch too, still upset by the trauma of seeing the doctor working so expertly and coolly upon her. 'Mary,' I asked, 'what happened to her?'

'She was climbing up the shelves of the bookcase,' Mary told me. 'I went into the lounge just as she got to the top – she fell off and her face hit the edge of the coal scuttle . . .'

Mary began to weep so I comforted her as, quite unabashed, Margaret continued with her meal.

In spite of our efforts to prevent her, she continued to climb for some years afterwards, but never with such dramatic effect.

Perhaps the funniest incident which involved both my

work and my private life occurred one Friday morning. This is the sequence of events – my involvement came some time after the beginning of the saga, but it is best to relate it from the start.

Around one o'clock on the morning in question, my mother and father were dragged from their bed by a telephone call from the CID at York. It came at a time when there was concern about letter bombs and the detective was calling from the GPO Sorting Office.

'Is that Mrs Rhea?' the detective asked my mother. He then provided the correct address to make sure he was speaking to the right person.

'Yes,' answered my mother, bleary-eyed and sleepy.

'This is York CID,' said the voice. 'I'm ringing from the GPO Sorting Office at York. This is a difficult enquiry, Mrs Rhea, and I don't want to alarm you, but are you expecting a parcel from anyone?'

'Well,' said my mother, not yet appreciating the problem, 'I might be. It's my birthday tomorrow . . . er today . . .'

'Ah!' There was some relief at this response. 'And you have no enemies? You, or your husband are not in sensitive work, are you? It's not the sort of work that would attract, well, a letter bomb?'

'No . . . well, I don't think so . . .'

'Well, the point is, there's a suspicious package here and it's addressed to you.'

The detective took immense pains to describe his problem without being too alarmist, but it seemed that as the GPO sorters were dealing with the night's influx of mail, one of them discovered a parcel which began to emit ticking sounds. As everyone dived for cover, the parcel was placed in a sand-filled bin designed to cope with exploding parcels. As it sat there, the entire staff of the sorting office took cover and waited for the bang. As they settled down behind whatever protection they could find, the police were called. And so the official procedures were set in motion.

The busy task of sorting the mail came to a halt and the district's mail was thus delayed until the CID arrived and the offending parcel was dealt with, probably by Bomb Disposal experts. One of the detectives, whom I shall call Gordon, arrived and looked at the offending object in the bin. It had now stopped ticking. Heads peeped above the counters and around walls as Gordon bravely scrutinized the parcel. Then he picked it up.

It promptly started ticking. Everyone dived for cover. He threw it back into the bin and vanished below a sturdy counter. Everyone waited for it to explode, but it did not. And so it lay at peace in its protective bin as the entire staff and the police hid behind their benches. They waited for a long, long time, but nothing happened. There was no bang and it had stopped ticking.

Gordon approached it again. The address on the parcel was legible; it bore my mother's name, hence the morning call to her.

'I've no idea what it might be,' she said. 'If it is a birthday present, it might have been sent by my daughter and son-in-law in London.'

'What do they do?' asked the detective.

'He's in the Metropolitan Police in London . . .'

'Then there could be risks . . . someone might be hitting back at him . . .'

Having elicited this information, Gordon rang Scotland Yard to check against the possibility of attacks against the police, and then rang my brother-in-law at his London home to explain the problem. But neither he nor my sister had sent the parcel. They were then asked if they knew anyone else who might have sent it; they suggested it could have come from my brother who lives in the Shetlands. He works for BP, and so there could have been some sinister links with a letter bomb.

As a consequence, he and his family were roused about 1.30 a.m. and the questions were repeated; they had not sent a parcel. Further checks were made with the security services, but there was no known campaign against our institutions.

My brother, however, was asked if *he* knew who might have sent a parcel, if indeed it was a genuine parcel, and he said, 'My brother at Aidensfield might have sent it. He's a policeman too.'

With the intrigue growing stronger, the mystery growing deeper and the mail growing further delayed, Gordon now rang me. By this time, it was around two o'clock on a chill February morning. I staggered into my cold office to take his call. At that stage, I knew nothing of the drama.

'Nick,' he said. 'It's Gordon at York.'

We had been at training-school together and knew one another fairly well.

'York?' I muttered through a haze of sleepiness. 'What's happened? It's two o'clock in the morning.'

'We have a parcel addressed to your mother,' and he patiently related the story so far. 'Now, I had no idea the lady was your mother – I've been ringing Scotland Yard, the Shetlands, the Special Branch, GPO Security, MI5 . . .'

'Oh?' This sounded important.

'So, Nick,' he asked, with a hint of exhaustion, 'yesterday, did you post a parcel to your mother?'

'No,' I said. 'I sent her a card with a gift token inside. I didn't send a parcel . . . it's her birthday today, so I suppose someone . . .'

'Oh, bloody hell . . .' There was a long silence at the other end of the telephone, then he said, 'Hang on, I'll have another look at it. We can't decipher the postmark, you see, and we're worried about touching it . . . I'm sure it's your mother's name on it . . .'

But he did touch it. It was sitting in its secure bin, and he lifted it to check the postmark. It started to tick again. He dropped it back inside the bin and dived for cover as I waited on the line.

Everyone was still under cover, but eventually he returned to the telephone, breathless.

'God, this is awful,' he said. 'The bloody thing could go off at any minute . . . I'm safe behind a screen here . . .'

'You're a brave bloke to tackle it like you have,' I said.

'I'm not,' he said. 'I'm stupid. I've been to a night club for a few pints and don't know what I'm doing really . . .'

As this conversation continued, Mary appeared at my side. 'What's the matter?' she asked. 'Are you talking about your mother. Has something happened? Is she ill?'

'No,' I said, 'it's the CID. They think someone's sent her a bomb . . .'

Mary began to chuckle. 'A parcel? Brown paper, with white string? A sticky label on the front? The address written in black ballpoint ink?'

As she described her parcel, I relayed the words to Gordon.

'This is the one,' he growled. 'Bloody hell! What a night! The description fits. Did your wife send it, Nick? Has she sent a bomb to her mother-in-law or something?'

'Did you send it?' I asked Mary, my feet like ice-blocks on the cold office floor.

'Yes, why, what's wrong?'

I explained about the chaos in York and the terror she had inflicted upon the Post Office, the police and probably GPO Security. The whole of the region's mail would be delayed and several sorters were close to having heart attacks.

'It's a pair of scissors,' she said. 'A pair of electric scissors, for cutting material to make dresses.'

My heart sank.

'Is there a battery in?'

'Yes, I fitted it before we posted it . . .'

And so, when pressure was applied to that parcel in certain places, the scissors began to snip within their box . . .

I apologized profusely to everyone and rang my mother to wish her a happy birthday.

8

The death of a dear friend would go near to make a man look sad.

William Shakespeare, 1564-1616

Every autumn, the children of Aidensfield waited for the donkeys to return to Lingfield Farm. These were seaside donkeys. During the summer, they spent their time on the beach at Strensford where, day after day, they patiently carried laughing children backwards and forwards along the sands. Adorned in brightly-coloured bridles bearing their names, with ribboned top-knots on their heads and neat little saddles on their backs, they had been a part of the Strensford beach scene since Victorian times.

They worked very hard but were always models of tolerance and patience. Perhaps their gentleness was due to the fact that they were not overworked; during their working week, for example, they were subjected to conditions about their rest periods. They enjoyed one day off in every three, with three meals a day and an hour for lunch. Their working day did not exceed eight hours and they were inspected regularly by a veterinary surgeon. In some respects, their working conditions were better than those of police-officers!

During the winter, they came inland for their holidays where they were boarded out at selected farms. Jack Sedgewick at Lingfield Farm, Aidensfield, had for years taken five of the donkeys from Strensford. As a rule, they arrived by cattle truck at the end of the summer season and remained until the Whitsuntide bank holiday. They occupied a rough, hummocky paddock where they seemed to thrive on the wealth of thistles and other vegetation which had little appeal to other beasts.

They had a range of small outbuildings, some without doors, which served as stables. These contained plenty of hay as bedding and for food, and there was an outdoor water-trough adequately fed with spring water. Some shrub-like hawthorn trees added variety to the paddock's undulating landscape and provided slender shelter against the winter storms.

Jack Sedgewick, a large and kindly man, knew that his guests required regular exercise otherwise they would grow fat and lazy. This presented no problem because he encouraged local children to come along and play with his little group of donkeys. He taught the youngsters how to care for them; to make sure their feet were trimmed regularly; to coax them to their halters and to feed them with the right kind of things. Some children rode them, and a little girl even persuaded one donkey, called Lucy, to jump over a small artificial fence.

It was very clear that the donkeys loved the children and the children loved the donkeys; indeed, there is some kind of mysterious affinity between small children and donkeys. These gentle and calm animals, with their big, soft eyes and cuddly long ears – called 'errant wings' by G. K. Chesterton – are so lovable. It wasn't all smooth and jolly, however. The occasional bout of stubbornness from a donkey who, for reasons best known to itself did not want to play, sometimes upset the youngsters, while a sudden session of braying made them jump with fright before dissolving into laughter. For the children, these minor upsets were lessons in themselves. For one thing, they taught the children they could not have all their own way, even with donkeys.

One winter, Lingfield Farm accepted its usual complement of five donkeys. They were Lucy, Linda, Betty, Bonny and Fred, and it was Fred who thought he was a human being. He loved to enter the house whenever possible; he loved to nose his way into small crowds and it was not unknown for him to poke his head through the open dining-room window of the farm whenever the family was having a meal. Calm, lovable and cuddly with his thick, grey coat and distinctive black cross on his back, he was a pet and a favourite.

Always popular with the children, he allowed them to ride him through the fields and lanes and when he got some distance from the farm, he would occasionally issue a blood-curdling braying noise, his way of checking whether any other donkey, male or female, was living nearby. The children used him in a Nativity Play at school where he stood as still as a rock and solemnly overlooked the model crib they had made. His acting was superb. From time to time, I saw Fred plodding along the lanes with his tiny charges making a fuss of him and I was pleased he provided the bairns with such pleasurable activity. These children would grow up to appreciate animals and their needs, and it was all due to their pal, Fred.

Then Fred disappeared.

It wasn't difficult to imagine the anguish and concern among the children and their parents. Indeed, poor old Jack Sedgewick was most upset too. He rang me just before ten o'clock one morning in April.

'Mr Rhea,' he said, with his voice showing traces of emotion. 'Ah've lost yan o' them donkeys. Fred, it is. Sometime since last night. Do you reckon 'e could 'ave been stolen?'

'I'll come down to the farm,' I assured him. To my knowledge, there had not been an outbreak of donkey thefts or moke-nappings and I couldn't imagine who would do such a thing. My own immediate view was that Fred had probably got through an insecure gate and wandered off. I felt he would turn up in due course.

When I arrived at Lingfield Farm, I found Jack Sedgewick and a small knot of children standing at the gate of the paddock which contained the other donkeys. The animals were standing together in a corner, watching us; if only they could talk, I thought. I halted my motor bike and parked it against a wall.

'Good of you to come down so quick, Mr Rhea,' he said.

'Fred's gone . . .' 'He was there last night . . .' 'I fed him, Mr Rhea . . .' 'I took his bridle off . . .'

The children were all talking at once so I held up my hands to indicate silence.

'Just a minute!' I laughed. 'I can't hear anybody if you all talk at once. So, Jack. You first.'

'I found him gone,' one little girl couldn't contain her worry.

'Aye,' Jack confirmed. 'Young Denise here came down to t'field about half-eightish. She came to feed 'em all, and noticed Fred wasn't there.'

'Was the gate open or shut, Denise?' I asked her. She would be about eleven years old.

'Shut, Mr Rhea. It swings shut by itself.'

I tried it. It was fastened with a hunting sneck, a type of fastening which comprised a length of wood suspended from two chains. It had a carved notch and it slotted into a bracket on the gatepost. It was easy to open when on horseback; this was done by easing it back with a riding crop, hence its name. I eased back the sneck and let the gate stand wide open, but it swung slowly shut by its own weight and the sneck slid home. The gate was then secure. For this reason, it seemed unlikely that the gate could be accidentally left open. But I knew it was not impossible. If it had been opened only sufficiently wide for a child to emerge, it might not have had the impetus or weight to latch itself properly after only a small movement.

'Who saw him last?' was my next question.

'We did,' came a chorus of voices.

'Where?'

'In the village, last night,' they told me. I asked one girl, the tallest of the group, to explain. She said half a dozen of them had taken Fred into the village for a walk and ride.

'Did anything happen, or did anyone say anything about him? Or to him? Can you remember?' I put to her.

'We all took turns riding,' she said seriously. 'He wasn't upset or anything.'

'Did anybody say anything to him? To you, maybe? About Fred? Was anyone angry or annoyed with him for anything?'

I was trying to establish whether anyone had threatened to take the animal away either as a joke or as a serious threat. The antics of the children and Fred could have upset someone.

'There was that man in the pub,' said one small girl.

'What man was that?' I asked.

'We got crisps and lemonade at the pub.'

'The Brewer's Arms?'

'Yes. We went to the door like we always do.'

'And what about the man? What did he do?'

'He smacked Fred on the nose,' said one of them. 'Just fun, though, he was just playing.'

'Maybe that's upset Fred!' I smiled. 'Maybe he's taken

the huff and gone off to sulk! So what happened exactly, Denise?'

'We had Fred with us. We wanted some crisps and things, so we went to the pub. Fred followed us in. Or he tried to. He poked his nose over the counter and this man clonked him on the nose, just in fun it was. Fred backed away . . . that was all.'

'And after your walk with him, you put him back in the paddock with the others?'

'Yes, we gave him some hay, patted him for a minute or two and then we went home.'

'And did you shut that gate?'

They all swore that it was properly closed. Jack Sedgewick said he did his rounds after ten o'clock that night and noticed nothing amiss. I looked at the lanes which led away from the donkey paddock; if it had got out, it could have wandered into the village, or into the surrounding woods and hills, or even along the river bank. It could be anywhere.

'What about your buildings, Jack? Have they been searched?'

The children provided the answer; they had searched everywhere on the farm before calling me.

'I'll report him as missing,' I said. 'Now, how about organizing a hunt for him?'

And so I organized a small hunt around the likely places in and around Aidensfield; there were empty farm buildings, woods, copses, fields and so on. I allocated a safe place for groups of these children to search; each group comprised three for safety reasons.

Jack said he would walk his own land this morning to check ditches and other likely places, and I decided to ask questions around the village. After all, someone might have spotted a lone donkey trotting along the road. I told them I'd keep Mr Sedgewick informed of developments.

A couple of hours later, I was in the Post Office asking about Fred. Several people were there, queueing for postal orders and stamps, and some were at the grocery counter. As I chatted and spread the news about Fred, a man in hiking gear walked in to buy some fruit and drinks. He noticed me, but he was not a local man. I didn't know him.

'Ah, Officer,' he said, his keen grey eyes showing bright in his weathered face. 'Just the fellow. I've just come through Plantation Wood,' and he showed me his route on a map clipped to his belt, 'and there's a dead donkey just off the footpath . . .'

'Dead donkey?' I almost shouted. 'Are you sure?'

'Well,' he seemed surprised at my reaction. 'Well, it was lying down . . . maybe it wasn't dead . . .'

I asked him to pinpoint the exact place, and noticed that everyone in the shop was listening. We identified the place as being about half-way along the bridleway between High Nab and Cross Plain, where it ran alongside Plantation Wood.

As I confirmed the details, the shop emptied rapidly and the customers scurried to their homes. They seemed to have been galvanized into action at the news. I decided to walk back to Jack Sedgewick's farm and break the news to him, then I would have to break the news to the children and decide whether or not to take them to the scene. I was sure Jack would help me to deal with the corpse.

'A dead donkey?' he gasped when I located him down his fields.

'So the man said,' I replied.

'Right, come wi' me, Mr Rhea, and be sharp,' and he led me to his implement shed. He started the engine of one of his tractors and bade me climb aboard. And off we rushed towards Plantation Wood, the tractor bouncing and bumping along the rough farm tracks. There was a definite note of urgency in his actions.

'What's the panic, Jack?' I shouted above the noise of the engine.

'A dead donkey!' he shouted back. 'I 'ope it's not poor awd Fred, but nobody's ever seen a dead donkey, Mr Rhea. Did tha know that? It's reckoned ti be good luck to see yan. An' we all need a spot o' good luck.'

He accelerated across the fields and from my uncomfortable perch beside his seat, I could now see a straggly line of local people. They were all rushing in the same direction, using a short cut from the village.

'Are they all going to see it?' I shouted at him.

'Aye, likely. Word soon gets about when summat like this 'appens. A dead donkey's a rare thing.'

As we drew nearer I could see the distinctive figure of the hiker leading the way. Several children had also joined the march. The news had spread with amazing speed. Jack's tractor pushed its way through the throng of people and we arrived, breathless almost, at the same time as the head of the procession. The hiker, baffled by this turn of events, was standing and pointing.

'It's gone,' he said, opening his arms wide in an expression of puzzlement. 'It was here, I saw it. And it's gone. It was lying right there!' and he stamped the ground with his boot.

And so the villagers never saw their dead donkey.

This is one of those peculiar legends which is supposed to have been started by Charles Dickens; it is said that no one has ever seen a dead donkey and if the news reached a village that a donkey was dying, everyone went to have a look. The legend has probably arisen from a belief that donkeys will wander off to seek a secret place to die.

We turned the tractor around and chugged back to Lingfield Farm.

'Could yon 'ave been Fred?' asked Jack.

'Who else?' I said. 'Mebbe he was just resting.'

'Aye,' said Jack. 'Mebbe. Mebbe he'll come back. Donkeys can live wild, tha knows. Ah've 'eard of one living twelve years in a wood . . . Fred'll come back.'

The children were pleased it wasn't Fred who had died, but the mystery caused all sorts of rumours. People went back several times to see if the donkey reappeared but it never did. And Fred never returned to the farm. His companions showed no sign of distress at his continuing absence and the children did get over their sorrow. Later that spring, Lucy, Linda, Betty and Bonny went back to their beach without Fred, and no one ever saw him again.

To this day, I do not know what happened to him. In my official report, I recorded him as 'Missing' because there was no evidence of theft.

But could that donkey have been Fred lying dead in the wood? Is there a mystery about dead donkeys that has never been revealed? Or did Fred find a new home somewhere?

I do not know. But I have never seen a dead donkey.

Among the lesser known duties of the village policeman are those connected with contagious diseases of animals. During our training-courses, we were told about anthrax, foot and mouth disease, sheep scab and sheep pox, swine fever, tuberculosis, cattle plague, fowl pest, rabies, atrophic rhinitis, epizootic lymphangitis, pleuro-pneumonia, bovine tuberculosis, sarcoptic parasitic mange, glanders and farcy and other exotic sounding plagues which produced devastating results and misery among farmers.

In the event of an outbreak, or even a suspected outbreak of any of these diseases, it was vital that immediate action was taken by the police, the Ministry of Agriculture, Fisheries and Food, and the owner of the livestock. Police action involved the enforcement of a multitude of rules and regulations and the serving of a document called 'Form A'.

As many of our training-school instructors were city types, I'm sure they did not know the effect of, or the reason for, Form A. The result was that we emerged from training-school with the knowledge that if a cow frothed at the mouth or a pig was sick we served Form A. It all seemed very puzzling, and it was not until I worked in a rural area, where domestic livestock is so important to farmers and to the nation's economy, that the real purpose and importance of Form A registered in my mind.

Form A was a printed document which had to be completed by a police officer who suspected an outbreak of one of the diseases I have listed. He completed the form with the name and address of the farm, or even a portion of the farm in question such as a cattle-shed or pigsty, and formally delivered a copy to the farmer. For most diseases, copies were also sent to the Ministry of Agriculture, Fisheries and Food at local and national level, the local council, and to various police stations. The effect of this document was to bring to a standstill all movements of animals in and out of the suspect premises until a Ministry vet had carried out his inspection. If he declared the animal(s) to be free from disease, the restrictions were lifted and life returned to normal. If he confirmed the disease, another set of procedures swung into action which could lead to the killing of a solitary pig on a small unit or the slaughter of a complete herd of pedigree cattle on a dairy farm. The precise action depended upon the disease in question; I have outlined the general procedures.

Form A was just one small part of the entire system, but as a whole, the impact of the rules and regulations did appear successful. For example, swine fever had practically been eliminated, sheep-dipping had virtually abolished sheep scab and strict import regulations kept rabies at bay. I never did know of a horse which caught epizootic lymphangitis and the last outbreak of pleuro-pneumonia was in 1898. We knew, therefore, that a major outbreak of a serious and contagious animal disease was very unlikely, although it's fair to say there were several false alarms, albeit with good intent. No chances were taken. Every suspicion was treated with the utmost care and attention.

In our county (the North Riding of Yorkshire), all police-officers were appointed inspectors under the Diseases of Animals Act; in some counties, only sergeants and those with higher rank carried this responsibility and in some city areas, there might be just one such designated inspector within a police force. In a large rural area, it made sense for all officers to have the powers thus conferred upon him or her and this meant that in addition to normal criminal law and police procedures, we had to be fully conversant with the statutes and procedures relating to this huge and at times complex subject.

In some areas, members of the Ministry of Agriculture's staff carried out these duties and during my time at Aidensfield, there was a growing feeling that all such work should be carried out by civilian inspectors. The authorities felt that this aspect of police work should be gradually phased out. Both the police and the farmers greeted this possible change with mixed feelings. For the police, it gave them a marvellous insight into rural life and helped them perform their wide range of other duties, while the farmers welcomed a uniform presence rather than a plain-clothes person wandering about their premises, especially in times of strife.

It was during these slow but relentless changes that the country suffered a huge and devastating outbreak of foot and mouth disease. The awful effects of it filtered down to

Reg Lumley's herd at West Gill Farm, Aidensfield.

I learned of the outbreak in October through the newspapers. A report said that foot and mouth disease had been confirmed at Oswestry in Shropshire, and that the police were faced with the task of tracing 2,500 animals which had been sold in the local market shortly before the disease had been discovered. It was a huge task; the cattle could be anywhere in the United Kingdom and every one of them could be carrying the virus. The problem was that the licensing system was not foolproof; bad writing on licences; missing ear-tag numbers which are so vital in the positive identification of a particular beast; and sheer carelessness in record keeping, meant that many cattle would never be traced. They could pass on the disease.

During an epidemic, a contact animal was often identified only when a new outbreak occurred many miles from the point of sale. Meanwhile, it had infected other animals, some of which had been moved away, and so the hunt continued. Foot and mouth disease spreads so rapidly that within five days of that original outbreak, fourteen English counties were declared Controlled Areas. Markets were prohibited and farmers guarded their farm entrances, allowing no one to enter unless their clothing and feet were disinfected.

This huge, fast spreading outbreak was one of the few occasions when members of the general public were inconvenienced. Its awful impact and consequences were such that it pricked the communal conscience of the public as never before. For probably the first time, the great British public knew something of the drama being played out on the farms of their countryside.

At Leeds and Bradford Airport, for example, passengers bound for Ireland had to walk over disinfected mats; the RAC Rally was cancelled; two hundred members of the

Second Battalion of the Royal Anglian Regiment were
drafted in to fight the outbreak near Shrewsbury; National
Hunt racing was called off; the import of fruit, nuts and
fresh meat was restricted on the Isle of Man; Christmas
trees became scarce due to the restrictions imposed on
movements to and from land, and farmers even had to get
permission to vote in a by-election. All dogs within five
miles of an infected place had to be confined and even
poultry movements were restricted.

300 extra veterinary surgeons were drafted in, along
with 2,500 ancillary workers; there were fourteen control
centres in the country and everyone involved worked
fifteen hours per day. All police leave was cancelled and
the troops were called in to help with many of the heavy
tasks. Burial of the slaughtered animals was one example
where military hardware and skills proved most useful.

One paper summed it up like this: 'Two brothers came
home to find a cow frothing at the mouth. They shut
themselves and their families inside the house. Men from
the Ministry came to slaughter and bury; the farm was
quarantined and red and white "Keep Out" notices were
erected around the boundaries. Policemen arrived and
moved into a hut near the farm gate to stop visitors; the
local market was cancelled and a pin was stuck in a map at
the Foot and Mouth Control Headquarters.'

The fear generated by this outbreak can scarcely be
imagined; the far-reaching consequences of the disease
caused every farmer to barricade himself in his farm and to
take every possible precaution to safeguard his own herd.
And it was during this atmosphere that I got a call from
Reg Lumley.

'Can thoo come, Mr Rhea?' He sounded almost in tears.

'What's up, Reg?' I felt that I needn't have asked.

'Yan o' my coos is frothing,' he said.

'Oh my God!'

My heart sank; it looked as if we had foot and mouth in this area, in Aidensfield. I could not comprehend the consequences.

'I'll call the Ministry,' I told him. 'I won't come down to the farm, I might pick up the disease on my feet. Can you arrange a system of disinfectant at the gate, Reg? A bath or summat will do for folks to walk through. Make folks paddle through it going in and out.'

'Aye,' he said slowly. 'Ah've been preparing, just in case. Ah've got a load of disinfectant and some waterproofs . . . Ah'll see to t'gate; Ah'll chain it up to keep traffic out.'

Over the past weeks, as the disease had spread across the nation, I had been issued with some red and white 'Keep Out' posters and so, for the first time during my duties at Aidensfield, I found myself typing out Form A. It had Reg Lumley's name and address on it, and where it asked for the name of the suspected premises, I typed 'The whole of the premises of West Gill Farm, Aidensfield.'

As Force procedure demanded, I compiled a telegram for transmission to the Ministry of Agriculture, Fisheries and Food (Animal Health Division) at Tolworth, Surbiton, Surrey. It said, in the jargon of the time, 'Important. Anhealth, Surbiton, Telex. Suspected foot and mouth disease. Reginald Lumley, West Gill Farm, Aidensfield, near York. N.R. Police, Aidensfield.'

Having despatched this, I next telephoned the local office of that organization and asked for the Divisional Veterinary Inspector. The Ministry now had vets working all over the county but I asked them to send one to Reg's farm; I then called the County Medical Officer's department and notified them, after which I rang my own Force Headquarters and finally Sergeant Blaketon at Ashfordly.

He asked me what I'd done and I told him; I assured

him I'd done everything necessary and that Reg was already providing disinfectant at his farm entrance. I explained that I was on my way to the farm within the next few minutes with my 'Keep Out' notices and to serve Form A upon poor old Reg to isolate his premises. I knew he would have quarantined his own farm, but the official wheels must turn.

I then put on my rubber leggings, a long waterproof mackintosh and wellington boots. Dressed like this, I decided to walk the half-mile or so, for in this type of urgency we were no longer thinking in terms of minutes or seconds. Everything had come to a standstill and would remain so until the Ministry's vets had examined the suspect cow or cows. With my notices under my arm, Reg's Form A in a buff envelope, I made my harrowing journey along the lane.

By the time I arrived at West Gill Farm, Reg was already in position at his gate. Dressed in oilskins and wellington boots, he was standing guard with a shotgun in his hand. A large zinc bath full of pale yellow fluid stood just inside the gate. A yard brush lay beside it and a tractor and trailer were parked nearby.

'Now, Reg,' I said.

'Noo then, Mr Rhea. Got all t'papers, hast tha?' His face was sad and drawn, and I knew I must be careful how I spoke to him. I must not be flippant at all, for farmers treat their cows like old friends. I knew he was on the verge of breaking into tears as he nodded towards the roll of notices under my arm.

'"Keep Out" signs,' I told him. 'I'll stick 'em up for you, on all your entrances. This makes all entrances forbidden areas, Reg. This is the only one that leads down to the house and buildings, isn't it?'

'Aye, t'others are just gates into my fields.'

'Good, well, I won't come through the gate. I'll do this job first – I've got some drawing-pins and string. I'll fix 'em on all the roadside trees and gateposts.'

'Thanks. Ah've already had two daft townies trying to walk their dog down my road. Ah told 'em it was an infected spot, but they didn't understand. They reckoned it was a public footpath down to t'pond, so Ah said it was out-o'-bounds now and anyroad anybody coming would have to paddle through that bath o' stuff. They didn't like that, nut wi' their townie shoes on. That's why Ah fetched my gun – folks don't argue wi' that, Mr Rhea. That lot sharp cleared off then an' Ah told 'em foot and mouth was catching for humans, an' all. It mebbe is, is it?'

'I'm not sure,' I had to admit. 'I know anthrax can be caught by people . . .'

'Aye, well, it's matterless now. You go and stick them signs up and Ah'll stop folks tramping down my lane. You'll 'ave called in t'Ministry vets, have you?'

'I have, and they'll be here as soon as possible. It might be a while, they've other suspected outbreaks.' I could see moisture in his eyes. His banter had concealed his genuine feelings, I felt, but now he would be alone once again with his thoughts. Before I left, I handed him his Form A, and then turned away to post the notices on his various entrances, eight in total. He was a sad and lonely figure as he waited with his gun in his hands, guarding his gate against ordinary people and a virulent disease. As I left, he opened my envelope, read the contents of the Form A and stuffed it into his pocket.

When I returned about forty minutes later, he was still there, pacing up and down as he looked out for the ominous approach of the vet's car.

'You go down to the house, Reg, I'll wait here,' I offered.

'Nay, lad,' he spoke softly. 'Ah couldn't. T'wife and our lad are so upset . . . they'd only upset me. Ah'd allus be wanting to look in on me cows . . .'

'It's not confirmed.' I tried to sound optimistic. 'It could be a false alarm.'

He shook his head. 'Nay, Ah doubt it. It's all around is that disease; somehow, yan o' my cows 'as picked it up . . . it's t'end, Mr Rhea . . . t'end . . . twenty years work . . . all for nowt . . .'

'Don't upset yourself.' I did not want to see this stalwart, tough farmer reduced to self-pity or tears, but he needed to talk to somebody. I happened to be that somebody; we were alone at the gate in our ungainly protective clothing, and we could look down the long straight track which led across his fields and into his compact clutch of farm buildings.

'Twenty years,' he repeated, almost to himself. I looked at him. A sturdy Yorkshireman, turned fifty I guessed; he had the round, weathered face of his profession, a face which had seen little else but long hours and hard work over those years. But that work had produced some pride, too, family pride I guessed.

'Twenty years, it's takken me to build that herd. Pedigree Friesians, they are. Eighty milkers, Ah've got. Eighty and Ah started wi' nowt.'

I glanced at the tall post which stood beside his main gate; it bore a small black and white sign which proclaimed that this was the home of the West Gill Farm Herd of Pedigree British Friesians.

'Ah did it for t'lad, for our Ted. Ah needed summat to pass on, Mr Rhea. He's grown up wi' them Friesians and knows 'em like they was bairns, Mr Rhea. We all do, every one on 'em. Me an' all, and t'wife. Seen 'em come along from calves, most of 'em. Bought some and bred some;

fussed over 'em, made sure they were just right. Bedded 'em down at night, seen to 'em when they were badly . . . best Friesians for miles, they are.'

He was staring into the distance as he talked, not looking at me and not looking down upon his farm in the shallow valley. He was gazing beyond all that, reminiscing and pouring out his heart in his own simple way.

'And now it's all gone . . . they'll be killed, all of 'em . . . put down like rats. Ah've been so careful, Mr Rhea, with foot and mouth about, taking care, watching where Ah bought things, where Ah went, disinfecting . . .'

'Don't,' I said uselessly. 'You're only making things worse. It might be a false alarm . . .'

I tried to give him a little hope.

'Nay, Ah knows foot and mouth when Ah sees it. Yon awd cow 'as it, there's nowt so sure . . .'

He went on to say how, as a young farmer, he had recognized the potential in a herd of Friesians; he'd seen them as ideal cattle for his plans, cattle which would produce first-class milk. They were useful beef animals too. So years ago, he decided to build himself a pedigree dairy breed, his own very special effort. And his idea was to introduce his only son, Ted, to the skills of dairy farming so that he, in turn, would continue with this herd. He wanted Ted to improve and expand it.

'Ah'd got all soorts of ideas in me head, Mr Rhea. Ah was gahin ti keep better records of 'em all, go for bigger milk yields an' that . . .'

It was good to hear him talking and I allowed him to ramble on, sometimes asking what I thought was a sensible question. I learned a good deal about Friesians that afternoon, but it also taught me enough about foot and mouth disease to make me realize the end had come. I didn't hold out much hope for his herd now, not after listening to his knowledgeable description of the disease and its drastic effects.

It would be over an hour later when a small car eased to a halt on the verge near the gate. A tall young man in a smart lovat green suit climbed out and announced that he was Alan Porrit, a vet from the Ministry of Agriculture. After shaking hands and expressing his sorrow at the awful news, he announced his approval of our immediate actions and donned his own waterproofs.

After swilling himself in the disinfectant, he said, 'Come along, Mr Lumley. Show me where to go.'

'Nay,' said Reg. 'Ah can't. Ah just can't go down there. Not now . . . you go and get it ovvered with.'

Tears welled in his eyes and he rubbed them roughly with his fist.

'Ah'm being right daft and sentimental, but you go. Ah can't . . .'

'I think you should, Reg,' I said. 'You'll be needed down there. I'll stay here.'

After some gentle persuasion from us both, Reg joined the vet and I watched them walk into the distance. Their sorry figures seemed to diminish as they approached the farm, and then, as they reached the paths which divided, one towards the byre and the other to the house, they halted.

From my vantage point on the lane, I could see them in deep conversation, then Reg began to shake his head. I saw him turn and walk towards his house. He left the vet standing alone. The vet turned on his heels and strode purposefully towards the byre which contained the suspect cattle.

As Reg approached the back of his house, his hands were over his face. He was sobbing like a child. Someone inside opened the door; he went in and the door closed behind him.

That epidemic of foot and mouth disease cost the country over £200 million. No one knows how much it cost Reg Lumley.

9

Is it, in heav'n, a crime to love too well?
Alexander Pope, 1688-1744

In the great and pleasant rural landscape which surrounded
Aidensfield during my time there, serious crime was
practically unknown. Certainly, there were many minor
thefts, most of which were never officially reported, and
I'm sure there were motoring offences which never came
to my notice. Other breaches of the law, such as drinking
late in the country pubs or petty acts of damage or vandalism
were dealt with in the spirit of the law rather than by the
letter of the law. A quiet word in the right ear usually
prevented further trouble.

It would be wrong to claim that Aidensfield and district
was totally free from crime. It was not; every so often, an
outbreak of criminal activity would occur, usually of the
kind described as petty damage, theft or the unauthorized
borrowing of cars. There were some house-breakings,
shop-breakings and poaching, and if we suffered three
crimes in the district during a month, the local papers
described it as a crime wave.

These waves were very tiny, therefore, more like ripples
on a village pond than the kind of waves that swamp ocean
liners. Nonetheless, they did cause distress to the victims
and this in turn caused anxiety among the villagers. From
my point of view, these crimes, minor though they were,

did involve my colleagues and me with extra duties. There were observations, report writing and court appearances, but I did not mind. In fact, I enjoyed the experiences they provided, albeit with deep concern for the victims, for the investigation of crime is fascinating. To investigate and detect crime is probably one of the major reasons for anyone joining the Police Service.

As time passed, and as each minor breach of the criminal law was dealt with, I did begin to wonder if a major crime or series of crimes would ever occur on my patch. I began to feel that this period of peace was too good to be true, and then, in the spring of one year, I was faced with an outbreak of arson.

Arson was, and still is, one of the most serious of crimes and the legal definition then said that arson involved the unlawful and malicious setting fire to buildings, including churches, warehouses, railway stations, shops and sheds, as well as crops, vegetable produce, coal-mines and ships. It was then categorized as a felony both at common law and by statute. The common law crime was confined to houses and their outhouses, while the statutory crime, featured in the Malicious Damage Act of 1861, involved a detailed list of the objects of the kind listed in the above definition. I remember that in those days, it was not legally possible to charge anyone with arson to a motor vehicle or television set because new fangled contraptions of that sort were not mentioned in that 1861 Act – other possible charges such as malicious damage to personal property had to be considered.

In the weeks following that first act of arson there developed a series of troublesome fires, all of which involved either haystacks or hay in barns. I could discern no pattern, except that the attacked barns or stacks were usually in isolated locations. Some, however, were in the centre of

our market towns and as time went by, I began to despair
of ever catching the fire-raiser. Some of the fires were on
my beat, and although all the local officers were involved in
the investigation, I felt it was my duty to arrest the culprit.
The battle both to halt and deal with the villain became a
personal challenge.

News of the first fire came in the early hours of a
Saturday morning in April. Just after 1 a.m. a passing
motorist noticed flames licking the asbestos roof of a
Dutch barn. He roused the farmer and his wife, who called
the fire brigade by dialling 999. As a matter of routine, I
was informed by our Control Room and clambered from
my warm bed around quarter past one.

Rather than waste time climbing into my motor cycling
outfit, I used my own car to rush to the fire. It was at Low
Dale Farm, Briggsby, less than ten minutes' drive from
Aidensfield. The farm, a small concern with livestock,
poultry and arable land, was owned by Arthur Stead and
his wife, Helen. When I arrived, the Fire Brigade was
already there. Hoses were spraying hissing water into the
fierce centre of the fire which had a very secure hold. Men
were working in the heat of the flames as the bales of hay
glowed in the night. The flames cast frightening shadows
upon the house and nearby buildings and showered
dangerous sparks across the dark countryside. Most of the
flames licked the exterior surface of the hay, while a stiff
night breeze carried sparks and more flames into the
interior of the barn. Small new fires were breaking out all
over the place; it looked like a lost battle.

With old raincoats over their nightclothes and wellingtons
on their feet, Arthur and Helen, both in their late fifties,
were using hayforks in an attempt to pull untouched bales
clear of the inferno.

Helpers had arrived from neighbouring farms and

cottages. Men and women were working around the barn, removing bales by hand. After announcing my arrival to the Fire Brigade, I used the Steads' telephone to relay a situation report to Control Room, and then joined the rescue effort. I began to haul bales from the barn and throw them clear of the spreading blaze.

One problem lay in a stiff easterly breeze which made the hay glow deep within the stack as the intense heat consumed the dry material. We tried to hoist some burning bits well away from the barn, but the speed of the fire's consumption beat us. Gallons and gallons of water were sprayed into the depths and we did manage to remove a considerable amount of uncharred hay.

During a lull, I spoke to Arthur.

'We've got a fair amount out, Arthur,' I commented, wiping my dirty hands across my face. We were all black from the smoke and sweating profusely in spite of the chill night air.

'T'cows won't eat it, Mr Rhea, even if it 'as been saved. It'll smell o' smoke, you see . . . might mak bedding or summat . . .'

'You'll be insured, are you?' I asked.

'Aye, but cows can't eat insurance money; they need fodder. It's a while yet before we can turn 'em out to fresh grass.'

I knew that the local farmers would rally to help poor Arthur with his forthcoming feeding problems; they always did when anyone suffered a loss of this kind. But we had fought a losing battle. As fast as we removed bales, others burst into flames; it seemed as if the blaze had crept deep inside the stacked hay and I wondered if our removal of the bales loosened the packed hay and permitted the air to enter. This would fan the flames. As things were, it wasn't long before the entire contents of the barn were a mixture of searing heat, smoke and untidy charred hay.

We kept an eye on the drifting sparks but they disappeared across the fields and missed the buildings. As dawn came to Low Dale Farm we could see the full extent of the devastation. The barn was burnt to a shell, some roof portions having collapsed when the supports gave way in the fire. It contained a jumbled mass of charred and useless hay which was still smouldering. It would continue to smoulder and smoke for days. All around were piles of hay which had been saved by the volunteers, hay which the cattle would not now touch because it was tainted by smoke. The entire area was saturated with dirty water and we stood in a sea of mud and straggly strands of hay.

Arthur and Helen gave us all a breakfast of ham and eggs with copious quantities of hot tea. As we stood outside and I gathered the information necessary for my Fire Report, one of the senior fire officers took me to one side.

'Constable,' he said, 'we feel this is a suspicious fire. We can almost certainly rule out spontaneous combustion which, I'm sure you know, causes a good many stacks and barn fires. That usually occurs within three months of a stack being built – this one is eight months old. Fire from spontaneous combustion works from the inside and moves to the exterior. This started on the outside walls of hay, so it looks deliberate. The seat of the blaze was on the outside of the hay, at the east end of the barn, low down upon the stacked hay but just off ground level. There was a platform of hay left where some upper bales had been removed, and the blaze was creeping up the outside walls of hay when our men got here. I am confident that spontaneous combustion is not the cause and that an outside agent is responsible. It could be an accident, but I'm calling in our experts for their opinions.'

This meant I must now inform the CID who would liaise with the Fire Brigade and a formal investigation would commence. It would be backed by statements from witnesses plus any scientific evidence salvaged from the scene. Inevitably, poor old Arthur and his wife would be under suspicion of having deliberately set fire to their hay for insurance purposes, and I knew the investigation had to be thorough, if only to exonerate them. I was sure they would never resort to this kind of evil. My witnesses were Arthur and Helen themselves, several fire officers and the motorist who had noticed the blaze, but none could provide any real evidence to show how the blaze had started. It remained a matter of opinion and speculation, but continued to be 'suspicious'.

A week later, there was a second blaze. Although this one did not occur on my beat, it was only four miles away at Seavham and the circumstances were very similar. Around two o'clock in the morning, Ronald Thornton and his wife Alice, who farmed at Home Farm, were roused by barking dogs. Wary of intruders, they had peered out of their bedroom window to see one of their haystacks ablaze. It was in the corner of a field, away from the buildings, but was valuable for livestock feeding.

I noted the date and time, and although I did not attend this one I did later contact the Fire Brigade to ascertain whether it could be linked to the blaze at Low Dale Farm. Other than to say the cause was not spontaneous combustion, the Fire Brigade would not commit themselves. Nonetheless, the similarities included an isolated haystack, an outbreak in the early hours of a Saturday morning, and the suspicious nature of the blaze. The Thorntons were not insured, I learned, which somewhat added to the mystery.

If they had not done it deliberately, which seemed most

unlikely, and if it was not an accident (there were no chimneys or exposed flames nearby), and if it was not spontaneous combustion, then who had done it and why? These were the questions we had to answer.

I tried to find links or more similarities with the Stead fire, but failed. My avenues of investigation included bad business deals; possible fraud; family feuds; jealousy, petty spitefulness or malice; the work of a pyromaniac and a host of other domestic and business likelihoods. To my knowledge, no known arsonist lived in the area.

The next blaze was three weeks later, on a Wednesday night at Crampton. It was discovered earlier than the others, around eleven o'clock. A neighbour had smelled smoke and had investigated the cause only to discover bales of hay well ablaze in the barn of Throstle Nest Farm. This barn was close to the centre of the village and happily, there was no strong breeze to fan the flames or to disperse the dangerous sparks among the houses.

Mr and Mrs Bill Owens farmed Throstle Nest; their splendid farmhouse occupied an elevated site surrounded by its spacious land, and a pair of Dutch barns stood at the bottom of a lane. This lane formed a junction with the road which led into the village, and their neighbour, Jack Winfield, lived in a cottage near that junction.

Jack's swift action and the rapid response by the Fire Brigade kept damage to a minimum, but the familiar story emerged. It was another suspicious fire, so like the earlier ones. As the Brigade fought the fire and helpful villagers removed bales of unburnt hay, the drifting smoke penetrated many nearby homes. The smell would linger for days afterwards. During a lull, I spoke to Jack Winfield, a retired farm worker.

'Now, Jack, did you hear or see anything? We've had a few of these fires now.'

'There was a motor bike about the village tonight,' he said without hesitation. 'I grumbled, 'cos it made my television picture go funny. Motor bikes do that, you know, sometimes.'

'What time?' I asked.

'Nine o'clockish,' he said. 'First time, that was. Then again later, before t'fire broke out. Not long before, but I couldn't be sure of t'time really. Same bike, I could tell by t'noise.'

'Has it been before?'

'Can't say I've noticed it. Mind, if I hadn't had my set on, mebbe I wouldn't have noticed.'

'Did you see it then? Do you know who it was?'

'Sorry, lad, no.'

After quizzing him at length, I took a written witness statement from him. For the first time, we had a hint of a suspect, slender though it was, and before the Fire Brigade left, one of their officers came to me.

'We found this,' he said, opening the palm of his hand to reveal a spent match.

'Where, precisely?' I asked, accepting this new piece of evidence.

'About five feet from where we believe the blaze started,' he said, pointing to a piece of muddy land. 'We think it started low down this side, where some bales have been removed . . .'

'Like the Low Dale fire?' I interrupted.

'Yes, in a similar position. The flames crept up the outside wall of hay before gaining a strong hold. This match, which is clean and new as you can see, was lying on the ground.'

'Thrown away, you think?'

'Its position suggests that.'

I pinpointed the precise location of this match and drew

a little sketch in my notebook so that it would be committed
to paper for future records. It was an ordinary match, not
from a book of paper matches or a short-stemmed Swan
Vesta. Its unweathered appearance said a lot; there was a
distinct possibility that it was associated with the blaze.

I reported these new facts to Sergeant Blaketon at
Ashfordly, and he decided to institute a series of nightly
police patrols. Their purpose was to trace the motor cyclist
and/or the fire-raiser. At this stage, we felt there was little
point stopping all motor cyclists, but did decide to record
the registration number of every bike seen during our
patrols. I was aware, too, that the fuel tank of a motor cycle
contains petrol and what better method is there for a fire-
raiser to carry this incendiary aid?

If and when another fire broke out, we could consult
our records and check the movements of all recorded
bikes. It would be possible to see if they tallied with the
date, time and place of the fire. Even so, with such a massive rural area to patrol, the chances of a police vehicle
crossing the path of the fire-raiser were remote to say the
least. But we had to try.

For the next couple of weeks there were no reported
stack fires. We began to feel that our presence on the roads
and the fact that our purpose was enhanced by local
gossip, had deterred the arsonist. But we were wrong.

The next fire broke out in the centre of Ashfordly.
Tucked into one of the side streets was a farmhouse and
behind it was a square stackyard and a motley collection of
implement sheds. The fields belonging to this farm were
some distance away on the outskirts of the town, but this
curious town centre farm, known as Town Farm, was a
thriving enterprise.

I was on night duty one Friday and was patrolling the
surrounding moors and hills when I spotted a bright blaze

in the centre of Ashfordly. It was 1 a.m. For a moment, I thought it was a bonfire in a garden, one which had been lit earlier and whose flames had been revived by a sudden night breeze; but in seconds, I knew it was too large for that and I feared the worst.

From my vantage point on the hills, it was impossible to say precisely where it was. All I could determine was a bright, flickering flame somewhere among a dark collection of houses and other buildings. I accelerated the little motor bike down towards the town and it was then that I recalled the tumble of farm buildings and sheds just off Field Lane. As I entered the town, I knew the worst. I roared towards the blaze. It was now showing as a bright orange and red glow against the sky above the houses, and I could see a pall of thick, black smoke. This was no garden bonfire and I feared another arson attack.

The moment I turned the corner and identified the precise location, I halted and radioed my Control Room. Through its radio network, the Fire Brigade was summoned and I asked the Control Room sergeant to awake Sergeant Blaketon. Then I began to rouse the sleeping occupants of the farmhouse and several nearby homes. The horrified farmer said there were horses in some of the buildings and so I helped him to evacuate his animals.

Two tractors were in the Dutch barn; they were already covered with blazing hay which had tumbled from the stacked bales and so began another battle to save his equipment and machinery. The farmer's wife was in tears; neighbours were terrified for their homes, and the horses were snorting and frisky in their fright.

We did not save the barn, the hay or the tractors but no human or animal life was lost. With Sergeant Blaketon at my side, I began a meticulous search of the scene. We were seeking that spent match which could be some distance

from the barn. He found it. Lying 5 or 6 feet away from
where the wall of hay had been, he located a clean spent
match, miraculously having avoided the trampling feet and
gallons of rushing water. He preserved it for evidence. It
was another important indication that the same person
was responsible for all the fires.

The Fire Officer in charge said he believed the blaze had
not been due to an electrical fault or to spontaneous
combustion; he expressed an opinion that the tractors
might, in some way, have been responsible. The possibility
of a short circuit from a battery couldn't be ignored.

A more detailed investigation would follow and the
charred remains would be examined. When we told the
firemen about the match, he said, 'That figures. We think
it might have started on that outer wall of hay, not far from
there . . . that's the second match you've found, eh?'

We began to ask about the motor-cycle noises in the
night and one of the neighbours, a retired bank manager,
did tell us he had heard a motor bike. It was not mine
because the timing was different. I hadn't been near the
place until just after 1 a.m. He had heard one about
midnight, he said, but could not say whether it was coming
towards Town Farm or leaving it.

But it was enough for us. After that, we intensified our
nightly patrols for the motor-cycling fire-raiser. At the
same time, we renewed our enquiries from earlier victims.
We asked them whether they had antagonized anyone who
owned a motor bike and we continued our efforts to
establish a link, any link, between all the scenes of the fires.

But we did not find any connection.

Then I had a stroke of luck. It was one of those
moments of good fortune that all detectives require and
with which some are blessed throughout their careers. In
my case, it happened while I was off duty. I recognized the

clue for what it was and became excited when I realized I might have found the arsonist.

It was a Friday, which was market day in Ashfordly. I went to market with Mary to help with the shopping and to look after the children. For me, it was a trying but enjoyable chore. I was wandering among the stalls in my off duty casual clothes, pleased that it was a fine spring day and that there were books and antiques to examine. I ran into friends and acquaintances to chat with and the entire experience generated a pleasing air of rustic contentment. It was a welcome break from my routine.

Then, as I poked among some junk on a stall, seeking old inkwells (which I collect as a hobby) I noticed the motor cyclist. He was sitting astride a green BSA Bantam in front of one of the pubs which overlooked the market place. He was laughing and chatting to a pretty girl. I watched and, because motor cycles were very much on my official mind, began to observe them.

I was in an ideal position. As I watched, I saw the youth dig into his trousers pocket, pull out a cigarette and light it. Then, having done so, he flicked the spent match over his shoulder and drew heavily on the cigarette. My heart thumped; I found a pen in my pocket and jotted the make and registration number on a piece of paper and followed with a description of him and his girl. Then, I ambled across to find that match. I had to have it for comparison with the others.

It was easy; it was the only one lying nearby. The youth was engrossed in his chat with the girl and didn't even glance at my approach. The match lay about 5 feet behind him.

Not wishing to draw his attention, or indeed anyone else's, to my curious behaviour, I 'accidentally' dropped my car keys close to the match then stooped to retrieve them and my valuable piece of evidence. Now, the match would be scientifically compared with those already in our possession, and discreet enquiries would be made into the owner of that BSA. The chain of evidence was growing stronger. I went straight to Ashfordly Police Station with the match, and Sergeant Blaketon said he would have it taken immediately to the Forensic Laboratory at Harrogate.

Prompt enquiries from the Vehicle Taxation Office at Northallerton told us that the youth lived at Malton; we learned he was called Ian Clayton. And so, at last, we had a very likely suspect.

The problem was whether to interview him immediately, in which case he could deny being near the fires, or to make some discreet enquiries and observations with a view to gathering more evidence and facts about his life and background. We decided we needed more evidence if we were to link him with the fires; after all, we had no proof yet, merely surmise, and so we circulated to all police officers, his description and details of his motor cycle. We would find out about his work and how he spent his leisure hours and if necessary, his movements would be monitored as he went out at night. We might even catch him in the act of lighting a fire.

Two days later, we received a telephone call from the Forensic Science Lab at Harrogate. Their experts had examined all three matches and said that, in their opinion, they were similar.

Scientific evidence confirmed they had come from the same manufacturer and even the same batch of timber, but the lab experts would not commit themselves to anything more positive. A written report would follow. As evidence of arson, this was, in itself, far too flimsy. Our suspect remained a mere suspect.

Two weeks later, the little BSA Bantam was seen heading

towards Ashfordly. It was discreetly followed and Ian Clayton collected his girl-friend from a house at 45 Stafford Road, Ashfordly. With each perched astride the tiny bike, it motored towards Waindale. It was about ten-thirty and it was dark. Having shadowed them into Waindale in his patrol car, PC Gregson radioed for me because Waindale was on my beat. He said they had driven along Green Lane. I received the call and set off for that hamlet. There was a feeling of excitement in my bones.

I used my own car because I felt this would be wiser than using the police motor cycle. A police motor cycle was far too prominent for this task. I parked in Waindale, making sure the car was out of sight, and began to walk along Green Lane, seeking haystacks and Dutch barns. I knew the location of most, and then, as I silently moved along the lane, I arrived at Green Farm. In the darkness, I could distinguish the tall supports of the Dutch barn, and then, as I padded silently into the complex, I came across the BSA Bantam. I could smell the heat of its engine as it leaned against a dry-stone wall, and a quick examination of its number plate proved it was the one we sought. My heart was thumping now; I had to find him before he fired this stack, but I also needed evidence of his crimes.

Other than the sounds of the night, including some furtive scuttlings from rats and mice, I could not see or hear anything. But he was here. Had he seen me? Was he watching me? If I wasn't careful, he might escape on his bike . . . perhaps I should have disconnected the plug lead?

All kinds of worries and plans crossed my mind, and then, as I stood in the shelter of a tractor shed, my eyes became accustomed to the gloom. Aided by a low light from the curtained farmhouse windows, I saw the flicker of a match. It burnt a hole in the gloom; it flickered for a few seconds and then flew in an arc to splutter into darkness. This was it!

I sped towards that place. The match had died now. It had not set fire to anything. But there was another tiny glow of red. And I smelt smoke. Cigarette smoke. Not burning hay.

I shone my torch. A pool of light burst upon the young couple, boy and girl, each partly dressed, each acutely embarrassed after their love-making in the hay. And in those moments, the youth's smouldering cigarette was cast away to land somewhere in the dry hay . . .

I found it before it ignited the hay, kept it as evidence and took them both to Ashfordly Police Station in my car. To cut a long story short, after a protracted investigation about their movements, Ian Clayton and Susan Longfield did admit visiting all the burnt barns and stacks. They identified them only when we took them to each one in turn. Susan, being new to the area, and Ian, living fifteen miles away, had seen the reports in the newspapers, but had never realized the fires had occurred in barns they had used. Names of villages and isolated farms meant nothing to them.

They had not known the names of the farms they had visited; they had simply jumped on the little bike and toured the lanes until they came to a warm and cosy barn or haystack. There they stopped and made love in the hay.

And afterwards, Ian always lit a cigarette which he discarded without thought . . .

He was charged with arson of each of those stacks and barns and appeared before the magistrates in committal proceedings. After considering all the facts, they found no case to answer because the fires were accidental. In their considered opinion, there was no malice in his actions and they accepted he had not unlawfully and maliciously set fire to the hay.

Another of my rare major criminal investigations concerned a case of housebreaking which even today remains unsolved.

Tucked discreetly behind the village street in Aidensfield is St Cuthbert's Cottage, a delightful small house which dates to the eighteenth century. With two bedrooms, a living-room and kitchen, it has beamed ceilings, pretty windows and roses growing around a rustic porch. When its elderly occupant died, it was bought by a Mr Lawrence Porteous of Leicester who wanted it as a holiday home. He retained most of the old lady's antique furniture, but modernized and decorated the little house until it was a veritable gem. It was the kind of home for which any romantic young couple would have yearned.

At this time, it so happened that one young couple from Aidensfield desperately needed a home. In their estimation, St Cuthbert's Cottage was ideal. They lacked the funds to buy it, but after the sale they did write to Mr Porteous to ask if he would rent them the cottage even for a short period, until they found somewhere of their own. He refused.

They wrote again a week or two later, pointing out that it was empty for most of the year, and that they had no home . . . but again he refused.

The situation had arisen like this. Jill Knight, née Crane, was the youngest daughter of Mrs Brenda Crane, a widow. Mrs Crane and Jill had lived in another Aidensfield cottage which was owned by a property company. When Jill married young Paul Knight, he moved into the same cottage and, with his new bride, shared the accommodation and its running expenses. Then Jill became pregnant. Through one of those awful quirks of fate, poor Mrs Crane suffered a heart attack and died about the same time.

The house had been in her name; consequently upon her death, the property company wanted to repossess it for another tenant, a retiring employee of theirs. Because Jill and Paul were not holders of the rent book, they were told to vacate the house. If they refused, then the due processes of civil law would be implemented to evict them. They were given three months' notice. This put them in a terrible dilemma. Paul worked for an agricultural implement dealer in Ashfordly and needed another home in the area, so that he was near enough to cycle to work. He couldn't afford a car and the buses were too infrequent.

Wisely, he applied for a council house but was told there was a waiting-list; his name would be placed on that list and in the meantime, he must find alternative accommodation. Not surprisingly, he got his eye on St Cuthbert's Cottage as an ideal short-term solution and that was how he came to write to Mr Porteous.

Repeated refusals from Lawrence Porteous put the youngsters in a real dilemma. I knew them both and liked them, but I could see the strain beginning to have its effect, especially upon the heavily pregnant Jill. The worry made her pale and constantly tired, and she began to neglect her appearance. Her mother's death, her own pregnancy and the housing problems were more than any young girl should have to tolerate.

'No luck?' I met her in the shop one day.

She shook her tousled head.

'Paul's been asking all over,' she said, her pretty face drawn with anxiety. 'We got a chance of a council house over at Scalby, but it was too far for Paul to get to work. If you see anything, Mr Rhea, you'll let us know? They can't put us on the street, can they? Me being pregnant and that?'

'No, I'm sure they can't and I'm also sure something will turn up . . .'

'We only need something till we get a council house near here,' she said. 'There's bound to be one soon, isn't there? The council said they come up fairly often.'

I did feel concerned for them. There were lots of suitable cottages in the surrounding villages, but this was the period when rich folks were buying them for holiday homes. Some were purchased as personal holiday homes or weekend cottages, and others were bought as investments to be rented weekly or for mere weekends to holiday-makers.

There is little doubt that the merits of this upsurge in buying country cottages did have a dual value; it did prevent many old cottages from falling into ruin and it did bring some welcome business into the village stores and inns. But on the other hand, it denied many young people a village home, either for rent or for purchase, because it made fewer local homes available.

This was brought home to me by the case of Jill and Paul Knight. I felt sure the council would never allow them to be thrown on to the street or taken into a hostel of some kind, but the wheels of official departments turn so very slowly and with such a lamentable lack of feeling or compassion. The officials would have no concept of the heartache involved in the long periods of waiting and hoping.

As I worried about the future for Jill and Paul, I received a visit from the postman.

'Mr Rhea,' he said as he knocked with my morning mail, 'somebody's broken into that little cottage down the village, St Cuthbert's.'

My heart sank.

'Much gone?' I asked.

'Dunno,' he shook his head. 'They got in by smashing a window at the back, in the kitchen. It's still open.'

'Right, thanks,' I said. 'I'll go and have a look.'

As he'd said, entry was by smashing a pane at the back. The burglars, or housebreakers, had opened the kitchen window and climbed through. Once inside, exit had been through the kitchen door by unlocking the Yale catch. I could not tell whether anything was missing for I had never previously been in the cottage, and the intruder(s) had not made a mess.

I now had a crime in Aidensfield. If the breaking and entry had occurred after 9 p.m. and before 6 a.m. it would be classified as a burglary. Outside those times, it would be recorded as a housebreaking. Since 1968, due to a change in the law, all such breakings have been categorized as burglary.

I contacted the key-holder, Miss Cox, who lived two doors away and together we made a brief examination. I asked her not to touch anything, but to look around and tell me what was not in its usual place.

'Oh dear, oh dear,' she muttered as she surveyed each room at my side. 'Oh, dear, oh dear, how awful.'

She was a fussy little woman of indeterminate age, probably in her sixties.

'Can you tell me what's been taken?' I asked, notebook at the ready.

'The television,' she said, pointing to an empty corner.

I quizzed her and found out it was a black and white Murphy set, with a 12" screen.

'The radio,' she said in the kitchen. This was a Bush portable in a red and cream case, with a plastic carrying handle. 'And a vase, a nice old vase in green glass.'

'Thanks.'

We searched the entire cottage, but nothing else seemed

to have been stolen. She checked it regularly, but could not say it was secure at 9 o'clock last night. So we recorded it as housebreaking, a lesser crime than burglary. I thanked her, and obtained the telephone number of Mr Porteous; then called in our CID and Scenes of Crime experts; they would examine the cottage for fingerprints and other clues.

My next task, apart from completing the formal written Crime Report, was to make house-to-house enquiries around Aidensfield in the hope that someone had either heard or seen something. The CID would do their skilled work after obtaining a key from Miss Cox and I asked the local plumber to reglaze the broken window.

From my office, I rang Mr Porteous to break the bad news. After assuring him that all that was possible had been done, and that his cottage would be secure before nightfall, he decided not to drive up from Leicester. I felt it was not necessary.

Funnily enough, another two cottages in a deep moorland village were raided about a fortnight later, but in each case, the MO was different from the Aidensfield crime. I was sure the Aidensfield housebreaker had not broken into the others but those crimes did prompt a telephone call from Mr Porteous.

'Ah, Mr Rhea,' he said. 'I've just seen the paper – two cottages have been burgled on the moors. Is this a regular happening in your area?'

'It's becoming more commonplace,' I had to admit. 'Some of these holiday homes, with expensive furnishings, are easy meat you know. They're empty for long periods and it doesn't take a genius to realize they've got things like TVs and radios inside; all easily disposable.'

He paused. 'We're going abroad for the summer,' he said, 'so we won't be using St Cuthbert's Cottage for our fortnight's holiday. It'll be empty from now until October; that's six months. Miss Cox will pop in from time to time, but you'll keep an eye on it for me, will you?'

'Of course,' I said, 'but it's always at risk, you know that.'

'I know. I heard about these people who live in houses for you, house-sitters or something. Have you anyone in your area who would do that? For a fee, of course.'

I was about to say I knew of no one, when I remembered Jill and Paul Knight.

'I know a young couple who would do a good job for you,' I said. 'They'd be willing to house-sit for you, for six months or whatever it takes.'

I told him all about Jill and Paul, and how they were now waiting for allocation of a council house. He recalled their pleading letters.

'I didn't commit myself before,' he said. 'After all, I don't know them and at that time I did intend using my cottage most weekends . . . but, well, for a gap of six months . . .'

'They are on the council waiting-list,' I stressed, 'but this would be useful to both you and them.'

'Ask them to ring me,' he said. 'I'll discuss terms; I was willing to pay someone, so I may decide to allow them the cottage rent free or possibly a nominal rent, for legal purposes . . .'

Three days later, they moved in.

Five days afterwards, the stolen goods were found in an old van which was rotting in a quarry. They were quite undamaged and after successfully testing them for fingerprints, they were restored to St Cuthbert's Cottage. It was good news for Mr Porteous.

My enquiries into the crime drew a complete blank but it was a remark I overheard from a drinker in the Brewer's

Arms which caused me to think.

'By gum,' said the man over his pint one night (he was chatting confidentially to a pal, but I heard him), 'it's a rum sort of a do when you've got to burgle a house to get folks to take notice of you. Still, yon lad's got a roof over his head now.'

From time to time, I still reflect upon that unsolved crime.

Constable
through the Meadow

1

'Meadows trim with daisies pied,
Shallow brooks and rivers wide.'
L'Allegro, John Milton, 1608-74

For the rural police constable going about his daily routine,
this is more than a poetic image; sights of this kind are a
pleasant part of country life and the constable's patrols
take him through a whole galaxy of meadows, sometimes
along major roads, sometimes along narrow lanes and
occasionally by little-used bridleways, green lanes or
tortuous footpaths with centuries of history beneath them.

On the edge of the moors where I used to patrol, some
of the fields are divided by rippling brooks which we call
becks or gills, other boundaries are marked by the sturdy
dry-stone walls of the region, and some make use of
hedgerows or even timber-and-wire fencing. There are
spacious flat fields used for the growth of cereals or the
nourishment of herds of milk-producing cows, and tiny
patches of grass which have the appearance of being
artificially created from the heather or bracken of a wild
moorland hillside.

Some of the meadows adjacent to the moorland are
almost too small to be considered fields or meadows,
perhaps being better described as paddocks. One local
name is intake because they have been cultivated after
being securely walled from the wilderness of pervading

heather, but they continue to provide a refuge for a few hens or moorland sheep, even a cow or horse.

Those on the edge of the moors usually contain a patch of smooth, short grass with very few flowers because the black-faced sheep of this region continually nibble at it until they produce a surface which is as smooth as a prize lawn. In the dales below, however, the meadows are more lush; on the fertile earth, they thrive upon the natural goodness which has accumulated over the years. They feature as parts of a beautiful green carpet decorated with profuse and colourful vegetation; in the spring and summer they are a delight, and in the winter they sleep unmolested.

There were times when I patrolled beside meadows filled with butterflies and bees busily exploring a bewildering range of blossoming wild flowers. Clovers and vetches patterned the greenery with tiny dots of colour and in the changing seasons I noted celandines, red poppies, sorrel, a variety of thistles, pretty red campions, cow parsley, buttercups, daisies and more besides, sometimes with a charming border of wild roses or honeysuckle along the carefully trimmed hedgerows.

In the late spring or early summer, before haytime, the meadows are rich with a multitude of pretty grasses and I learnt there are about a hundred and fifty varieties in this country, our farmers knowing which will produce the best nourishment for their grazing livestock, or which are most suited for transformation into hay and silage. I discovered that after the grass has been cut for haymaking, the coarse grass which follows is called fog by some Yorkshire farmers.

'By, yon fog's leeaking well,' a moorland farmer noted one morning. I looked for the familiar wispy clouds in the valley and wondered why he had made this comment on a clear sunny morning, but was later to learn he was speaking of the grass in a recently mown hayfield. I believe there was an old Scandinavian word 'fogg' meaning a limp type of grass.

In addition to this form of fog, there is a variety of grass called Yorkshire Fog which is most attractive and very widespread throughout Britain and Europe. Growing up to two feet in height, it has a soft green/grey stem and when it flowers in the summer, it produces a most delightful pink and white hue which turns to purple as the long days of summer edge towards another autumn.

Whatever their functions, these meadows and the highways and byways that knit them together like a huge patchwork quilt are an echo of history. Many of the fields which today support livestock or produce crops have been fulfilling this role for centuries, altering their functions and appearance to keep pace with the requirements of good husbandry. The changing techniques of farming and the increasing use of large agricultural machines mean that the size, shape and uses of our fields must alter to keep pace.

Some of us grumble about the removal of hedges with all the consequent upheaval among the wild life that depends upon them, but we may not appreciate that this results from the desperate need to feed the expanding human race by making the best use of modern machinery.

We grumble about the disappearance of footpaths or the use of chemicals, the removal of small copses or the way new roads and buildings encroach upon the natural landscape. We may not like these changes, but they are part of the moving pattern of the landscape which has been occurring since man first cultivated the land and made the countryside his home.

History has noted that fields existed more than 3,500 years ago; there were fields in medieval times, fields born from the enclosures of the eighteenth and nineteenth centuries, and the extensive but controversial fields of modern times.

Throughout history, the countryman has loved the fields which surround his home, so much so that they have been given names. For the village policeman going about his daily business, it was necessary to know these names because they cropped up in his work. They were just as important as other place-names in and around the village and I was soon familiar with names like Hundred Acre, Highside, Beckside, Rough Edge, Stoney Heights, Back Lane, Maypole Hill, The Bottoms, Low Leys, Croft End, The Carrs, Hagg End, Manor Intake, Hob Hole, Castle Lands, Hawthorn Leys, Lucy Ings and others.

Some of these names are self-explanatory, and others are widely used to describe the nature of a field. For example, a carr or The Carrs refers to an area of heavy, rough marshy ground which is not close to the moors, often being used in connection with a low-lying area.

Ings is another word for a pasture with these features – many local ings are covered with water and there is a fine example at Fairburn Ings, a modern haven for wild life close to the A1 near Ferrybridge in West Yorkshire. A ley is a rich arable field which has been put down to grass, while an intake of the kind mentioned earlier is generally a patch of land which has been reclaimed from the moor. In our local dialect the word is often abbreviated to intak. Of some curiosity-interest is the prefix Lucy, as in Lucy Ings mentioned above. This word is spoken and written in different ways, such as Lousey Lane, Lowsey Ings, Lucy Field and so forth. It is nothing to do with a girl called Lucy nor does it mean lousy (as in awful); it comes from an old word meaning pig-sty, one derivation of which is loosey. So Lousey Lane, Lowsey Ings or Lucy Field refers to places where pigs were once kept.

Another interesting word is neuk; it means the corner or angle of a field and is perhaps more widely known as nook, as in nooks and crannies. This also appears in some locations such as Cocquet Nook or Blew Neuk, both being place-names on the North York Moors.

During my patrols, I was frequently traversing the heights of the moors from which magnificent vantage points were available. Time and time again, it was possible to park my police motor cycle and sit astride it as I gazed across the panoramic landscape below.

The fields and meadows decorated the countryside in a manner which has become so much a part of the English country scene, and from these lofty positions I could only wonder at the range of colours, shapes and locations. From a distance and from a height, those meadows were truly a gigantic patchwork quilt, but in the course of their history, they had witnessed a thousand stories, ancient and modern. They had seen more changes and innovations than we might hope to recall, and many of them remained stubbornly silent about their experiences. Some, however, did contain relics of earthworks, old tumuli, bygone settlements and even Roman remains, and from these sources the history of our district could be told.

Sometimes, at the crack of dawn, I would sit upon my police motor cycle and gaze in wonder at the illusion of history before me; later, I came to realise that my own duty was somehow reflected by the changing circumstances of those meadows. Just as they appeared in many shapes and sizes, so did the duties I was bound to perform. Large tasks and little tasks, major incidents and minor jobs all came my way, and just as the meadows changed during the year, so did my work. It was altering all the time, with constant innovations forcing changes upon the entire police service, changes which eventually filtered down to my level. In a lifetime, those meadows would evolve beyond all present recognition but in spite of that, they would remain English meadows.

My work would be transformed too, but an underlying feature was that it would always be police work, albeit of a very special kind. Whatever variations were wrought upon society and upon the police service, the vital ground-level work of the constable would continue. With an air of permanence that can be under-estimated, those meadows and the British police constable will modify and be modified to accommodate society's needs.

I had arrived at Aidensfield just as the era of the pedal-cycling village constable was ending; I enjoyed the swift transportation offered by a little Francis Barnett two-stroke motor-cycle, even if that transportation was tainted with the need to cater for the British climate. To perform a patrol, however short, I had to smother myself in oily waterproofs and if I visited anyone's house, I had to stand outside lest the oil from the bike or water from the road caused damage to the home. Carrying papers and documents was fraught with danger and there were immense difficulties in conducting a roadside interview in pouring rain.

But, in many ways, I did enjoy my motor-cycle patrols. The power of freedom and the rush of fresh air combined to give a tremendous feeling of elation and I like to think this open-air life kept me healthy and free from colds. But change was on the horizon.

One day in early summer, I was informed that I was to be issued with a mini-van.

It would replace the motor cycle I used for my patrol work and at first I welcomed the news. A four-wheeled vehicle with a roof and comfortable seats would be so much better for my duties; I'd be able to carry equipment, forms and circulars and it would in all respects be a great improvement upon the motor bike. But there was one snag. I had to share the van with the constable on the neighbouring beat whose house was seven miles away. If the authorities could not appreciate the problems this would create, then I could. The chief snag would be the possibility that the little van would be miles away when I required it urgently. I might be marooned with no official transport. When a constable lives on official premises as I did, he must be expected to cope with any emergency that occurs, even during off-duty periods. And there would be complications in making the change-over at the end or the beginning of each shift whether it was then in my possession or the possession of a colleague. On paper, it seemed a feasible idea; in practice, I knew it would generate problems. But the police service, always a Cinderella when it comes to local authority expenditure, could not afford to supply every rural constable with a van.

Its arrival, however, signalled another change in the methods of patrolling a policeman's rural patch. Instead of being on duty twenty-four hours a day, the village bobby would now work in shifts of eight hours, sharing his beat with other constables and performing duties away from his own beat.

It meant that I must now patrol an expanded area, albeit for only eight hours a day, but my work would thus become more formalised and regimented. I would have to work shifts to accommodate the changing work pattern because, in order to ensure a full twenty-four hour cover every day of the year, the system requires about five officers. Three are needed every day to span the twenty-four hours in eight-hour shifts; to cater for days off, sickness, courses, holidays, court appearances and other absences, expected or unexpected, extra officers must be available. And so, with the stroke of a pen and the gift of a van, the policing of Aidensfield changed. I would be expected to patrol other parts of the district, while constables from afar would be invading my patch.

I did not welcome this; I would far rather have been fully responsible for the Aidensfield beat for twenty-four hours a day, and allowed to work at my own discretion. But it was not to be; progress had arrived and it could not be halted.

On the day the van was to be issued, I had to drive my little motor cycle over the hills to Police Headquarters. This was its last trip as a police motor cycle and it was rather sad; quite unexpectedly, I felt a twinge of sorrow at its departure and was tempted to try and buy it. But official wheels had already started to turn, and the Francis Barnett was to be sold, along with other redundant motor cycles, to the dealer who had won the contract to supply the vans. The outdated bikes were therefore part-exchanged for up-to-date transport in the shape of little grey vans.

Having said a rather emotional farewell to my bike, I relinquished my protective clothing, crash helmet and gauntlets and handed over the bike's log-book to the admin. department of our Road Traffic Division. Thus I severed all links with my motor cycle. I was shown to my new van which stood among rows of others awaiting their drivers; each was gleaming in the morning sunshine and they were all alike. There seemed to be hundreds of them, all in symmetrical rows with their bonnets facing east, but there were probably about fifty! Each was a brand-new Morris mini-van clad in a pleasing grey livery; this surprised me. I had expected black or navy blue, but it seemed the service was moving away from its past stereotype colours. Furthermore, none of the vans bore police signs, the only visible link with the service being the blue lamp perched in the centre of each roof. Inside the cab, however, there was a police radio set plus an official log-book for recording dates, times and distances of journeys, petrol issues, oil consumption and the name of each driver. There was a tool kit, a spare wheel and nothing else.

The rear of each little van was completely bare and empty; the ridged metal floor had no covering and there were no shelves or compartments for storage or for conveying the paraphernalia of constabulary duty. In truth, that empty rear compartment was of a very limited value; no one (except a child) could sit there although I did note the huge battery strapped down near one of the rear-wheel arches.

This had replaced the original car battery because of the additional power required for the radio which would be functional virtually round the clock, and for activating the flashing blue light should it ever be required. After a short course of instruction about operating the mini-van, the radio and the blue light, and a lecture about the need to regularly clean the vehicle inside and out, to rigidly abide by servicing dates and oil changes, to enter details in the log immediately upon completion of each journey and to report any fault however minor, I was allowed to leave.

It was at this point that another problem faced me and countless other constables. It was a simple problem – police officers are among the largest of people and mini-vans are among the smallest of motor vehicles. Getting some officers into those driving-seats was rather like a size 6 foot being squeezed into a size 4½ shoe. Not being as tall or as broad as some, I found that I could get into the driving-seat and, with the seat pushed back to its maximum, I could operate the foot pedals and hand controls. But I could not wear a cap while driving. Even though we wore peaked caps and not helmets, I now knew the purpose of that empty rear part – it was to carry the caps of constables at the wheel, even if they were liable to rattle around in that empty bare area. Once inside, however, I started the engine, listened to the crackle of the tiny exhaust and switched on the official radio. Having booked on the air, I found first gear, noted the fuel tank was full and set a course for Aidensfield.

On the journey home, I gained impressions of my cap bouncing around in the rear, of me bouncing around in the front and the little van *et al* bouncing across the moors. I was later to learn that passengers in mini-cars are nervously aware of this bouncing motion because their rumps hover dangerously near to the road surface while the suspension of the vehicle gives the overall feeling of riding in a high-speed motorised trampoline. But we made it.

During that half-hour trip, I learned to drive with my head slightly bowed to avoid crowning myself on the roof, and managed to manipulate the miniature pedals by judicious use of my police boots. Sometimes, however, the expanse which formed the soles of my boots made me strike two pedals at the same time, but protests from the mini rapidly corrected that fault. The simultaneous operation of a brake, clutch or accelerator is enough to confuse the cleverest of transmission systems and the mini had the sense to protest loudly and actively at this abuse.

Once at home, the children were delighted. Tiny as they were, they thought it was my personal van and so I let them sit in the back; for them, the experience was wonderful and they squeaked with delight as they tumbled and rolled about the bare metal floor. Lots of little faces peered out of the rear windows like miniature prisoners in a miniature Black Maria, and more squeals of delight occurred when one of them tweaked the switch of the rotating blue light which flashed and reflected brightly in the windows of the house.

They spent a few minutes playing in the van, sometimes listening to the burble of voices that muttered eternally from the official radio and sometimes pretending to drive it to an accompaniment of suitable brum-brums and pip-pips. It was a moment of fun in a vehicle that had a very official function to perform. After a coffee, I rang Sergeant Blaketon to announce my return to Aidensfield with the van and he ordered me to drive to Ashfordly Police Station so that he could formally inspect this newest of acquisitions. Before leaving, I made sure the children hadn't left anything in the van, because Oscar Blaketon was not the sort of person to appreciate a child's desperate need to play 'going to Nanna's' in Daddy's new police car.

I parked it outside the square brick-built police station at Ashfordly and entered; Sergeant Blaketon was writing something at the front desk and actually smiled at my arrival.

'All correct, Rhea?' he asked; this was his way of saying 'Hello.'

'All correct, sergeant,' I chanted the ritual response.

'The section's new vehicle functioning all right, is it?' he continued. 'No breakdowns, mechanical defects, malfunctioning of equipment, unnecessary rattles, squeaks or groans? Damage or wear and tear? Punctures or oil leaks?'

'No, it seems to go very well,' I said. 'Good acceleration, the braking seems OK and it corners very well. I didn't hit anything on the way here either,' I added.

'You're to share it with other beat men, Rhea.' His face never cracked at my veiled sarcasm, for his smile was now stored away for use at a future time. 'That van does not belong to Aidensfield beat, you appreciate?'

'Yes, I know that, sergeant.' I was now behind the counter and had removed my cap. I had some report writing to complete, and this seemed the ideal opportunity to do it on the office typewriter. 'You wanted to see the van?'

'In a moment, Rhea. I'm busy compiling a set of instructions right now,' he said. 'You'll have to familiarise yourself with them, so you might as well type them out for me. Copies to all users of the van, copy for the office notice-board, copy for Divisional HQ, and a copy to be stuck inside the van's log-book. All to note and sign as having read and digested the said instructions.'

I knew Blaketon's obsession for detail and his practice of committing his orders to writing; I could visualise the contents of his order. I was not disappointed when he presented his neat handwritten work for me to type. After identifying the vehicle by its registration number and the call sign of the radio set, he listed a host of 'do's and don'ts'.

These included the following:

'Members *will*, repeat *will*, maintain the vehicle in a roadworthy condition. Under no circumstances will road traffic laws and regulations be infringed. Members will therefore inspect the van before and after each journey.

'Members *will*, repeat *will*, inspect for defects such as faulty lights, worn tyres, defective windscreen wipers, brakes and steering, and any other fault, mechanical or otherwise, which might infringe either the Road Traffic Acts or the Construction and Use Regulations. The van will *not*, repeat *not*, be driven upon a road if it is in such a condition that statutory provisions are infringed.

'It will be the responsibility of drivers to thoroughly check the roadworthiness of the van; responsibility will be deemed to devolve upon the person driving it when such a fault develops. It will therefore be in the interests of all members to check the vehicle meticulously before taking it on the road. Any defects or damage then discovered *will*, repeat *will*, be reported immediately.

'Members *will*, repeat *will*, ensure that the vehicle is filled with petrol at the conclusion of every tour of duty, and that the oil, water and tyre pressures are checked, and if necessary, replenished. Details *will*, repeat *will*, be entered in the log-book, and in the pocket-books of the officers concerned. It is imperative that this instruction is obeyed. Failure will be considered a disciplinary offence.

'Members *will*, repeat *will*, ensure that the vehicle is driven courteously at all times and that drivers set an example to the public by the high standard of their driving.

'Members will *not*, repeat *not*, consume food or drink within the vehicle.

'Members *will*, repeat *will*, at all times be correctly dressed when using the vehicle. Caps *will*, repeat *will*, be worn, tunics will be fastened correctly and ties will be knotted. When meeting a senior officer of or above the rank of Inspector, members will emerge from the vehicle before saluting.

'Members will *not*, repeat *not*, carry unauthorised members of the public, friends or family in the vehicle, unless their presence is necessary in the performance of their duty, eg upon arrest or other emergency.

'Members *will*, repeat *will*, ensure that ashtrays are emptied regularly and that the vehicle is thoroughly cleansed inside and out at the conclusion of every tour of duty, unless the exigencies of the service prevent otherwise. In these circumstances, a report will be submitted to explain those exigencies.'

Having written out his instructions, he handed them to me and as I began transferring them to paper, he went outside to examine the van. He spent some minutes and I

saw him stooping to examine the tyres and to seek evidence
of any damage, however minor, that might be present. He
looked inside, checked the radio for its effectiveness and
the ashtray for residue, looking into the log-book and then
lifted the bonnet. He dipped the oil and spent some
minutes tugging at plug leads and checking internal engine
matters. Next he tested all the lights, the flashing indicators,
the windscreen wipers and washers and even the interior
light.

Then he took it for a brief drive around the block, and,
satisfied that it was absolutely correct, took out his own
pocket-book and made a note to that effect. Woe betide an
officer who might suggest the vehicle had been delivered
with a fault. Blaketon's record showed that it was in perfect
order upon arrival, therefore any faults which developed
would be the responsibility of the driver at the time. I knew
that we must all treat the van as if it were our very own and
I also knew that some officers, upon damaging an official
vehicle (even accidentally) would not mention the matter,
hoping that a subsequent driver would be careless enough
not to check the vehicle before taking it out. Thus blame or
responsibility could be avoided and the unwary innocent
saddled with another's sins. We all knew the value of being
ultra-cautious in such matters.

I completed Blaketon's piece of typing and made no
comment as I passed it to him for signature. By the time I
had finished my own work, copies had been signed and
one was prominent upon the office notice-board.

'So the van's yours for today and tomorrow, Rhea?' he
said.

'Yes, Sergeant.' After studying the duty sheets, I
understood the arrangements.

'So when you knock off duty tomorrow night, at ten,
you will deliver it to Falconbridge beat?'

'Yes, sergeant.'

'Make sure it's filled with petrol?' he said. I nodded.

'Shall I book off duty late then, or will PC Clough come on duty early?' I asked.

'I don't follow your logic, Rhea.'

Knowing his attitude for precise timing, I said, 'If I arrive at PC Clough's house at 10 p.m. to hand over the van, and he then drives me home, I will not be able to book off duty until 10.20 p.m. or thereabouts. I will be in uniform, in an official vehicle, with an officer who is on duty. So I will be on duty, won't I? And this will happen every time the van is handed over. One of us will have to work extra time either before our shift or after it. Shall we all claim overtime for the hand-overs, sergeant?'

He looked at me steadily, his dark eyes never showing any emotion . . .

'Rhea,' he said, 'a constable is never off duty.'

'So if the van is involved in a traffic accident as I am being taken home, and I am injured, will I be able to claim that I was injured on duty? It makes a huge difference if there is a question of compensation or an entitlement to an ill-health pension, sergeant.'

He knew I was right, and I guessed this aspect had never occurred to him, or to those who had dreamed up the system of change-overs in this way. He was thinking rapidly, mentally assessing the enormous legal complications which could accrue from any incident which might happen within those disputed few minutes.

'I will ask the superintendent to authorise half an hour's extra duty for at least one of the officers involved in every change-over,' he said. 'I will ask for it to be included on your overtime card and to be taken off when duty commitments allow.'

'Thank you, sergeant.' He knew, and I knew, that this

matter had to be determined right from the outset; minor though it appeared on the surface, there could be immense ramifications which might affect the officer or his family if something went wrong during those contentious few minutes. For an officer to be killed or injured when on duty differed hugely from one killed or injured when off duty.

The next problem, unforeseen by Sergeant Blaketon, occurred when the superintendent visited me at the beginning of one of my tours of duty. The little van was parked on the hard-standing in front of my police house and the superintendent parked behind it, awaiting my emergence from the house. He did not come to the office which adjoined, but preferred to wait outside to see if I was late on duty; that's how some senior officers operated. But I had seen the arrival of his black car and went outside prompt on the stroke of two o'clock. I was to perform an afternoon shift from 2 p.m. until 10 p.m., and had custody of the van because PC Clough of Falconbridge was enjoying a rest-day.

As I emerged, therefore, I slung up a smart salute and smiled as the superintendent clambered from his car.

'Now, Rhea,' he said. 'Anything to report?'

I updated him on events which had occurred on my beat over the past few days and he nodded approval at the way I had dealt with them. Then he turned his attention to the mini-van and asked my opinion upon its suitability.

I enthused over it, but refrained from mentioning the hand-over complications. Sergeant Blaketon would have seen to that – it was a matter of internal politics.

Then the superintendent began, 'I came past your house last night, Rhea, around midnight.'

'I finished at ten last night, sir. Same hours as today.'

'Yes, I know. And when I drove past, I saw the van parked there, on the hard-standing.'

'Yes, sir.'

'It was not in the garage, Rhea. There is a garage at your police house and I would have expected you to garage the van there, for security and safety.'

'It's a private garage, sir, my car's using it.'

'The official motor cycle used it, Rhea.'

'There was plenty of room for both, sir, I could park the bike alongside the car. That garage was added to the house long before official cars and motor bikes were issued. Garages adjoining rural-beat houses have always been used for the officer's private car.'

'Then I feel the practice must cease, Rhea. Now that you have the official use of a van, the van must surely take precedence over your private vehicle.'

I noticed that he did not directly order me to garage the van nor was I ordered to remove my car. I felt there was scope for manoeuvre which in turn suggested there was some official doubt about the rights of the occupants of police houses. After all, the police house was my home but unlike some civilian tenancies, there was no rental agreement. A police officer simply moved in and out when instructed and obeyed orders if there was a dispute. I knew of no order which dealt with the current matter and the only condition of occupancy that came to mind was that I could not take in lodgers without permission!

As I pondered the superintendent's remarks, I realised that if I was unreasonable in my attitude, he might post me to a less-than-pleasant urban area, and I felt sure there was scope for discussion or flexibility.

'You are responsible for the care of the van while it is in your possession,' he reminded me. 'It is a police vehicle and it does contain valuable police equipment, such as a radio. The van and contents are your responsibility, Rhea.'

'Yes, sir,' was all I said. I understood the import of his remarks.

'It will not be resting at your house every night,' he reasoned and I saw a twinkle in his eye. 'Others will be making regular use of it and it will be used for night shifts, so I think a little common sense will sort out this dilemma, don't you, Rhea?'

'Yes, sir,' I agreed.

And so it was. My private car continued to occupy the garage at my police house, and from time to time, I would give the mini a treat by placing it inside for the night. Then I discovered that if I parked the mini on the front lawn, it was obscured from the road by the privet hedge. Neither the superintendent nor Sergeant Blaketon was in the habit of coming into the house or office, preferring to wait outside at the other side of that tall, thick hedge. And if they could not see into my garden, then neither could potential breakers-in of police vans . . .

Common sense did prevail and no one grumbled about the van's open-air life.

The van, its other drivers and I soon settled into a trouble-free working routine and we had no problems; indeed, the little vehicle proved its worth over and over again. Its tiny engine and small size coped with the large constables it had to carry, and the steep hills of this dramatic part of Yorkshire. It was most useful for carrying assorted objects and for protecting us from the English weather, thus enabling constabulary duties to be performed with far greater ease than hitherto. But on one occasion when I was surreptitiously carrying a load of rather doubtful legality, I found myself face to face with the redoubtable Sergeant Blaketon.

It happened around 10 o'clock one Wednesday morning. I was working a day shift from 9 a.m. until 5 p.m., a rare treat. Such routines are few in a police officer's life and I was looking forward to the evening off. At 9 a.m., therefore, I began work in the office which adjoined the house and by 9.45 a.m. was ready to begin my patrol.

Just as I was leaving, my wife, Mary, rushed in.

'Oh, thank heaven I caught you!' she panted. 'The car won't start.'

An immediate problem was presented, for it was Mary's turn to convey seven or eight children to the village play school. Elizabeth, our eldest, had started play school and thoroughly enjoyed it, and the mums worked on a rota system, each taking their turn to tour the nearby farms and cottages to collect pre-school-age youngsters. It was an important part of village life, a bonus for the children and a welcome tonic for the mums.

I had a quick look at our car and decided the battery was flat; it had been causing problems in recent weeks and I had never got around to replacing it. Now I had no choice and would obtain a battery today, but first, we had pressing commitments to keep. Those youngsters and their mums would be awaiting collection at farm gates, isolated spots and remote cottages.

'I'm going out on patrol,' I said. 'I'll collect them. Give me a list.'

And so, armed with a list of children's names and addresses, I set about this mission. Most of the mums saw nothing odd in their local constable collecting their offspring in a police van, while the children thought it was marvellous. Squatting on the cold, hard metal floor, they pretended they were chasing robbers as they listened to the dour voice from the police radio. They blew the horn and Elizabeth showed them how to flash the blue light, as a result of which we flashed the light at every halt to announce our arrival. By the time I returned to Aidensfield, the rear of the van, and the front passenger seat, were full of small, noisy but excited children. I had lost count of the number on board, but they seemed so happy at this change in their routine.

They babbled and chattered, made police siren noises, caught robbers, arrested thieves, chased speeders, battered my brain with questions, and generally created something of a party atmosphere in the back of the little van. The bouncing didn't seem to bother them, for in their minds, they were keen police officers engaged upon a matter of grave importance. I've no idea how many villains we arrested on that trip, but I reckon each child caught several and tonight they would recount their experiences to their dads. As a public relations exercise it was marvellous and as a means of getting those children to school it was a success.

But the noise they generated within the confines of the van was colossal and I was pleased I was not a play-school teacher having to tolerate it for longer periods. On the last lap, I turned into Aidensfield and was about to drive down the lane to the house which hosted the school, when I saw the tall, severe figure of Sergeant Blaketon standing on the corner of the road. My heart sank. Of all the people to meet this morning of all mornings . . . I thought of his instructions about using the van, about unauthorised passengers, about disciplinary proceedings, about the law on overloading, about insecure loads . . .

I had probably broken several laws on my goodwill mission.

I could not avoid him. I eased to a halt before him, flushing furiously as I anticipated his wrath. I switched off the engine and climbed out, my mind full of excuses, reasons, apologies . . .

'It was urgent . . .' I began.

But he ignored me and thrust his head inside the van and I heard him say, 'Now then, what's going on in there?'

There was an instant babble of juvenile response; I heard tiny voices shouting at him about catching robbers and poachers and making people drive better and then, after asking more questions and generally joining in the chit-chat, he emerged.

'Is this the village bus service, Rhea?' he asked me.

'Er, no, sergeant, you see . . . well . . . they're going to play school . . . er . . . the car taking them wouldn't start, you see, so they were stuck . . . I . . . well . . .'

'Got a Public Service Vehicle operator's licence, have you?' was his next question. 'Know about seating requirements in vehicles, do you? Safety of passengers?'

'Er, well, sergeant,' I babbled. 'It was an emergency . . .'

'So all you lot have been arrested, have you?' He poked his head inside again.

'Ye . . . e . . . e . . . e . . . s . . .' came the sing-song response. He emerged, smiling with joy.

'Nice one, Rhea. Creating goodwill with the public and making the kids happy, eh? All right, carry on.'

And so I did.

I learned afterwards that the play-school teacher had asked them to draw a police van and, without exception, they had included Sergeant Blaketon's big smiling face.

2

Our deeds still travel with us from afar,
And what we have been makes us what we are.

George Eliot, 1819-80

Patrolling in the warmth and comfort of the mini-van was
heavenly after the inconvenience of the motor cycle and I
think it is fair to say that one adverse effect was to make us
rather lazy. When using the motor cycle, particularly during
chilly weather, it was sensible to walk as much as possible,
if only to keep warm. But that exercise was unnecessary
with the mini-van. We were cosseted in an all-embracing
warmth from which, especially in the chill of a long night,
we were unwilling to emerge. This tended to make us drive
where we should have walked; we took the van around all
manner of unlikely places, roaming behind buildings,
through factory premises, into farmyards, along narrow
alleys and over fields, all of which were the kind of places we
should have walked in our efforts to prevent and detect
crime.

Our supervisory officers and our own consciences told
us it was not a good thing to spend so much time sitting in
a van, that exercise was necessary for continuing good
health and that foot patrols were a vital part of the constable's
crime-preventing and public relations repertoire. Each of
us appreciated such precepts and although we began our
patrols with those aims uppermost in our minds, they soon

evaporated once we settled into the cosy routine of heated and motorised patrolling.

We learned, for example, the best places to park in order to shine either the van's headlights or our own torch beams upon vulnerable windows and doors; we located places in which the van could be concealed for a short nap, a tasty but forbidden sandwich or sip of coffee from a flask. We knew where to hide from Sergeant Blaketon or which unmapped track offered the best short-cut through the lush and scented meadows of Ryedale.

It was a bout of idleness of this kind which led me into a spot of bother one night. It happened like this. Tucked in the centre of my beat, well away from urban civilisation, was a derelict airfield. The nearest village was Stovensby, a tiny collection of pretty stone houses on a gently rising street, and everyone knew this patch of cracked concrete and unsightly old huts as Stovensby Airfield even though no aircraft had used it since the end of World War II. Leading from the village into one corner of the airfield was a narrow, unmade lane, across which someone had, years ago, erected a gate.

As time passed, however, that gate had fallen into disrepair which meant that courting couples, trespassers and all manner of other inquisitive folk ventured on to the airfield from time to time, perhaps to steal bits and pieces from the derelict buildings or perhaps to conceal themselves in the old ruins so that their love-making was kept a secret from prying eyes, as well as from suspicious husbands, wives and neighbours.

Squatters, tramps, down-and-outs and persons on the run from life, from HM Forces, from the police or from their families would sometimes hide here too.

The area covered by the old airfield was huge; remnants of the Air Traffic Control Tower remained, as did buildings which had been Station Headquarters, Squadron offices, hangars, sleeping accommodation, etc. Many of them were windowless, some were roofless and none had been officially occupied or used for almost a quarter of a century. In the broad light of day, the airfield reeked of dereliction and decay, although the old runways themselves were in fairly good order. They were like huge modern highways which crossed and re-crossed this patch of Ryedale and they had survived surprisingly well without any formal maintenance. The area between them comprised overgrown grass, weed and scrubland, although some of the fertile areas had been leased to a local farmer who managed to grow wheat there.

No one seemed quite sure who owned the airfield; perhaps the Air Ministry had forgotten it was there, perhaps someone had purchased it years ago and had no idea what to do with it . . . I never knew. What I did know, however, was that the deserted runways were regularly used by learner drivers, by young men who fancied themselves as racing motorists, by teenage motor-cyclists who roared about the place doing crazy things with their moving machines such as wheelies or headstands on the saddles, and even by pedal-cyclists who organised time trials and races around the perimeter track.

The old notices saying 'Trespassers Will Be Prosecuted' or 'Air Ministry Property – Keep Off' had fallen down and although there could have been a question of illegal use, it was not the job of the civilian police to enforce any such rules. We knew that the public, rightly or wrongly, made use of the old airfield and we did not raise any formal objection because we knew where many of the youngsters got to. They were safe here, far better using this enclosed area for racing or showing off than attempting their doubtful skills on the open road.

So we closed our 'official' eyes to the many trespassers although, at night, we did make routine patrols through the airfield, checking for possible lawbreakers who might dump stolen cars here, steal bits from the buildings, cause damage or perform a host of other illegal acts. Children on the run from school or home were another aspect of our searches, as were depressed folks who wanted to be left alone with their thoughts, or even to commit suicide.

One night in early May, I was performing an all-night duty, having started at 10 p.m. I booked myself on duty from home by ringing Eltering Police Station at 10 p.m. and asked for any routine messages. I was given a list of unsolved crimes committed locally during the day, plus details of a car which had been stolen from Scarborough. It was a Ford Consul, five years old and a dark green colour, and it had been stolen from outside the Spa before eight that evening.

According to the police at Eltering, a villager from Stovensby had telephoned at quarter to ten to report a car with blazing lights repeatedly circling the old airfield at high speed. There was just a possibility that it was the missing vehicle in the hands of joy-riders, as other cars stolen from the coast had been found abandoned here.

I was therefore asked to check out this report.

It was a foul night with pouring rain and lingering mist as I arrived in Stovensby village. The time would be around 10.20 p.m. and the late spring dusk had matured into a heavy darkness due to the weather. I drove the little van down to the fallen gate which marked the entrance to the airfield, the windscreen wipers having trouble coping with the teeming rain. I extinguished the van lights as I peered through the gloom, hoping to catch sight of roving car lights somewhere in that vast expanse of misery and darkness. I saw none, so maybe my own approaching lights had alerted the thieves. Perhaps they'd gone? Perhaps it was just a local lad having a fling around the place in his own car? Maybe it was thieves who had run for shelter and were hiding in one of the many disused buildings? The lights could have been anything or anyone, harmless or potentially harmful.

I waited for five or ten minutes; there was no sign of activity on that airfield, not a hint, not a light. But if a car had been seen earlier – and not all that much earlier – then a full search would have to be made.

To make a proper search, I should really walk; I should take a torch although, strictly speaking, I should make a search in complete darkness so as to surprise the villains in possession of the stolen property. In the darkness, I could creep up on them . . . But, I reasoned, if they were in a car, they could escape simply by driving off and I would be marooned in the middle of the airfield with no car, no radio and no chance of catching them. I reckoned that if I circled the airfield in the mini-van, shining my lights into and behind all the old buildings, I might flush out the thieves. Then I could give chase, and my radio would allow me to summon any necessary aid. That seemed a far better idea.

So I switched on my lights, crossed through that tumbledown gate and found myself driving along the glistening wet concrete of an old wartime runway. The rain, the mist and the darkness made driving very difficult, and without a detailed knowledge of the layout of the airfield, I really had no idea where I was heading. My only hope was to pick out the buildings one by one and then scan them in my headlights. If I did detect anything or anyone suspicious, then a more detailed search could follow.

With the excitement of the chase making my heart pound just a little faster, I located the first of the buildings and drove towards it; it was an old hangar, vast and empty in the darkness so I drove right inside, did a sweeping turn in the mini and watched as the beams explored every corner.

Old oil drums littered the floor, a few rats scuttled off at my intrusion and there was an old settee against the far wall, but it was otherwise deserted. I moved to the next location, another hangar similarly deserted. As I searched each building, the radio in the van burbled into life and I recognised my own call sign.

'Echo Seven,' it said. 'Location please.'

Every half-hour, our Control Room sought our location in this manner, then plotted our movements on a map so the most conveniently-positioned vehicle could be directed to any incident. It was also a means of checking our individual safety; if we failed to respond, we might be in trouble.

'Echo Seven,' I spoke into the mouthpiece. 'Stovensby Airfield.'

'Received. Echo Nine?' the next car was requested.

As locations were sought from every mobile on duty, I continued my search. Sometimes, I walked in the light of those headlamps, sometimes I drove around a block or behind the more remote buildings, but I did make sure that every possible hiding place was examined. As I progressed, I found it was becoming more difficult to see the buildings ahead; the rain and mist obscured them and so I found myself having to drive at a crawling pace in the gloom. From time to time I'd leave the van with its engine running and lights blazing as I fought my way through the thickening mist to a building with a difficult access.

I must have searched every conceivable nook and cranny without finding anything remotely suspicious, by which time I had decided that no stolen car was hidden there.

There was nothing and no one lurking on that deserted airfield. Of that, I was positive.

I radioed Control. 'Echo Seven,' I announced. 'Have completed search of Stovensby Airfield for reported stolen vehicle from Scarborough. No trace. Am resuming patrol. Over.'

'Received Echo 7. Control out.'

With the windscreen wipers assailing the tumbling rain, and the dense fog now blanketing the entire airfield, I screwed my eyes against the white screen outside. While I had been busily searching the buildings, the fog had dramatically intensified and now I could barely see the runway ahead of me. I could not determine the edges of the concrete . . . I moved to one side, swerving to catch a glimpse of the runway's extremities. I failed. The twin beams cut into the fog like two long shafts of solid light, but they did not penetrate it. The light simply reflected back at me. I was moving at less than walking pace now, my head out of the window hoping to see where I was heading . . .

But I was hopelessly lost. I'd lost all contact with the buildings which had, to some extent, broken the fog's density and I was encircled by a thick white blanket of dripping clinging mist. I was somewhere inside a dark fog-bound wilderness and had lost all sense of direction.

I found myself fighting the onset of panic; I knew that I was only a few miles from home and from civilisation, but at the same time, could not find the route which led off this old airfield. It was almost like being trapped, like driving through a black, unlit tunnel and into a massive blockade of cotton wool; the mist was so thick that it had become a wall of brilliant white through which nothing could apparently pass. Although I was still driving, I had no impression of movement or distance for I could see nothing but the reflected glow of my headlights. I was upon a featureless plain and the headlights would not even pick out the surface of the runway. I had no idea whether I was in the middle, on the edge, doing a circuit of the perimeter track or simply driving around in circles on an expanse of featureless concrete. I have never been so helpless. It was like one of those nightmarish dreams that childhood worries can cause and there seemed no immediate relief.

I knew it would become easier in daylight, but dawn was hours away, and I felt such an idiot. I was lost within such a small patch of England . . . but I could not stay here all night. I had to find a way off, and so I kept moving. Once or twice, I ran off the edge of the runway, but fortunately the ground was solid enough to carry the weight of the mini-van, and after each mishap I managed to regain the solid surface. I had no idea how long I'd been looking for the exit until my call-sign sounded from the radio.

'Echo Seven, location please,' asked the voice.

I must have been chugging around for nearly half an hour! I did a rapid mental calculation. If I failed to reply to this request, Control would think I was missing or injured, and a search would be established. And in this fog, more officers could get lost as they hunted for me! Furthermore, at the last 'locations' I'd already said that I was resuming patrol and if I now announced that I was lost in the airfield, I'd look a real idiot in the eyes of our Control Room staff.

Surely I would soon find the exit? I'd been going round in circles for ages, and must have covered miles, however slowly I'd been driving.

'Echo Seven, not receiving. Echo Seven, location please,' repeated the voice.

'Echo Seven.' I decided to pretend I was patrolling normally and made a guess about where I might have been if I'd emerged from the airfield. 'Echo Seven. A170, travelling east and approaching Brantsford. Over.'

'Received, Echo Seven. Echo Nine, your location please,' all cars were now being asked this question.

As the half-hourly ritual continued, I renewed my efforts to drive off the runway. Travelling at less than walking speed in the darkness, often with my head out of the window for better vision, I continued to search. But it was hopeless. By the time of the next 'locations' call, I was still on the airfield. But I daren't admit it.

When Control Room next asked Echo Seven for its location, I said, 'Echo Seven. Eltering towards Cattleby.'

'Received Echo Seven,' responded the voice. 'Echo Nine?'

And so it continued. I daren't halt the vehicle for any length of time in the fog to search on foot in case the battery could not cope with the demands upon it from the combined effects of the heater, radio and the lights; I did not feel inclined to switch off the lights in this ghastly silent world. So I continued to drive around; in any case, I wanted to find my way out! For each half-hour, therefore, I provided a fictitious location when asked, and when the time came for my refreshment break at 2 a.m., I took a gamble.

We were supposed to take our refreshment breaks at police stations and not in our vehicles; I knew Ashfordly was unmanned at night and hoped no one would attempt to contact me there by telephone. So, when I would normally have broken my tour of duty for refreshments, I radioed to Control 'Echo Seven, refreshments Ashfordly. Over.'

'Received, Echo Seven.'

I halted in the gloom and had my break at the wheel, in contravention of Sergeant Blaketon's rule about not eating or drinking in the mini-van. I kept the engine running and the equipment and lights operating, for I needed light and heat, and then, after enjoying my sandwiches and flask of coffee, I decided to risk a brief exploration on foot. I'd leave the lights on and the engine running so that I could re-trace the van. Perhaps this would help me find the exit?

With my hand torch, I tried to determine my whereabouts but failed. In whatever direction I walked, I found nothing but more featureless expanse of runway and the thickest fog I'd ever encountered. I daren't stray too far from the car either, in case I failed to re-locate it. And so, at 2.45 a.m. at the official termination of my break, I had no alternative but to recommence my circuits of the airfield.

'Echo Seven,' I introduced myself. 'Resuming patrol at Ashfordly, towards Gelderslack.'

'Received Echo Seven,' acknowledged Control.

And so the second half of my shift began. The rain had ceased now, but the fog had not lifted and the darkness was just as intense, but I knew that before my knocking-off time at six o'clock, daylight would arrive. This would help me find a route off this awful place.

For the next two and a half hours or so, I continued to provide fictitious locations, listing places I would have visited during a normal night patrol. Happily, it was a very quiet night and I was never directed to any incident. And then, soon after I'd given my final location at 5.30 a.m., the fog lifted. A gentle breeze had risen as dawn was pushing the darkness aside, and I saw the distinct movement of the thick fog. Wisps began to float away and then, with remarkable speed, it began to disperse. In the daylight, I could now see the outline of some buildings and hazy roofs of the village on the edge of the airfield.

And I was less than a hundred yards from the exit!

I need hardly express the cheer that I felt as I drove out of that old gate, and with considerable relief, I made for home. According to the log-book which I had to complete,

I had covered nearly forty miles around that airfield, a useful distance for a night patrol. My eyes were red-rimmed and sore with the strain of staring into that wall of fog, and I was mentally shattered.

I arrived home at six o'clock to find Sergeant Blaketon and PC Clough waiting for me. They were in Sergeant Blaketon's official car. Clough was to take the van out from 6 a.m. until 2 p.m., and on this occasion, Sergeant Blaketon had decided upon an early visit to both Ken Clough and myself. And he had undertaken to ferry my colleague to Aidensfield Police House to collect the van.

'Morning, Rhea,' he said as I emerged, bleary-eyed and very anxious to get some sleep. 'All correct?'

'All correct, sergeant,' I managed to say.

'The duty chap at Eltering said something about you searching for a stolen car on the old airfield.'

'Yes, sergeant. I searched for it just after commencing my shift. It wasn't there.'

'You sure?'

'Yes, sergeant!' I snapped the answer. 'I searched every possible place. The airfield was deserted.'

'Good. I thought you'd have done a thorough job.'

'Is there a problem?' I asked.

'It's just that Eltering Police Station got one or two calls during the night from residents at Stovensby. They reckoned cars were running round the airfield all night. They reported seeing lights and hearing engines in the fog. Eltering's sending a car to have a look in daylight – apparently, a road-traffic car attempted to investigate last night, but turned back because of dense fog.'

'I've just come from there, sergeant,' I decided to tell him. 'I did a final search myself, in daylight with the fog thinning. I saw nothing – that was only half an hour ago.'

'They must have imagined it, Rhea. So, nothing else to report, eh?'

'No, sergeant,' I said with determination.

'Good, then sleep well,' and they left me.

It was a long, long time before I returned to Stovensby Airfield and I never ventured there during a fog!

Mind, there were times when I wondered how those wartime pilots had coped with these Stovensby pea-soupers. Perhaps they had never become airborne, pretending instead to fly upon long circuitous missions into enemy territory?

There was another occasion when a duty trip in the little van caused something of a headache, and again it involved a journey which would certainly have caused Sergeant Blaketon to consult his book of rules. Happily, he never learned of this particular mishap.

Like so many memorable incidents, this one happened through a chance conversation. I was on patrol in the mini-van with instructions to deliver a package to a member of the Police Committee who lived on the edge of my beat. The package had come from the Chief Constable via our internal mail system and I was the final courier in this postal routine. I think it contained a selection of local statistics and pamphlets required for a crime prevention seminar in which she was to be involved. She was out when I arrived, but I spotted a gardener at work in the grounds of her spacious home and he told me to leave the mail in the conservatory. She'd find it there, he assured me. He pointed me towards the door and then, eager for a moment's respite, asked me how my family and I were settling in. I did not know the man, but saw this as yet another example of how the public knows the affairs of their village constable!

As I'd been at Aidensfield for a year or two by this time,

I was able to say we were very happy and enjoying both the area and the work.

'Got the garden straight, have you?' he asked with real interest, and perhaps a little professional curiosity.

'Not really,' I had to admit. I love a well-tended garden which comprises vegetables, flowers and shrubs, but I never seemed to have the time to create the garden of my dreams. Mary, however, in spite of coping with four tiny children and a hectic domestic routine, did manage to spend some time tending the garden.

I told him all this and he smiled.

'Tell her not to be frightened to ask if she needs owt,' he offered. 'Cuttings, seeds, bedding plants, that sort o' thing.'

'Thanks, it's good of you,' I responded.

'Well, we've often a lot o' spare stuff and t'missus is happy to give bits and pieces to t'locals.' By 't'missus' he meant his employer. 'You've only to ask.'

It was at this point that I remembered Mary asking me to keep an eye open for horse manure during my patrols; she'd mentioned it some days ago and it had slipped my mind until now.

'That reminds me,' I said half apologetically, 'she did ask me to look out for some horse manure. That was ages ago.'

'Ah, we don't have any o' that,' he said. 'But there's plenty at Keldhead Stables. They can't get rid of it fast enough. It's free to take away. Just go along and help yourself.'

'They're the racing stables, aren't they?' I asked.

'Aye, they get some good winners from there if you're a betting man. Grand National, Cheltenham, Lincoln, Derby – they've won some big races. You can't go far wrong if you follow them – they've often winners at Stockton, Thirsk, Ripon, Beverley and Wetherby an' all. I don't mind admitting I've won a bob or two on 'em.'

'So their manure should make our rambling roses gallop along, eh?' I laughed. 'Thanks, if I'm ever out that way, I'll pop in.'

We chatted about other trivia then I moved on. Keldhead Stables was off my beat in another section and it was highly unlikely that I would be able to pop in during a duty patrol, so I made a mental note to tell Mary. Perhaps we'd make a special trip there on my day off.

Then, through one of those flukes of circumstance, I was directed there within a week of learning about their manure offer. It was a Saturday evening in late May and I was making a patrol from 5 p.m. until 1 a.m., being responsible for the entire section in my little van. Shortly after 7 p.m., I received instructions over my radio to proceed immediately to Keldhead Stables where a prowler had been sighted – by chance, I was the nearest mobile.

This was not uncommon – people did trespass upon the stables' premises, sometimes just out of curiosity or to see a famous winning horse in its home surrounds. The motives of some, however, were a little more suspect because, at some other stables, there had been attempts to dope horses which were favourites to win. Scares of this kind had led to increased security at all racing-stables (and many existed in our area), consequently reports of such trespassers were fairly frequent.

I rushed towards Keldhead and drove into the stable yard. Waiting for me was J.J. Stern, the noted trainer, and his face bore clear signs of relief at my arrival. After a very brief chat, he pointed towards the stable block and said a lad had seen a man creeping furtively about. By now, something around half an hour had passed and I felt sure any visitor would have left, but I made a thorough initial search of the premises. Stern had already examined his

horses without finding a fault and nothing appeared to
have been damaged or stolen. With a stable lad in tow to
guide me through the complex of buildings, I made a
second very detailed examination. It took some time, but I
found no one.

Afterwards, I detailed my actions to J.J. Stern and
advised him that if other uninvited guests trespassed on his
premises, he should take care to record a detailed
description of the visitors, and to obtain the registration
number of any suspect cars that were around. So many
people fail to do this when they see a suspect car – a car
number in these circumstances is vital to an investigation
and can very swiftly help to trace the culprits.

He thanked me and said he would issue instructions to
his staff to follow my advice. Then he asked if I'd like a
coffee. It was at this point that I remembered Mary's wish
for some manure – and at this very moment I was
surrounded by a huge amount of surplus horse muck.

I hesitated to ask, but he had guessed I was about to
make a request of some kind. He must be plagued with
people asking for winning tips, but I was not seeking this
kind of information . . .

He smiled as if not to discourage me.

'Er,' I began. 'While I'm here, I was told you had some
horse manure to get rid of.'

'Manure? Tons of it! Want some, Mr Rhea?'

'I wouldn't mind some, not a lot . . . I'll pay,' I offered.
'I can help myself . . .'

'Nonsense. It's free to any good home! We just want
shot of it. Look, you've earned a coffee for your advice, so
come into the office and I'll get young Christine to pop
some in your van. Are the rear doors open?'

'I'll unlock them,' I said, and I did, leaving them standing
open.

In the office, he picked up the intercom telephone, dialled an extension and a girl answered.

'Christine,' he said. 'There's a police van in the yard. Pop some manure in the back, will you? The doors are open.'

She agreed and he replaced the phone. 'She's new here,' he said. 'Only sixteen, but she's mad on horses. It's only her first week, so it'll do her good to see what goes on.'

He organised a cup of coffee, asking if I would like a touch of Scotch with it, but as I was on duty and driving, I declined the latter offer. The coffee would be fine.

We chatted for about quarter of an hour, he telling me about his life in horse racing, and me trying to explain a little about the work of a rural constable. He was a charming man, I decided.

Just as I stood up to depart, his telephone rang so I excused myself and left him to deal with his caller. When I got outside, the van doors were closed and there was no sign of Christine; I had never even seen the girl and could not even thank her for her trouble.

But when I opened the driver's door, I was horrified. The stench that met me was appalling, and as I stared into the rear compartment, I saw that it was full of hot, fresh horse manure. It was neatly spread across the width and along the length of the back of the van.

She had filled every space, but she had not bagged it; she had simply shovelled muck into the back of the van, as a farmer would have shovelled muck into a cart. I could have died on the spot. What on earth could I do?

I thought fast, closing the door to shut off some of the stink; if I returned to complain to J.J. Stern, he'd probably fire the girl . . . and it would look as if I was rejecting his generosity . . . I decided to drive away.

Gingerly, therefore, I climbed into the malodorous

interior, already feeling itchy as flies were buzzing around, and began the trip home. The weight in the rear was enormous and it affected the steering, making it dangerously light as I took to the winding lanes to avoid being seen.

I opened all the windows and found that the flow of fresh air did keep some of the powerful pong at bay, but it was a terrible journey. My uniform and hair would reek of the stuff when I emerged.

After radioing Control to say I had searched Keldhead Stables but had found no intruder, I decided to sneak home and remove the muck. But on the way, I got a call to a road traffic accident about two miles from Aidensfield. Groaning, I could not avoid this duty; happily, it was not serious and no one was hurt. A farm lorry and an old Ford Cortina had collided on a junction near Briggsby, but the lorry had been carrying farm manure too, several tons of it. Due to the accident, it had been catapulted from the lorry and had almost smothered the car and peppered both drivers.

The Cortina, a battered old vehicle, had been carrying a drum of waste oil on the back seat. The oil drum had overturned inside the car, resulting in a terrible mess to both the car and its driver. The fulsome smell surrounding this scenario was dreadful, so much so that the contribution made by my uniform and van was of no consequence. After dealing with the accident and arranging for the load, the vehicles and the mess to be removed, I chugged home.

There is no need to explain the effects of this combination of events upon my person and upon the little van, save to say that Mary and I spent the next three hours frantically trying to remove the muck and then attempting to rid the van of the lingering effluvium.

But the manure had filtered into every possible crevice; try as we might, we never did remove it all.

I bathed and changed my uniform for the second half of my patrol, but the miasma remained; I cleaned the rear several times afterwards, using all kinds of disinfectants and smelly things, but it seemed that for ever afterwards, the mini-van smelled of horse muck. Some of the other drivers, including Sergeant Blaketon, did from time to time refer to the redolence; I said it had come from dealing with the accident to the muck-carrying lorry, some of which had penetrated our official vehicle. I'm sure he did not believe me, but he never questioned me further. After all, it was I who had to live with the unwholesome results of my manure venture.

In spite of everything, we should not criticise that young girl – after all, she had obeyed her boss's instructions to the very letter. However, the incident did teach me that orders must be precisely and clearly given if they are to be properly obeyed. And so Mary got her muck and the garden did benefit from it.

On another occasion, a car also landed me in trouble, but it was not a police car this time. It was my own.

Even though we had been issued with our little van, the faceless powers-that-be felt it was prudent that, from time to time, we patrolled on foot.

I think this idea came to them because there were, inevitably, occasions when two rural beat constables were on duty at the same time, when both simultaneously required the official van.

Clearly, we could not patrol together, consequently when our duties overlapped in this way, one of us was scheduled to work a foot patrol, perhaps for four hours or even for eight. Now, in a city or town, this is a splendid idea and there is no finer way for a constable to meet the public and for them to meet him. But it does not quite operate the same way in rural North Yorkshire.

For one thing, villages or centres of population are several miles apart. Another thing is that such centres may contain only six or eight houses and a telephone kiosk, added to which many of the farms which created our work were located some distance away from these little villages. Furthermore, our patrols were governed by the location of telephone kiosks because we had to stand beside a nominated kiosk every hour on the hour in case our superiors wished to contact us, or in case there was an emergency.

How we would have travelled to any emergency was never discussed, but this system meant that we spent about an hour walking along deserted country lanes between villages, following which we stood beside a telephone kiosk for five minutes. After that, it was time to walk to the next village which meant we never had time to meet people or time to perform any duty of more than a minute or two's duration.

To my simple mind, it seemed very silly to spend periods of almost one whole hour beyond communication with the public. Virtually the only companions I had upon those long country walks were the beasts, birds and insects of the fields and hedgerows. Cars carrying people did flash past and occasionally one would halt to ask whether I required a lift anywhere, but such occurrences were rare. More often than not, I simply left one village telephone kiosk and walked to the next without meeting a solitary person.

From a purely selfish point of view, it was marvellous. It meant I was getting paid for regularly taking a most enjoyable walk through some of England's most beautiful countryside, a pleasure for which many were prepared to pay considerable sums or to travel long distances. But from a police efficiency point of view, it was ridiculous. The amount of official time wasted was considerable and besides, what aspects of police work could I engage upon in such circumstances? The answer was nil, other than a spot of musing upon aspects of the profession.

I had a word with the Inspector about this ludicrous situation, but his response was simple. 'If it says foot patrol on the duty sheets, then that's what you must do.'

I attempted to defend my logic by saying that an hour spent in every village *en route* would be far more beneficial than an hour spent plodding along an empty road; if I spent time in a village, I could meet the people and undertake the traditional role of a village constable.

There were always enquiries to complete about local crimes or happenings, investigations to be made and contacts to be established. But my reasoning fell on deaf ears. Foot patrols were foot patrols and there must be no arguments against the system. Try as I might, I could not persuade anyone to change the useless ritual. Then, one foul and rainy day, I hit upon a solution.

Rather than endure many hours walking to nowhere in the pouring rain, I decided to use my own private car to transport myself between the villages. I would not claim anything by way of expenses from the police authority; I would quietly drive between points for my own convenience and peace of mind. This would enable me to spend the best part of an hour in each of the villages upon my route, so giving me a greater opportunity for solving crimes, meeting people, getting acquainted with the locality, absorbing knowledge about the area and its personalities and, in fact, doing all those varied jobs a police officer should do.

None of my superiors knew about this little scheme, and so when I was next detailed to undertake a foot patrol of this kind, I decided I would once again use my own car to transport me between points. Upon arrival in each of the villages, I would conceal it well away from the telephone kiosk, just in case the sergeant, the inspector or the superintendent called on me and objected to my enterprise. So far as they were concerned, I was still spending all my time on foot.

I almost fell foul of the superintendent on one occasion because I arrived in Elsinby by car, only to find him standing at the telephone kiosk, awaiting me. And he was a witness to my arrival in this very unofficial transport.

With some apprehension, I parked and walked towards him, throwing up a smart salute upon my approach. He chatted amiably for a while and then threw in the barbed question, 'Why are you using your private car, PC Rhea?'

'I've a firearms certificate to renew, sir, at Toft Hill Farm. It expires this week. It's a mile and a half out of the village, and I wouldn't have had time to do that, and then walk to my next point on time.'

It was true, as it happened, and he accepted my excuse.

'Well, so long as you don't do this regularly, PC Rhea. Remember, this system is designed as a foot patrol.'

'Yes, sir.' I had become too wise to argue and quietly determined that I would studiously ignore this instruction, albeit with the knowledge that he would inform the inspector of my transgression. But I could easily conceal the car in countless hiding places at every village I visited. And so that is how I conducted my foot patrols.

Then, on a damp, cold and foggy evening one November, I was performing yet another of these marathon patrols. This one, whether by accident or design I am not sure, took me to the more remote corners of my patch. I had started at 5 p.m., and was due to patrol, on foot, through those remote lanes until 1 a.m. with a refreshment break around mid-way.

In my view, to patrol on foot along unlit roads in the foggy darkness was rank stupidity. It was both dangerous and futile, and so I decided to use my own car. Things went well until I arrived at my 8 p.m. point in Ploatby; in that time, I had managed to call at local inns, to chat to residents and to conduct a miscellany of minor enquiries. And then, as I stood beside the lonely kiosk in the thickening fog, the inspector arrived in his official car.

'Ah, Rhea,' he smiled. 'Nasty night. Anything to report?'

I detailed some of the duties I had performed since starting work at five and he expressed his satisfaction. Then, after signing my pocket-book to record this conference, he appeared to have an attack of benevolence.

'Shocking night, Rhea.' He regarded the deepening fog. 'Where's your next point?'

'Nine o'clock, sir, at Waindale, then I'm off duty at ten o'clock at home for my refreshment break.'

'With a long wet walk in between, eh? In that case jump in. I'll give you a lift to Aidensfield, you can make your nine o'clock point there instead of Waindale. Then you can patrol your own village until refreshment time. I'll inform Control of the change. It's silly tramping these lanes in this fog.'

For a moment, I wondered if some of my earlier protestations had had an impact, then I realised with horror that it would mean leaving my own car abandoned out here.

And if I left my car here, it would mean a long walk back for it! Or, I might cadge a lift . . . As I dithered in my momentary indecision, he unlocked the passenger door and waved me in.

'Come on, Rhea, I haven't got all night.'

As he issued his order in those curt words, all thoughts of refusing his offer evaporated and so, with my heart sinking at the thought of a long trek back here, I settled in the warm and comfortable front seat of his fine vehicle. He drove confidently and smoothly away and within quarter of an hour was dropping me in the splash of light outside the Brewer's Arms in Aidensfield.

'Goodnight, Rhea,' he said, and vanished into the misty darkness.

He left me standing in the pool of warmth outside the pub, so I went in, half deciding to regard this as an official visit when I might chase out of the premises any stray under-age drinkers, and half to see whether any of the Ploatby farmers were in. Maybe I could persuade one of them to give me a lift back to my car? But I was out of luck. The pub contained no one from that part of the dale and I had no wish to intrude upon the drinking-time of anyone else.

By the time I'd chatted to some of the locals about crimes reported in the national papers, to others about the state of the weather, refused several offers of a drink and checked two youngsters for their ages, it was nine-thirty.

A quick peramble through the village took the time around to ten o'clock and then I knocked off for supper. I had a grumble to Mary about the inspector's actions, but she didn't offer much sympathy.

'If they say foot patrol they mean foot patrol,' she said with feminine simplicity. 'You haven't forgotten I need the car early tomorrow, have you?' she added. 'I'm going to see my mother and I must get some shoes for Elizabeth. She's got a hole in hers.'

I decided not to pursue the matter; I would endeavour to retrieve my car sometime during the remainder of this tour of duty. After all, when I resumed my work at

10.45 p.m., there would be a couple of hours left before 1 a.m., and I might still beg a lift from some of the pub regulars. But when I looked at my points and predetermined route, I saw it took me well away from the local pubs. The short second half of my patrol took me through some lonely poachers' territory, not villages.

At the end of this marathon shift, therefore, I still had not regained my car. Tired and footsore at 1 a.m., I trudged into my little office beside the house and rang Eltering Police Station to book off duty. The duty PC wished me goodnight. Mary was in bed and had left a mug and biscuit on a tray; I would make myself a cocoa. But she needed the car first thing tomorrow . . .

And there was no local officer performing night shift who might come to my aid . . . I daren't ring Kit Clough at Falconbridge who was in possession of the official van. He'd completed a 2 p.m. – 10 p.m. shift and was due out at 6 a.m. so he'd be fast asleep; I couldn't rouse him for this and did consider rising early myself, to beg a lift from him as he began his tour. But I couldn't guarantee he'd be free to do the trip – the inspector might go out early to meet him or there might be some other commitment.

It was my very own problem, so I crept out of the house and started the long, weary, wet and dark walk back to Ploatby to collect my car. I've never known such a long, foot-weary trail. In the pitch darkness and in thickening fog, I slowly made my way to Ploatby, the time ticking away and my energy being sapped at every step.

But I made it. Somehow, I managed to reach it and with a sigh of relief, opened the door and sank into the driving seat. For an awful moment, I thought it might not start due to the damp atmosphere, but it burst into life and carried me safely home.

As I sank into bed just after two o'clock, trying

desperately not to rouse Mary, she muttered, 'Busy night? Working late?'

'Yes,' I said, drifting into a blissful slumber against the warmth of her resting body.

That night, I dreamt I was trekking to the North Pole in my sore, bare feet.

3

'Aye, marry, is't; crowner's-quest law.'
Hamlet, William Shakespeare, 1564-1616

The romance and excitement of finding buried treasure was something fairly common in the countryside around Aidensfield. It happened to residents and visitors alike, and I became involved in many of these occurrences because of the fascinating and ancient law surrounding treasure trove.

The reason for so many discoveries is that the district around Aidensfield is rich in historic ruins. They include castles, abbeys, churches and even battlefields and, over many centuries, these have attracted pilgrims and travellers both from our country and from foreign lands. Because those ancient visitors were careless like the rest of us, lots of them mislaid things like coins, swords, jewellery and other personal valuables, then through the passage of time these became buried in the earth. Many years later, due to the use of modern technology in the form of metal detectors, deep ploughs or sheer good fortune, these were found amid scenes of great excitement.

One source of discovery was the humble footpath. Linking these establishments, and indeed linking the tiny villages between them, were footpaths and bridleways through woodland and along the banks of our streams and rivers. Those villages also boast origins which can be traced across the centuries, and in more than one case, evidence can be found in the village churches, some of which date as far back as the seventh century.

For example, modern visitors can examine two tiny minsters; one can be seen at Kirkdale (*circa* AD 654) over whose doorway is a Saxon sundial, the most complete in the world, which bears the longest-known inscription from Anglo-Saxon times. The other is at Stonegrave (*circa* AD 757) and each gives some indication of the immense span of English heritage which is present in this beautiful area of Ryedale in North Yorkshire.

This sense of history continues with abbeys founded some five hundred years later, such as those at Rievaulx and Byland, whose grandeur was reduced to ruin by the Reformation, while some four hundred years after their destruction more abbey-building took place at Ampleforth.

Castles like those at Ashfordly, Eltering, Elsinby, Helmsley, Pickering and Gilling East add to the majesty of the locality, and it was to these places via remote villages and hamlets that travellers came. They have travelled these byways for many centuries, rich and poor, royal, noble and common, British and foreign. And in many cases, they lost their personal belongings, perhaps the odd coin or jewel, or even a goblet or defensive weapon.

In the case of places liable to be raided either by villains or tax-gatherers, however, the people concealed their hard-earned wealth. They hid coins in the walls of castles and abbeys, up the chimneys of cottages and mansions, or buried them in earthenware jars in the gardens or fields. And, of course, many local folks lost the occasional coin.

The result of all this is that the fields, woods, paths and gardens of Ryedale, and indeed the whole of England, are rich with buried treasure. Every year, thousands of pounds' worth is discovered, some by accident, some by the use of metal detectors, some during road works or building construction and some by sheer good luck. There are many recorded instances when ordinary people have suddenly found themselves in possession of a fortune – one example occurred when workmen were excavating the site of a new building at York University. They uncovered 2,880 Roman coins, while in 1966, a hoard of twelfth-century coins then worth £30,000 was found near Newstead Abbey in Nottinghamshire. Twenty years later, treasure-hunters at Middleham in North Yorkshire found a unique fifteenth-century jewel of gold with a sapphire inset. It was sold for £1,430,000. In cases of this kind, the rule is not 'finders keepers', because when certain treasure is found the law of England, with its curious provisions for dealing with treasure trove, steps in. And this is how the police and the coroner become involved.

The coroner generally concerns himself with sudden or violent deaths, so why does he supervise the laws on found treasure? The answer lies far back in our history and a little explanation is now called for: in dealing with several cases of this nature and to satisfy my own curiosity, I delved into the reason for this odd aspect of our legal system and discovered a fascinating trail of legal history.

The first thing to remember is that treasure trove is defined as gold or silver, whether in the form of plate, coin or bullion, which has been deliberately hidden in the earth or in a house or in any other private place. This immediately rules out other valuables such as precious gems, bronze, pottery and glassware etc, unless these are set in either gold or silver. It also rules out gold or silver coins, plate or bullion which have been lost. The law on treasure trove does not concern itself with lost articles, but merely those which were hidden, however long ago.

If the owner is not known, treasure trove belongs to the

Crown, i.e. the State, but before being handed over, a decision must be made as to whether a particular item is or is not 'treasure trove', i.e. *hidden* treasure which has been found. This is the duty of the coroner who must hold an inquest (that is an enquiry) to determine whether or not the gold or silver object in question was lost or hidden. This can often be determined by the circumstances of its discovery. In very simple terms, a gold coin found under two inches of earth beside a well-used footpath was probably lost. There is no clear evidence that it had been concealed, therefore it would not be declared treasure trove, and would probably belong to the finder or perhaps to the landowner.

On the other hand, if a cache of gold coins was found in a leather bag or a container of some kind, perhaps buried beneath a tree or lodged up the chimney of an old house, then this suggests a past and deliberate concealment.

These are the kinds of decision which must be made by the coroner, usually based on evidence obtained for him by the police. The reason for his involvement goes back to the twelfth century at least, and possibly further. Once known as 'the crowner', the origins of the coroner are lost in time, but the office was mentioned in 1194 in Richard I's Articles of Eyre. They provided for the election of three knights and one clerk as custodians of the pleas of the Crown. From this, the early coroners were known as Keepers of the King's Pleas (*Custos Placitorum Coronae*) and their duties were to keep 'the pleas, suits and causes which affected the King's Crown and Dignity'.

The task of an early coroner was really to record matters rather than determine them, but one of his jobs was to ensure that any 'chance revenues' were paid to the King. These included money from 'the forfeited chattels of felons, deodands, wrecks, royal fish and treasure trove'. In other words, the early coroner was little more than a tax-gatherer, although he did enquire into sudden deaths and did supervise the disposal of a deceased's lands and goods. Indeed, his official interest in sudden deaths was then to ensure that the Crown received all its dues.

The forfeited chattels of felons were the belongings of a man who had committed some felony (i.e. serious crime like theft or murder). If he was convicted, all his belongings were forfeited to the Crown and it was the coroner's job to see that it was done.

It is now easy to understand why the coroner had to enquire into every sudden death – it was to determine whether or not it was the result of a murder so that, when a culprit was convicted, the Crown would receive its dues. Deodands are now obsolete: these were the objects which had caused the death by misadventure of a person. For example, if a cart accidentally ran over and killed a man, the cart or even just the offending wheel might be declared deodand and forfeited to the Crown. In days of old when this happened, the King would donate the object to the church or to the family of the victim, so that money could be raised for the sufferers. This scheme was abolished in 1846 when it was feared that entire railway trains or ships might be forfeited!

Wrecks at sea are now subject to their own procedures which were recently up-dated by the Protection of Wrecks Act 1973 and the coroner is no longer involved. So far as Royal Fish are concerned, it was Edward II who ruled that all sturgeon caught in British waters belonged to the sovereign and it was the coroner's duty to make sure this was done. I know of no modern law which enforces these provisions, but the practice continues as a matter of courtesy and custom. These, plus treasure trove, were the chance revenues which had to be handed to the King; of them, only treasure trove legally remains, and even now, if objects are declared treasure trove, they must still be handed to the Crown. But now, of course, this means the British Museum.

Upon the coroner declaring a discovery to be treasure trove, the goods will be handed to the British Museum who will then determine the current market value of the find. The finder will then be paid that sum, which shows that, in this case especially, honesty is by far the best policy. In recent years, many rewards totalling hundreds of thousands of pounds have been paid to lucky finders.

The old common-law misdemeanour of 'concealment of treasure trove' has been abolished, but if anyone now finds treasure trove and does not declare it, they can be charged with theft under the Theft Act of 1968 and their find will be confiscated. No reward will be paid either. It is so much wiser to report any of these discoveries, both from a criminal liability aspect and from the nation's need to conserve treasures which might otherwise be lost for ever.

It is not the job of a coroner to determine *ownership* of any treasure found on private land or in private premises; if it is *not* declared treasure trove, it might belong to the finder or the owner of the land or occupier of the house, or indeed to anyone else. That kind of decision is a matter for the civil courts if there is a dispute and so, with this background in mind, I found it both interesting and simple to deal with people who found things in their homes, or in the fields and surrounding countryside. And the number and variety of things discovered was truly amazing.

It is not easy to select the most interesting of the finds which occurred in and around Aidensfield – every one was fascinating in its own way. Mundane objects like old bikes, oil drums and even motor-car spare parts were constantly being located in the lakes, ponds and streams while our woodlands produced cast-off refrigerators, ovens, settees and a bewildering selection of household offal, most of which resulted from the actions of those ghastly people who dump their unwanted rubbish in the countryside. In our streams and waterways, old guns have been found too, and so have Victorian lemonade and beer bottles which are so desired by collectors. There were modern ones too, along with kettles and bedsteads, and in one miraculous case, a diamond wedding ring was discovered in a tiny beck. This was returned to the owner who had lost it several years earlier; she had reported the loss to the police, and our records turned up her name. Needless to say, she was delighted.

But none of these objects was remotely within the scope of treasure-trove rules, neither was an antique flintlock pistol found in the thatch of a cottage, or a beautiful unmarked glass goblet which had been tucked into a hole in a wall, and then boarded over for a couple of centuries. Because our area had been colonised by the Romans, we were often told of discoveries from that era; items of pottery galore like bowls, plates and urns turned up, usually broken into fragments, although very occasionally a complete and flawless example would be found.

These caused immense excitement, and although such finds were always of tremendous archaeological interest, they were generally not of police interest, nor was the coroner officially involved. Sometimes, however, we had to bear in mind the likelihood that any found object might be the subject of a crime – people did steal valuables and then dump them, but in most of our cases they were genuine discoveries from the distant past. Our procedures referred the finder to a local museum or archaeologist; sometimes, Roman coins would be unearthed and we had all coins examined by experts to determine whether or not they were struck in gold or silver; I don't think we ever dealt with a gold or silver coin from Roman times, although I understand that the Anglo-Saxons made gold copies of some Roman coins – these are now very rare. Most of the Roman coins we dealt with looked a dull bronze colour with the head of an emperor crudely portrayed on one side with various inscriptions on the other. None was particularly valuable and there seemed to be so many different types.

In one case, a very enthusiastic and slightly dishonest hunter discovered a hoard of Roman coins on private land and kept them; he was charged with stealing them from the landowner, as he had not obtained permission either to go on to the land nor to seek the coins. Some bore the head of the Emperor Septimus Severus who died at York around AD 211; this gave them a very local interest, but because they were neither gold nor silver, they were not treasure trove.

There was a burst of tremendous excitement at Elsinby when a local farmer turned up an ancient sword. He was ploughing close to the stream which flows through this pretty place when he struck the long, stout metal blade. His fields occupy a patch of land beneath the castle walls where there are strong links between Elsinby Castle and the Civil Wars; it was a regular occurrence for Fred Pullen to find relics of this kind. He regularly turned up cannon balls, musket balls, buckles from belts and spearheads.

But this sword was different. Although the long, heavy blade and hilt had suffered years of rust, he was alert enough to notice two narrow bands of what appeared to be gold which had been incorporated in the hilt. He brought this discovery for me to examine but I could not determine whether or not the bands were fashioned from real gold. That could only be decided by an expert, so we arranged for the sword to be examined.

And those bands were of gold; furthermore, the expert who hailed from the Yorkshire Museum said that the sword was not from the Civil War period. It was very probably an Anglo-Saxon warrior's sword dating from the seventh century, and he believed the gold bands had once bound a leather handle to the sword. But those tiny bands of gold made all the difference to Fred's discovery – because of the gold content, I now had to consider the law on treasure trove and this meant that Fred could not keep the sword – unless the inquest decided it was *not* treasure trove.

I made a formal report on the matter, and included a detailed statement from the museum's expert together with the circumstances of its discovery in that field beside the stream. The coroner said he would hold an inquest at some future date – he always kept such matters on file until a number of cases had accumulated, and he would then hold several treasure-trove inquests on the same day. Each lasted but a few minutes.

In this case, he decided the sword was not treasure trove – clearly, it had not been deliberately hidden and had, more than likely, been abandoned or even thrown away. And so Fred Pullen was allowed to keep it, but he donated it to the museum for display.

'It'll be safer yonder, Mr Rhea,' he said with simple logic. 'If I keep it and then pass on to that big hayfield in the sky when my time's up, it could get chucked away again. Folks round here don't recognise history, tha knaws, 'specially them relations o' mine. They see sike stuff as nowt but old bits o' junk. In my mind, them bits an' bobs are all a part of history and should be kept where folks'll appreciate 'em and where they'll never get lost again.'

I told him I couldn't agree more, and from that time, he donated many more pieces to local museums.

If Fred's discovery was rather unusual, so was that of Mrs Dolly-Ann Powell, a delightful lady of mature years who earned a living by lecturing upon and arranging beautiful displays of flowers in hotels, shops and other places.

Dolly-Ann was a tiny, slender and very pretty widow of about forty-five who lived in a picturesque thatched cottage at Briggsby. When dressed in her best clothes, she reminded me of one of her own flower arrangements, so delightfully neat and attractive was she. Our paths seldom crossed for she went about her business in a brisk and efficient manner and her work was something that rarely, if ever, warranted attention from a policeman. Every so often, however, I would spend time patrolling around her village and very occasionally I would find her in the garden, tending her beautiful collection of exquisite flowers. Many of these were used in her work and I do know that she sold lots to florists for wreaths and bouquets, or even to customers who came to the door. To say that her house and garden were a picture was a great understatement – they were a sheer delight. On such occasions, we would chat amiably over the hedge, passing the time of day and issuing the customary British small-talk about the weather and gardening.

One of Dolly-Ann's strengths was that she did most of her own renovations to the cottage; rather than employ builders or craftsmen, she would tackle most jobs and, surprisingly, achieved a great deal. It was while undertaking one of her improvements that she made a discovery which puzzled and then intrigued her.

It occurred when she decided to re-lay the sturdy path of sandstone paving-slabs which led to her honeysuckle-covered porch and front door.

Over the years, they had become rather uneven and

maybe dangerous, and so she decided to level them all. To make a good job, she lifted every one, including that which formed the threshold. It was here that she made her discovery. Underneath the threshold she found an old glass bottle dirty with age. Some six inches tall with a wide neck, its top contained a large cork which was thoroughly sealed and had remained intact in spite of many years in the ground. She had wiped off much of the grime to find the bottle contained some very strange objects and ingredients, so strange in fact that she was baffled by them.

By chance I arrived just after she had cleaned the bottle, when she was endeavouring to determine the contents, so she invited me in for a look at it. She put the kettle on and sat me in her pretty kitchen among countless vases and arrangements of flowers.

'So here it is.' She plonked it on the table before me. It was a clear bottle, although the glass had a faint greenish tinge to it, and I could see a dried-up, dark and almost glutinous substance covering the bottom. This had congealed many years ago, judging by its appearance, but there were other small metal objects stuck into it, rather like pins or nails, some rusted and others still clean; I could see what appeared to be human hairs and nail clippings too.

And then I knew what it was.

At that point, she arrived with a mug of hot tea and settled down at my side.

'Well, Mr Rhea, have I discovered hidden treasure?'

'Not really,' I smiled, thanking her for the drink.

'Oh.' Her face showed just a hint of disappointment.

'You've no idea what it is?' I asked.

'Not a clue,' she was honest.

'Well, suppose I asked you if your house is troubled by witches?' I smiled at her. 'What would you say?'

'Witches? No, of course not!' she laughed. 'Why, was this a witch's cottage?'

'On the contrary, witches were not welcome here!' I told her. 'This little device was to stop them, to ward off witches and to prevent them from bewitching the house or its occupants. It's obviously done a good job!'

'Really?' She opened her eyes wide with surprise and smiled at my attempt at joking. 'I had no idea!'

I explained my own interest in the folklore of the North York Moors and how, even until little more than a century or so ago, the country folk believed in witches and the power of the evil eye. Even today, some cottages contain witch posts whose original purpose was to protect the occupants from the attentions of witches, and there are other devices which served this purpose: for example, iron nails in beams or bedsteads, circular stones with holes in the centre, horseshoes on the walls of houses and outbuildings and even rowan trees planted close to the dwelling. All were used to deter witches.

She listened as I explained, and when I had finished, asked, 'So what is this bottle?'

'It's a witch bottle,' I told her. 'It was customary to bury them beneath the threshold, or sometimes under the hearth.'

'Really?' She picked it up and tried to identify the contents. 'What's inside?'

'Do you really want to know?' The ingredients were rather revolting and I wondered if she was squeamish.

'Something odd, is there?' she asked, suspicious of what was coming next.

'Ordinary things, really,' I smiled. 'But gruesome at the same time.'

She plonked the bottle on the table and stared at it, her pretty face screwed up in concentration.

'Go on, Mr Rhea,' she said at length. 'Make me squirm!'

'I'm not sure precisely what's in this particular bottle,' I said. 'But the sort of ingredients they put in would include samples of human hair, nail cuttings and metal objects like pins or nails. They'd put urine in too, and human blood . . .'

'Urggh . . .' she shuddered.

'And,' I was in full flow now, 'some of them contained the liver of a live frog stuck full of pins, or the heart of a toad which had been pierced with the spikes from the Holy Thorn of Glastonbury.'

She stared at the bottle on her table.

'How revolting!' she shuddered again. 'Why did they make such horrible things?'

'They really worried about the effect of witches on their children and cattle,' I explained. 'If things went wrong, things that couldn't be easily explained, they would blame the local witch. She was usually some poor old woman who dabbled in herbs or reckoned to foretell the future. And to stop any evil that she might perpetrate, they made these bottles as safeguards.'

'So the contents acted as a charm?'

'Yes, they were put under the door to prevent entry by evil spirits or witches. The presence of iron has long been a means of keeping witches at bay, hence the horseshoes, nails, pins and so on. The hair and human nail-parings come from the most indestructible part of the human body, and they believed that if included in a bottle, their presence would stop the witch injuring the family. I'm not sure what the blood was for. The addition of the urine was a terrible thing – they believed this caused the witch's death because she would be unable to pass water!'

I went on to say these charms were used beyond our shores too, examples having been found in Sicily and

Germany, and that in some cases three earthenware jars were used with similar contents, in this case each being buried beside a churchyard footpath seven inches below the surface and seven inches from a church porch.

When I had concluded my lecture on local witchlore, she smiled. 'So what am I going to do with this bottle? Is it something you should know about, officially, I mean?'

'No, but thanks for showing it me. You could replace it!' I suggested. 'Or keep it as an ornament . . .'

'No thanks! I wouldn't want that collection of stuff on my shelves.'

I mentioned the local Ryedale Folk Museum and felt it would be a suitable place to keep this bottle and its odd contents. She agreed.

'Mind you,' she smiled with a twinkle in her eye. 'I suppose that if I remove it from the house, I'll then be open to the machinations of the local witches? They might ruin my flowers, cause them to wilt or die, or even create havoc in the house itself.'

'That's the risk you take,' I confirmed with a chuckle. 'It seems this cottage has been free from strife over the years!'

'It's always been a happy house,' she said. 'Always.'

Draining my mug of tea, I left her to make her decision and never asked what she had decided. I felt I should not mention the bottle again, and although I did see her from time to time, she refrained from bringing up the subject. But I have never seen that bottle in the folk museum, and so far as I know Dolly-Ann's cottage and business have remained free from trouble. And her front path is now neat and level, with the threshold firmly in place.

Among the other discoveries was a magnificently ornate silver spoon which a householder found buried in the thatch of his cottage; this was identified as a seventeenth-century dessert spoon worth around £2,500, and the coroner decided that it *was* treasure trove. He said due to the peculiar place in which it was found, it must have been deliberately hidden for reasons which we shall never know. So much treasure seemed to be discovered in the thatched cottages around my beat that I was almost tempted to buy one!

But perhaps the most satisfying discovery was the one that occurred at West Gill Farm, Aidensfield, the centuries-old home of Reg Lumley and his family. Only months earlier, I had seen Reg devastated by a terrible outbreak of foot and mouth disease. It had resulted in the slaughter of his entire herd of pedigree Friesians, a herd which had taken him twenty years to establish but which had been wiped out in hours by that most dreaded of cattle diseases. The story is told in *Constable along the Lane*.

I knew that Reg, his wife and son Ted, were struggling to re-build their lives but no new cattle had yet appeared on the farm. I did not like to pry into their affairs nor discuss matters like insurance or compensation, nor did I wish to cause anguish by reminding them of the outbreak, so it was a pleasant surprise when I received a call from Reg. On the phone, he sounded in unusually high spirits.

'Can thoo come, Mr Rhea? Ah've summat to show you.'

'Sure Reg, when's a suitable time?'

'Any time, we're about t'spot all day.'

'How about just after two o'clock?'

'Champion,' he said and rang off.

When I arrived just after lunch, I found the family in the kitchen. They were sitting around their massive scrubbed pine table with huge mugs of tea, and in the centre was a tray full of muddy coins and bits of broken pottery.

Reg, beaming with happiness, shoved a mug into my hand and pulled out a chair. I settled on it, staring at the treasure before me.

'That's it, Mr Rhea. How about that?'

'Reg!' I said. 'Is this yours?'

'That's for you to say, Mr Rhea. Our Ted dug it up wiv 'is plough this morning, down in oor fifteen-acre.'

'Did he now!' I couldn't resist running my fingers through the pile of ancient money. The coins, most of which appeared to be of silver and from the sixteenth and seventeenth centuries, tinkled and rattled back on to the tray, and there seemed to be thousands of them. Upon some of them, I recognised names like Carolus I, Jacobus, Elizabeth, Edward VI and Carolus II. So they were from the reigns of Charles I and II, James I, Elizabeth I and Edward VI. I believe at least one was from the reign of Henry VIII.

'Wonderful!' I beamed. 'Absolutely wonderful.'

'Are they worth owt, Mr Rhea?'

'They must be,' I said, 'but I'm no expert.'

'Can I sell 'em? We could do wiv a bit o' cash.'

'I'm afraid not, Reg. But you could still get money from the find, although it'll take time,' and I told them about the procedure relating to treasure trove. Ted showed me where he had ploughed them up and I noted the place, then took a formal statement from him.

Next, we counted the coins. It took a long time because there were almost 2,000, and I had the unpleasant task of taking them away from the Lumleys in a large sack. I gave a receipt for 1,985 coins. I explained they would have to be examined by experts to determine whether or not they were silver or even gold. The Lumleys probably thought it was the last they'd ever see of them, knowing they were now subjected to red tape and officialdom.

As expected, the coroner declared them treasure trove which meant they were handed to the British Museum, and they would make their customary valuation based upon the prevailing market prices. It was some months later when I got a telephone call from Reg.

'Can thoo come, Mr Rhea? I've summat to show you.'

'Not another batch of coins, Reg?'

'Nay, summat else.' His voice contained an air of mystery. 'Thoo'll like this.'

'I'll be there in ten minutes,' I said, curious to learn about his latest discovery.

This time, there was a whopping glass of whisky on the kitchen table when I arrived and the family sat around with huge grins on their faces. Even Mrs Lumley was smiling.

Reg made sure I was settled and insisted I drink the whisky, even though I was in uniform. I didn't like to offend by refusing! After this performance, I was handed a letter. It was still in the official buff envelope which had been opened, but it bore the logo of the British Museum.

'Tak a leeak at yon, Mr Rhea,' invited Reg.

I did. I read the formal letter and was astounded. It itemised every single coin and identified them by year, reign and designation, and an individual valuation had also been added. The letter said that the total official value of the hoard of coins found at West Gill Farm, Aidensfield was £47,884 and a cheque for that amount was enclosed.

I held the cheque . . . I'd never seen, let alone held, such a huge amount of money.

'Whew!' was all I could say.

'That caps owt, Mr Rhea,' said Reg. 'That really caps owt.'

'It does, Reg. It really does cap owt. And I'm delighted for you all.'

Mrs Lumley, a woman of few words and a severe hair-do, just smiled again.

'Nay, it's thanks to thoo,' said Reg. 'I read summat in t'*Gazette* about thoo and another inquest on summat found at Elsinby, so thowt I'd better tell thoo. If thoo hadn't said what we had ti deea wiv 'em, Ah might have stuck 'em in t'loft and said nowt. I mean, thoo can't spend 'em, so in my mind they were worth nowt.'

That was a typical Yorkshire attitude, and he continued, 'Ah mean to say, who'd have thowt they were worth all this? So we'll have a party, Mr Rhea. Your missus'll come, eh?'

'We'll be delighted,' I said, and I meant it.

'It'll be soon,' he said. 'I'll ring wi' t'date.'

'Don't spend it all on a party!' I cautioned him with a laugh. 'Make the money work for you!'

'Ah shall, Mr Rhea. Starting next week, me and Ted'll be off to a few cattle marts. There's a few young pedigree Friesians we'd like to get oor hands on.'

I was so happy for the Lumleys, and their party was marvellous. With a farmhouse full of friends and relatives, it was a wonderful event, especially as Reg seemed to have overcome the depression which had plagued him for so long. And he did get his new herd started. Now, when I drive past his farm, I see his fields once again full of beautiful Friesians and Reg has still not retired. He continues to build that 'new' herd with just a little help from some past occupants of his lush farmland.

But of all the discoveries made on my patch, it was the one involving Mrs Ada Jowett which was the most intriguing. Ada, a stout and oft perspiring lady in her late sixties, was the church cleaner at St Andrew's Parish Church, Elsinby, a job which she did voluntarily. She had been St Andrew's cleaner for more years than anyone cared to recall, and the lovely building sparkled through her efforts.

The brasses always gleamed, the altar cloths were ironed to perfection, the surrounds were tidy and neat, and she managed to ensure that the flowers were always fresh and readers' lists and other notices were tidily displayed.

In short, Mrs Jowett was a treasure.

The church, always short of money and in need of constant maintenance and repairs, was soon to learn just how much of a treasure she really was. Conscientious as ever, she decided one year to spring-clean the hidden corners of the church. In addition to her normal brushing and polishing, this meant clearing out cupboards and corners, getting rid of years of accumulated rubbish and paper and generally ridding the church of unwanted junk. The job was long overdue, but no one had dared suggest it to Mrs Jowett. For all her skills, she cleaned only what could be seen . . .

No one knew what had prompted her to tackle the cupboards and corners, but she attacked the job with much gusto, lots of mops and dusters and gallons of perspiration. The stuff that was thrown out was bewildering – old curtains and cloths, ancient notices and posters, stacks of battered hymn books and a load of assorted jumble which would have graced the best junk-sale for miles around. It is just feasible that some important documents got lost in her enthusiasm, but she operated like a whirlwind. There was no stopping her once she had started and for days the church was almost lost in a cloud of dust or bonfire smoke.

And then, right at the back of a massive oak cupboard in the vestry, she found a chalice. It had obviously been there for years for it was dirty, very battered and full of dust. Like most other discoveries, she decided to throw it in the bin, so removed it from the shelf and took it outside. Then she had a second look in the strong daylight and for some reason changed her mind about casting it in the bin. It was at that precise moment that I arrived. I was undertaking a patrol around Elsinby and had noticed the frantic activity within the church. Attracted by the piles of rubbish outside, I thought I'd pop in to see what was going on and to pass the time of day with Ada.

As I strolled up the path towards the porch, I saw Ada clutching the chalice; she was peering intently at it.

'Morning, Ada,' I greeted her. 'Still busy, eh?'

'Never been so busy,' she grumbled. 'Wish I'd never started this. The more I chuck out the more I find inside, it's never ending. Makes you wonder where it comes from.'

'You're doing a good job.' I decided to praise her efforts. 'It must be benefiting the church. So, what's that you've found?'

'An old cup,' she said, holding it up for me to see. 'Been stuck in the back of a cupboard for years, it has. Junk I'd say, by the look of it. It's made of tin, I think, been battered about a bit. They'd never use this sort o' thing now for communion.'

She passed the chalice over to me and I held it, weighing it in my hand.

'It's pewter, I think,' I told her. 'And very old by the look of it.'

'It'll not be worth owt, then? It's not gold or silver, is it?'

'No, so what are you going to do with it?'

'I was thinking about chucking it out,' she said. 'Then when I got out, I had second thoughts. I'd like to show it to t'vicar, but he's away at a conference.'

The Rev. Simon Hamilton, Vicar of Elsinby, was away at a Diocesan Conference; I knew that because he'd told me that the vicarage would be empty for a whole week and had asked me to keep an eye on it during his absence.

Still holding the chalice and turning it in my hands, I said, 'I think he'd like to see this,' and then, in the strong light of that morning, I noticed the faint engraving on the face. It was very difficult to determine but it looked rather like a crowned sovereign in a sailing ship; he was carrying an upright sword and a shield.

'You take it and get somebody to look at it,' she said quite unexpectedly. 'Then I can tell t'vicar what we've done. You deal with found treasures, don't you?'

'Yes, if they're treasure trove.'

'Well, mebbe it's a good thing you turned up like you did. Do you happen to know anybody that'll look at it, say what it's worth or summat?'

'I'm going into York tomorrow,' I said. 'Off duty, but I've a pal who's in the antique business. I'll show it to him if you like.'

'Aye.' She looked relieved, for the decision had now been taken out of her hands.

And so I took the chalice from her. I found a piece of brown paper among the rubbish and wrapped it up, then placed it in the cubby-hole of the mini-van. Next day, I popped it into a carrier bag and took it to York. Mary and I did a little shopping, had a meal and then I remembered the old chalice. I went back to my car and removed it, then walked along Stonegate to my friend's antique shop.

'Hello, Paul, how's things in the antique world?'

'Hi, Nick,' he said. 'Things are bloody fine. So what brings you here?'

'This,' I said, and I placed the battered old chalice on his counter. 'I think it's pewter but wondered if it's worth anything.'

He took it and held it very carefully, turning it in the strong light of an angle lamp as he first studied the cup itself, and then examined the engraving on the front.

'Bloody hell!' was all he said. 'Where's this come from?'

'One of the churches on my patch,' I said. 'The cleaning

lady found it in a cupboard. Been there years by the look of it.'

'Centuries more like,' he said, and I saw his face was flushed. 'You've no idea what this is?'

I shook my head and said lamely, 'A chalice?'

'A chalice, yes. But what a bloody chalice! Worth a bloody fortune,' he whistled. 'A bloody fortune, or I'm stupid. You say she found it in a bloody cupboard?'

I explained the circumstances of its discovery, and then asked why he was so enthusiastic about it.

'Here,' he said. 'Take a look at this engraving. What is it?' he shone the light upon it and pointed to it.

'I think it's a king in a ship.'

'Right, with a sword and a shield, eh? The sort of arms you'd get on a bloody coin, not on a bloody pewter chalice!'

'Oh,' I said.

'This might have belonged to a King, see? Or to the priest who was the King's confessor or something. Henry IV it would be,' he continued. 'Reigned 1399 to 1413, he did. And see this?' He pointed to the shield, but I could not determine precisely what he was showing me. 'His shield, it's only got three fleurs-de-lis, not four. He changed his royal arms, you see; coins with only three fleurs-de-lis are so bloody rare it's unbelievable. And see this rudder on the ship? There's a star on it. Now most rudders on Henry IV coins are blank, but some have crowns on and some have bloody stars. Nick, if I'm not mistaken, this is a bloody rare find – a really rare bloody find.'

'No kidding?' I was awestruck by the thought.

'No kidding,' he said. 'You need expert valuation of this, my lad. Try Sotheby's.'

'I don't know anybody there.'

'I do, and he's a whizz-kid on medieval pewter. I'll fix up

a bloody appointment, right now if you like.'

'The vicar hasn't even seen this yet; if it's what you think it is, no doubt he'll want to be involved, and maybe even bring his bishop or the Archbishop into this find.'

'Too bloody right he will when he finds out what it is. Right, show it to him, tell him what I said, then ring me and I'll fix up an appointment at Sotheby's for it to be expertly assessed. Somebody'll have to take it down to London.'

'Right, Paul, thanks. I appreciate your advice.'

'And if your church wants to sell this bloody thing, let me know! I'd mortgage my shop to get my bloody hands on that.'

When the vicar returned, I informed him of this conversation (although I omitted Paul's colourful flow of expletives) and he promptly rang the Archbishop of York who suggested we let the Sotheby expert have sight of it. And, he said, the diocese would pay the train fare of the person who took it. We nominated Ada, with the proviso that she be told to take great care of the chalice at all times. Simon Hamilton felt she could be trusted to look after it – after all, who'd think this countrywoman was carrying treasure?

'I'm off to London,' she said next time I saw her. 'With that cup, Mr Rhea. To show a chap down there. I've never been to London, you know, never even been on a train.'

And so, dressed in her heavy brown shoes, lisle stockings, headscarf and her only overcoat which was of heavy tweed, Ada Jowett set about the journey of a lifetime. Excited both at the prospect of travelling to London and of riding on a train, she was driven to York Station by the vicar and would be met at King's Cross by the man from Sotheby's. He'd promised to care for her during her visit, bearing in mind the circumstances. I've no idea what he made of Ada when they met, but she had a most enjoyable day. Upon her return that same evening, she was collected from York by taxi and the vicar invited me to go along and hear how she'd progressed at Sotheby's.

The vicar's wife had arranged a late supper for her and I was invited. And when Ada came in from the taxi, she was carrying the chalice in a brown carrier bag; in fact, she'd put one bag inside another to give greater protection to the chalice! That was her notion of taking care of it.

'Well, Ada,' began Simon Hamilton. 'How did it go?'

'By, yon train goes fast,' she said. 'And then in London, they rushed me down some stairs under t'ground and there was more trains, coming every few minutes . . . I've never seen owt like it . . . and folks! Thousands of 'em all pushing and shoving . . . there's no wonder folks get bad-tempered with all that rushing about.'

'Yes, but the chalice . . .'

Ada ignored the vicar and continued to enthuse about London, giving her highly colourful interpretation of life in the capital. She rambled on about guards in funny hats at Buckingham Palace, messy pigeons, Eros, Big Ben, the Houses of Parliament, the department stores, the different nationalities she noticed, buses that came every few minutes instead of twice a week and trains whose doors shut without being pushed by the travellers.

Eventually, she ran out of talk of the city and Simon took the opportunity to mention Sotheby's and the chalice.

'They would have nowt to do with it, Mr Hamilton.' She shook her heavy grey head. 'Didn't want to know. This young chap met me off t'train and took me in a taxi where I saw the chap you mentioned, him what reckons to know summat about cups like that.'

'And he examined it?'

'He did, in a manner o' speaking. It took nobbut a minute or two, and that was that.'

'And what did he say?'

'Not a lot.'

'You offered to leave the chalice for a more thorough examination, as I suggested?'

'Oh, aye, I made that clear. I said I'd leave it for him to have a better look and he could mebbe post it back, but he said he'd have nowt to do with it, Mr Hamilton.'

'Nothing to do with it?'

When I heard this, I wondered about Paul's assessment – Paul would never have allowed Ada to go all the way to London with a dud. I was sure Paul knew his antiques . . .

'Nay, nowt. Summat to do with insurance, he said. He wouldn't take it off me, so I had to fetch it back.'

And she dug into the paper carrier bag and lifted it out.

'Is that all?'

'Well, he said he'd be having words with you about it, I told him your telephone number. Tomorrow, he said, all being well. He'll ring.'

There was clear disappointment on Simon's face and I knew mine also showed similar feelings. It seemed that the so-called experts in London had merely fobbed off poor old Ada. The vicar should have gone, he should have taken it and presented it in a more sophisticated manner.

'Leave it with me, Ada,' said Simon. 'We'll see what they say tomorrow, eh?'

'Aye, and it's my bedtime now. See you tomorrow,' and off she went.

I remained with Simon for a while, each of us expressing our sorrow at her apparently callous treatment in London, and then I went home. Then at lunch-time the following day, I got a call from Simon Hamilton.

'Can you spare ten minutes, Nicholas?' he asked.

'Of course,' I said. 'I'll come now.'

When I arrived at the vicarage, he showed me into his

kitchen where Ada was seated at the table. Mrs Hamilton was also present and I noticed a glass of wine at each place setting. And in the centre was the dirty old chalice.

When we were all gathered together, Simon said, 'Ada, PC Rhea, I'd like to thank you both for your work in rescuing this chalice. I've had a call from Sotheby's this morning, Ada, and they thank you for taking it to them.'

'The cheek of 'em!' she pouted. 'Nearly threw me out they did . . . didn't want to know about me . . .'

'I think you have misunderstood them, Ada.' He spoke softly. 'They did a proper and expert examination; it's a Henry IV pewter chalice, a very rare object and more so because of the arms which it bears. It seems pewter chalices were used in medieval times, but most of them were buried with the priests when they died. Very few from this period have survived, especially of this quality. Now, did he say what it was worth?'

'Well, he muttered on about it being worth summat in the region of half a million pounds. Now I ask you, Mr Hamilton! Half a million pounds for that bit of awd tin?'

'And you didn't believe him?'

'I did not! I reckoned he was having me on 'cos I'm a country woman who doesn't know about such things.'

'Ada, he does genuinely believe it would bring that amount in a sale at his auction rooms. It is unique, Ada, a real treasure.'

'You're all having me on!' She flushed deeply now and looked very embarrassed. 'That's why I said nowt to you about what they'd said it was worth. A bit of awd tin can't be worth that much, it just can't.'

'No, we're not teasing you, Ada, none of us. His problem was that he could not keep it overnight because he was not insured for that particular cup. So you took it sight-seeing . . .'

'Aye, and I nearly lost it over London Bridge, an' all,' she said grimly. 'Can't say I'd have missed it.'

'So you've a problem now,' I put to him. 'Your church will never afford the premiums to insure this!'

'I must speak to the Archbishop,' he said. 'This is a real shock, Ada, a massive shock. I'm reeling from the thought that this has been standing in my vestry for years and, but for you, would have been thrown out . . .'

'Half a million pounds!' she repeated. 'For that bit of awd tin? I'd not give it house-room!'

She was steadfastly refusing to accept the truth of that statement, and left the vicarage shaking her head. After being assured Simon would place it in a bank vault for safe keeping, I followed her out, stunned that I'd carried it around in my car and had left it unattended in a York car-park!

It would be about a month later when the Rev. Simon Hamilton called me again. 'I thought you'd like to know the outcome of the chalice saga,' he said.

'Love to,' I said, and drove to his vicarage for a coffee with him.

When I was settled, he said, 'As you've been involved with this from the start,' he strode up and down his spacious kitchen, 'I thought you'd like to hear the Archbishop's decision about the chalice.'

'Yes, thanks, Simon. I appreciate that.'

'It is a problem, Nicholas,' he said. 'We cannot keep it because of the risks and the necessarily high insurance premiums. We could not afford them. And, as you know, we do need a regular supply of money for upkeep of our church.'

I let him take his time on this explanation.

'If we allowed Sotheby's to auction it on our behalf, it might raise that huge sum; half a million pounds does seem excessive, but I am assured it could bring as much as that on the open market, maybe from international buyers.'

'So you're selling it?' I asked.

'Not by public auction. As the Archbishop says, if we did sell it through Sotheby's, it might go out of the country. There is no telling where it might get to. We don't want that – we want such a unique chalice, our chalice, kept in England, Nicholas. It must never leave these shores.'

'But you're in a cleft stick, Simon,' I said. 'You can't afford to keep it, and you can't dictate where it goes if it is sold. You cannot issue conditions for sales of that kind.'

'A solution has been reached, Nicholas,' he said. 'A museum has offered us £45,000 for it; it will be put on display and kept in this country for all time.'

'But that's a fraction of its true value,' I protested.

'Perhaps, but it's all that museum can afford. If we invest that cash, it will give the church a very nice income for years ahead and that will safeguard it and permit us to maintain it in the manner it deserves. After all, we want nothing more than that. You see, this method pleases everyone because the chalice can be viewed by the public, we get some income from it and it will never again be lost or taken out of England. It's an admirable solution.'

'But you're throwing money away!' I said.

'Not really, because we're getting more than we've had before, and we don't really need half a million, Nicholas.'

'It's a real Christian decision,' I heard myself say.

'It was made by the Archbishop, I might add,' said Simon as if that explained everything.

Today, Ada's name is upon the notice which provides a history of the chalice as it stands in a famous museum, and soon after the sale, Ada got a new apron, and some new brushes and dusters. So the chalice was of benefit to her as well.

And she still refuses to believe that such a 'piece of awd tin' was worth so much money.

4

'They inwardly resolved that . . . their piracies
should not again be sullied with the crime of stealing.'
Tom Sawyer Abroad, Mark Twain, 1835-1910

The crime of theft, known legally in England as larceny until 1968, is among the earliest of criminal offences; not only is it a crime, however, it is also a sin, and as such features in the Ten Commandments. 'Thou shalt not steal' could hardly be a more direct prohibition.

A universal loathing of theft has, over the centuries, provided it with many penalties, some of them dreadfully severe. Some five hundred years before Christ, for example, the Romans hanged those who stole crops at night. They were executed at the scene of their crime as a sacrifice to Ceres, goddess of the harvest. Here in England during Danish times, a thief could be killed without fear of having to pay compensation to his family because his act of stealing had rendered him valueless. During medieval times, theft continued to be a capital offence along with others such as murder, treason, arson, burglary and robbery; Henry II, however, said that crimes which involved the theft of five shillings (25p) or less could be punished by amputation of a foot instead of death.

By the middle ages, reforms were gradually reducing the barbarity of our penal system, although as late as the seventeenth century a woman was drowned in Loch Spynie in Scotland for committing theft, and across the Channel in France the infamous guillotine was utilised against thieves.

After many tests, France's wonderful new death-dealing machine was perfected by Tobias Schmidt and fitted with a slanting blade on the advice of Louis XVI. In fact, he was later to die by that very blade. However, after being installed on 15th April 1792 as the official method of execution, the guillotine's very first victim was a thief. He was Nicholas-Jacques Pelletier who was guillotined at 3.30 p.m. on 25th April 1792 by the Executioner of Criminal Sentences, Charles-Henri Sanson. The machine was thoughtfully painted red and white, and Pelletier's execution had been delayed so that he could have the honour of being the first to be executed by the guillotine.

Even by the early years of last century, some forms of theft in this country carried the death penalty. In 1810, the reformer Samuel Romilly was horrified by the number of offences which did carry the death penalty, and he tried to introduce bills in Parliament to change these laws. At first, he failed; he tried, for example to remove the death penalty which had been reinstated for stealing objects up to the value of five shillings (25p), and also for stealing objects to the value of £2 from houses and for stealing from ships in navigable waters.

He achieved partial success when Parliament abolished the death penalty for stealing from bleaching-grounds. In spite of his efforts, in 1819 there were still over two hundred capital offences on the statute book, one of which was impersonation of a Chelsea Pensioner!

Examples of the contempt in which theft was held occurred in 1827, when a man called Moses Snook was awarded ten years' transportation for stealing a plank of wood, and another man was sentenced to death for stealing

2s 6d (12½p). But the spirit of change was moving, and Robert Peel, founder of the modern police service, made a tremendous impact upon legal reform. His influence reduced three hundred Acts of Parliament to only four, and drastically reduced the number of capital offences. The death penalty continued to exist, however, even for some crimes of theft such as stealing goods to the value of £2 or more from a dwelling-house.

But the juries hated the death penalty for such crimes and they would deliberately undervalue the stolen goods to save a criminal from death. One jury valued a £10 note at £1 19s 0d (£1.95) to save a criminal from death; other examples involved sheep-stealing and horse-stealing, both of which carried the death penalty. A jury found a thief guilty of stealing only the fleece of a sheep instead of the whole beast, and guilty of stealing only the hair of a horse instead of the entire animal.

By 1956, when I joined the Force, theft, in its many and varied forms, carried penalties which ranged from a maximum of five years' imprisonment up to and including life imprisonment, although fines were often imposed in the less serious cases. It was then called larceny, a term which still creeps into some publications.

Stealing from one's employer, for example, carried a maximum penalty of fourteen years' imprisonment; an officer of the Bank of England who stole securities or money from the bank could get life imprisonment. The stealing of horses, cattle or sheep carried up to fourteen years, while stealing postal packets carried life imprisonment. In 1957, a murder committed during the course of, or in the furtherance of theft carried the death penalty, and on 13th August 1964, Gwynne Owen Evans and Peter Anthony Allen, two Lancastrians in their early twenties, were hanged for murdering a van-driver during the course of theft. These were England's last judicial hangings.

In 1968, the law of theft was completely overhauled. The definition of the crime was both altered and simplified, and from that time it has carried a maximum penalty of ten years' imprisonment, with associated offences such as burglary and robbery carrying a maximum of life imprisonment in some cases. Those penalties still apply, for theft is still regarded by some as a sin, by others as a major crime and by yet more as a normal part of life.

People help themselves to 'souvenirs' from hotels, restaurants and cafés; they take stuff home from work and fiddle expense accounts. They 'borrow' with no intention of returning, lift plants from garden centres, purloin precious objects from stately homes and have expeditions to our cities for shoplifting. And it is all theft with a ten-year maximum jail sentence.

In our modern society, the scope for theft is infinite; hundreds of thousands of such crimes are committed daily but massive numbers go unreported because they are accepted as 'normal', and so the true incidence of theft in this country can never be known nor even estimated. But taken as a whole, and supported by most police officers, this will suggest that we live in a very dishonest society.

A statement of this kind, taken from knowledge but unsupported by statistics, will anger politicians who are to the left of centre, but such a claim will be agreed by most business and professional people. They know that thefts occur from their premises and many are dealt with internally, so why report those for which there is no chance of detection? A café-owning friend of mine cheerfully told me that he had about a hundred and twenty teaspoons and thirty-six ashtrays stolen *every week*, but he never reported any of these crimes to the police. The incidence of unreported theft would make a marvellous study for a university student . . .

But while the Church continues to denounce theft as a sin, and socialists continue to regard it as a symptom of a society deprived of its basic needs, police officers continue to regard it as a crime committed not by those in need, but by those who like to get their hands on something for nothing and don't mind who suffers in the process. I must confess that I know few, if any, thieves who genuinely had to steal in order to survive; they stole out of pure greed. And that is why thieves are so despicable.

Although so many thefts are not notified to the police, considerable numbers *are* formally reported and investigated before being fed into the nation's crime statistics. For the operational police officer, however, such academic matters are of little importance; his work involves knowing what constitutes a theft, and how to catch the villain responsible. Statistics are of little interest to him.

The 1916 definition of larceny was as follows, and this was the wording which we had to learn parrot-fashion. It was the equivalent of learning the Lord's Prayer or the alphabet, and although I learned this more than thirty years ago I still remember it. Since then, of course, I had to learn the new definition of theft which is contained in the Theft Act 1968, but the old words stick in the memory. The 1916 wording may seem ponderous, but it does have a certain rhythm and indeed one poet wrote it down in verse form.

The definition is as follows, according to section 1 of the Larceny Act 1916, now repealed. 'A person steals who, without the consent of the owner, fraudulently and without a claim of right made in good faith, takes and carries away anything capable of being stolen, with intent at the time of such taking permanently to deprive the owner thereof.

'Provided that a person may be guilty of stealing any such thing notwithstanding that he has lawful possession thereof, if, being a bailee or part-owner thereof, he fraudulently converts the same to his own use or to the use of any person other than the owner.'

I frequently imagine a Shakespearian actor quoting this definition, with due pauses at all the commas and full-stops, but our task was to learn it and understand it, along with all the other variations of larceny such as stealing by finding or by intimidation, stealing by mistake or by trick, larceny from the person, larceny of trees and shrubs, and a whole range of other associated crimes like embezzlement, burglary, housebreaking, robbery, false pretences, frauds by agents and trustees, blackmail, receiving stolen property, taking of motor vehicles, etc.

It was fascinating stuff and the precise interpretation of that definition has kept lawyers occupied and earning fat fees for years. We had to know it in our heads so that we could instantly implement its provisions in the street, even if our actions did result in appeals to the High Court or House of Lords in the months to come. But in a volume of this nature, there is no space to enlarge upon the wonderful range of legal fiction which resulted from this and similar statutes. But imagine a thief maliciously cutting someone's grass and leaving the clippings behind on the lawn . . . would it be larceny? Were the clippings 'taken and carried away' or indeed, is grass capable of being stolen? And, how many crimes would be committed? One only? Or one for each blade of grass? Was there intention permanently to deprive the owner of his grass? Or was the whole affair a crime of malicious damage? Such points could keep a class of students occupied for hours and reap rich fees for lawyers.

But police officers tend to deal more with the ordinary

crime than the exotic, and few interesting cases of larceny came my way at Aidensfield. Most of them were very routine, often committed at night by pilferers who sneaked around the village picking up things left lying around. For example, one farmer had a brand-new wire rat-trap stolen from his barn, a householder had a selection of pot plants stolen from his greenhouse, a child's tricycle was stolen having been left outside all night, and someone managed to steal a full-size horse trough. Coal was occasionally nicked from the coal yard, wood was taken from the timber yard and, as happens in most villages, there was a phantom knicker-pincher who stole ladies' underwear from clothes-lines. It seems that almost every village, and in towns every housing estate, has a resident phantom knicker-pincher, most of whom are peculiar men who operate under cover of darkness, many of whom are usually caught in the act of satisfying their weird addiction. When their houses are searched, a hoard of illicitly obtained exotic and colourful underwear is usually found. Publicity rarely brings forth claimants because many ladies are too shy to report the initial theft or to admit ownership of some of the magnificent and strikingly sensual underwear thus recovered. The courts are then left with the task of ordering suitable disposal.

Apart from the mundane thefts, several interesting cases did cross my path and one of them involved a picture hanging in a village pub.

It was one of those background pictures, some of which are delightful, which adorn the walls of village inns but which are seldom appreciated until someone steals them or mutilates them in some way during a fit of pique or drunkenness. In this instance, however, the picture remained safely in its position above the black cast-iron Yorkist range, enhanced in the colder seasons by the flickering flames of the log fire below and in the warmer seasons by a vase of flowers positioned on the mantelpiece.

The picture was an oil painting of Winston Churchill as the British Prime Minister and it depicted him with his famous cigar between his lips. It showed him at the height of his powers, a confident and forceful personality who had guided our nation to victory during World War II. In the picture, he was contemplating something across to his left (maybe the Labour party!) and was shown seated in his study with books around him and papers scattered across his desk. It was a fine picture of a widely respected statesman and it had been in the Moon and Compass Inn for several years.

It was one of those pictures which brighten the bars of our village inns, and many a glass had been raised to Winston, later Sir Winston, in his silent pose above the cosy, welcoming fire of the Moon and Compass. During my official visits to the inn, Sir Winston was still alive and I had admired the picture and complimented David Grayson, the landlord, upon its merits. This pleased him, although he had acquired the painting with the fittings of the pub.

The possibility that there could be a problem associated with that picture never entered my head until I received a visit from a tourist. He arrived on the stroke of two o'clock one Wednesday afternoon just as I was about to embark upon a tour of duty in the mini-van. I noticed the sleek grey Jaguar 340 glide to a halt outside my house and a smart man in his sixties emerged. He was dressed in light summer clothes of the casual kind, and his wife remained in the car. I met him in the drive to the police house.

'Good afternoon,' I greeted him.

'Ah, I've obviously just caught you, constable. Are you in a hurry? You can spare a minute or two?'

'Yes, of course,' and I offered to take him into my office but he said he could tell me his business where we stood in the front garden.

'You know the Moon and Compass Inn, at Craydale?' he put to me.

'Yes, it's on my beat,' I said.

'Ah, well, there is a problem. A delicate one, I might add,' he began. 'I hate to make accusations which I cannot substantiate, but I feel you ought to be aware of this . . .'

I wondered what was coming next, but waited as he gathered his words together.

'It's the picture of Winston Churchill,' he said eventually. 'You know it?'

'It hangs over the fireplace in the bar,' I informed him. 'A nice picture, very realistic. I know it well.'

'And so you should!' His voice increased in pitch. 'It was commissioned from a special sitting – Churchill actually posed for that picture, constable. It's not a copy, not a print but the original by Christopher Tawney. It's the only one in the world, constable.'

'It must be valuable, then?' I said inanely.

'I have no idea of its value,' he said shortly. 'No idea at all; it's not an Old Master so we're not talking in huge sums, but I'd guess it can be measured in thousands, if not tens of thousands. And this is why I've called, constable. That painting has been stolen. It should not be there; that pub has no right to that picture, no right at all.'

'Stolen? But it's been in that pub for years,' I told him. 'Long before I came here. Eight or ten years even. Are you sure it's the one you think it is?'

'I've never been so sure in my life, constable. You see, I had it done, I was the person who commissioned the artist and persuaded Winston to undertake that sitting. I know that picture like I know my own belongings. If you care to examine it, you'll see Tawney's signature in the bottom left-hand corner too.'

'You'd better come into the office,' I said.

I asked Mary to make a cup of tea, and to include the gentleman's wife who waited in the car. She was persuaded to come into the lounge where Mary and the children entertained her as I discussed this matter with her husband.

His name was Simon Cornell and he was a retired director of one of Britain's largest and most famous manufacturers of cigars.

'I retired about six years ago,' he said. 'And now Jennie and I spend a lot of time touring England, seeing places we've never been able to visit until now. Always too busy, you know, leading the hectic life of a businessman.'

'So what about the painting?' I was taking notes. 'What's your involvement with that?'

'It was done for an advertisement series,' he said. 'Winston was happy enough for us to use that picture in our adverts – restrictions weren't so rigid then, although he did ask for us to give the equivalent of his fee to a charity of his choice. So we had the oil painting executed by Christopher Tawney; several prints were run off it and you might have seen copies of them on cigar-box lids, adverts in the papers and magazines and so on.'

'Yes,' I admitted. 'I thought I'd seen that picture before. To be honest, Mr Cornell, I didn't pay a great deal of close attention to it . . .'

'Exactly, because there are so many copies still around, a lot of them hanging in pubs, by the way, like this one. They're the same size too. But the one in the Moon and Compass is the original. I can vouch for that.'

I took a long handwritten statement from him which confirmed what he had told me, and then noted his address and telephone number for future use.

I did extract from him that he was not acting in any official capacity on behalf of the company for whom he had worked; he was merely drawing police attention to a theft which had occurred many years ago. He did inform me that, so far as he could recall, the picture had been hanging in the boardroom and it had been painted soon after Churchill had won the Nobel Prize for Literature in 1953. Some time around 1956, it had disappeared.

'Company records will give the exact date of its disappearance,' Mr Cornell informed me. 'But that's roughly the sequence of events.'

'So it might have been here at least ten years?' I said. 'And I do know the present landlord has been here only four years. He bought the picture with the inn, by the way; he told me that when I was admiring it some time ago. He did not bring it with him – it was part of the fittings.'

'So who does it belong to now, eh?' smiled Cornell.

'I think that's a matter between the company and the landlord of the Moon and Compass,' I said. 'But clearly, you'd be interested in tracing the thief?'

'I think that would be impossible now,' he said. 'But perhaps you will contact the company and inform them of my discovery, and perhaps warn Mr Grayson, your landlord, of this conversation?'

'Yes, of course. And I'll let you know what progress I make.'

And so Mr Cornell left me with this problem.

As he drove away, his wife chirping with delight at her warm reception by our little brood of four children, I was left with the thought that David Grayson had no idea he was in possession of stolen property. I was equally aware that the matter could not be ignored, but knew that if I mentioned the affair to Sergeant Blaketon, he would charge into action like the proverbial bull in a china shop. His heavy-handed, rule-bound methods would wreak havoc every inch of the way as he had me arresting everyone in sight for theft or for receiving stolen property. It was my belief that this allegation, for it was nothing more than an allegation at this stage, required some rather delicate handling.

And so I waited for Sergeant Charlie Bairstow to come on duty. I felt he would adopt a more reasoned approach. It meant a delay of just one day, but I felt it was justified. I caught him during a quiet moment over an early-morning cup of coffee in the office at Ashfordly, and presented him with the story. He listened carefully and I showed him the statement made by Simon Cornell.

'A tale of villainy if ever there was one,' he smiled. 'What do you reckon?'

'About the truth of it, you mean?' I asked.

'Yes. Is Cornell having us on, or is that picture the genuine thing as he says?'

'I believe him.' I spoke as I felt and, of course, I had witnessed Cornell's reaction as he had relayed his tale.

Sergeant Bairstow thought for a while and I knew he was weighing up all the problems that might accrue, both emotional and legal, and then he said, 'We'd better go and have a look at it. And we'd better warn Grayson of this.'

'He bought it legally,' I pointed out.

'Yes, and that gives him a claim to the painting,' he said. 'A claim of right made in good faith, as the Larceny Act so aptly puts it.'

And so we drove out to Craydale and popped into the Moon and Compass. David was working in his cellar when we arrived, stacking crates and cleaning out his beer pumps. He was happy enough to break for a coffee.

'Well, gentlemen.' He took us into the bar which was closed to the public as it was not opening hours. 'This looks businesslike, two of you descending on me.'

'It is a problem,' Sergeant Bairstow said. 'Nick, you'd better explain.'

I told him of Cornell's visit and allegations, and he listened carefully, a worried frown crossing his pleasant face as I outlined the theft of the picture from the cigar company. We closely examined the painting and it was clearly executed in oils and signed, and on the back was a certificate of authenticity. It was the genuine thing; of that, there was no doubt. David kept looking at the image of Sir Winston and was clearly upset at our unpleasant news.

'So what do I do now?' he asked us both, looking most anxious and apprehensive.

'Nothing,' said Charlie Bairstow. 'Just sit tight; there's no suggestion that you stole it, we want you to know that. Our next job is to contact the cigar firm and tell them the picture has been found. But you do have a claim to it, David, because you bought it in good faith, as part of the fittings of the pub.'

'When did you say it was stolen?' he asked.

'1956, as near as we can tell,' I said.

'That was two landlords ago,' he added. 'I took it over from Jim Bentley, and he came here in 1959. I'm not sure who was here in 1956.'

'Our liquor licensing records will tell us,' said Bairstow. 'We'll chase up that angle.'

'But I don't want that bloody picture hanging here if it's worth a fortune!' he cried. 'Somebody might pinch it!'

'It's been there years without that happening,' Bairstow said. 'Anyway, I'd say it's yours now, David, but you might need a solicitor to do battle for you, from the ownership point of view, especially if the cigar people decide they want it back and make a claim upon it.'

'I think I'll hide it upstairs,' he smiled grimly. 'So what happens now?'

'Leave it with us,' said Charlie Bairstow. 'We will contact the cigar company and see what they say.'

'Thanks for telling me all this first.' David was clearly grateful for our action. 'So I might be sitting on a fortune after all this?'

'Cornell thought it was worth a lot of money,' I said. 'But he wouldn't commit himself to an amount. Don't forget that this is the original, David.'

'How can I? It's funny this has arisen,' he added. 'I've often said to Madge – my wife, that is – that this looked like an oil painting and not a copy. I know some copies look so realistic now, even down to a rough surface, but well, this did have a genuine feel to it. I never thought of looking at the back for that certificate!'

'Well,' said Sergeant Bairstow. 'You hang on to it, and we'll see what happens next.'

'Thank you, sergeant,' and we left him to his thoughts.

Back in the office, I compiled a report on the matter for despatch to the Chief Constable of Surrey Constabulary in whose area the cigar factory was based. In the terminology of the time, I asked him if he would allow an officer to search his records in an attempt to locate the report of the original theft, and then allow an officer to visit a senior official of the cigar company to inform him of the painting's present whereabouts. Sergeant Bairstow also asked me to include a paragraph to ask whether, in view of the passage of time, Surrey Constabulary required any further action by us in this matter.

The reply came ten days later. A detective sergeant in Guildford had established that the crime had been reported on 28th April 1956, the picture then being worth £850.

The original's disappearance had not been noticed for

some time because one of the copies, in an identical frame, had been substituted. It had never been recovered, nor had the thief been arrested. Enquiries at the time had revealed that one of the suspects had been a salesman who had subsequently resigned from the company, but nothing had ever been proved against him. That man's name was not supplied, but Surrey Police did say the file had never been closed; they went on to add that it would be appreciated if steps could be taken to ascertain the name of the person who had sold the painting to the landlord of the Moon and Compass.

We did trace the long-retired landlord, an old character called Ralph Whalton who now lived with his married daughter in a bungalow at Eltering. He did not remember anything of the painting, but his daughter did. A plain girl approaching her thirties, she remembered its arrival.

'Oh, yes,' she said. 'You must remember, Dad!'

The old man shook his head. 'I'm too old now, Jill. They gave me all sorts of publicity stuff, I stuffed most of it in the cellar. I couldn't put it all up in the bar.'

'Well, I remember it well. I was about eighteen or nineteen at the time, and helping behind the bar. A salesman came in, not the regular one, with a box of those cigars you always bought. And he had the picture of Churchill. He said every pub was being given one and he hoped we would display it in a public area.'

'Was I there?' he asked, clearly puzzled.

'You might not have been,' she now realised. 'Maybe not, maybe that's why I was helping out. Mebbe you'd gone away somewhere. Anyway, we took a picture down, it was one of those pen-and-ink drawings of a Scottish mountain scene, and hung Sir Winston instead. He's been there ever since.'

She was unable to provide a description of the salesman

and did not know his name. We passed this information to Guildford Police and it was about three weeks later when I received a telephone call to say that Guildford Police were closing this file because (a) the picture had been located and (b) their suspect salesman was now known to have died in 1962. Apparently, their records showed he was working in the North Riding for a short period during the spring of 1956. He was a very positive suspect.

So who did the picture now belong to? I knew that if someone was convicted of stealing it, the court could make an order for its restitution to the cigar company, but this was impossible in this case because several innocent buyers had since been involved and, apart from that, no one had been convicted of its theft. This latter fact alone ruled out this form of restitution through the criminal courts; now, of course, no one would ever be convicted for stealing it.

David Grayson, landlord of the Moon and Compass, now had a strong legal right to that picture, and I do know that he changed his mind about hiding it upstairs.

He was very proud of it, particularly as it had spawned so many copies throughout the country, and he told me that the cigar company had eventually offered him one of the many surplus copies in an identical frame, but he had refused. They desperately wanted the original to be returned for display in the company head office, but they did not offer him any money or compensation for it. After all, he had paid good money to acquire it quite legally and perhaps the company should have made some form of financial gesture.

Instead, following David's refusal, the company had made a half-hearted threat of attempting to recover the painting through the civil courts, but that was never proceeded with. I don't think it would have succeeded. So even now, if you go into the bar of the Moon and Compass

at Craydale, you will see Sir Winston Churchill's image
beaming over the customers. And no one knows how or
why it came to be in this remote North Yorkshire pub.

One theory is that the salesman managed to steal it from
his head office and that he mistakenly gave it away while
delivering the advertisement copies. Or, of course, he
might have become terrified at the thought of being
captured with it in his possession, and decided to get rid of
it in this way, hoping that no one in remote North Yorkshire
would realise it was something special. But David Grayson
did tell me that, when he decided to leave the pub, he
would return the picture to the company for display in
their boardroom above a little notice saying 'Donated by
Mr David Grayson.'

I thought it was a nice gesture, a moral compromise and
a means of ensuring the picture never again went astray.

While that episode caused more than a flicker of professional
interest, there were countless mundane crimes and one of
them, or to be more accurate, a series of them, involved the
village store at Crampton. It was a typical village store, the
kind of emporium found in every self-respecting small
community. It dispensed almost everything from
lawnmowers to tins of beans by way of socks, bread loaves,
paperback novels, eggs and some of the finest cooked ham
in the area. The high walls were filled with shelves of
wines, exotic foods and sweets, tins of fruit, boxes of
screws, nails and washers, dishcloths and kitchen utensils.

The owner was a small sprightly bachelor of
indeterminate age. He was called Mr Wilson and had run
his well-stocked shop for as long as anyone could remember.
No one seemed to know his Christian name because
everyone called him Mr Wilson and no one knew much
about his private life. A secretive but marvellously tidy

little fellow, he seemed to be involved in no social or community activities, for his entire life was spent running his shop. It was his pride and joy, and if he could not supply any requested item from stock, he would always obtain it from somewhere. On one occasion, I asked if he knew where I could find a belt for our twin-tub spin-dryer, for the existing one had become worn and stretched until it would not properly turn the pulleys. Mr Wilson had one in stock.

His range of cheeses was remarkable, as were his liqueurs, chocolates, fresh fruit and beautiful vegetables, and I know one man who even bought a wheelbarrow wheel from Mr Wilson's stock – and it was the right size.

During the course of my duties, I learned that people respected Mr Wilson highly and relied upon him to cater for all their daily requirements. 'You'll get it at Mr Wilson's,' was the slogan, and so I was a frequent visitor, both on duty and off. He never complained, never seemed flustered or worried and was always in complete control of his stock and in touch with his customers' changing needs.

And then, one breezy day in May, he rang me and asked if I would pay him a visit, preferably between 1 p.m. and 1.45 p.m. when he would be closed for lunch. I was asked to go around the back, to his cottage door, because he wished to discuss a matter without interruption by his customers.

Intrigued by this, I drove across to Crampton and knocked on his cottage door. When he met me, he had a deep frown on his small, pink face and for the first time, to my knowledge, his immaculate head of pure white hair looked untidy. I detected worry in his eyes and there was no doubt he was more than a little agitated.

'Come in, Mr Rhea,' he invited. 'You'll have a coffee with me? Have you eaten?'

'Yes, thanks, I had lunch before I came out, but a coffee would be very welcome.'

He led me into his neat living-room; it was very plain and lacked the touch of a woman. There were no flowers, for example, and everything was in its place, untouched by children, visitors and family. There was not a speck of dust anywhere and his collection of brasses sparkled in the light of the bright spring weather. He indicated a plain leather easy chair and I settled in it as he busied himself with the coffee.

'You'll be wondering why I've called you in,' he said, sitting opposite me and crossing his legs. I was surprised at the tiny size of his shoes, so highly polished and well kept. I'd never seen his feet before, because he was always behind his counters. Now, without those protective barriers, he was like a little elf as his bright blue eyes scrutinised me.

'It must be important,' was my response to that remark.

'Yes, and confidential,' he said. 'Er, am I permitted to discuss something with you unofficially, off the record in a manner of speaking?'

'Of course, we are allowed discretion, you know. We do not enforce every rule by the letter – that would make it a police state!' I wondered what was coming next.

'I have a shop-lifter among my customers.' He drew in a deep breath and then spat out those words. 'A clever and persistent shop-lifter, Mr Rhea. I do not know what to do about her.'

This problem was the scourge of many city shops, and it was also affecting some rural ones which encouraged self-service by their customers. Mr Wilson's was such a shop, for the three counters which formed an open square as the customers entered each bore a selection of goods upon their tops. Sweets, cakes, delicacies, preserves, novels in paperback, spoons, fruit and so forth occupied space upon them.

'You know who it is?' I put to him.

He nodded. 'Yes, it's been going on for some time now, months perhaps, but I've been keeping a careful eye on things recently. I have made myself certain of the identity of the culprit, Mr Rhea.'

'You've confronted her about it?' I asked.

He shook his head this time. 'No, that is the problem, that is why I need your advice.'

'So what's she been doing?'

'General thieving, I think you'd call it,' he smiled a little ruefully. 'She is a good customer, Mr Rhea, a very good one. But I noticed that she began to linger in the shop when other customers were present, allowing me to serve them while she examined my stock. Then she would make her purchases, but I began to realise things had disappeared from my counter surfaces after each of her visits. She was picking things up while I was busy, you see, and hiding them in her shopping-bag.'

'Valuable things?' I asked.

'Not really, more like silly things. Apples, plastic teaspoons, tins of sticking-plasters, tubes of toothpaste, indigestion tablets, bars of chocolate or tubes of sweets, a bottle of wine on one occasion, biscuits, cakes . . .'

'If I am to prosecute her, I'll need to catch her in possession of the stolen goods,' I said. 'I cannot take a person to court without real evidence.'

'No, I don't want that,' he was quick to say. 'I don't want to prosecute her, that's the problem. I just want to stop her.'

'Confrontation would be advisable in the first instance,' I advised him. 'You'd have to catch her in possession of something that you could positively identify as having been stolen from your shop. Then threaten her with court action. That might stop her.'

He hesitated and then said, 'I did halt her on one occasion,' he said quietly. 'I had placed a bottle of French perfume on the front counter, where I knew she had been taking things from, and it disappeared when she was in my shop. As she was leaving, I said, "Miss Carr, the perfume, that will be £3 17s 6d please".'

Unwittingly, he had revealed the name of the shop-lifter but I did not comment on this just yet.

'And what did she do?' I asked.

'She looked at me full in the face and said, "Mr Wilson, I have no perfume. I never use that horrid French stuff".'

'And did you search her bags?'

'Oh, no, I couldn't do that,' he said. 'That would drive her away.'

'You want her driven away, surely?' I put to him.

'On the contrary, Mr Rhea, I do not. That is my dilemma. You see, she is a very good customer. She spends heavily in here, buying all sorts and she always pays cash, except for the silly things she steals. She is not like some customers, Mr Rhea, who run up bills and need pressing to pay them. She pays cash for every honest purchase, so she's a very valuable customer in that sense.'

'You couldn't afford to lose her then?'

He shook his head. 'No, but there's more, you see. She is aunt to lots of people around here. She's one of a very large family, the Carrs, most of whom live around Crampton. Farmers, villagers, professional people – you'll know them as well as me. They're related to the Bennisons, the Tindales, the Haddons, the Newalls, the Lofthouses and others too. Many have accounts with me, Mr Rhea, they're all good spenders. She buys for them, as well; she's very generous you see, always buying things for her army of nephews and nieces, always giving them presents from here. Bottles of wine, expensive cheeses, perfume, tins of exotic fruit and so on. They're things she pays for, by the way.'

'Are you saying that if you banned her, they'd all stop coming as well?'

'It's a fear at the back of my mind,' he admitted. 'They are a very close family, Mr Rhea, and I know they'd never believe that their generous Aunt Mabel was a cunning thief.'

In some ways, it was the classic case of a nasty thief taking advantage of a kindly village storekeeper, and in real terms this was a case which well justified prosecution. I explained to Mr Wilson that we could secrete a camera inside the premises to catch her actually stealing an item, and then take her to court by using that film as evidence. Or we could mark certain objects with a fluorescent powder which would adhere to her hands and clothes, and which would glow under certain lights. By using technology, we could catch her in the act – all this presented no problems.

'No, I couldn't bear that,' he said. 'Not for such a good customer, Mr Rhea, and I must think of her reputation and that of all her relations. The publicity would be terrible in a community of this size.'

'So how can I help if you do not want official action?' I asked.

'I thought you might have knowledge of other methods of prevention, Mr Rhea. I know shop-lifting is a problem, and I thought you might know of some way I could prevent her, for her own sake really, without resorting to court action.'

'I could have a word with her,' I offered. 'I could try to

warn her off. Maybe a lecture from a policeman would
help. I could frighten her off, maybe.'

'She might take umbrage, Mr Rhea, and boycott my
store if she thought I'd been making accusations behind
her back.'

'So we've reached an impasse,' I said. 'You will not
confront her with your suspicions, and you will not allow
me to confront her either. Really, Mr Wilson, if you do not
want official police action, the remedy must come from
you. You've got to decide either to let her continue, or to
ban her from the shop, with all the possible consequences.'

'Oh, dear,' he said. 'I know that if I do ban her, the
others will boycott me, and I could not afford that. There
are some very good customers among her relations, Mr
Rhea. It seems I must grin and bear it, then.'

'Sorry,' I said. 'I only wish I could be more helpful.'

'Well, I had to talk it over with someone impartial,' he
said. 'I shall keep a closer eye on her, that's all.'

And so I left him to his worries. But later that afternoon,
as I drove around my picturesque beat, I felt I'd let him
down. Even though he did not wish me to take official
action, I felt there could have been some advice or help I
might have produced. But what?

How could I involve myself in this problem in an
unofficial capacity? In some ways, Mr Wilson had placed
me in a dilemma too and as I drove around, I passed Miss
Carr's fine house. A magnificent detached stone-built
house, it occupied a prime site about a mile out of Crampton
and as I went past, she drove out of her gate in her new
Volvo.

Money for Miss Carr was no problem; a confident,
fine-looking woman in her early fifties, she paid her way
and was openly generous to her nephews and nieces and
indeed to others who needed help. The village could tell

of many acts of kindness by Mabel Carr. For these reasons, it seemed very odd that she was systematically stealing from this hard-working little shopkeeper. My own instinct was to prosecute her for this unkindness towards him, for I felt it was the only answer. I drove on, and it would be about a week later at lunchtime when I was next in Crampton. Mr Wilson's shop was closed so I decided to walk around the village, then pop in to see him. And as I walked among the pretty cottages and flowering meadows, I had an idea.

'Ah, Mr Rhea,' he beamed. 'Good of you to call.'

'Good afternoon, Mr Wilson,' I smiled. 'How's things?'

'Very well, thank you,' he said. The shop was empty, so we chatted about the weather for a while, and engaged in our usual small talk, and then I asked about Miss Carr.

'Is she still stealing?' I asked.

'I'm afraid so,' he said. 'As bold as brass, really. She got away with a small liqueur on Monday, slipped it into her shopping-bag as quick as lightning. I think she's getting bolder, Mr Rhea. I do wish I could find a way of halting her.'

'I think I have an answer,' I said. 'Highly irregular, I'm afraid, and very unofficial, but it might work.'

He smiled. 'I'll listen to anything.'

'First, I must ask this, you're not making it easy for her to take things, are you? Putting temptation in her way? Placing things where she can't resist them?'

He shook his head. 'No, the stuff she takes is my normal stock which is regularly on the counters for sale. I've always displayed it there, Mr Rhea; in fact, I've been trying to make things a little more difficult for her by putting out larger items, like the bottles of liqueur. But after she'd been in, one was missing. She was too quick for me, Mr Rhea; it had gone in a twinkling and she was out of the shop before I realised what she'd done. That's how she operates; I have kept an eye on her and she knows it, but she's too quick and clever, a real expert. I can't clear my counters because of her; besides, that kind of open sales technique is a valuable source of income.'

I knew that his neat and tidy mind would instinctively realise when something had been taken; he'd know if a solitary tomato or roll of mints was stolen from his stock, so organised was his mind and his business.

'I had to ask,' I said, 'because it's the sort of question that you might get asked by her relations if you implement my little scheme.'

'Short of banning her, Mr Rhea, I've done everything to make it harder for her to steal. So what is your plan?'

'Her relations, nephews, nieces, cousins and so on, how many of them are your customers?'

'Most of them who live hereabouts,' he said, opening a drawer behind the counter. 'I'll check for you.'

He lifted out several small red notebooks, each with a customer's name on the front, and sorted through them. He put several to one side, and then counted them.

'Seven,' he said. 'Seven have monthly accounts with me, these are their books.'

'And are there others without accounts?' I asked.

'Just one,' he said. 'Mrs Ruth Newall, Mabel's elder sister. She pays cash for everything. Why do you ask?'

I side-stepped that question for the moment by asking, 'And are they fond of their Aunt or Cousin Mabel? They'd not want her to get into trouble with us, the police?'

'Oh, they love her, Mr Rhea, they're a lovely family, so close.'

'Good, so this is what I suggest. I suggest that every time Miss Carr steals something, you add its cost to one of those relations' accounts. In other words, you make the family pay for her sins through a form of communal responsibility.'

'They'd know they hadn't bought the goods in question, Mr Rhea, and query it. It's almost dishonest . . .'

'But that's the idea, Mr Wilson, to encourage them to query their account. Then you tell them why, you tell them it's for a bottle of liqueur that Miss Mabel, er, took, without paying. You tell them quite clearly what she's doing, Mr Wilson.'

'I think they'd be very upset.'

'Yes, but that's where you score because you say that she's been stealing for many months, that you've done all in your power to stop her, and short of taking her to the magistrates' court, this is your only redress. I'm sure they'll appreciate your actions in not prosecuting her – after all, she is giving them presents and money . . . besides, that bottle of liqueur, for example, might well be sitting on one of their own shelves right now . . .'

'Yes, I suspect it is, Mr Rhea.'

'The idea is that the responsibility is placed upon her family; it lifts the burden from you and it means you are not losing money or sleep because of her actions.'

'I'll think about it,' was all he said.

It was several weeks later when he called me into his cottage behind the shop.

'Mr Rhea,' he said over a coffee. 'That system you suggested for Mabel Carr. I thought I'd let you know that it is working very well.'

'Is it? Then I'm delighted!'

'I must admit I was uncertain at first, and indeed I ignored it, but then she got away with a full bottle of brandy. I put it on Mrs George Haddon's bill – George is a nephew, and I explained why. It seems Mabel had given him the bottle anyway! But he called a family conference and they invited me up to the Haddons' house to explain things to the whole family, without Mabel's knowledge, of course.'

'That's an excellent move, so they took it well?'

'Yes, very well. They were sorry that she had placed me in such a position, but they fully understood. And they agreed to my actions. They were pleased I had told them.'

'And they will be trying to persuade her to stop shop-lifting?' I smiled.

'Er, no,' he said. 'They do not want to upset her, so we will all allow it to continue, and they will pay for everything she steals. They feel it is a symptom of her time of life, you see, and that she will overcome it eventually. So they're keeping my actions secret from her.'

'And does this please you, Mr Wilson?' I asked.

'Yes, it does, Mr Rhea, and thank you.'

In the days that followed, I wondered whether the actions of Mabel Carr now amounted to the crime of theft and felt this could produce a marvellous challenge for a defence lawyer if such a conspiracy ever reached court. But it never did. Mabel's huge complement of relations continued to pay for her indiscretions and I heard no more about it.

Years later, though, I did learn by sheer chance from one of her sisters that, throughout her youthful and indeed middle-aged years, Mabel Carr had conducted a very one-sided love affair with Mr Wilson. And not once had he shown the slightest romantic interest in her – I don't think he ever knew of, or suspected, her yearnings and devotion.

Maybe her shop-lifting was a last desperate attempt to attract his attention?

5

'Where is the man who has the power and skill
To stem the torrent of a woman's will?'

Anonymous

It was Shakespeare who said that a railing wife was worse
than a smoky house, and Thomas Moore who wrote in his
'Sovereign Woman' that 'Disguise our bondage as we will,
'Tis woman, woman, who rules us still.' Those poets, and
the anonymous gentleman who wrote the opening lines at
the head of this chapter, must have had some personal
knowledge of the awful effect that a nagging wife can have
upon the happiness and peace of mind of a husband.

Down the ages, and in spite of modern scientific progress,
it has been impossible to stop some women from nagging.
One terrible attempt was made by the introduction of the
brank; this was an iron framework which was placed upon
a woman's head and padlocked in position. At the front, it
had a plate from which protruded a spiked or sharp edge,
and this fitted into the mouth of the woman. If she moved
her tongue, therefore, she injured herself; if she kept quiet,
she was not hurt.

With this upon her head, the scold, as she was called,
was paraded through the streets by one of the community
officials. This object, known variously as the brank or
scold's bridle, was thought to have been first used in 1623
in Macclesfield, although there are hints that it was used in

Scotland as early as 1574. In 1600, it is thought, the brank was used in Stirling to punish 'the shrew'.

Around the country, some branks are preserved in our museums, and a famous one is linked to the church at Walton-on-Thames. It was presented to the parish in 1632 by a man called Chester because he had lost one of his estates through the actions of a lying and gossiping woman. Mr Chester presented the brank with this accompanying verse:

> 'Chester presents Walton with a bridle
> To curb women's tongues that talk too idle.'

It is difficult to ascertain when the brank was last used, although there is an account of one in the early part of last century. At Altrincham, a woman who caused great distress to her neighbours by her ceaseless and malicious gossip was punished by being paraded around the town wearing a brank. But she refused to walk with it on and would not agree to this punishment. As a result she was then placed in a wheelbarrow and wheeled around the principal streets and market-place. History assures us that this had the desired effect of curbing her tongue.

Another device for dealing with scolds was the ducking-stool; this varied in detailed construction but was based on something akin to a long plank, rather like a see-saw, which had a chair or seat at one end. It was positioned with the chair over a pond or river, and so the scolding woman, after being tied into the chair, was lowered repeatedly into the water to cool her tongue. This punishment usually attracted a crowd of local folks who came along for the so-called fun.

One account dated 1700, written by a Frenchman upon a visit to England, says, 'The way of punishing scolding women is pleasant enough,' and he then describes the ducking-stool, after which he adds, 'They plunge her into the water as often as the sentence directs, in order to cool her immoderate heat.'

Like the brank, the ducking-stool's last known use occurred in the early years of last century, probably in 1809 at Leominster. The lady was called Jenny Pipes and the first thing she did upon release from the stool was to utter a string of foul oaths as she cursed the magistrates.

Of these two methods, contemporary reports said that the brank was better than the ducking-stool because 'the stool not only endangered the health of the party, it also gave her tongue liberty 'twixt every dip.'

The nagging woman has been a topic of writers, poets and comedians for years, and remains so. I like the story of a man who called his wife Peg, when her real name was Josephine. Someone asked him why he called her Peg and he said, 'Well, Peg is short for Pegasus; Pegasus was an immortal horse and an immortal horse is an everlasting nag.'

There is also a view that nature has given man the apparatus for snoring to compensate for the woman's capacity for nagging. She nags him during the day, so he retaliates by snoring at night, for which she nags him during the day . . . and so a type of noisy if uneasy balance is achieved.

But not all naggers are married to snorers and not all snorers are married to naggers, which means that many innocent people suffer from vitriolic and poisonous tongues while others must tolerate nights of oscillating and very tuneless olfactory muscles.

One would hardly expect the village constable to become involved in marital battles of this kind, but in fact all police officers, whether rural or urban, do find themselves involved in what the police call 'domestics'. These are breaches of the peace which generally occur among families; if the battles remain behind closed doors, we are not too concerned, but when warring women spill into the street armed with frying-pans, rolling-pins and sharp tongues, then we are sometimes called in to quell what could otherwise develop into a breach of the peace in a public place. As a rule, we try to avoid these because the moment the peace-making constable arrives, the sparring partners both turn upon the unfortunate constable. But at least that stops the quarrelling and perhaps personifies the constable's unsung role in maintaining public tranquillity. He keeps the peace while being attacked from all sides.

It would not be possible in this book to list all the 'domestics' in which I became officially involved, but they did conform to this pattern and few terminated in court. They were usually settled by a stern talking-to or threats of having 'binding-over' orders levelled against the parties, for most were of a sudden and temporary nature.

But there were cases when nagging wives caused domestic upsets of a more permanent kind. One involved a man called Joseph Pringle who had a wife called Roberta. They lived in a neat little bungalow in Aidensfield, just off the Elsinby Road, where it nestled cheerfully among trees with a fine view to the south. With no children, the Pringles were a quiet couple who rarely involved themselves in village matters. Mrs Pringle's socialising was done in York.

I first became aware of Joseph when I noticed his car halting outside the Brewer's Arms at Aidensfield around seven each weekday evening. He always popped in for a swift half of bitter on his way home from work, and sometimes I came across him when I was on official business in the pub. If I had any confidential enquiries to make of any landlord, I would pop in before the customers filled the bars. And so I became acquainted with Joseph Pringle.

Aged about forty with a balding head of greying hair, he was one of those insignificant men who are hardly noticed among a crowd of three. Of average height and average build, he wore average clothes and drove an average car at an average sort of speed. He lived in an average house on an average income, but, as I was to learn later, he suffered from a higher-than-average amount of nagging. He had married a true virago, a real warrior of a woman who constantly and cruelly nagged him during his every moment at home. She never gave him a moment's peace; she nagged and nagged and nagged.

Roberta Pringle was a loud-mouthed, energetic and very forceful woman who played hell with everyone; good-looking in some ways, she was approaching forty and had a fine figure topped with an equally fine head of dark hair which framed a handsome, rather than pretty, face. Slightly taller than her husband, she was always very well dressed, but went about her daily routine playing hell with the postman, the dustman, the milkman, the paper-boys, the butcher, the grocer, the vicar, the policeman, her neighbours and anyone else with whom she had any dealings. And of course, when they were not available, she played hell with Joseph.

Because most of them learned, by experience, to keep out of her way, Joseph bore the heaviest burden. He was continuously told off because of the government, the rates, the parish council, the state of the nation, the cost of living, the sloppy work of builders, plumbers, electricians, motor mechanics, doctors, dentists and nurses; she played hell about the roads, snowploughs, weather forecasters, British Rail, bus timetables, canteen ladies, rubbish bins, café proprietors, village shops, the Post Office, tinned beans, the telephone system, television, women's fashions, men's trousers, hotel beds, the water supply, long grass, bruised apples, cold Yorkshire puddings and fatty ham.

And she never stopped complaining and nagging, which meant that her range of subject-matter was never exhausted. Indeed, it expanded, with the meek Joseph having his ears lambasted during all his precious moments at home.

As a result, of course, he started to come home later, a ploy which enabled him to avoid some of her vitriol and which was part of the reason he paid his nightly visit to the Brewer's Arms. It gave him peace from both work and wife.

Joseph owned and ran his own gentlemen's outfitters in Eltering. It was a modest shop which sold fairly cheap clothes whose quality was not of the highest. He now faced competition from the major department stores in York and elsewhere for they stocked good clothes within the cheaper range, while those men with money patronised their own bespoke tailors. Joseph had no drive and ambition; he did not wish to become the owner of a chain of shops nor did he strive to change his own dwindling circumstances. He seemed content to let things drift downwards, and I began to learn of his shrinking fortune in the course of my patrolling.

Some hint of his problems arose when I popped into his shop to buy some black socks. He was on the telephone, and was saying words like, 'Yes, dear. No, dear. Yes, I will. No, I will not be late tonight. There isn't much in the till today. Yes, I know the car needs attention, the brakes, yes. I'll see what the garage says.'

When he saw me at the counter, he said, 'I have a customer, dear. See you tonight,' and he replaced the handset.

'Women!' he said, recognising me. 'All they think about is money and status! Well, Mr Rhea, what can I get you?'

'Two pairs of black socks please, Joseph,' I said.

He obtained them and I paid, then he said, 'There are times I wish I had your job, Mr Rhea. A regular salary, interesting life, varied work and the means of travelling around the district. I'm stuck in here, day in and day out, it does get a bit monotonous.'

'It's funny, you know,' I said. 'Lots of policemen say they'd like their own business.'

'It has some advantages, Mr Rhea, but times are not good for my trade. Multiple stores, cheaper mass-produced clothes, foreign imports – small shops are finding it hard, very hard to compete. I'd pack it in tomorrow if I could.'

'You surprise me.' I was honest when I said that.

He seemed anxious to talk so I did not rush away.

'Roberta likes to live well, to dress well, to socialise and have a nice home. I can't give her all she wants, Mr Rhea, it does worry me.'

'Could you sell up and try another business?'

'I would have trouble selling this shop, I feel. But you don't need burdening with my worries! Thanks for listening, I needed someone to say that to. Not that you can help, but at least you did listen.'

'I'll listen whenever you want, Joseph.' I tried to show a little understanding. 'Maybe I will come across someone who wants a shop just like yours. As you say, I am out and about a lot.'

'Thanks, I'll buy you a half next time you're in the Brewer's Arms,' he offered with a sad smile.

Further hints of Joseph Pringle's problems came to me over the next few months. A businessman friend from York, for example, asked if I knew the Pringles of Aidensfield; my friend's wife was a member of a York Ladies Luncheon Club where Roberta Pringle was also a member. It seemed she had told her fellow members that Joseph ran a men's clothing manufacturing business with outlets all over the country. In fact, there was an internationally known manufacturer of men's high-quality clothing at Eltering, but it was not Joseph's business. Roberta's skilful story-telling had led her friends to believe he was a very successful businessman and that those premises were his. I began to see that Roberta was living a life of fiction, a life of fantasy, a life of dangerous expense for poor old Joseph.

It explained why she socialised away from home, why she kept away from those who knew her well, why she dressed so expensively, why she was always nagging at the tired Joseph to improve his status and income. And, as eventually I learned, she was spending all his cash.

I met him on a walk one Sunday morning and he wanted to talk again. 'You've not found anyone who might want my shop, Mr Rhea?' was his opening gambit.

'Sorry, Joseph.' I had asked around, and had in fact come across a retiring police sergeant who was thinking of starting a shop in Eltering. Not a clothes shop, however, although he did express interest in the premises. But he never went ahead.

I promised Joseph I'd keep my ears and eyes open on his behalf.

'I'm getting to the point where I can't pay my bills,' he said. 'I can't get credit to buy my stock . . .'

'How about a sale?' I suggested. 'Why not sell off some older stock?'

'I have,' he said. 'It's Roberta, you see, she is a partner and she never stops buying clothes for herself. She does need them, you see, for her luncheon clubs and theatre outings and so on, and it's not fair if I stop the only enjoyment she has in life. She has to be smart, she's mixing with the right people, you see . . .'

It's all right telling a man to be firm with a wife who is

ruining him, but it's a different thing persuading that same man to take positive action. I never knew why Joseph did not take a firmer stance for I'd heard that she demanded a new outfit every month so that she could keep up her social appearances . . . poor old Joseph. Much of his dilemma was due to his own fault and his weakness with his awful wife, but I could only commiserate with him. Tentatively, I asked whether Roberta might help in the shop, perhaps by selling other lines, baby clothes, for example, or ladies' wear.

'Oh, no, she wouldn't do that, Mr Rhea, not Roberta. She doesn't believe in women having to work.'

'But if it's to save your business, your livelihood . . .'

He shook his head. 'She won't, I've tried that idea. In fact, I think a general clothes shop would go well, but I'd need finance to establish it, and I'd need staff to run it, but can't afford either.'

Surely Roberta would have worked with him, for no wages, to establish a thriving business and to enable her to continue her desired way of life? But she would not. He was adamant about that. After this chat, there was no doubt in my mind where his problem lay. Over the weeks that followed, I saw him spending longer and longer in the Brewer's Arms, not getting drunk because he wasn't that kind of man. He just wanted relief from her nagging, but then she started ringing the pub. She began nagging at George, the landlord, demanding that he send Joseph home, and when Joseph got home, he was faced with more nagging.

Roberta continued to nag George day in and day out until, whenever poor Joseph went in for a quick half, George would say, 'Come on, Joseph, don't spend all night here, I don't want that wife of yours hogging my telephone and nagging me. Folks come here to get away from nagging.'

Poor old Joseph. There was no escape.

As for Roberta, she continued to strut around the village in her finery, holding her head high and nagging at everyone she met until the end came. Joseph went bankrupt. It was all done quietly with very little noise from Roberta, but his ailing shop closed, and they sold their bungalow. But this did not stop Roberta.

I was to learn that they had moved into York where, according to Roberta, Joseph had become a director of one of the city's department stores but where, in fact, he was an assistant on the men's shirt counter.

And she continued to attend her important social functions in the finest of clothes. Looking back, she would have been a fine candidate for the brank or the ducking-stool, and I'm sure plenty of volunteers could have been found to administer that punishment.

Since then, I've always felt sorry for the Josephs of this world, but really, who was to blame?

Another case of a nagging wife had a very different outcome. Benjamin Owens was a hill farmer in a fairly small way and his untidy clutch of ramshackle buildings occupied a remote hillside in Rannackdale. Always in need of painting, glazing, tidying-up and general maintenance, his mediocre spread barely earned him a living. He managed to scrape together a few pounds every week by selling milk from his small herd of cows, and by selling eggs, poultry, sheep for mutton and some wool when he sheared his little flock of moorland sheep. A tiny patch of land was cultivated and he would sometimes sell turnips, potatoes or cabbages to the local shops. He earned just enough for subsistence; he never bought clothes nor went out socially, except once a month to Eltering Market to sell his stock and to buy more. Even then, he went in his scruffy old clothes which he'd worn every day for about fifteen years.

Benjamin, who was about sixty-two years old, had farmed at Helm End, Rannackdale, all his life; his parents had run the tiny farm before him and his grandfather before that, so there was no mortgage to worry about. The farm had been handed down from father to son for generations, but Benjamin had no heirs. His massive wife, Kate, who was perhaps a couple of years younger, had never produced a litter, as he once said.

The income from such a small hillside small-holding did not allow luxuries or extras; Benjamin ran a battered old pick-up, an even more battered old tractor and his untidy wife never worried about dusting the house, washing their clothes regularly or doing any form of extra housework. She did the essentials like baking, cooking their meals and some shopping, but little more.

As I got to know them better, I realised they never went anywhere together. Benjamin's only outing was to Eltering Cattle Mart once a month. The rest of his time was spent at home. Kate, however, did go out once a week. Dressed in her long, scruffy overcoat and black wellington boots, she caught the bus to Eltering every Friday to do her shopping and seemed to enjoy these trips. She also went to the WI meetings once a month and on special occasions, such as the Anniversary, would visit the chapel high in the dale.

In those early days, I wondered whether they shared a bed, for they seemed to live separate lives, seldom speaking to one another but never fighting. Each got on with his or her own work as they had done for years, and they ate together, their main meal, a hot dinner, being at 12 noon prompt. It was a mutual understanding, a convenient arrangement and neither seemed to mind this form of life.

I saw them once a month when I went to inspect their

stock registers, and Kate always produced a mug of hot tea for me, along with a plate of fine home-made scones or rock buns. Benjamin would join us at the kitchen table, we'd discuss business and local matters, and then I'd leave.

I must be honest and say that I never noticed any discord between them but, on reflection, never noticed any warmth in their relationship. They seemed to exist side by side, to live beneath the same roof without any overt problems, but without the love or understanding that one finds in most families.

But, as I grew to know them better, and as I gained the confidence of other local farmers, especially those in Rannackdale, I learned more of the Owens' way of life.

'Never slept in t'same bed ever,' one stalwart informed me. 'She's never let him near 'er; poor awd Benjamin's nivver covered that missus of 'is, nivver. He was a bit of a stallion as a lad, but she's kept him short. It's a bit late now, mind, 'cos t'farm'll etti be sold up when they're called up ti yon small-holding in the sky.'

As I was realising I'd never heard of a child of their union, he continued, 'Ah doubt she'll produce a lad noo. She's ovver awd for that sort o' caper; if she was a coo, they'd have her put down. She's neither use nor ornament, if you ask me.'

He was right, because Kate was far from pretty. In fact, she was downright ugly, a large, loose and untidy woman with hairs on her upper lip and a floppy body which seemed to spill at random out of her ill-fitting clothes. Her iron-grey hair was pulled tightly back into a bun behind her head and she had awful teeth, many of which were rotten or missing. I could fully understand why Benjamin had never 'covered her' as his colleague so aptly put it.

But Benjamin wasn't much of a catch either. A wiry

fellow with freckles all over his balding head of thin gingery-grey hair, he looked more like a retired jockey than a farmer. Bandy-legged, thin as a lath and often unshaven, he was not the kind of man who would appeal to a woman.

I was to learn also that Kate nagged him. She nagged him about getting more work done around the farm. The poor little fellow seemed to work every hour except those trips to mart, but Kate demanded more. On one occasion when I called, I could hear her lashing him with her tongue.

'If thoo didn't spend si much time messing aboot wi' these coos, you'd have more time ti spend on yon field, growing crops, selling tonnups, cabbages and t'like.'

'Coos need care,' he countered. 'We need coos for t'milk cheque . . .'

'That's a woman's job, our Benjamin. Coos is for milkmaids, not fellers.'

'Then you do it.'

'Nay, Ah've enough on what wi t'hens and t'house.'

From what I gathered in my rounds, she did nag at him, her chief antic being that whatever he was doing at any particular time, she thought he should be doing something else. If he worked on his sheep, she thought he should be working on the cows; if he was with the cows, he should be in the fields, and if he was in the fields, he ought to be tending his sheep. If he settled down for a rest at night, he ought to be fixing the tractor, and if he was fixing the tractor, he should be tidying the garage.

I understand that poor old Benjamin had tolerated this for years. Her constant irritation had led him never to argue or talk with her, except when it was essential during moments like 'Pass t'tea pot, will yer?' or 'Get us a roll o' binder twine if you're in Atkinson's.'

Then I had a spell doing pig-licence duty at Eltering Cattle Mart and noticed Benjamin with his cronies. He was in a group of farmers of his own age, and was clearly enjoying himself. He noticed me and came across for a word.

'They've let you away from t'missus an' all, have they?' he said, grinning from ear to ear.

'Now, Benjamin,' I greeted him. 'Good to see you out and about, getting away from that busy spot of yours. And, yes, they have let me loose for today!'

'That's what cattle marts are for, Mr Rhea, to get us fellers away from them wimmin folk. Ah mean to say, we could sell cattle in other ways, but, by gum, it's a grand way of having a day out.'

'You've left your missis at home then?' I knew he always came without Kate, but used the phrase to make conversation with him.

'Aye, she's better off there. Couldn't fetch her here, tha knaws. If she saw me standing here, she'd say Ah should be standing ovver there, and if Ah was looking at them Red Polls, she'd say Ah should be thinking of Jerseys and if Ah took her into t'Black Swan for a beef sandwich, she'd want to go to t'Golden Lion for a ham sandwich. As things are, Ah can do as Ah like; Ah allus does, mind, 'cos I don't let that nagging get to me. It just maks her go on a bit more, but doon here, wiv me mates, I can have a day off nagging.'

'Enjoy it,' I smiled.

'Don't you worry, Mr Rhea, Ah shall.'

I could appreciate his genuine need to get away from the farm, and then, as I performed more of those market duties, I noticed that Benjamin's group of market friends included a tall and very attractive blonde girl. She would be about twenty-five years old at the most, and I noticed he spent a good deal of time talking to her.

So fascinating was her style and beauty that most of them were taking a keen interest in her, and I noticed that she attended every mart. My own curiosity was such that I wanted to find out more about her, and the opportunity came through Benjamin himself. He came to my little wooden shed at the mart for a pig-movement licence, saying he thought he'd try a few store pigs for fattening in the hope that the bacon factory would eventually buy them from him.

'Who's your friend, Benjamin?' I asked him, nodding towards the direction of the tall blonde.

He blushed just a fraction when he realised I was speaking particularly of her, then said, 'Oh, yon's awd Harry Clemmitt's lass, Rachel. Fine lass, that. She does all his buying and selling at mart; knows her beasts, she does. Ah gets all my stock from her, Mr Rhea. Knows his breeding stock does Harry Clemmitt, and she does, an' all. You can rely on Harry Clemmitt for good breeding stock.'

'She's taken a shine to you!' I laughed, for she seemed to be very happy in Benjamin's company, even if their ages and appearances were poles apart.

'Ah used to be a good 'un at chatting up the wimmin, Mr Rhea,' he chuckled. 'Ah reckon Ah've lost nowt o' me touch!'

'I can see that!' I said, and he walked off, beaming with pride at his achievement with the girl. But I was not to realise, until some time later, that Benjamin and the girl were considerably more than just good friends. For one thing, they met here regularly and he took her to lunch.

The full realisation came to me about six weeks later when I called at Helm End Farm to make my routine check of the Owens' stock registers. I went into the untidy kitchen for my customary mug of tea and buttered scone, and was welcomed by Kate. As she fussed over me, the door opened and in walked Benjamin, followed by the tall blonde girl.

'Morning, Mr Rhea,' he beamed. 'Good to see you.'

'Hello, Benjamin.' I couldn't take my eyes off the girl; even when dressed in her rough working-jeans and old smock, she was gorgeous. Her erect bearing, long blonde hair, smooth skin and lovely features were so out of place here. I could even visualise her on the catwalk of a fashion show, such was her elegance and stylishly slender build.

'This is Rachel,' he introduced her. 'My new milkmaid.'

'Milkmaid?' I said, puzzled.

'Aye, Kate said coos were wimmin's work, and 'cos she wouldn't take 'em on, Ah thought Ah'd better get a milkmaid. Rachel here knows about coos and got a bit sick o' working on her dad's farm, so I've takken her on. She sleeps in, Mr Rhea, so she's part of t'family now.'

'Hello, Rachel,' I said to the milkmaid.

'Hello, Mr Rhea,' she said, moving sensually across to the cupboard for a jug of milk for our tea.

It was impossible to guess what was going through Kate's mind at this time, but I think she felt this stunning girl would never be interested in her thin, scruffy and ageing husband. But Kate was wrong.

One night, she came back early from a WI meeting because the speaker had failed to turn up for his engagement, and poor Kate caught Benjamin and the girl together in bed. The outcome was not one of the famous 'domestics' we were so accustomed to on council estates, but merely a rapid and discreet exit by Kate. She simply packed her bags and left that same night, without a fight and without an argument. She stayed that night with a friend, and told her, 'I would never let him touch me, the filthy old brute, so she can't be very choosy! I'll not live in the same house as a hussy like that and he's welcome to her!'

Even now, I do not know what happened to Kate, for no one saw her again. So far as I know, she never returned to the district and I never heard of any divorce. But Rachel Clemmitt continued to live with Benjamin at the remote farm, and during my monthly calls, I noticed the transformation to the premises, and to Benjamin himself. The entire place was smartened up, the house was cleaned from top to bottom, new licks of paint were added, the farmyard was tidied up and the whole enterprise appeared to be buzzing with new life. Rachel had transformed the farm.

She had transformed Benjamin too. Uncharacteristically, he appeared in the pub one night with Rachel, and he sported a smart new jacket and trousers; his face was bright and alert and he behaved like a prosperous farmer, and a happy one. I was later to learn that he was prosperous; in spite of outward appearances, Benjamin had made lots of money.

Another benefit of his life with Rachel was that he looked and behaved as if he were ten years younger, and in time, Rachel started to call herself Mrs Owen. She looked very happy too and it wasn't long before she was pregnant. At this news, Benjamin strutted around like a proud bantam cock, as pleased as any man could be, and in due course, a son was born.

I called about a month afterwards and saw the baby in his smart new pram. Rachel was fussing over her son, whom she called Patrick, and Benjamin insisted on lifting him out for me to examine.

'Marvellous,' I congratulated them both. 'How marvellous for you both. You must be very proud!'

'Ah allus said t'Clemmitts had good breeding stock, Mr Rhea, and Ah was right. There'll be a new line of Owens to continue this farm now. Ah did it just in time.'

I smiled and said, 'So you did, Benjamin.'

'Ah was a bit oot o' practice, mind, but wiv a bit o'

training, Ah soon got caught up again. Like a lad Ah was, in full strength. And see that, a fine lad, as bonny as you could wish to see anywhere. And he's mine, all mine.'

'And mine,' said Rachel gently.

I was pleased for Benjamin, but even now I cannot understand why such a lovely young woman had given herself entirely to this curious old character. She'd seen him as a poverty-stricken, unkempt old hill farmer during his visits to the mart and she knew his background and his age.

In spite of all that, she had fallen in love with him and had then transformed his life. Albeit at the unfortunate Kate's expense, it was something of a miracle and it only served to make me more curious about the way a woman's mind operates. That is something I have not yet discovered! But Benjamin became a local legend because of this romance; his prowess as a lover was the talking-point of the market and of the surrounding villages, and none of the eligible young men of the area could understand why they had lost to this ageing Lothario from Rannackdale. Nor could anyone else.

As one envious old farmer said to me: 'He got shot o' that nagging awd bitch of a wife and won hissell yon fit-looking lass who looks good enough for a duke and fit enough for a young buck of a lad. And he did it all without missing one hot dinner.'

Another character with a chattering wife was Horace Pitman who ran a small garage and taxi-service in Waindale. His was an old-fashioned garage which had been operating since the first cars came to these dales. Stocked with spare parts in neatly marked and carefully arranged boxes, and with a pair of tall green petrol pumps outside, Horace's garage was always busy. He worked from seven each morning until ten each night, except when he was on rural or county council business. On those occasions, he would take a day off and hire a driver/pump attendant should anyone require a taxi or some petrol.

I seldom saw Horace dressed in anything but a pair of navy blue overalls heavy with grease and equally greasy black boots. He did all the mechanical work himself and somehow coped with everything that came his way.

Horace was a big man. In his late forties, he must have weighed at least sixteen stone and had a jolly, calm face which never seemed troubled by anything or anyone. Balding on top, and with a monk's hair-style of sandy hair, he wore rimless glasses and, oddly enough, always sported a crisp white shirt and coloured tie beneath his overalls. I think that was in case he got a sudden taxi job – he could throw off his overalls and put on a blazer type of jacket he kept hanging in his garage.

Everyone liked Horace, which is probably why he found himself elected to the rural district council, and then to the county council. With so little spare time, he did manage to accommodate his council duties, and often went to meetings at Northallerton in his white shirt and working clothes. These comprised a pair of dark crumpled trousers, that blazer-like jacket which he kept in the garage, and his greasy black boots. One snag with his trade was that his hands were never clean; black oil had engrained itself into the skin of his hands and his fingernails were always black. Scrub as he might, he could never get his hands clean. Those who knew him paid no attention to his mode of dress or dirty hands, but I often wonder what the other councillors thought.

But Horace was a good man, a fine councillor and a very able person in every respect; perhaps in other circumstances, he would have become a top-flight businessman or even a politician. But he was utterly content with his busy village life – he loved cars and he liked being a councillor, and his way of life gave him the best of both his chosen worlds.

His wife, Dora, was an ideal companion for him. A tiny, active woman in her early forties, she was a bundle of energy who had a family of three fine teenage children and who busied herself with the Red Cross, Women's Institute, night classes and various other charities. She was secretary to countless village organisations, including the parish council and parochial church council, and she also did the office work and accounts for Horace's garage.

And she was a non-stop chatterer, unlike Horace who was a man of very few words. What he did say usually made sense, but she could not stop talking, and the village knew that if she cornered anyone for a two-minute chat, it would continue for half an hour if her time was short, and for well over an hour if things were progressing in a more leisurely manner. Horace, however, allowed her flow of constant chatter to drift away to oblivion over his head and he had that happy knack of saying 'Yes, dear,' at frequent intervals while never listening to a word she said. For Horace, Dora's voice was nothing more than background noise, there to be ignored where possible.

He did respond when she called 'Coffee's ready,' or 'Dinner' or 'Tea's up,' usually by simply arriving at the table or desk where she placed his morning cuppa. Even in council meetings, he said very little, consequently when he did say something, everyone listened. With his wife, however, no one listened, least of all Horace.

For all her chattering, she was a lovely woman and he was a fine man; they were a popular and hard-working pair of people who deserved the best. If anything, Dora was perhaps a little more ambitious than Horace although not in the same league as Mrs Pringle. Dora loved and respected her husband and felt that his work for the council, both at local rural level and at county level, deserved some recognition.

But Horace was not interested; he went along to the meetings, said his brief piece and came home to his garage. And that, in his mind, was that. He rarely told Dora what had transpired and if she asked what had happened, he would usually say, 'Nowt much.'

I caught a hint of Dora's ambitions one day when I was in his garage. I was asking about stolen cars, and had provided him with a list of their registration numbers in case any were brought in for petrol; he would ring me or our Divisional Headquarters if he spotted one. As we chatted, Dora came in with his coffee and invited me to have one. I agreed, and she joined us, chattering non-stop.

'I mean,' she said, 'they never say thank you, not one of them out of the whole village and they expect Horace to trek over to Northallerton month in and month out to say his piece for them and to fight their fights about rates, drainage, the water works and sewage and I mean, he does do well for the village, don't you think, Mr Rhea? More than some I know, more than some who make much more of a fuss about it and you'd think they would make a bit of a fuss about a man who works so hard for other folks and who's got a business, two businesses in fact, taxi and garage, to run as well. It's not as if he's retired or on a private income, you see . . .'

I wanted to say that councillors did not work for thanks but she would not let me get a word in.

'Dora . . .' I began.

'Well, you would think they'd do something for people like my Horace, Mr Rhea . . .'

And so she went on, so I drank my coffee while Horace rubbed at a piece of car engine with some emery paper.

She rabbited on for a long time and I found myself becoming like Horace. Everything she said drifted over my head and once I caught sight of Horace, smiling to himself. This was a regular event for him.

I could see that his wife had some social ambitions for Horace even if he did not have any for himself, and it would be about a month later when I next came across the voluble Dora. I was on duty in Waindale when she was shopping and she spotted me; before I could leap into the mini-van to avoid a marathon session of her brand of verbal diarrhoea, she had presented herself before me.

'Ah,' she began a little breathlessly. 'Just the man who might help me. Mr Rhea, I know you are familiar with the county council and how they operate because our Horace never tells me a thing because he just goes along to those meetings and says nothing, then comes home and says nothing has happened until I read in the paper that they're building new schools here, police stations there, libraries and fire stations, new roads and putting the rates up and he would know all that and yet he never says a thing to me about it. You'd think he would, wouldn't you, I mean I am his wife but the reason I've stopped you, and I won't keep you because you must be a very busy man with lots of enquiries to make and jobs to do apart from talking to women like me, is that I thought you might know something about the Buckingham Palace thing. I met this lady at WI whose cousin is a councillor from Malton just like my Horace and he's been on years, she says, sitting on the Finance Committee and the Highways Committee and really getting involved . . .'

'The Buckingham Palace thing?' I was baffled and managed to register my curiosity as she turned to smile at a friend.

'Yes, you know,' she said. 'You must know, being a

policeman, but that lady didn't know much about it because her husband had never gone on it and I wondered if you knew what it was, Mr Rhea, and whether I, well, Horace really, could go along as well, I mean, it would be nice, wouldn't it? It would be a sort of thank-you for Horace for all he's done and I could wear a new hat and lovely coat and meet the Queen and all those important people. I've always wanted to go to a posh place like that, Mr Rhea, in one of those large hats with a wide brim, you know, the sort society ladies wear at races and operas and things like that . . .'

As she chattered on, I began to gain a glimmer of understanding.

'You mean the selection procedure for the Garden Parties?' I said during another momentary lull in her chatter.

'Yes, so you do know! How marvellous. What do I have to do, well Horace really, what does he have to do? I mean, does he write to the Queen or how does he get there? I mean, I'm sure Her Majesty has never heard of my Horace even though he does do an awful lot of good work for the council and the village but he's so quiet about it and never makes a fuss while other folks who don't do so much seem to get down to the Palace for tea with the Queen.'

Now I realised what she was talking about because my own grandfather, himself a county councillor, had once been invited to Buckingham Palace for a garden party.

Dora stopped chattering to say a long 'Hello' to a passing friend, and this gave me the chance to say, 'Horace will have been told about the system, you know.'

'He never tells me anything, Mr Rhea, you know my Horace, tight as the proverbial duck's, well, you know what and he always says nothing's happened at the meetings, then I hear of Mr and Mrs So-and-So, then Mr and Mrs

This-and-That going off to London to meet the Queen and I ask myself why isn't our Horace getting himself there, and why isn't he taking me? I would love to go and wear my new hat, Mr Rhea, I really would, it's not as if I get far, you know, what with the business and my other interests, so this would be a once-in-a-lifetime outing, a really lovely one . . .'

'There's a draw for tickets,' I managed to tell her. 'I'm not sure when it's done or how often, but according to my grandfather, all councillors who want to be considered must put their names forward, and then a draw is made. Those drawn out of the hat, in a manner of speaking, are then invited to the Palace Garden Party. But Horace would have to find out exactly how the system operates. Get him to put his name forward, Dora. But you realise it's something of a lottery – not everyone can go, so there's no guarantee Horace would win an invitation.'

She beamed with happiness.

'Oh, Mr Rhea, I know he'll get there if only he'll do something about it . . . I will have a word with him straight away; now I mustn't keep you, I know you're very busy.'

She kept me standing there another ten minutes, saying how busy I was and how busy she was, and then she sailed away home in a very cheerful mood. Horace, I knew, was in for a session of chatter from her, with strict instructions to put his name forward next time Buckingham Palace asked the county council for Garden Party nominees.

It would be four or five weeks later when Horace mentioned this; I had popped into his garage on a routine enquiry and he said, 'Mr Rhea, our Dora said summat about you suggesting I put my name down for t'Buckingham Palace jobs?'

'Yes,' I said. 'She was asking how councillors like

yourself managed to get invited to Buckingham Palace, so I told her about the draw they have.'

'Aye, well, I can't say sike affairs are much in my line, but my name's gone down. They asked us at t'last meeting, and a few councillors sent their names in. I thought I would, then if our Dora goes on at me, I can allus say I put my name forward. That'll keep her quiet, 'cos I shan't win. I never win owt, Mr Rhea.'

I was surprised that he had bothered to actually do this, for it would have been easy to tell a white lie, to tell Dora he had submitted his name even if he hadn't. But the surprising thing was that Horace won. His name was drawn from the list and he was notified by a telephone call, following which detailed instructions about the event would be sent to him.

Dora spent hours rushing around the village telling her friends, and then she went off to York to buy an entire new outfit, including one of those huge wide-brimmed hats that were her heart's desire.

Then the formal instructions arrived by post.

And Dora's world fell apart.

Horace had certainly submitted his name, but he had failed to understand that he had also to nominate his wife; he had failed to include her name, and so the invitation was for him and him alone. A maiden lady councillor from Whitby had also won an invitation – she had been issued with the one that should have gone to Councillor Horace Pitman's lady.

Dora's anger and disappointment was acute and she kept herself hidden from the public for some weeks after this bad news. Then on the day before the event, I saw Horace getting into one of his cars, and went across. He was dressed in the dark blazer he used for taxi-driving; he had on a dark tie and white shirt, and some crumpled trousers which he usually wore under his overalls. His boots were clean but very greasy and he carried a brown paper carrier-bag.

'Going shopping, Horace?' I asked.

'Nay, it's for t'hotel tonight, Mr Rhea. I'm off to London. A clean collar and me razor and toothbrush. I need nowt else. I'm off to Buckingham Palace.'

And so he was; thus equipped, he got into his car and started the engine. I had no idea whether he intended to drive all the way to London or catch a train from York, but he sat there, smiling at me but saying nothing as he ran the engine of his car.

And then Dora came rushing out, looking like a dream. She wore a beautiful new suit, a matching wide-brimmed hat and high-heeled shoes. She carried a small suitcase and a matching handbag.

'Off to see the Queen, Dora?' I asked.

'I am not, and I'm glad I'm not, not with our Horace looking like that. You'd think he would have got some new clothes if he's to shake Her Majesty by the hand . . . no, Mr Rhea, he's not getting away with this! I'm going to London to see the sights, a play maybe, and then the shops. I wouldn't be seen dead with our Horace dressed like that . . .'

And Horace engaged first gear and drove off with a big smile on his face. I wondered what Her Majesty would make of him. Upon their return, Dora never stopped talking about her trip. She'd had a marvellous time and had crammed a host of exciting events into her short visit to the city. As for Horace, I asked him what he thought of the Buckingham Palace Garden Party.

'Not much,' he said. 'T'food was nowt but a load o' ket.'

A translation of that dialect word would, I doubt, not please those who arranged the teas.

6

'If this be not love, it is madness,
and then it is pardonable.'
William Congreve, 1670-1729

One of the recurring duties of the sympathetic police officer involves dealing with people in distress; there are times when that distress is self-inflicted either by accident or design, and there are times it is inflicted upon us by other people or by a single event or even a series of unfortunate occurrences. Officialdom, bureaucracy and red tape can also inflict distress in their own inimitable manner, the latter being revealed when puzzled pensioners receive threatening letters from computerised accounts departments when their rates or other bills have been paid.

Minor examples of distress might include those who lock themselves out of their homes or whose motor cars run out of petrol, or who are locked out of their homes by others during arguments or stupidity, or whose cars run out of petrol because their teenage son has surreptitiously done a trip to Scotland and back. Other people can inflict distress upon us, by simple things like persistent telephone calls or playing football in our front garden, or by greed such as burglary or through dangerous actions like reckless driving, playing about with firearms or indeed anything else. The possibilities of trouble are endless and it seems we are continually at risk either through our own behaviour or from the actions of others.

In the course of police work, therefore, the constable often comes across examples of this kind and seeks to comfort the victims where possible. A kind word and some assurance that the world isn't going to end is generally sufficient, albeit tempered with advice on how to cope with the unexpected and harrowing predicament.

In dealing with jobs of this kind, however, it becomes evident that of all the root causes of man's predilection for disaster, that which causes most problems is man's love for woman. Through their vast experience of people, police officers know that men get themselves into some of the most curious situations in their undying efforts to prove their love to the lady of their dreams. Constables know that love is one of the most powerful of urges, so strong that at times it removes every scrap of common sense from the skulls of those whom it infects. A poet who remains anonymous once said that 'Love is a passion which has caused the change of empires' – in short, men do the daftest things when they are in love, and I have mentioned some of their misadventures in previous 'Constable' books.

But because this symptom provides a never-ending series of dramas, sagas, mishaps, problems and (to be honest) a few chuckles in the process, every constable has witnessed and can recount stirring tales of love. They would fill a volume, so I thought I would place on record a few more tales of the love-lorn countryman.

One example occurred during the depths of winter. While I was the village bobby at Aidensfield, one of my less pleasant duties as Christmas approached was to man road-checks at various lonely points. This meant stopping all cars to check them and their boots for stolen chickens, turkeys, drinks and other festive fare. We were also seeking those who stole holly from gardens and Christmas trees from our acres of local forests. It was a task that country constables had undertaken for years and the only time I found any game in a car was when I halted and searched a Rolls-Royce which, it transpired, had a boot full of pheasants. His Lordship was not too pleased; he was delivering them to his tenants.

The timing of those road-blocks varied, but they were usually of two hours' duration, perhaps starting at 8 p.m., 9 p.m., 10 p.m., 11 p.m. or even midnight, and on each occasion we selected a different check-point. Word generally got around the local pubs that the police were checking cars at Bank Top or The Beacon or Four Lane Ends, which probably meant the poachers took alternative routes. But we did get results – we found cars with no insurance, drivers with no licences, cars not taxed, cars with dirty number plates and cars in a dangerous condition. We caught drunken drivers, car thieves and burglars and, once in a while, we caught a Christmas poacher with a boot full of illicitly acquired game or liquor, or a hard-up dad who had risked digging up a Norway spruce from the local Forestry Commission plantation.

We referred to these duties as turkey patrols, although I've never known an arrest for having a boot full of turkeys. On one occasion, however, I caught a youth riding a bike without lights. It happened like this.

It was a pitch-black night with no moon and I was manning a road-check at Elsinby Plantation. It was about 8.30 p.m. and I was alone for it was a very minor road which ran right through the centre of the conifer plantation which comprised Norway spruce, Scots pines and larches. We'd had reports of Christmas-tree thefts and so I was out to catch a thief.

Almost numb with cold, I suddenly heard the distinctive

swish-swish of bicycle tyres and as I peered into the pitch blackness, I could not see any lights. And then the noise came closer and I could hear the sound of breathing as the rider pedalled up the slight gradient. And so I shone my torch upon him.

He cried with alarm, for my sudden action had terrified him. In the light of my torch, I saw it was young Ian Spellar from Elsinby and he stopped when he realised it was me.

'Oh, Mr Rhea, hello.' He was slightly out of breath.

'Now, Ian, what's all this then? Riding without lights, eh? You could get yourself killed on a night like this, you know. Car drivers can't see you; you realise you're putting drivers in an impossible situation?'

'Aye, sorry, Mr Rhea. I won't do it again.'

'Where are you going anyway? It's a bit off the beaten track up here!'

I shone my light on his bike and upon his back to see if he had anything which might carry a small tree or any other Yuletide trophy, but he wasn't equipped for transporting anything save himself. I knew he wasn't stealing.

'I'm not pinching things, Mr Rhea, honest. I'm off to see my girl-friend.'

'And who's she?' was my next question.

'Linda Thornhill,' he said. I knew where she lived and this was on the route to her parents' isolated farm.

'Right,' I said. 'Off you go, but be careful. And next time, get some batteries in those lights, and get them switched on, OK? Or I'll book you!'

'Yes, Mr Rhea. Sorry, Mr Rhea.'

'And be careful – remember you can't be seen!'

Knowing few cars used this quiet track, I allowed him to continue to see his love, although the lad might be a danger to other road users. Maybe I should not have relented, but

I decided in his favour. Ian was a pleasant youth. Just turned eighteen, he worked in a local timber yard and was a hardworking lad from a decent working-class background. I'd had to tell him off once or twice about drinking under age but he never got into serious trouble. Under-age drinking and riding a bike without lights was the extent of his lawlessness.

Then, only a week later, I was manning another check-point in that vicinity, this time at Flatts End, when I heard the same swish-swish of bicycle tyres. I shone my torch upon the oncoming rider and again it was Ian.

'Same rider, Mr Rhea!' he said, halting at my side.

'Same constable, Ian!'

'Same excuse!' he countered.

'Same warning!' I said. 'Now what about those lights?'

'I never got round to putting them on, Mr Rhea, sorry,' and he bent over his lights, back and front, and switched them on. After telling him once again of the dangers, I let him go.

'It'll be a summons next time, Ian!' I shouted after him as his red rear-light disappeared into the gloom.

It puzzled me that he should be riding in such darkness without lights when both his lamps were in good working order. It didn't make sense. Then some ten days later, one Saturday night, I was manning yet another check-point, this time at Swathgill Head, and once more, I heard the panting sound of someone pedalling heavily, and the accompanying swish-swish of bicycle tyres. I groaned. I would now have to be harder with this youth.

I switched on my torch and waved him to a halt. I was right; it was Ian Spellar.

'Same cyclist, Mr Rhea,' he said, this time not so chirpily.

'Same constable,' I retorted, sternly.

'Same excuse,' he said, wondering what my reaction would be as he switched on both lights.

'Same threat, Ian!' I sounded angry. 'Now look, this is getting beyond a joke. This is your final warning, right? Next time, you go to court. I can't have you putting yourself and car-drivers at risk . . .'

'If I hear a car coming, I stop and put 'em on,' he said. 'I'd never let 'em run me down, Mr Rhea, I'm not as daft as that.'

'Why ride without lights when your lamps are in working order?' I asked. 'There's nothing wrong with them!'

He just shrugged his shoulders in reply, and I watched him ride off once again. Each time I'd seen him, he'd been on a different road, albeit within the same general area of the heights above Elsinby. Any of those roads would take him to Linda Thornhill's remote home, but this attitude defeated me. It wasn't defiance of the law, it was more a strange sort of lethargy. Now, however, I felt he had got the message. But I was wrong. Only a week later, I was again on the lane running through Elsinby Plantation when I became aware of an approaching cyclist without lights. My heart sank. I could distinguish the swishing of the tyres and the sound of a man breathing as he climbed the gradient, and so, once more, I shone my torch on Ian Spellar.

'Same cyclist, Mr Rhea.'

'Same constable, Ian.'

'Same excuse,' he recited what had become a kind of ritual response.

'Same results, Ian.'

'Same apologies, Mr Rhea.'

'And this time, it's the same summons, Ian. You're clearly ignoring my warnings, so it's a summons this time,' and I took down his name, age, address and occupation, then reported him for riding a cycle without obligatory lights.

'I'm really sorry, Mr Rhea,' and he switched on his front and rear lamps.

'Look, Ian, this is serious, you're risking an accident and putting too much faith in other drivers . . . they just cannot see you in darkness. Why are you doing this?'

He hung his head, embarrassed at my questioning, but his demeanour told me there was a reason for his odd behaviour. Even so, he did not reveal this to me. I must admit that I was against submitting a formal report against him; on paper, it seemed such a trivial matter and my superiors would probably think I'd become drunk with power. But Ian had to be taught a lesson, and so I did submit a report with an accompanying account of the reasons for my action.

And then, even before a decision had been made upon that report, I caught Ian once again.

'Same constable, Ian,' I shouted at him. 'And it'll be another summons for the same offence. What on earth are you playing at?'

'Same cyclist, Mr Rhea.' He sounded very subdued now. 'And same excuse.'

'You're going to see your girl-friend again?'

'Aye,' he said. 'I am, and well, Mr Rhea, I'm sorry, I really am. I know it's wrong, but, well, it's so important . . .'

'Go on, Ian, I'm listening,' I said.

'Well, you know where the Thornhills live, down at Birch Bower Farm?'

'I know it well.' I paid a visit to this farm about once a month and it was an awful trek from the road. The farm lay at least a mile and a half from the road, and although the first quarter of the track leading to it was surfaced, the remainder was an unmade lane full of ruts and pot-holes and littered with partly buried rocks. It was a diabolical road and Ted Thornhill never seemed inclined to repair it. Everyone who used it grumbled.

'Well, old Thornhill doesn't like me courting his lass, Mr Rhea, so I go in secret. Linda can't get out at night, you see, being only sixteen anyway, so I have to ride out there if I want to see her. She goes into her room to do her homework, you see, but she sneaks out at nine o'clock. Well, her dad might catch me riding down that lane if I show lights, Mr Rhea, and 'cos I need to adjust my eyes to ride down when it's pitch dark, I practise on these quiet roads . . . I allus have lights on in the village, or on main roads, but not here where there's nowt but trees.'

I believed him. I knew the value of working without light when operating at night because one's eyes do become accustomed to the darkness.

'So you're practising that ride and using different roads to avoid me, eh?' I put to him.

'Yeh, well, when you first nabbed me I reckoned you'd often be on that road, seeing Christmas is coming up and there's poachers about. So I went the other way round, then you were there an' all, Mr Rhea . . .'

'And I've no doubt you've been riding those roads other nights, Ian, when I've not been on duty?'

He laughed with a silly sort of giggle. 'Aye, well, you have to, haven't you? Just the quiet bits, mind, and that lane down to Birch Bower.'

'I'm not interested in Birch Bower Farm Lane,' I said. 'That's private property. I'm concerned with public roads.'

'So will they take me to court, Mr Rhea?'

'It depends on the superintendent,' I said, which was the truth. 'He'll read my report and decide what to do.'

'Tell him I'm sorry, then. But mebbe he was a lad an' all, at one time? Going courting.'

'I'll see what he says,' was all I could promise.

The superintendent met me at one of my rendezvous points a few days later and took the opportunity of asking me about my 'no bike-lights' report. I explained the situation and included Ian's odd reason.

'Christmas is coming up, PC Rhea,' said the superintendent. 'Would you agree that a written caution is appropriate in this case?'

I smiled. 'Yes, sir. I think it would be very appropriate.'

And so that was Ian's punishment. Within a few days, he would receive a written caution from the superintendent which would inform him that he would not be prosecuted on this occasion, but that the letter must be regarded as a warning. Any future offences of this nature could result in a court appearance.

I saw Ian in Elsinby one Sunday afternoon just before Christmas and told him what to expect.

'Thanks, Mr Rhea, I'm grateful.'

'Wish Linda a happy Christmas from me,' I said.

'Thanks, Mr Rhea. I will. And I'm sorry I've been a nuisance, I was daft really. But there was nowt else I could do, was there, if I wanted to see Linda?'

'I can't encourage you to break the law.' I smiled at him. 'Mind,' I added, 'I'm not sure how you'll sneak down to Birch Bower in the summer without her dad knowing.'

'Me neither, Mr Rhea. I'll have to find a way in somehow, although she might be able to go for walks when it's light at night.'

'Let's hope so, Ian. Oh, and by the way,' I said. 'We finish those check-points this coming Saturday night.'

'Thanks, Mr Rhea,' he said. 'Happy Christmas.'

One of the funniest incidents involved a man whom I shall call Ronald Youngman, a salesman who lived in Ashfordly. I was never very sure what he sold, although I think it was something linked to the building-industry like scaffolding. A dark-haired, attractive man in his early thirties, he was a lively character who played a lot of tennis, cricket, football and badminton. When he was not selling scaffolding or playing one of his sports, he was exercising his considerable charm upon the local ladies.

In the latter case, he made ample use of his company car which was a Ford Cortina with reclining front seats; he used this to take his many conquests for outings, frequently making trips to rural pubs after which he would take his charmed girl to a remote rustic location, there for mutual enjoyment. For this reason, his distinctive gold-coloured car was often to be seen parked in lonely places, sometimes with steamed-up windows and generally in complete darkness.

Most of the local police officers knew the car and they knew of Ronald's insatiable appetite for lovely ladies, consequently they never checked over the car or its occupants when they found it in a far-away place. Normally, our procedures were to check every car found in a remote place to see if the occupants were safe and sound, to see if it was someone trying to commit suicide or whether the car had been stolen and abandoned. It might contain the proceeds of crime, or it might be used for crime – there were many other valid reasons for checking such vehicles.

If I was patrolling late, therefore, and came across Ronald's car upon the moors or deep in a forest, I ignored it. After all, I didn't want to embarrass either Ronald or his lover of the evening and if neither was breaking the law there was no need to make myself a nuisance.

But late one night – in fact it was after midnight – I was working a patrol and around 1 a.m., my route took me high into Waindale. Tucked away in the corner of a quarry behind Wether Cote Farm was an explosives store; it belonged to the quarry owner and because it contained explosives and detonators used for blasting, we had to check it regularly for security. It was little more than a very solidly built chamber, part of which was underground, and it seldom contained a large amount. But it had to be checked and our checks had to be recorded.

With this in mind, I parked my mini-van off the road near Wether Cote Farm and decided to walk the couple of hundred yards to the explosives store. The route was along an unmade lane, full of pot-holes and with the quarry gates closed, there was very little room for turning a vehicle around. It was much safer to walk. And so, in the gloom of that night, albeit armed with a torch which I did not use during the walk, I made my way along the track. Rather like young Ian Spellar, I found I could see without the light from a torch. And then, in a corner right next to the store, I came across Ronald's car. It was in darkness but I could recognise the outline. Ronald was at it again.

Having no wish to become a Peeping Tom or to disturb him in his moments of bliss, I tried to creep past the car to carry out my essential check. But as I was going past, I could hear cries for help . . . and they were being sounded in a man's voice! I halted a while, listening; I thought it might be the car radio, a disc jockey fooling about or perhaps a character in a play or it could be Ronald playing games. After all, he had no idea that I, or indeed anyone else, was standing just outside his passion-wagon.

But the cry was genuine . . . and a woman's voice was calling too. Who on earth they were hoping to attract in such a remote part of the moors was beyond me, but I listened carefully, just to ensure that these were genuine cries for help. I did wonder if it was some odd part of their love-making, but in spite of being muffled by the closed windows, they were, I felt, very genuine cries of distress.

And, they sounded rather weak.

I had to investigate.

I switched on my powerful torch and pulled open the driver's door. The interior light came on and there, in the most bizarre situation upon the passenger's reclining seat was Ronald. He was face down and beneath him was a woman. Both were completely naked. And neither could move.

'Who's that?' he asked, with a mixture of relief and embarrassment, unable to turn his head towards the door.

'PC Rhea, Ronald.'

'Oh, thank God . . . get me out . . .'

In the weak glow of the interior light, I could distinguish a tangle of bare legs; I could not identify the woman, and she was saying nothing. In fact, she was hiding her face by turning her head towards the wall of the car. But Ronald was saying 'My foot, Mr Rhea, my leg . . .'

'What's the problem?' I asked, baffled by this discovery.

'My legs . . . my feet . . . they're trapped . . . can you loosen them . . .'

I could now see that his right foot had disappeared through the cubby-hole of his car; it seemed he had been exerting pressure with that foot as a result of which it had dislodged the plastic back panel of the cubby-hole. His foot and much of his lower leg had then slipped through the hole to become trapped among the wires and bodywork, and he could not pull it out. That sudden action had then caused his left leg to make an involuntary movement, and his foot had gone through a gap between the spokes of the steering-wheel. That leg was also trapped due to the weight upon it.

'Interesting position, Ronald,' I said as I examined his predicament.

'I can't move, Mr Rhea. I just can't move . . .'

His entire body weight was resting upon the woman beneath; she could not roll free because the driver's seat was not in a reclining position, nor could she slide towards the rear due to the slope of the seat upon which she was trapped, and Ronald's position prevented a forward escape.

Besides, one of her legs was somehow curled between his which well and truly anchored her. Unfortunately for Ronald his own trapped position and the weight of his body meant he could neither rise nor free his own legs.

'I wish I had a camera, Ronald, this is one for the record books!'

'Give over, Mr Rhea, just get me out . . . I've been here ages . . . I thought nobody was going to come . . .'

'They wouldn't, at least not until the quarry opens in the morning – it would give the lads summat to talk about. I just happened to be coming to the explosives store. Now, let's see if I can shift one of these legs.'

I went around to the passenger side and opened that door, upon which the woman turned her face the other way. It was almost the only part of her that I had not seen, but I set about removing Ronald's foot. By pushing my hand through the cubby-hole, I could dislodge the panel which had secured his foot, and then, by heaving on that leg and getting him to bend his knee, I could release that foot. But he could still not help himself. Gradually, I eased the other foot out of the spokes of the steering-wheel, got into the rear of the car and dragged him towards the back seat by his shoulders, and then he was free. Aching, stiff with cold and very, very embarrassed, he rolled into the driver's seat.

And then the woman could move and I recognised her.

'Good evening, Mrs Stamford,' I greeted her.

She was the wife of an hotel owner in Ashfordly but she made no response, not even a thank-you. As I clambered out of their car, she began to get dressed in total silence as Ronald grabbed his clothes and began to pull them on in the lane as he talked to me.

'Look, Mr Rhea, we're men of the world. I mean, I've committed no crime, no offence . . . You don't have to take action, do you? Report this, or anything? She is a respected lady from the town, you see, she's never done this before, not with me anyway. Her husband's away, he's at an hoteliers' conference in Harrogate . . .'

'There's no need to say anything, Ronald. Rescuing damsels and knights in distress is just part of our service. Well, it's made my night interesting, but, Ronald . . .'

I paused.

'Yes?' He was fastening his shirt by this time.

'I'd love to know how on earth you managed to get yourself into that position. I'll bet a contortionist would have a job to achieve that!'

'You'll not tell a soul, will you, Mr Rhea?'

'It's our secret, Ronald, ours and Mrs Stamford's.'

And I have never mentioned it to anyone. Ronald often greets me and insists on buying me a drink when I'm off duty, but the humiliated Mrs Stamford never speaks to me.

But when I returned home and booked off duty that night, I realised I had omitted to do one vital thing. I'd completely forgotten to examine the explosives store.

Possibly the most dramatic love story that came my way involved Mr and Mrs Colin Blenkiron and a notorious crossroads called Pennyflats Cross. So difficult and accident-prone was this stretch of road that my predecessor, and then I, kept a stock of blank scale-drawings of the roads for use in our accident reports. The number of traffic accidents which happened at that point kept us in regular work!

Wherever a road traffic accident occurred which resulted

in a need to examine all the evidence with a view to prosecution, we had to submit detailed plan drawings of the scene. These were carefully drawn to scale and contained the positions of the vehicles involved both before, during and after impact. This was for the benefit both of our senior officers in deciding whether or not to send the case to court, and later the magistrates if it did get to court. This system helped enormously to simplify a difficult explanation of the events. A stock of neatly drawn plans depicting this road, with all the constant measurements, the position of warning signs, indications of gradients, type of road markings, etc., did save a lot of time.

At Pennyflats Cross, the main road, which had a 'B' classification, ran from Ashfordly to York and crossed Pennyflats, an area of elevated scrubland covered with small conifers, gorse bushes and heather. As it reached the crossroads, the road dipped suddenly and quite steeply, although this short gradient was well signed in advance.

Nevertheless, many drivers who were strangers to the area were, when approaching from Ashfordly, largely unaware of the undulating nature of the road. They sailed over the summit without knowing and apparently without caring what lay beyond. That in itself could be regarded as careless driving or even dangerous driving because, just over the summit, within a matter of very few yards, was a minor road. It crossed the Ashfordly-York road at an oblique angle, emerging almost unseen from a plantation of conifers at one side and a copse of young silver birch at the other.

Defence solicitors always maintained that these crossroads were badly placed and it was unfair to convict anyone of driving carelessly here. The police, however, assured the court that the crossroads were well signposted from all directions, and that, in any case, a driver should always drive at a speed and in such a manner that he or she could deal with any unexpected hazards.

But a similar problem afflicted drivers coming out of the side road on to the main road. Upon emerging on to the main road, their vision was grossly impaired by the angle of the road and the profusion of trees. The chief problem was that those on the main road often crested that hill at speed only to find a slow car emerging into their path. So short was the stopping-distance that very few could pull up in time, not even those who pottered along in a leisurely style. Fast or even moderately fast drivers had no chance at all.

Accidents were inevitable, and although we, the police, grumbled at the Highway Department and the district council for improvements to be made, nothing was ever done. Their argument was that the crossroads were not dangerous because no one had been killed there, and, oddly enough, that was true. There never had been a fatal accident there, although some nasty injuries had occurred. Everyone said that, one day, somebody would be killed, but happily in my time at Aidensfield that did not happen.

I was not surprised therefore, one Sunday afternoon in May, when I received a frantic phone call from a passing driver to say he had come upon two cars which had clearly just been involved in a traffic accident. He was chattering nervously as people tend to do when they are reporting urgent matters to the police, but I tried to calm him down by slowly asking the obvious questions.

I learned that the location was the infamous Pennyflats Cross, and that both drivers were injured. In his view, the injuries did not appear to be too serious although he said an ambulance was required. The road was not blocked and he had not witnessed the accident; he had come upon it moments after it had happened. I thanked him and said I would be there in less than ten minutes; I assured him I'd call the ambulance before I left home. He said he would wait and attend to the injured drivers.

The accident was one of the kind that regularly happened here. A young woman in an Austin mini-car had come out of the minor road on to the main road just as a young man in a sports car had crested the brow of the hill. He'd reacted quickly and had attempted to swerve to his right to avoid a collision, but she'd kept coming across his path from the left. He had collided with the front of her car. This had spun her off the road and she had collided with a telegraph pole while he had veered further to his offside, ending his short trip by crumpling his MGB around a sturdy ash tree.

A quick visual appraisal of both drivers showed that neither was too badly hurt; happily, neither was unconscious and I could detect no arterial bleeding; the girl, however, did say that her right arm hurt a lot and the youth complained of intense pain in his left leg. Tenderly, I examined both their injured limbs and was in no doubt that each was fractured; there were abrasions too, and some degree of shock. Hospital was a necessity for both.

At that stage, the ambulance arrived. The injured pair were well enough to tell me their names and addresses before the skilful ambulancemen lifted them out of their vehicles, wrapped them in blankets and in no time had placed them aboard stretchers. In seconds, they were being borne towards York County Hospital for treatment. I thanked the passing driver for his assistance and confirmed that he was no longer required as he was not a witness. Then I radioed our Control Room with a request for a breakdown truck.

The rest of my action was routine. I obtained measurements of the positions of their cars, cleared the scene, swept up the broken glass and made arrangements for relatives to be informed. The breakdown truck took away both cars, lifting one on board and towing the other, and I went home. Using my stock plan of the crossroads, I entered the position of each of the cars and completed my accident report as far as I could. I rang York Police with a request that an officer be allowed to visit the hospital when the injured couple were well enough, and that the officer be allowed to obtain from each their version of events.

If they were not well enough, then other arrangements would be made; I also had their driving licences and insurance certificates to check.

When all this was done, I submitted my report to the sergeant for onwards transmission to the superintendent and I was to learn later that he recommended 'No prosecution' on the grounds that there was no independent witness. No one could say precisely what had happened, for it was a case of the man's word against the girl's. And that, I thought, was that.

But there was more to follow.

Some time during the November that followed, I received a telephone call from a Mr Colin Blenkiron.

'It's Colin Blenkiron speaking. Is that PC Rhea?' the voice asked.

'Speaking,' I confirmed.

'Ah, good, well, I wondered if you'd like to come to a party, you and your wife.'

'Me? Well . . .'

At that instant, I couldn't recall knowing anyone called Blenkiron and I was hesitant until he said, 'That accident at Pennyflats Cross last May, Mr Rhea. It was me in the MGB Hardtop.'

'Oh!' Now it all came flooding back. 'I remember now, that Colin Blenkiron! Well, thanks, what sort of party and where is it?'

'It's my engagement party, Mr Rhea, and it's at the Hopbind Inn, Elsinby, a week on Thursday night. Half eight.'

'Well, that's very kind of you.' I was surprised at this. 'Very kind. I'm off duty that night,' I said. 'And I know my wife would love the outing, but . . .'

I was about to say that I was surprised at the invitation because Colin's parents' farm, which he ran in partnership with his father, was not on my beat. I did not know him or his parents, although I did know they were very wealthy and successful.

'It was because of that accident, Mr Rhea. You looked after me, and Susan. Got us to hospital, and there was no court appearance for us either. So we'd like you to come to our party.'

'She's your fiancée?' I was surprised.

'Not then, she wasn't. I didn't even know her then! She's my fiancée now, we met in hospital, you see.'

'What a way to meet!' I laughed.

'Yes, well, it was. Actually,' he chuckled, 'we met in the ambulance, but we weren't exactly on speaking terms then! I was blaming her for the pile-up . . . I still am, by the way, and she was blaming me . . . anyway, in hospital, one thing led to another and here we are, getting engaged!'

'What a lovely tale!' I said. 'Yes, then we'd love to come and wish you a happy future!'

'Marvellous. We're inviting those ambulancemen as well, they were great. See you then.'

And he rang off.

Mary was delighted. From time to time, one of my 'customers' produced an offer of this kind, a form of genuine and heartfelt 'thank-you', even if my part in their romance was very minor. We went along to the party and met their respective families, friends and relations. Susan

Ascough, Colin's fiancée, was a secretary in a big department store in York and lived in Ploatby, which was on my patch. She drove into York every day. I knew her parents by name, but had never met Susan until this evening.

During the party, there were ribald jokes about their method of meeting, their respective injuries, their time in bed in hospital and the prospects for their future together. It was a very happy gathering and a real tonic for me, and even more so for Mary. Diplomatically, we left the party at closing-time for I did not wish to make them feel uncomfortable if they decided to stay awhile at the pub.

'I enjoyed that,' said Mary on our way home. 'They seem a real nice couple, and their families are nice too.'

'It makes you think that that accident was fate,' I said. 'I wonder if they'd have met each other if it had never happened?'

'We'll never know,' she said. 'And thanks for leaving the pub at closing-time!' she added. 'I hate people staring at you as if you're a leper when the landlord calls time.'

'A little drink after hours always tastes better,' I said. 'It's like kids pinching apples – they're always better than the ones at home, and drinks laced with a spot of law-breaking taste all the better for it. A hint of naughtiness will put the final seal on their celebrations!'

'That's if they *do* drink after hours!' she laughed. 'You'll never know, will you?'

'I don't want to know,' I said, truthfully.

I thought that would have been the last we'd see of Colin and Susan, but it wasn't. The following March, we received an invitation to their wedding. It was fixed for the weekend before Easter in Elsinby Parish Church, with the reception at Craydale Manor. This was a fine country house which had been converted into an hotel and restaurant, and we looked forward to the whole celebration.

The wedding was superb. In Elsinby's historic parish church, the atmosphere and setting were both dramatic and moving. Susan looked a picture in her long white wedding dress with its train and eight tiny bridesmaids in the most delicate of pinks.

Colin and his best man looked handsome and splendid in their top hats and tails, and the happy couple were united before a full congregation of family, friends and well-wishers. Beyond doubt, it was this district's wedding of the year. Mary and I thoroughly enjoyed the occasion; we lingered as the photographs were taken outside the church, savouring every moment and participating in the sheer happiness of the newly-weds. As the village constable, it was so nice being part of this joyful event.

Eventually, the photographer had taken all that he wished and the best man shouted for us to rejoin our cars and follow the bridal procession to the reception, after which the presents would be on display at the bride's home in Ploatby. And so we all went off to Craydale Manor in a long procession of gleaming vehicles led by a silver Jaguar car with white ribbons fluttering from its bonnet.

The reception was splendid; the excellent meal was run with flair and efficiency, Colin's speech and those of the other dutiful men were fluent and entertaining, and the toasts were drunk with style and aplomb. The wedding had started at 11.30 a.m. and by the end of this reception the time had crept around to 2.30 p.m.

At this time, the best man, a friend of Colin's, said, 'Ladies and gentlemen, the presents are on display at the bride's home, Sycamore Cottage, Ploatby – you are invited to view them. The bride and groom will leave the bride's home for their honeymoon at four p.m. You might like to see them off.'

Mary, who always loves a wedding, said she'd like to

view the presents and see Susan's going-away outfit, so we agreed to visit Sycamore Cottage, Ploatby. As we were leaving the reception, several other cars were doing likewise, and leading the first flush of departing vehicles was the silver Jaguar containing the bride and groom.

The uniformed chauffeur had been hired with the car, both coming from a York firm which specialised in this kind of service. In an orderly fashion, the procession of cars filed out of the spacious grounds of the hotel and began to speed through the lanes towards Ploatby.

I was somewhere towards the rear with perhaps ten or a dozen cars ahead of me. I simply tagged on behind and others followed me, for some of the guests were strangers and did not know the route. I made it clear I would show them the way. As we moved off, there was a good deal of merriment with people waving at each other out of car windows, flying their silk scarves, throwing confetti, shouting and laughing as we passed through the splendid Ryedale countryside.

And ahead was the fine Jaguar, its polished silver bodywork glistening in the bright sunshine of the day as the happy couple waved and blew kisses to everyone. It disappeared around the sharp corners and was frequently hidden from my view by the high hedges and the distance between us.

As we motored along Hazel Burn Lane which joined the Ashfordly-York road, I lost sight of the powerful Jaguar; its lead had become quite substantial but I did not try to keep pace with it, for I had no wish to lose those behind me who were relying on my guidance. And then we were on the main road, the B-class highway which led towards York. Driving steadily, I was approaching the dangerous portion over Pennyflats Cross, and even as I neared the place, I saw several smart-suited gentlemen waving us to a halt.

'Oh, no!' I groaned at Mary. 'What now! Don't say there's been an accident today of all days!'

With every passing yard, it was clear there had been an accident, for cars were strewn across both lanes of the highway and people were milling about, shouting at us to slow down and stop. I pulled on to the grass verge, making sure my car was clear as I went to investigate. Upon my advice, Mary remained in her seat – the fewer people about the scene, the better.

When I crested that notorious hill, my heart sank. The silver Jaguar was on its side, its roof crushed against the very same ash tree that Colin had hit only months ago. Also lying on its side in the middle of the road was a tractor and trailer, the trailer having carried a load of manure. It was spread across the carriageway and other cars were scattered randomly about the road with anxious people milling about . . .

I ran to the Jaguar.

I knew Colin and Susan were inside and the awful silence about the car made me fear the worst; I was no longer a wedding guest, but a policeman who had suddenly found himself on duty. As I ran down the road, weaving between irregularly parked cars, I saw that several had been slightly damaged. The accident was one of the shunt type when each car runs into the back of the one ahead. Seven or eight had been damaged, but I was not concerned with those. I arrived at the Jaguar to find a knot of helpers trying to reach the bride and groom who were in the rear seat. No one seemed to be worried about the chauffeur, and at this stage I was not even aware of the tractor driver's injuries.

Susan, her wedding dress stained with blood and dirt, was crying as she lay on top of Colin; he was curled up in an untidy heap as he lay among the broken glass and shattered metalwork of the car body, and he was bleeding about the head and face. I told the helpers who I was and they stood aside as I wrenched open the rear door which now lay uppermost and somehow, I don't know how, I found myself crouched inside the rear compartment, mysteriously avoiding trampling on the couple.

They were conscious but hurt; I shouted for someone to call two ambulances and to stress the urgency due to the number of casualties, then call the police, a local doctor and finally a nearby garage to arrange lifting-gear and cutting equipment. I asked the volunteer to give a detailed account of the multiple accident; he said he would cope.

I thought Colin or the chauffeur might be trapped, such was their position in the wreckage. Each was lying on the side of the car which was on the ground, the roof being caved in around them. I asked the gathered menfolk to care for their ladies and other guests, and to ensure that there was adequate warning for approaching vehicles. I didn't want more pile-ups and I asked them not to move their cars; their position was vital for the subsequent official report.

But I must see to Colin and Susan. Speaking to them in what I hoped were soothing terms, I managed to move Susan to a more comfortable position. Then I made a very brief and almost cursory examination of Colin. He was sighing with pain and I daren't move him in case he had broken bones or internal injuries which could cause further damage. One of his arms seemed to be trapped somewhere beneath him and careless handling could aggravate any injuries he might have.

Relieved that he was alive, I now looked to the unfortunate chauffeur; he was lying trapped too, unconscious and pale with a spot of blood on his face, but he was breathing quite smoothly. I did not touch him. This release required the skill of experts and the injured people needed medical attention. I hoped the messages for help would receive the attention they required. And I was not disappointed.

The sequence of events moved rapidly ahead. In what seemed a very short time, the emergency services arrived; a motor patrol car based at Scarborough had happened to be patrolling nearby and two capable officers, not closely known to me, came and dealt very efficiently with the multiple accident, paying immediate attention to the casualties. Two ambulances came and, with the help of us all, and the garage's lifting-gear, we soon had the casualties free and on their way to hospital.

The chauffeur was placed in a second ambulance and the tractor driver, who seemed to be forgotten by most of us, was also placed on board. The other casualties were all suffering from minor injuries and shock, and Doctor Archie McGee, summoned from Elsinby, was able to treat most of them without hospitalisation.

I sent Mary home while I remained to help the two officers with the statement-taking, clearing the scene and generally making myself useful. Under the circumstances, I'm not sure if anyone went to the house to see the presents, but we didn't. I was shattered by the awful turn of events, the enormity of which did not register until some time later.

This is a feature of police work; you deal with a harrowing incident in a cool and professional way, and it is later, when relaxing at home, that the sheer horror of the incident registers. I'm sure many police officers have wept with sorrow and anger after dealing with terrible incidents.

But this was not such a serious case for there were no fatalities. That, I felt, was another example of fate. With so many cars involved, there could have been carnage.

I rang the hospital to enquire after each of the casualties and learned that Susan had fractured an ankle and had suffered lots of bruising to her body. Colin had a broken arm, a minor fracture to his skull and lots of cuts about the face; the chauffeur, a man from York called Eric Wallis, had fractured six ribs and had facial injuries due to impact with the steering-wheel and windscreen. The tractor driver, a 56-year-old farm worker called Eddie Harper, had been knocked from his machine to suffer a broken shoulder blade, a broken arm and severe lacerations to his face and hands.

The following day, I rang the two motor patrol officers to explain about my battles to get the junction made safer either by more signs, better advance warnings and a clearer view from the minor road and they assured me this would be incorporated in their report. Their enquiries, based on witness statements, suggested that poor old Eddie Harper had pulled out of the minor road with his slow-moving tractor and trailer, and the fast-moving Jaguar had crested the blind summit of that hill driven by a man who was accustomed to city traffic, not country roads. The Jaguar had hit the tractor, and the following cars had each collided with another vehicle. Nine of them were damaged, and fifteen people had been injured.

It was the worst accident on my patch and I hoped it would result in some improvements to that road. And then, about six or seven weeks later, I received a phone call.

'It's Colin Blenkiron,' said the voice. 'We're out of hospital, Mr Rhea, Susan and me, and we wondered if you and Mrs Rhea would like to see the wedding presents? I know it's a bit late, but we're having friends in, a few at a time . . . how about Sunday afternoon, say three-ish?'

'We'd love to!' I enthused.

'Drive carefully!' he said, laughing.

It was pouring with rain as we went along to their lovely cottage and we found both of them still wearing dressings on some of their injuries and both chuckling at the absurdity of the situation.

'That crossroads has got it in for us,' Colin laughed as he poured the wine. 'It's put us in hospital twice now . . . I never go that way when Susan's with me. I'm not risking another accident, I can tell you!'

'You met me because of Pennyflats Cross!' she retorted with good humour.

'And I got put in hospital twice because of it,' he said. 'And that first accident was all your fault . . .'

'It wasn't! It was yours!' she cried. 'You were going far too fast . . .'

'Here's to the pair of you!' and as the driving rain beat upon their cottage, a flash of lightning was followed by a crack of thunder which rattled the windows.

I raised my glass to them and then, for some odd reason, I remembered the words of Samuel Beckett in, I think, *All That Fall*. I quoted them as a toast, 'What sky! What light! Ah, in spite of all, it is a blessed thing to be alive in such weather, and out of hospital!'

And Colin kissed Susan.

7

'A difference of taste in jokes is a great
strain on the affections.'

George Eliot, 1819-80

Society will have its jokers. Throughout the ages there
have been many classic pranks, some on a large scale and
others of a very minor nature. In the countryside, April 1st
has always been a good time for practising pranks upon
one's friends, relations and workmates. I remember one
joker who claimed that hens' eggs could be stretched if
they were collected immediately after being laid because at
that moment, their shells are still soft. He said they could
be stretched to appear larger and so fetch a better price.

In our area, one newspaper printed a story that Barnard
Castle was to be demolished to make way for a bridge
across the River Tees, and there was a joke that almost
went wrong when a man walked into a park and picked up
a new park bench under the nose of a policeman. He was
stopped on suspicion of theft and claimed he wanted the
seat for firewood. He was promptly arrested and when he
explained that it was merely a joke no one believed him.
He did, however, manage to prove that the seat was his
own, as he'd bought it specially for the joke only the day
before.

One Yorkshire lad tricked his family and friends when
he organised a spoof wedding. He and a girlfriend had

apparently got married, had their photographs taken, and then driven around town in their wedding outfits for all to see.

One of my favourite jokes was the news that British time was to be decimalised. It claimed that, in order to rationalise Great Britain with the move towards metrication and decimalisation, the year would no longer have twelve months. Instead, Britain would have ten months, each comprising ten weeks; there would be ten days to each week, and ten hours to each day. Each hour would have ten minutes and each minute would be split into ten seconds. A year would be called a Kiloday, a month would be a hectoday, a week would be known as a decaday, while a minute would become a centiday and so forth.

Furthermore, to coincide with the change, Big Ben would become digital and there would be wage adjustments to cope with each Leap Kiloday.

Harmless, and at times very believable, jokes are great fun, such as the time our local zoo claimed they had found the Loch Ness Monster and even fooled the Scottish police into halting them at the border as they tried to smuggle out the carcase. It was in fact a huge type of seal, but the police had unearthed a byelaw which forbids the taking of certain rare species out of Scotland and so they were halted at the border in the belief they had the Loch Ness Monster in their possession!

One 'animal' which is a regular victim of April Fool jokes is the famous White Horse of Kilburn. It overlooks the North Yorkshire countryside from its vantage point just below the rim of the escarpment near Sutton Bank.

This huge white shape of a horse, over 105 yards long, was cut from the hillside in 1857 from plans drawn by John Hodgson, the headmaster of Kilburn village school. Helped by his pupils and a group of local men, Hodgson carved the horse from the hillside where it remains a landmark for miles around. It is the only hillside sculpture of its kind in the north of England and can be seen from over 70 miles away. It was filled with white lime and so the outline of this magnificent horse continues to dominate the countryside around Kilburn, not far from Aidensfield. But on April Fool's Day, the horse is liable to change! From time to time, it has been transformed into a zebra, a cowboy's horse with a rider and, in recent times, a well endowed stallion.

I think it is fair to say that most of us enjoy a clever but harmless joke and police officers are no exception. A clever April Fool joke is always appreciated and so are jokes perpetrated at other times of the year.

I well remember one young rookie constable who was ordered to place traffic cones around York Minster one Sunday morning which happened to be April 1st. He had been told that today was the annual Archbishops' Foot Race, when every clergyman in the York Diocese was expected by the Archbishop to run a short race around the Minster, all dressed in their cassocks and surplices. The lad had therefore coned off the entire Minster moments before the regular services were due to start. If he kept his cones there, no one could enter the Minster.

The situation was rectified at the last minute when he received a radio call, supposedly from Police Headquarters, to say the race had been cancelled because the Archbishop had influenza.

Other jokes included leaving notes for the night-shift sergeant to the effect that the Chief Constable had requested an early call at 5 a.m., and a similar one backfired when an unsuspecting constable was ordered to wake up the warden of the local dogs' home at 5 a.m. by knocking on his door. He was told that the warden had made this request and that he had insisted that the police keep knocking until he answered the door. He was a noted over-sleeper and had a very important meeting that day. The truth was that the warden didn't live on the premises; in fact, no one lived on the premises except hundreds of dogs, and the resultant continuous loud barking roused the entire town.

It was when I called at Eltering Police Station one day on duty that I found myself involved in a practical joke on a new constable who had recently arrived. His name was Justin Pendlebury, a man of about twenty-eight years of age, and he came from a very wealthy background; it seemed his family were from the stockbroker belt of Surrey, but Justin had decided to break away from both family and environment to become a constable in the North Riding of Yorkshire. We never knew why he had done this, but in fact he proved himself a very capable young officer.

But he had one annoying character trait. He was rather pompous and always boasted about the style and quality of his clothes. Certainly, he dressed well, far better than the rest of us. His suits were beautifully cut, he wore hand-made shirts and shoes, exquisite silk ties and his casual wear was of the very highest quality.

Justin certainly looked very stylish and smart, but he made everyone aware of the fact, telling us tales of how his tailor was the very best in London's West End, how the fellow made all his suits by hand and dressed film stars, politicians and City business people. Justin scorned the cheap suits and flannel trousers that we wore, saying we ought to be more clothes-conscious. But none of us copied him or ever tried to emulate his style. If our clothes kept us warm and dry, then that was good enough.

Although everyone liked Justin and admired his professionalism when on duty, we did get sick of his continual talk of fine clothes, men's fashions and popular styles. He talked of Ascot, Glyndebourne and Epsom as we talked about the back row of the Empire Cinema or the cheap end at Thornaby Races and Cargo Fleet Greyhound Track.

As I entered Eltering Police Station that day, I walked into a discussion about clothes. And, as usual, it was led by Justin. He was having an animated conversation with PC Alf Ventress and two visiting officers, PCs George Henderson and Harry Pitts.

Alf Ventress was known to us all as Vesuvius because his uniform was always covered in ash and he was likely to erupt at any time; he was a huge, grizzly-haired constable of the old-fashioned type whose trousers always needed pressing, whose tunic was constantly smothered in dandruff and cigarette ash, whose boots always needed cleaning and whose shirts always sported crumpled collars. He was the last person to be discussing smart clothes with Justin.

'Ah, young Nick,' he said as I walked in. I had my bait-bag with me, bait being the name for my sandwiches and coffee. I was to take my meal-break here this evening.

'Hello.' I nodded at them all as they were seated around the kitchen of the police station, with the kettle boiling and a bottle of milk on the table.

'Just the chap!' said Vesuvius to me. 'Nick, a few months ago, you were telling us of a tailor you knew, one of the old-fashioned kind who makes suits by hand. He sits on his table cross-legged, you said, and you can see him at work through his window.'

'Golding,' I said. 'John Golding,' for this was his name and I remembered telling them about him.

'The best for miles around, you said,' continued Vesuvius and he winked at me in what I recognised as the beginnings of a conspiracy of some kind.

'He does a lot of work for the local folks,' I agreed. 'Yes, he turns out some good stuff, our farmers love him.'

'Justin here was saying he needed somebody local to make him a good suit,' Vesuvius continued. 'I was telling him of that chap you mentioned; couldn't think of his name or where he works.'

'Ah, well, John Golding,' I said to Justin. 'He's a bit old-fashioned, but he sits there in full view of the street making suits, jackets, trousers and so on. He'll tackle women's costumes, children's coats and, well, everything, even rugs for horses or car travellers. He's always busy.'

'Really, where's he operate?' asked Justin.

'Elsinby,' I said. 'If you're ever out there patrolling, park near the church and then go up the little alleyway just opposite. You'll see his window. It's a little stone cottage and there's a sign on the top of his window with his name, and it says, "Ladies' and Gentlemen's Alterations".'

This was true; people from far around took pictures of that curious sign with its double meaning, but John reckoned it brought him customers!

'And can you recommend him?' asked Justin. 'I need a brand-new suit, you see, urgently. I've been invited to the wedding of Lord Gauvey in Westminster Abbey and I must have a new suit. Duty commitments mean I cannot get to London to be measured, and Vesuvius recommended this fellow.'

At this stage, both the other constables began to praise the old tailor and I suspected a plot of some kind.

I had no idea what they'd been saying before my arrival, so I adopted an impartial stance by adding, 'I've never had anything made by him.'

'But your local farmers use him?' Justin said.

'Oh, yes.' I knew this to be the case. 'They keep him going with their jobs.'

'Just like your farmers from the south, they are,' said Vesuvius. 'Smart, plenty of cash, and always out to impress. Gentlemen farmers, you know, stylish and up-to-date.'

Now I knew something was going on. Many of the local farmers didn't care two hoots how they dressed or what they looked like. If they had one smart suit for funerals and weddings, that was sufficient; the rest of the time was spent in any old working-togs they could muster. They would rarely buy a new outfit, the main visits to Golding being by bachelor farmers who wanted to have tears mended or patches sewn on knees and elbows of worn-out clothes which they thought had ten or twenty years of wear left in them. Those who were married received this attention from their wives.

I realised no one had told Justin that Golding's suits never fitted anyone properly; they were always far too big or far too small; one sleeve or one leg would be longer than the other and the general rule was that his clothing only fitted a customer who was misshapen. Throughout the district, John Golding was known for his awful tailoring, although the material he used was of very superior quality. 'It's stuff,' said one farmer to me. 'Real stuff.'

John Golding always used the finest of materials and we never really knew his source, although it was thought he had family connections with the textile industry at Halifax, West Yorkshire. But his cloth was his strength, and those who commissioned John to tailor their clothing invariably knew the outcome. They would receive an ill-fitting outfit made from the very best of materials, so they would take it to another tailor to have it altered. Because he was more than generous with his sizes, making clothes that were far too large, such alterations could usually be achieved. This system kept John in work, for his fees were modest, and at the end of the operation, the customer did have a very fine article of clothing which would last a lifetime.

The outcome of that visit to Eltering Police Station was that Justin Pendlebury did call on John Golding. He was duly measured and ordered his suit. He selected the very best Yorkshire worsted and was highly impressed by the quality of material kept in this tiny village tailor's shop.

'Amazing,' he said to me over the telephone. 'You'd never expect quality of that kind up here! It's top quality, you know, genuine too, the real stuff.'

Two or three weeks later, I received another telephone call from Justin. 'Nick,' he said. 'Can you do me a favour? I've had a call from Mr Golding to say my suit's ready. I wondered if you could pick it up for me and drop it off at Eltering Police Station? I see you're covering the whole section next Friday.'

'Yes, of course,' I offered.

That Friday morning, I called at John Golding's little shop and collected the parcel. I completed my morning's patrol and at lunch-time telephoned Justin who was on duty in Eltering until 3 p.m. He was working 7 a.m.-3 p.m. that day, and I said that I had the parcel and would bring it to the police station around 3 p.m. I arrived just before three o'clock and Justin was already there, awaiting his treasure. The wedding was the following day, and he was to travel to London later that afternoon.

Vesuvius had obviously spread the word around because four other constables from the villages had, apparently by sheer coincidence, come into the office at that time, and Sergeant Charlie Bairstow was there too. They had brewed a cup of tea and it seemed that Justin, even though he didn't realise it yet, was about to have a fitting.

'I had one earlier, you know,' he told us when we pressed him to try on the suit. 'Mr Golding called me in last week . . . the final fitting . . . it was a really good fit.'

'Come on, Justin,' pleaded Vesuvius. 'Let's see how a city man should look. We know nowt about smart clothes up here on t'moors, you know. You've been telling us to dress well, so now's your chance to show us how to do it, right from scratch.'

The rest of us echoed those thoughts and pressed Justin to try on his new suit. In the face of such demands, he disappeared down the cell passage to change.

A few minutes later, he emerged in his new outfit. In a handsome dark worsted, it was a three-piece in the very latest style and it was a perfect fit. Justin was the epitome of a smart and successful City gentleman.

There was a stunned silence from his audience.

'How about that, then?' he beamed, doing a twirl. 'This is style, gentlemen,' he said. 'I never knew such clothing was obtainable in the north.'

'Bloody hell, you must be deformed!' laughed Vesuvius, going across and tugging the jacket. 'It's perfect . . .'

And so it was. We admired the suit; it was superb in every sense and the quality and fit was undeniable. Justin was so proud and, to be honest, we were all pleased for him. Looking back, it would have been a tragedy if it had been a gross misfit, and so later that afternoon he hurried away to travel down to the wedding in London.

Our joke had misfired, and perhaps it was a good job it had. But later that evening when I was relaxing at home, the telephone rang. It was John Golding.

'That suit you picked up this morning, Mr Rhea,' he began. 'Have you still got it?'

'I haven't, John, no. I delivered it to my colleague.'

'Where is he now?' he asked.

'In London, I'd say,' I told him, and explained the reason.

'Oh, crumbs,' he said. 'That's torn it!'

'Why?' I asked, wondering what John's problem could be.

'Well, it was the wrong one,' John said. 'That should have gone to a chap in Thirsk, and I reckon he's got that 'un your friend ordered. He reckons it doesn't fit him.'

'I think he's mistaken, John,' I said, trying to cover for Justin. 'Justin's was perfect, he's gone to a wedding in it and he was delighted. I saw him wearing it, he got the right suit, I'm sure. Maybe you could alter the Thirsk one and say nothing about the possible mistake?'

'Aye, mebbe I should. I'll tell yon Thirsk chap he's got the right 'un, they're t'same cloth. Thanks, Mr Rhea.'

I never told Justin he'd been given the wrong suit, nor did I tell Vesuvius and the other constables. I let Justin think we could produce the finest suits, and it was several weeks later when there was another repercussion.

'How did the wedding go?' I asked Justin one day when we were chatting.

He told me all about it and then, as an afterthought, he added, 'Oh, by the way, that suit you helped me with. You should have seen the admiring looks I got; my family and friends were most impressed, Nick, most impressed. In fact, several of them are ordering suits from Mr Golding. I can't wait to see their faces when they receive them.'

'Neither can I,' I said with some honesty.

One of the funniest jokes was the one played upon poor Douglas Gregson and his girlfriend Deirdre. Douglas was a farmer's son who lived in Crampton with his parents.

Aged about twenty-five, Douglas was not the brightest of lads; in fact he was very simple-minded and worked as a labourer on his parents' large and busy farm. He was capable of doing as he was told, and his physical strength enabled him to undertake most of the tasks about the farm.

A very good worker, he was not mentally handicapped, but merely rather slow when it came to using his brain.

He was strongly built with powerful shoulders and a neck like a bull, although he was very gentle-natured. With his short brown hair and big brown eyes, he was a fine-looking lad, but as his father said, 'Oor Douglas was at t'back o' t'queue when God was dishing out brains.'

His parents were ordinary hard-working farmers, and his father enjoyed working with horses; indeed, he kept several on the farm, as well as a collection of fine horse-drawn vehicles including a stage coach and several traps. He would take these to local agricultural shows and galas, where he would provide rides in them for charity. Douglas was quite a capable driver too, and would often take the reins of his father's coaches, carts and traps.

Then Douglas found a girlfriend. Deirdre was the niece of a couple in Crampton and she came to visit them from time to time. She was not too bright either and was a plain but pleasant girl a couple of years younger than Douglas. She wore her dull brown hair in a bobbed cut and had pretty pink cheeks and grey eyes. Heavily built and somewhat slow in her movements, her surname was Wharton.

Deirdre lived in Middlesbrough where she had a mundane job with the Corporation and she loved to come to the countryside. Her long-standing, platonic friendship with Douglas meant she paid regular weekend visits to Crampton and there is no doubt the couple were ideal for one another. She loved to go on outings alone with Douglas and they were sometimes accompanied by his family or her aunt and uncle.

It was during one of those outings on a lovely summer day in June, that someone played a prank on the happy pair. Douglas had been allowed to take a pony and trap for a drive and this delighted Deirdre. With her sitting in the trap like a lady, Douglas had driven along the lanes until he had found a place to halt. It was a field through which a footpath led to a lovely walk along the banks of the river to an old mill, and then across the water via a footbridge and back to this field over another packhorse bridge. The local people enjoyed this as a Sunday afternoon walk, for it took a little over an hour.

At the entrance to the field, Douglas had tied the horse's long reins to a small tree beside the five-barred gate and had then escorted Deirdre upon this delightful stroll. The horse could move around and was able to munch the grass, even though it was still between the shafts of the trap. But a prankster saw a wonderful opportunity for a joke upon Douglas. This unknown person had discovered the unattended pony and trap and had clearly known it belonged to Douglas.

He had unhitched the pony and, with considerable skill, had manhandled the light trap. This was really a governess cart of the kind used for taking children on outings; it had two seats facing inwards, mudguards over the wheels and a low rear door. Ideal for country lanes, it was very light and manoeuvrable, even by hand. The prankster was able to place the tips of its twin shafts between the bars of the gate and the gap between the bars was sufficient for the entire length of the shafts to go through. Thus the front panels of the cart were tight against the gate, with the shafts protruding at the other side, and then the joker had backed the pony between the shafts and had rehitched it.

When Douglas and Deirdre had returned, this sight had baffled them. Neither could understand how the pony had somehow caused the gate to become inextricably intertwined with the shafts of the trap. And Douglas, not being the brightest of lads, could not see a way to undo this problem. His answer was to use his strength. The space between the bars allowed him to lift the gate off its hinges, then he put Deirdre aboard the trap and jumped up himself.

And then he set a course for home with the gate still fastened in position; its width filled the lane and provided the wonderful sight of a mobile five-barred gate being carried between a pony and trap. And that's how I found them. I was driving my mini-van towards Crampton when this sight confronted me. I could not get past on the narrow road and pulled on to the verge where I signalled Douglas to stop.

'Now then, Douglas,' I said. 'What have we got here?'

'A five-barred gate, Mr Rhea, from yon field down by t'beck.'

'Ah.' I knew the field in question. 'And how's it come to be here? Did you run into it or something?'

'Nay, I didn't, but how it's come to get tangled up with my cart is summat I shall never know, Mr Rhea,' he said with all seriousness.

'Why, what happened?' I was now very curious about it for at this stage, I did not know what had occurred. As he pondered aloud, Deirdre sat silently in the trap, frowning as she puzzled over the answer.

'Well,' he said slowly. 'I got into t'field, tied up my awd pony and set off walking. I mean, we didn't crash through t'gate or owt like that. It was in t'field by this time, safe and sound, Mr Rhea, both t'pony and t'trap. And when we got back, yon pony must have got loose or summat, because it had got itself tangled up like yon. Now how it managed to do that, I'll never know, so I thought I'd take it home and get yon gate off. I might have to saw it off, it looks fairly well fastened on, eh?'

'If we unhitch your pony,' I said, 'we could slide that

gate off, eh? And then we can put it back before somebody thinks you've stolen it.'

'Stolen it? I'd never do that, Mr Rhea.' He looked very worried at this suggestion.

'I know you wouldn't, Douglas, so let's get it off.'

I felt that the best way would be to drive pony and trap back to the field, for this was the easiest way to carry the gate to its former position. To manhandle that gate off those shafts as the trap stood here on its two wheels wouldn't be easy, so I jumped aboard and Douglas drove us back to the field. There, he skilfully positioned the trap into the space between the hedges and we inched the gate into its former position. There was sufficient room for me and Douglas to manipulate it back on to its hinges while still resting upon those shafts, and when it was secure, we unhitched the pony, withdrew the trap from the gate, and re-assembled the unit.

'There,' I said to Douglas and Deirdre. 'Now you can go home without this gate.'

'By gum, Mr Rhea, that was a clever move. Who'd have thought of that, eh?'

'Who indeed?' I wondered who had done this to Douglas and guessed that, sooner or later, the culprit would approach him to find out how he'd coped with the gate. Maybe I would never know of that discussion.

But the happy couple then drove home and I heard no more about the prank with the five-barred gate. I'm still convinced, however, that neither Douglas nor Deirdre thought it was the work of a prankster. They thought the pony had done it.

Prominent among the wonderful aspects of welfare within the police service are the police convalescent homes. There are two in England and they provide facilities for serving or

retired officers who are recuperating from sickness or
injury. Supported by voluntary contributions from every
serving officer, they are havens of rest for those who wish
to recover quietly from a serious ailment or injury. Many
officers make use of them, for it is here they can enjoy a
relaxed and cheerful atmosphere coupled with the undivided
attention of dedicated staff. These are not hospitals; their
function is to consolidate the work of the doctors and
hospitals by providing after-care facilities for rest and
recuperation away from domestic and professional
pressures. And most certainly, they do a fine job.

The following account is not mine, therefore, because it
comes from a friend who spent some time in one of the
convalescent homes, and I feel it is worthy of inclusion at
this point as we are discussing practical jokes.

I will call my friend Dave; after a serious illness he was
advised to spend some weeks in the Northern Police
Convalescent Home in order to encourage a full recovery.
Once inside, he was one of a group of about thirty officers,
men and women of all ranks representing most of the
northern police forces. The friendly atmosphere was evident
from the moment he stepped inside, and one of the things
he noticed, as a constable, was that the rank structure was
abolished.

In the workaday routine of the police service, especially
among the provincial forces, ranks are strictly honoured,
with sergeants always being called 'sergeant' by the
constables. Sometimes, very unofficially, they would be
called 'Serge', but the lower rank must never address
anyone of higher rank by his or her Christian name.

Sergeants and constables then address inspectors and
anyone above that rank as 'sir'; inspectors call chief
inspectors 'sir'; both call a superintendent 'sir', and so
forth up the scale. Chief superintendents, assistant chief

constables, deputy chief constables and chief constables are all 'sir' to those who are subordinate to them. In the London Metropolitan Police, the higher ranks include commanders, deputy assistant commissioners, assistant commissioners and a deputy commissioner with, of course, the Commissioner himself, all of whom are addressed as 'sir'. In the case of lady police officers, sergeants are called by that name, whereas inspectors and those of senior rank are addressed as 'ma'am'. Within the CID hierarchy, the ranks are the same, i.e. detective constables, detective sergeants, detective inspectors, detective chief inspectors, detective superintendents and detective chief superintendents.

Throughout the service, this hierarchy is strictly honoured because police officers are members of a highly disciplined body with an enormous amount of formality; inevitably, this leads to a powerful consciousness of rank through every aspect of a police officer's life.

For officers of all ranks to be thrown together into a common pool can be a traumatic experience, especially if they are supposed to be off duty and recovering from sickness in a friendly environment. No one wants his boss breathing down his neck when he is recovering from sickness. This was recognised by those in charge of the convalescent homes, and it was felt that, within those walls, all distinction between ranks should be abolished. After all, a constable could hardly feel relaxed if his table companion or snooker partner was known to be a deputy chief constable, albeit from another police area.

When officers were admitted therefore, their ranks were not known to the other residents. They were simply Miss, Mrs or Mr. Obviously, instances did occur when one officer was known to another which meant that his rank was also known, but this was a comparatively rare event because of the huge catchment area. Many officers found themselves sharing their convalescence with complete strangers, and this was the ideal situation. The decision whether or not to reveal one's rank rested with individuals.

It was Dave's misfortune, therefore, to be admitted at the same time as his own deputy chief constable. Within moments of arriving, the Home's insistence that ranks should be ignored was made known to them, and to give the deputy his credit, his first words to Dave were, 'Ah, Dave. I'm Bill. I mean that; I'm Bill, so forget my rank. I'm Bill Short, got it?'

'Yes, sir, er . . . Bill . . . sir . . .'

'Bill,' said the deputy.

'Yes, sir . . . er . . . Bill.'

It was very difficult to abandon that habit which had developed over many years in the service, but Bill Short did his best to make Dave relax. The others, a mixture of men and women of all age groups and from widely varying aspects of the job in distant police forces, had no trouble referring to Bill as Bill. They did not know his rank, and he did his best to ensure Dave didn't tell them. But for Dave, it was not easy; it took days for him to be able to refer to his second most senior officer as Bill.

Inevitably, he did slip up from time to time and called Bill 'sir' in front of the others. They, of course, did not mind for there were other 'sirs' among them, happily unaware even then of the precise ranks involved. And then there developed a strange situation which completely relaxed Dave and put his boss in a wonderful new light.

One Friday evening, the residents gathered around the notice-board to study the list of forthcoming arrivals who were due at the Home on the following Monday.

'Bloody hell!' cried Stan, a man from Lancashire

Constabulary. 'See that? He'll not go along with this "no rank" idea. He's the most rank-conscious man I know – he even gets his wife to call herself Mrs Superintendent Welsh. He never speaks to lower ranks when he's off duty – he's a right pain, I can tell you!'

The rest of them crowded around the board in an attempt to read the name of this unwelcome guest, as Stan went on: 'He crawls to the bosses – he'll grovel like hell to anybody higher than himself. He'll put a right damper on this place, you'll see.'

'Who is he?' asked Bill Short.

'Superintendent Adam Welsh, the Admin. Superintendent in one of our Divisions in Lancashire. Special-course man, a flier, passed all his exams and shot up the tree. He's a right toffee-nosed bastard! He doesn't know me, thank God, but we all know *him*!'

Bill laughed.

'Right,' he said. 'If he's coming here to flaunt his rank, we'll be ready for him. I have a plan. We can take him down a peg or two, as they say. Everyone agreed?'

They asked Stan to give a detailed account of the behaviour of the newcomer, after which they agreed they would listen to Bill's idea. In short, Welsh seemed a most objectionable man whose chief aim in life was to rise through the ranks by creeping to those who were senior to him. After hearing this, Bill took them all into the lounge and explained his system.

'Right,' he said. 'The first thing is not to react to him if he toes the Home's line; I mean, he might join in with everyone and forget his exalted rank. If he does, then we don't bring our plan into action, OK? We let him set the pace – we must give him a chance to join us.'

They all agreed to that.

'But,' he continued, 'we shall need plans if he tries to

pull rank on the rest of us. To get the maximum benefit from this, you should know that, although I'm Bill to each of you, I am really a deputy chief constable. But from the moment this man enters this Home, you will let him know that I am a constable. I'm the sort of constable who has never been in line for promotion, never passed any exams, and at my age there is no hope for promotion!'

They smiled at the idea.

'Now,' said Bill, addressing a man called Keith who came from Newcastle upon Tyne. 'Keith. You are a very well-spoken man, if I may say so. You do not have a Geordie accent, not even a trace of one and you do have the presence of a senior officer.' Bill's ability to assess a person shone through.

'I'm originally from Surrey,' said Keith.

'You sound very like a deputy chief constable to me!' smiled Bill. 'At least a deputy, perhaps even a chief constable. You're not, I know, because I know all the chiefs, deputies and assistants in the north. So do you mind telling us your rank – for this important exercise?'

'No, I'm a constable, that's all. I never got promoted because I never passed my exams.'

'Right,' said Bill. 'From the moment this Lancashire character arrives and plays the rank game, you will be a deputy chief constable. I shall inadvertently call you "sir" from time to time and we'll see how he reacts.'

'I'll love that!' said Keith.

To avoid further confusion, the little meeting of conspirators decided that no one else would adopt a false rank, although there was nothing to prevent them pretending they were higher than superintendent if the moment justified it. They all agreed that Keith would be their deputy chief constable for this exercise, and that Bill would be a constable on a beat in Scarborough.

It was with some interest, therefore, that the company awaited the arrival of Mr A. Welsh. After being attended to by the receptionist, he settled in his room and came to join the rest of the guests in the lounge just before lunch.

His first remark, to a grey-haired man called Cyril was, 'Where are the officers' toilets, please?'

'There aren't any,' said Cyril. 'Men's and women's are separate, but we don't use ranks here, Mr Welsh.'

'This is a police establishment,' was his retort. 'I should not be expected to share toilets with the lower ranks. I shall speak to the management. And for lunch? There will surely be officers' tables? With linen cloths and napkins?'

'No,' said Bill Short, entering the conversation. 'We all muck in, we don't ask for ranks here, Mr Welsh.'

The cheek muscles in the taut white face of this man tightened noticeably; he was a tall, thin man with an almost gaunt expression and his fair hair was cut short and plastered back with hair oil.

He showed no inclination to smile and his eyes, darting rapidly around the room for indications of support, rested on Keith. As Bill Short had recognised, Keith, for some reason, had the demeanour of a very senior officer and Welsh addressed him.

'Is this true? Am I to believe that in this police establishment, the achievement of rank is not recognised?'

'Yes, Mr Welsh, that is so,' said Keith in his finest voice. 'We are all guests, men and women of equal status as we recuperate.'

'Then I think this is appalling. I haven't worked my way up to superintendent rank for nothing! I am Superintendent Welsh, I wish everyone to know that and to remember and respect that fact during my stay here!'

And with that statement, everyone knew what to do.

'What do you think, sir?' Bill Short asked Keith, slipping

in the rogue 'sir' with astonishing ease. 'Should we revert to our ranks?'

'I think it is a matter for individual choice,' said Keith. 'Speaking purely personally, I am happy to be called Keith by everyone here, including Superintendent Welsh.'

Keith played his part with such aplomb that the others almost applauded him and this set the scene. Later, they learned that Welsh had quietly sought the advice of one of the guests about Keith's rank, and was told, in the strictest confidence, that he was deputy chief constable from Newcastle upon Tyne City Police.

In the days that followed, Welsh followed Keith around like a pupil with a crush on a teacher, having been assured that everyone else here was below his own rank and therefore unworthy of his companionship. He carried Keith's golf clubs, invited him out for drinks, joined him at snooker and card games, discussed policy matters with him and generally shut the others out of his short convalescence.

For Bill Short, this was excellent and he was enjoying himself testing Welsh's reactions; he tried to win his confidence by inviting him out for a drink, by offering to play snooker with him, by inviting him for walks into town for shopping or sightseeing, but each of Bill's overtures was politely rejected. Welsh made it abundantly clear that he did not consort with lower ranks, especially constables who drank pints and played snooker.

Stan's assessment of Welsh had been absolutely accurate for he was a snob, and a rank-conscious snob into the bargain. By the end of the week, everyone was wondering how to reveal to Superintendent Welsh the fact that he was being led gently along a path that led to nowhere in a wonderfully false world. It was learned that he would be going home on the Sunday, and in order to make the necessary impact upon him, the truth should be revealed.

The opportunity came during the dinner on Saturday night. It was made known that the Chief Constable of Newcastle upon Tyne City Police would be attending the evening dinner as a guest of the Home.

He was chairman of the management committee and was attending in that capacity. Chief constables were regular visitors, for most of them served on the management committee or supported the work of the convalescent home in various ways. As the dinner gong sounded, therefore, the residents moved into the dining-room and Superintendent Welsh made sure he shared a table with Keith. There was an even more important reason for this because Welsh realised that Keith was from the Newcastle Force. Perhaps he thought the Chief Constable would come over and express interest in the health of one of his most senior officers. Everyone was seated prior to the Chief Constable's entry and, as was his custom, he toured the tables to speak to the guests before settling down to eat.

When he arrived at Keith's table, his eyes lit up.

'Ah, PC Burton, good to see you. How's it going?'

'Fine, sir,' beamed Keith. 'This break has done me a world of good. I feel much better now.'

'Summonses and Warrants is having a busy time without you, you know. I'll tell Sergeant Helm you're doing fine; I know he's anxiously awaiting your return!'

'Another week should do it, sir,' said Keith, pleased his Chief had recognised him.

'Good, well, nice to have seen you looking so fit. And you,' he now addressed Welsh. 'Are you recuperating nicely?'

'Yes, sir,' beamed Welsh.

And before Welsh could announce his name and rank,

the Chief Constable moved on and stopped at Bill Short's table.

'Bill, good to see you! Are you coping with these rebels around you? It's time you were getting back, you know, your Chief hasn't had a day off since you went sick!'

Everyone in the room heard his friendly exchanges and all eyes were now on Superintendent Welsh. For a long time, he said nothing, his eyes flickering as the full impact of the Chief's words began to register.

'PC Burton?' Eventually he quietly asked Keith to tell the truth. 'Did I hear your Chief correctly?'

'You did, Mr Welsh,' said Keith with an air of pride. 'I am PC Keith Burton of the Summonses and Warrants Department of Newcastle upon Tyne City Police.'

'And that other man, that Bill Short, he led me to think he's a constable at Scarborough. If my ears don't deceive me, your Chief knows him well and that smacks of a rank much higher than constable! The others haven't mentioned their ranks.' Already there was a look of impending horror on Welsh's pale face; he realised he had been deliberately tricked.

'He's a deputy chief constable, Mr Welsh. With the local force.'

For a long time, Superintendent Welsh did not speak. He ate his dinner in silence, often playing with his food and allowing the conversation to bubble around him. No one could tell what thoughts were buzzing through his head.

At the end of the meal, the Chief Constable left the room with other members of staff, and only then did the grim-faced Welsh make his move.

'I would like a word with all of you,' he said to the residents. 'In the lounge, if you don't mind, in five minutes.'

It was almost like a command, but it was clearly tempered with a note of sorrow and even regret. As the others looked to him for guidance, Bill Short nodded his agreement to Welsh's request and they all assembled, wondering what was in store. They settled on the easy chairs which lined the walls, awaiting Welsh's comments. He came in and stood before them, a tall, pale and now rather fragile figure. The arrogance had been knocked out of him.

'You've made a fool of me,' he said, without smiling. 'I fell into your trap. I am a fool,' he suddenly added with a smile. 'An utter stupid fool. It's people that matter, not ranks. So if anyone wants to go out for a drink, there's a nice hostelry down the road, and the drinks are all on me. I am sorry for my behaviour.'

There was a momentary silence, then Bill Short said, 'It takes a man to admit he's wrong, so you're on – er, sir!'

'Thanks – er, Bill,' smiled Welsh. 'You've made me realise we're human beings, not machines with pips on our shoulders!'

Everyone started chattering and then Welsh turned to Keith Burton. 'Coming – er, sir?' he asked with a smile.

'You try and stop me – er, Adam,' said PC Burton.

8

In previous 'Constable' books, I have provided accounts of fascinating people in the twilight of their years; some of their stories are included in *Constable around the Village* and I thought I would elaborate upon one or two of those tales and include a few new ones.

So far as old folk are concerned, caring for them is very much a part of the village constable's life. This is not formal care of the kind expected from the multitude of welfare and charity services nor does it impinge upon their family's own responsibilities, but it means that the village constable, while on patrol, does keep an eye open for signs of need or distress among the older folk. Sometimes this continuing observation results in a telephone call to the family concerned or perhaps to one or other of the welfare services or charitable organisations. More often than not, however, the constable is able to cope with any immediate need and his work goes unpublicised, save for a word of thanks, or a cup of tea, from a grateful senior citizen.

I found that the elderly who lived in and around Aidensfield were highly independent country folk who hated the idea that they might have to depend on charity or the welfare state. In helping them, there was a need to exercise discretion and to show them that any help given was not an adverse reflection upon their own capabilities.

Having led a life of self-sufficiency founded upon hard work and enterprise, their advancing years made them less able to cope physically, although their mental state and belief in themselves remained undimmed. Many of them felt they could achieve just as much at eighty years of age as they had done at thirty, and that did cause some worries.

One shining example of this philosophy was eighty-three-year-old Jacob Broadbent. Officially, he was a retired farmer and he and his wife, Sissy (81), lived in a neat bungalow in Aidensfield. Built specially for them in their retirement, it was fitted with the latest work-saving ideas and boasted a large garden full of mature soft-fruit bushes, fully grown apple and plum trees and a patch for vegetable cultivation. The garden had once been part of a larger house and Jacob's son had succeeded in buying the plot upon which to build his parents' retirement home.

The inclusion of a large garden had been a brilliant idea by Jacob's son, Jesse, a man in his late fifties. Jesse knew that his father would require something to occupy him during his so-called retirement, and this was the garden's purpose. In spite of tending his little patch, however, Jacob made regular visits to the farm where Jesse found the old man various jobs to keep him busy. Jacob, as one would have expected, couldn't understand the new ideas and machinery that Jesse introduced, but contented himself by looking after the pigs and sheep, feeding the hens and recording their egg production as he had in years past.

The result was that in his retirement, Jacob was kept busy and that made him very happy. Sissy, his down-to-earth wife, kept out of his way. She knew better than to interfere with his daily routine. Always on the go, she fussed over her new bungalow, visited people in the village and, even at eighty-one, made sure she was involved in village activities such as the church and the Women's Institute. This kept her fully occupied, and for a couple in their eighties, they were remarkably alert, active and energetic.

There is no doubt that one of Jacob's joys was his orchard. Having grown apples at the farm, he had continued this enterprise at his new bungalow, another example of Jesse's foresight in providing something for his father to do. And so, in the autumn, Jacob supplied the local shops, hotels and village people with a variety of fresh and tasty apples. It provided him with some pocket money, out of which he enjoyed a regular pint in the Brewer's Arms, a daily pipe or two of strong-smelling tobacco and weekly trips to all the local cattle markets and, where possible, sales of antiques or house-contents.

It was during a late September afternoon that I was attracted to his orchard by a cry for help. By chance, I was walking through Aidensfield, intending to call at the garage on a routine enquiry about a recent accident. The garage had recovered from the scene the vehicles which had been damaged, and because I needed precise details of the damage for my report I was on my way to inspect them.

As I walked beneath the high wall which concealed the Broadbents' home from the street, I became aware of a hoarse cry. It was very faint. At first, I could not decide what it was or where it was coming from, but as I stopped to listen more carefully, I realised it was a man and it was coming from Jacob's orchard. Sensing trouble, I rushed into the garden and hurried around the back of the bungalow to the orchard from where the calls were being repeated. And there, as I rounded the corner past the greenhouse, I found Jacob.

'Mr Rhea!' he breathed as he saw me. 'By, it's good thoo's come along now . . .'

He was lying on his back beneath a tall, sturdy apple tree and his right leg was held high in the air among the lower branches. A basket of apples was lying upturned near by with its contents spilled across the grass.

'What's up, Jacob?' I asked, hurrying to his aid.

'I tummled doon this tree, Mr Rhea, and that trouser leg's gitten hooked up somewhere . . .'

'Jacob!' I tried to sound angry as I examined his elevated leg. How did he come to tumble down the tree? But I had no time to ask that sort of question just yet. I had to release him first. The material of his trousers had 'snagged' on a short, strong stump of a branch, and it had pierced the cloth. This now held Jacob's leg in the air and from his position on the ground, he could not free himself. He was a prisoner of his own apple tree!

'This is a right mess you've got yourself into, Jacob!' I said, trying to free his leg. 'Are you hurt?'

'It winded me, Mr Rhea,' he said. 'Knocked the stuffing out of me, landing flat on my back like this. But I've got me breath back now. I think I'm all right.'

'No injuries, then?' I was struggling to free the trouser leg from the tree but his weight made it difficult.

'Nay, nowt.'

'How long have you been lying here then?' was my next question.

'Ages, Mr Rhea. She's out, you see, our Sissy, I mean. Gone to see a friend, she has. I've been laid here shouting for hours . . . nobody heard me . . . I got frightened, thoo knaws.'

'Lift your backside in the air a bit, can you?' I asked him. 'Then it'll take some of the weight off this leg and I'll be able to lift you off this branch.'

His overall trousers were made of tough denim and I had to cut the cloth to effect his release. My pocket knife made short work of that problem and once his leg was free, I lifted him to his feet. He hobbled around a bit, stamping his foot and holding his aching back with his hand. I looked around for a ladder, but found none. Maybe a rung had snapped or its wood was rotten?

'How did you get up that tree, Jacob?' I asked.

'Climbed up,' he said.

'Without a ladder or steps?' I put to him.

'There's no need for owt like that, Mr Rhea,' he said with just a trace of contempt. 'Why bother with ladders when t'trees grow their own steps?'

'You shouldn't be climbing trees at your age!' I shook my finger at him in a mock rebuke. 'You could break a leg or something if you fall down – these are big trees and it's a long fall from the top. Look how a tumble bruises apples that come down. You'll be covered with bruises tonight, I shouldn't wonder.'

'Thoo'll not tell our missus, wilt thoo?' he asked with a note of pleading in his voice.

'Why not?' I put to him.

'Well, she's allus going on at me about climbing trees and picking apples, Mr Rhea, and it's only way I can pick 'em. So say nowt to her, eh? About me tummling doon.'

'So long as you're not hurt,' I submitted.

'Fit as a fiddle,' he said, straightening his back as if to emphasise his words. 'There's nowt ailing me.'

'OK, but remember, no more climbing trees.'

'You sound just like my missus,' he grumbled as he stooped to begin picking up the spilt apples, groaning with pain as he did so. I helped him and when we'd collected the lot, he went indoors.

'Thoo'll come in for a cup o' tea, Mr Rhea?' he invited me.

'No thanks, Jacob,' I said. 'I'd love to, but I've got to get on. I'm supposed to be visiting the garage.'

Happy that his fall had not resulted in any permanent damage, I left him to recover over a cup of tea. I thought little more about the incident until I saw his wife, Sissy, in the village street a couple of weeks later.

'How's your Jacob these days?' I asked after a general chat.

'Fine,' she said, 'but his rheumatics is bothering him a bit. He reckons his back hurts; I say it's with climbing apple trees but he says it's not. Mr Rhea, mebbe you'd have a word with him about climbing trees at his age. He'll fall down one of these days, mark my words, and that could be t'end of him. I shouldn't want to deal with him if he cripples hisself 'cos he's tummled oot of a tree at eighty-three, Mr Rhea. He's a bit awd for that sort of a caper.'

'I'll have a word with him,' I promised her.

I did speak to him and said he was too old for that sort of a caper, as Sissy had put it. But it made no difference. He continued to climb apple trees until his death at ninety-two.

Another tale involved Sidney Latimer who was eighty-six. A retired lengthman, his work had involved keeping the roads tidy and well maintained. And, so I learned from the older folks, Sidney had done a very thorough job. In winter especially, he had kept them gritted and open when others near by had been closed in the grip of the weather. Sidney had always taken a pride in 'his' roads.

He lived alone in a pretty cottage just off the main street at Aidensfield and he coped very well with his daily chores, albeit with the help of a lady who popped in to care for him. Like so many of the elderly in and around Aidensfield, he would emerge on a fine day to sit on the bench near the war memorial, there to observe the passing show and to chat with three or four pals of similar age.

Then he became ill. I was not aware of this for some time, but realised that he was not enjoying his daily walk or his sojourns to the village seat and so I asked after him from his cleaning lady.

'Oh, he's in hospital, Mr Rhea, at York.'

'Oh, I had no idea! What's wrong with him?' I asked.

'Old age mainly,' she said without a hint of sympathy. 'And his waterworks are giving him pain. They're seeing to him there, he might be in for a week or two.'

I rang the hospital to enquire after his progress and was given the usual response: 'Mr Latimer is as well as can be expected.'

That did not say a great deal so, one afternoon when Mary and I, with the family, went shopping to York, I decided to pop in and see Mr Latimer. I found him in a ward full of elderly gentlemen, some in a very poor state and clearly approaching the end of their lives. Assailed by the distinctive smell from this geriatric ward, I settled at Sidney's beside.

'Now, Mr Latimer,' I said. 'How's things?'

'Hello, Mr Rhea.' His old eyes twinkled with delight because he had a visitor. 'You are looking slim. How's Mrs Rhea?'

This was his usual greeting; whenever he met anyone, man or woman of any shape or size, he complimented them upon looking slim.

'She's fine thanks,' I told him, pulling up a chair. 'She's in town shopping, she sends her best wishes and hopes you'll be home soon.'

'It's my waterworks, Mr Rhea, they say. I reckon I need

a good plumber not a doctor. But they say I'll be home before long.'

He was very alert and we chatted for some time about village matters. He was a big man, well over six feet tall, and in his younger days must have been an impressive sight. He had married, I knew, but his wife had died several years earlier and, so far as I knew, there had been no children. Sitting propped up on that hospital bed, he did look rather vulnerable and somewhat smaller and more fragile than usual. During the course of our conversation, he said he got a bit lonely.

'It's not like being at home, is it? At home I can pop out and see folks, there's allus somebody about, or something to do, even if it's just popping into a shop or the Post Office for my pension. Here, I just have to lie down and do as I'm told. These old lads in here aren't much company, are they?'

He looked along the ward at his companions and sighed.

'Just lying there fading away, that's all they're doing. There's not a lot of excitement unless it's some poor sod who's cocked his toes.'

It must be awful, seeing one's companions dying one by one, but he seemed unperturbed. He was fully convinced he would be allowed home very soon.

'There must be somebody I can tell about you being in here, Mr Latimer,' I suggested. 'The village folks know you're here . . .'

'They never come!' he grumbled.

'Relations, then? Old friends? Shall I write to them and say you're here?'

'Apart from folks around Aidensfield, there's only my old schoolteacher. Taught me when I was a lad, she did. You might tell her, I allus send her a Christmas card.'

Now I thought he was going senile but wary of his

reactions if I showed disbelief, I said, 'Where's she live? I'll tell her.'

He delved into his bedside cabinet and pulled out a battered old pocket diary, years out of date. Flicking through the pages until he found the place, he said, 'No 18 Ryelands Terrace, Eltering. Miss Wilkinson. Taught me my three Rs at Ashfordly Primary she did. 1886 she was there. Lovely woman. Lovely as they come. She'll be interested to know I'm here. Allus kept in touch, she has.'

To humour him, I made a note of the name and address in my private diary and promised I would tell her. This seemed to please him greatly and our next half-hour was spent in casual chatter about nothing in particular. I could see he was tiring so I said my goodbyes.

'Goodbye, Mr Rhea,' he smiled as I stood up. 'My word, you do look slim. Now, you won't forget to tell Miss Wilkinson, will you? And you will come again?'

'Yes, I'll come again,' I assured him, and left to collect my wife and family from the café where they'd been having tea with one of Mary's friends.

I must admit I gave no more thought to Mr Latimer's supposed schoolteacher, but a few days later, I was patrolling Eltering. I had driven there in my mini-van because I was scheduled for a two-hour foot patrol in the town; there was a shortage of local officers that afternoon. And then, quite unexpectedly, I found myself walking along Ryelands Terrace. The name had meant nothing until now and when I saw the nameplate on the wall of one of the houses, it caused a flicker of reaction in my mind. At first, I could not determine why it should interest me and then I recalled my chat with old Mr Latimer.

Pulling out my diary, I found my note about Miss Wilkinson, the primary schoolteacher who'd taught him around 1886; she had lived at No 18. Now full of curiosity, I decided to walk along to No 18.

When I got there, I found an elderly lady tidying her front garden. She was slender and small, with a neat head of tidy grey hair and she carried a paper sack. She was collecting fallen leaves which had been blown from some nearby sycamores. She smiled warmly as I approached.

'Leaves are such a nuisance, constable, aren't they? Every autumn, they blow into my garden, and every autumn I clean them out!'

'They are,' I sympathised with her. 'My wife makes compost from them, we find them a nuisance really, but we can make use of them.'

'Yes, I give mine away,' she smiled. 'To the old gentleman who lives next door. My garden is much too small for me to worry about compost.'

I wondered if I dare ask about Miss Wilkinson, Mr Latimer's old teacher, for it was such a long time ago that she'd taught the old man. Maybe she had married and this was her daughter? Or a younger sister? Maybe this lady had no idea who had lived here before her . . .

'Excuse me,' I said, 'but now that I'm here, I wonder if you know of a Miss Wilkinson who used to live here? She was a teacher in the primary school at Ashfordly in 1886.'

'That's me,' she said primly. 'I'm Miss Wilkinson.'

'You!' I did not know what to say. 'But, she must be older than you . . . she taught a friend of mine, a Mr Latimer . . .'

'Sidney Latimer,' she smiled. 'Yes, of course. He was in my class, a very good pupil and very bright. He did nothing with his life, Officer, yet he could have done anything he wanted, that man. Wasted his talents. Such a shame.'

I was still not sure we were discussing the same Sidney Latimer, so I said, 'Well, he's in hospital actually, in York.

He's had a minor operation and asked if I would inform Miss Wilkinson, his teacher . . .'

'Yes, that's me. He must be, oh, what? Eighty-six now? He was eight when I taught him, Constable, and I would be getting on for twenty, I think.'

'So you really were his teacher?' I was astounded.

'Yes, of course! I'm well into my nineties now, you know, but still going strong!'

'But . . .'

'Sidney was a nice boy, Constable, and I've always been interested in his welfare. Always. I shall go to visit him in hospital.'

'Shall I arrange a lift for you?' I heard myself offering.

'Thank you, but no. I will use the bus. There is a very good bus service from Eltering to York and I will enjoy the outing. Thank you for telling me about Sidney, I will certainly pay him a call.'

And so she did. He was delighted and I was amazed.

I sat down and worked it out; if he was eight in 1886, he'd been born in 1878 and at the time I met him, he was about eighty-six. If she was twenty in 1886, which was feasible for a teacher in a primary school, she'd have been born in 1866 which meant she was around ninety-eight!

Even now, I find myself surprised that a man of eighty-six could keep in touch with his primary school teacher. And, following her visit, Sidney Latimer did get well and returned home to continue his life in Aidensfield.

Another sad but funny tale occurred during a summer soon after I arrived at Aidensfield. It involved a pair of twin bachelor brothers and their aged father who farmed in an isolated dale to the north of Aidensfield. The sons were Angus and Fergus MacKenzie, and their father was Alexander Cameron MacKenzie, a man in his eighties. No one was quite sure of the twins' age, but they must have been around sixty years old.

In spite of their names, they were Yorkshiremen, although I'm sure a distant ancestor must have journeyed this way from the Highlands. They occupied one of the most remote farms in the moors; it was called Dale Head and it stood high on the slopes of Lairsbeck, at the end of a long, rough track. The MacKenzies dealt chiefly in sheep, although they did breed Highland cattle, and seemed to scrape some kind of a living from their lofty farmstead. Theirs was a life of constant work with no time for relaxation.

Money was always short; they were clearly hard up and were seldom seen in the village or nearby market towns. Mrs MacKenzie had died some years ago, but the twins had never married; they'd never seen the point of having to keep one or two extra people in the house. And so, over the years, they existed in the little stone farmhouse with its stupendous views across the moors. I called infrequently to check their stock register, and that was my only contact with them. I called, drank a mug of tea, signed their book and departed. I probably called once every month or even once every two.

On one occasion when I called in late May, Angus met me and produced the necessary book which I signed. I had seen Fergus in the foldyard and on this occasion, I was not invited to stay for a cup of tea in spite of my long drive.

'We're getting set up for hay time, Mr Rhea,' Angus told me. 'It's allus a thrang time for t'likes of us.'

I knew what he was saying. Thrang is the local word for 'busy', and for a moorland patch like this, every day counted. Hay time up here was fraught with risk from the weather, and so they had to work rapidly and positively to succeed, taking swift advantage of the limited sunshine and drying winds. And with only two fit men and one old man to do all the work, it was a lengthy procedure. Later, however, I thought about that missing mug of tea. It was unusual, but at the time I did not pay any heed to this departure from the normal.

Later, I realised, I had not seen the old man around the buildings either, and once more, this was unusual. Down in the dale and in the surrounding hamlets, no one thought it odd that old Mr MacKenzie had not been seen. He seldom ventured out anyway, his lads making sure they did any shopping that was necessary. I must admit that his absence did not bother me, for I knew of his habits and routine. It was more unusual to see him than not to see him! It was only after the events which occurred later that I realised the significance of all these odd facets.

It began with a call from Harold Poulter, the undertaker.

'Mr Rhea,' he said quietly over the telephone. 'I've a rum sort of a job on. I thought I'd better give you a call.'

Harold dealt with most of the local funerals and we had a good working liaison due to my own official involvement in the investigation of sudden, violent or unusual deaths. Harold knew which deaths should be investigated by the police and so a call from him had to be taken seriously.

'Yes, Harold, what is it this time?'

'It's poor awd Alex MacKenzie, you know, from Lairsbeck. He's tipped his clogs.'

'Ah,' I said partly to myself, 'that's why I haven't seen him around, he must have been ill.'

'Well, I'm not so sure about that, Mr Rhea,' he said. 'But it's a funny affair if you ask me.'

'Go on, Harold,' I invited him to continue.

'Well, them twin lads of his, they've had him up there for weeks, Mr Rhea, never got around to fixing a funeral. I mean, I wonder if you fellers'll need a PM or inquest or summat. Seems he's been dead for weeks.'

'Weeks? How many weeks, Harold?' I asked.

'Dunno, and they're not sure either,' he said. 'They've had no doctor in, they say they know when a pig's dead or a cow, so they know when a feller's gotten his time overed.'

I groaned.

'Where is the body now?'

'In a pigsty,' said Harold. 'They put him there because it's a cool spot and he would keep a while. He wouldn't stink the bedroom out, so they said.'

'I'd better get up there,' I said. 'Have you told Doctor McGee?'

'No, I thought you'd best know first.'

'OK, right, I'll have a ride up to Dale Head and let you know what happens. I'll ring Doctor McGee before I go.'

When I spoke to Doctor McGee, he asked whether I thought it was a suspicious death, like a suicide, or even murder. I had to say I had no idea at this stage; a visual examination would help to determine the future police action, but in view of what Harold had told me, I felt the presence of a doctor was advisable.

'Right, I'll see you there,' he said.

I arrived in advance of Doctor McGee and knocked on the tatty kitchen door. In need of a coat of paint, it was opened by Angus, a thin, large-boned fellow with gaunt cheeks and an unkempt head of sparse ginger hair which was greying around the temples. He smiled a welcome, showing a mouth full of huge yellowing teeth which looked as solid as the rocks around the farm and which had probably never seen a dentist in half a century.

'Noo then, Mr Rhea,' he said, opening the door. 'We was expecting thoo.'

Inside, Fergus, who was almost identical to his brother, albeit perhaps a little more robust in his appearance, was sitting at the end of the plain wooden kitchen table. Around him was a collection of mugs along with the teapot, a half-full milk bottle and a sugar bowl.

'Thoo'll have a cup o' tea, Mr Rhea?' Fergus asked. I was pleased to see this routine had been re-established.

'Thanks, Fergus,' and I settled at the table with Angus at my side. I waited until I had the mug in my hands and said, 'Harold Poulter would tell you why I had to come?'

'Aye, 'e did, Mr Rhea. Unusual death, 'e said. But, Mr Rhea, there's nowt unusual aboot oor father's death. 'E just passed on, like awd folks do. In 'is sleep, no fuss or bother. We've 'ad cows pass on like yon. Nice as yer like, Mr Rhea, so, well, Ah'll be honest, Ah can't understand why awd Harold wouldn't just let us git on wi t'funeral and git t'awd man buried. It's time we did summat wiv 'im.'

'There are always formalities when a person dies.' I tried to be courteous. 'Forms to fill in, a doctor's certificate to obtain, the registrar to see, things like that. You can't bury a human being like you'd bury a sheep.'

'When they're dead, they're dead,' said Angus. He was probably harking back to the days when the procedures surrounding death were less strictured. Certainly in some remote places, people died in circumstances which today would warrant a full investigation – but all that was in the past.

'Doctor McGee is following me along,' I said. 'He must see the body . . . er . . . your father . . . and certify that he is dead. That's his first job. Then if he cannot certify the cause of death, I'm afraid a post-mortem must be held. That means examination by an expert who determines precisely what caused death; he'll find out if it was a heart problem, or something else. Once that's been established, the funeral can go ahead, with the permission of the coroner.'

''E's as dead as a doornail,' cried Angus. 'There's neea need for t'doctor to come and tell us that! And as for t'reason 'e died, it was age, nowt else. 'E was tonned eighty-eight, and 'e just faded away in 'is sleep.'

'I'm sure you're right, but we do have to do things the proper way.'

I could see they did not understand the need for all the fuss, and then Dr Archie McGee arrived. Fergus took him to the table and he sat down with a mug of tea, then looked at me for guidance.

'Well, Mr Rhea, what's the score on this one?'

'It seems that Mr MacKenzie, senior, died in his sleep, Doctor.'

'He'll be upstairs now, is he? I'll have a look.'

'No, he's outside in a pigsty,' I said. 'We are waiting to take you there, after you've had your cuppa.'

'Pigsty? Did he die there?' he asked the twins.

'Nay!' said Fergus shortly. ''E died in bed, but because it was hay time, we couldn't stop work to git 'im buried. There was no time, Mr Rhea, not a minute to spare. You'll know what t'weather's been like, we daren't miss a day just for a funeral. So we laid 'im in yon pigsty till we got finished haytiming; it's not in use and we cleaned it out, then put 'im in straw and salted 'im, making sure we turned 'im twice a week. 'E's out there as fresh as a posy, waiting to be buried. I mean, there's nowt wrang wiv 'im, except he's dead o' course. 'E didn't suffer, 'e wasn't badly, 'e never fell off a ladder or banged 'is head on owt . . . 'e just faded away like Ah said.'

Doctor McGee raised his eyes as if to heaven. 'And how long has he been there?'

'Since just afore we started hay time. Four or five weeks, mebbe. Actually, Doctor, we got finished haytiming a while back, and we was that relieved we'd got all t'hay ladened in, we forgot aboot 'im for a day or two. It was only when Ah went in t'sty for summat that Ah saw 'im there, so Ah turned him over and rang Harold to git 'im buried.'

McGee grinned ruefully at me, as Fergus continued, 'I thought it was time we were gitting summat done with t'awd feller. Not that 'e'd have minded waiting, thoo knaws, 'e allus was a patient chap, oor dad.'

'You are supposed to organise the funeral straight away, gentlemen,' Doctor McGee sighed. 'You must call a doctor who'll certify death and get things moving.'

'We couldn't see t'point in that,' said Fergus. 'Ah mean, once 'e was dead, there was nowt 'e could do and nowt we should do, and besides, 'e wouldn't take any 'arm waiting awhile to get buried. Ah reckon this is a fuss about nowt.'

McGee drained his tea. 'I'd better have a look at him. Take us to him, gents.'

The brothers led us to a row of pigsties and pointed to one with its door closed. 'In there,' said Fergus.

'You wait outside,' he said to them. 'I'll have a look at him, PC Rhea had better come with me.'

Inside, there was the stench of death which is always present around a corpse, but it was tempered by the stronger smell of salt and there, packed in lots of dry straw, was the body of old Mr MacKenzie. It had not decomposed as one would have expected, and no doubt the salt treatment had done something to preserve it. And the straw had kept it cool too, rather like the old system of storing blocks of ice in straw deep within the ice-houses of country mansions. Ice blocks kept in straw could survive for many months without melting . . .

Corpses were kept in mortuary fridges for months or even years, and those old ice-houses would keep game fresh for months too. This pigsty was beautifully cool and dry; it was also rat-proof and I wondered how long old Mr

MacKenzie would have kept 'as fresh as a posy' in here. Maybe for months, if it was an English summer.

McGee began his examination; it was very thorough due to the curious circumstances, and he stripped the nightshirt off the stiff old man to check for wounds or marks of violence, turning the body over and meticulously inspecting it. From where I stood, I saw no marks likely to raise suspicion, but I watched the doctor's careful work.

'You never treated the old man, Doctor?' I asked as he conducted his examination.

He shook his head. 'Once, years ago, he went down with a stomach problem, but that was ten or twelve years since. Looking at him, and bearing in mind he's been out here for weeks, I'd say he died from old age, from natural causes.'

'Would you certify that?' I put the important question to him.

'It would require a post-mortem to determine that with any accuracy.' He spoke honestly. 'The pathologist would have to examine the heart, brain, internal organs, lungs, throat muscles, the lot – you know the routine as well as I do. There are ways of despatching old folks, as you well know, to make it look like a natural death.'

'So do you think this is a suspicious death?' I put him on the spot once again.

'To be honest, no. These chaps are too basic for that. Besides, if they had done the old chap in, they'd have got rid of the body, not kept it in cold storage until they could fix a proper funeral. Look, PC Rhea, if we go through all the official motions, with a PM, the coroner, publicity and so forth, these old characters are going to be made to look fools, aren't they? And nothing will be achieved.'

'Yes,' I agreed. 'They will look a bit daft.'

'I am prepared to certify first, that he is dead, and

second, that he died from natural causes, from old age in fact. In spite of these odd circumstances, there is no doubt in my mind that the old boy died naturally, although, to be totally honest, we should really have a post-mortem due to the time lapse since he died. But I will stick my neck out and issue the necessary certificate, without going through all those formalities. I think it is totally unnecessary in this case.'

'Fine, that's all I need, and thanks. We can get this over now. That's all Harold needs to organise the funeral.'

And so Doctor McGee wrote out the necessary certificate and gave it to the brothers.

'That's all you require,' he said. 'Give this to Harold Poulter and he'll attend to the rest of it. He'll see the registrar for you as well, leave it all in his hands.'

'Thanks, Doctor,' said Fergus. 'Ah never realised dying meant sike a carry-on.'

'I've dated the death certificate for today,' said McGee. 'That means the official date of your dad's death is today, do you understand?'

Angus nodded. 'A bit like t'Queen, eh?' he said slowly. 'She's got an official birthday and a real one, so our dad's got an official day for dying and a real one.'

'Yes,' said McGee, 'but don't mention the real one!'

'Do we 'ave to do owt else, then?' asked Angus. 'Is that it? Is t'official bit ovver with?'

'Nearly, but Harold the undertaker will see to the rest of it for you. You've done your bit.'

'Dying's fussier than Ah thought it would be,' said Angus to his brother. 'So think on, and get me buried quick if Ah goes afore thoo!'

'And we'll 'ave to get yon pigsty disinfected, we've a sow due to farrow next week, and we can't let t'young 'uns live in a sty that needs disinfecting. It's time we got oor awd dad shifted somewhere more permanent.'

And so the funeral went ahead and they made their 'more permanent' arrangements for their father's long-term rest. So if you visit the churchyard at Lairsbeck, you will see the tombstone of Alexander Cameron MacKenzie who died aged eighty-eight. The date on his tombstone is 4th July, but that is neither the date of his actual death nor of his funeral.

It is the date Doctor McGee examined him in that pigsty.

9

'Something very childish, but very natural.'
Samuel Taylor Coleridge, 1772-1834

Children take part in a large proportion of a police officer's work, sometimes through the fault of others such as cases of neglect or cruelty, sometimes as victims through the commission of crimes, sexual assaults, family arguments and maintenance defaulters, sometimes by accident when they are knocked down by motor vehicles or suffer death by drowning or from any other cause. Other matters within our scope were the employment of children, dangerous performances in places like circuses or theatres, harmful publications which might affect them, smoking by juveniles, their general care and protection, their education and a whole host of other matters. Abortion, child destruction, infanticide, concealment of birth and the abandonment of children all came with the realm of our duties.

Our law books and police procedure volumes devoted entire chapters to the law, practice and procedure relating to children and young persons but I cannot determine precisely what proportion of my duty time was spent on matters relating to them. It was certainly a substantial amount and indeed, the criminal law of England does rightly devote many statutes or parts of statutes to children and young persons. Indeed, it divides them into neat categories and we had to learn, parrot fashion, a table of relevant ages at which certain crimes and offences might be committed against youngsters.

For example, a mother causing the death of her child under 1 year old could be convicted of infanticide; it was an offence to abandon a child under 2 so as to endanger life or health; there was a crime committed by suffocation of a child under 3 when it was in bed with a drunken person over 16; intoxicants must not be given to a child under 5 unless for medicinal reasons, and children over 5 must receive a proper education. It was an offence to be drunk in charge of a child under 7 in a public place or on licensed premises and, at that time, a child under 8 was not held criminally responsible for his or her acts. That age was subsequently raised to 10.

This table of ages included youngsters up to 24, with a mass of information concerning those in their teens – there was drinking in pubs, owning and using firearms, driving motor vehicles, marriage, betting, pawning goods or dealing in rags plus a list of penalties open to them if they committed offences or crimes. Much of this legislation was designed for the care and protection of children and young persons and it was our duty to enforce those laws.

In criminal law, the word 'child' meant a person under the age of 14, and 'young person' meant a person who had attained the age of 14 but was under the age of 17. The term 'juvenile' included both children and young persons, thus referring to all those under 17, while 'adult' was a person aged 17 upwards, but aspects of these definitions have now been changed.

It follows that we spent a lot of time learning the mass of laws which affected children and young persons, and we also spent considerable time enforcing the awkward laws which seemed to attract rebellious youngsters, such as drinking under age, driving under age, betting under age, smoking under age, using firearms under age, having sex under age and being employed under age. There were times when even police officers felt the law was silly – for example, a person can take the responsibility for getting married and having children at 16, but cannot buy a pint of ale in the bar of a pub until reaching 18. A person of 17 could be in sole charge of an aircraft in motion but should not be sent betting circulars until reaching 21.

However, it was not the task of the police service to question the laws of the realm, however illogical they might be, for those laws were made by Parliament and our job was to enforce them without fear or favour. In fact, our enforcement of the law is always tempered with discretion for without that, the country would become a police state. If we rigidly enforced every law, life would be intolerable; imagine the furore if we prosecuted everyone who drank, smoked or placed bets while under age or experienced their first groping sexual encounter with someone under the permitted age. One learned judge made it clear that the latter laws were not for the prosecution of youngsters having a tumble in the hay.

But many of our dealings with youngsters were outside the scope of the law; they were simply ordinary everyday happenings which involved a policeman and a child, and I had a marvellous example of this when Mrs June Myers lost her purse. A pretty young mother with two children, she came to my police house at Aidensfield to report the loss.

When the doorbell rang that Saturday lunchtime, I answered it to find the fair-haired June standing outside with her daughter; this was Melanie and she was seven. I invited them into the office, but June turned to look behind herself, and there, hiding behind the hedge at my gate, was her son. This was Joseph and he was nine.

'I won't come in, thanks, Mr Rhea, it's Joseph, he won't come near you.'

'Why not?' I asked as the little face peered at me through the foliage.

'He's frightened of policemen,' she said. 'He thinks you'll lock him up!'

'I'm not frightened!' beamed Melanie from her mother's side.

'Of course you're not,' I smiled, 'so what on earth's given Joseph that idea?'

'Some of the kids at school, I think. He won't say much about it, but I don't like to leave him there with all the traffic passing . . . so . . .'

'Joseph is silly,' said Melanie.

'Be quiet, Melanie,' said her mum.

'I won't hurt him,' I said loudly so he might hear, 'so what's the problem, June?'

She explained how she had been to Ashfordly on the bus only this morning to do some shopping and had lost her purse. It contained a few personal belongings and about £10 in cash, too much for her to lose.

With Melanie adding her comments, I took details and promised I would see if it had been handed in. As she waited at the door, I rang Ashfordly Police Station, but at that stage, there was no record of it. However, I assured her that if it was handed in, it would be restored to her in due course. Off she went, with Joseph running ahead to keep out of my clutches and Melanie waving a brave goodbye.

That afternoon I had to visit Ashfordly Police Station on a routine matter and was in time to see a middle-aged lady departing. As I entered, PC Alwyn Foxton said, 'Ah, Nick! Just in time. That purse you rang about, it's been brought in. Found in the market-place under a seat. The finder's just left.'

I checked the contents and sure enough, it belonged to
June Myers, and the money was intact. I told Alwyn I'd
deliver it to Mrs Myers later in the day, and would provide
her with the name of the lady who had been so honest in
handing it in. And, of course, I would obtain the necessary
official receipt for it and its contents.

I knocked on the door of the Myers' council house at
teatime and it was opened by young Joseph.

Upon seeing me standing there in full uniform, he gave
a sharp cry of alarm and bolted back indoors, shouting and
crying for his mother. Alarmed at his outburst, she rushed
from the kitchen and expressed relief when she saw me at
the door. I gave her the good news about her purse and she
invited me in while she signed my official receipt. During
this short item of business, Joseph hid behind the settee,
peering out at me with tearful eyes. I learned that Melanie
was out playing with friends.

'Mr Rhea isn't going to hurt you!' she said to the child.
'He's brought Mummy's purse back, look!'

He looked at it, apparently puzzled that a policeman
should be doing something helpful, and then he retreated
behind his protective settee.

'I'm not here to hurt you, Joseph,' I spoke to the unseen
lad. 'I'm here to help your mum, we've brought her purse
back.'

There was no reaction from him. I didn't seek him out;
that would have raised his fears even more, so I left quietly
with June's delight being my reward. She said she would
write a letter of thanks to the finder.

It was some three weeks later when I received a phone
call from Alan Myers; he was June's husband and he
worked at an agricultural engineers' depot in Ashfordly. I
think he was a welder and he rang me from work.

'It's Alan Myers, Mr Rhea,' he said. 'I've just had a call

from our June. Somebody's pinched Joseph's bike, it's a new one an' all. We got it for his birthday . . .'

'Where did it go from?' I asked.

'Outside our house, sometime since last night. It got left out, Mr Rhea, by accident; it's our own fault, but I thought you might come across it.'

'I'll have a walk down there this morning, Alan,' I assured him. 'Is June in? I can see her for a description of it.'

'Aye, she rang me from a neighbour's, said she'd be in all day.'

'Good, I'll do my best.'

When I arrived, both Joseph and Melanie were at school and I obtained the necessary written statement from June Myers. This included an account of the bike's location, its description and a sentence to say that no one had any authority to remove it. It was a Hercules, a small blue cycle with white mudguards and a white pump. The seat was white too and it had a chainguard and lamps back and front. Almost new, it was clean and in very good condition. It was the miniature of a gents' full-size bicycle.

I promised June I would circulate its description to all local police stations and patrolling officers, and that it would appear in our monthly Stolen Cycles Supplement which was distributed to all cycle dealers. But, in my heart of hearts, I was doubtful if we could recover it.

Having undertaken these routine matters, I decided I would tour the area around Aidensfield, making a search of hedgebacks and likely dumping places. An adult could not have ridden it away; it was far too small for that, but another child might have taken it for a joy ride and abandoned it. Or, of course, a thieving adult could have picked it up and transported it away to sell for cash.

But I was lucky, or rather Joseph was lucky. Later that

afternoon, I decided to visit the village sports field at
Maddleskirk, a couple of miles away. I knew it attracted
youngsters from the local villages and many rode there on
cycles. And there, parked behind the cricket pavilion, I
found Joseph's bike. It was undamaged and there was no
one on the field at the time. I was tempted to leave it and
keep observations upon it, for the thief would probably
return and collect it. Then he could be dealt with. But
there was no hiding-place for me here and if I left it
unsupervised in the hope that I might later catch the thief
riding it, it might be stolen again or lost forever. I decided
against those risks. I had found it and it was safe, so I put
it in the van and drove to the Myers' home.

When I arrived, the family was having a cooked tea and
Alan answered the door.

'Hello, Alan,' I smiled. 'I've good news,' and I led him
to my van. I lifted out the cycle and, of course, he was
delighted. He looked at it and was pleased it had suffered
no damage.

'Come in, Mr Rhea, and show it to our Joseph. He's
scared of blokes like you, this might make him appreciate
you fellers a bit more.'

Following Alan indoors, I wheeled the little bike into
the front room and Alan called for Joseph, Melanie and
June. They came from the kitchen, and when Joseph saw
me holding his precious bike, his little brown eyes showed
a mixture of fear and amazement.

'Here, Joseph,' I invited him to come closer. 'Come and
have a look – is this your bike?'

'Go on, Joseph,' urged his mother. 'Tell Mr Rhea if it's
yours.'

The little lad, brave but somewhat shy, moved towards
me and I crouched down to welcome him. 'Well?' I asked.
'Is this yours, Joseph? I found it on the cricket field.'

He took hold of its handlebars and nodded.

'Yeth,' he said.

'Say thank you to PC Rhea,' said his mother. 'Thank you for finding my bike.'

'Thank you for finding my bike,' he said.

'There,' said his mother. 'That wasn't bad, was it? You see, policemen are not here to hurt you, Joseph, they're here to help you.'

'Shall I ride it for you?' He suddenly asked me.

'Can you ride a two-wheeler?' I asked.

'Yeth, of courth I can,' and he proudly wheeled it outside as I followed with June and the others.

Melanie suddenly decided she should ride a bike too, for she said, 'I can ride a bike, Mr Rhea,' and dashed back indoors for her red three-wheeler. On the footpath, I was then treated to a display of cycle-riding by Joseph who did tricks like ringing his bell while riding with one hand, riding with his feet lifted from the pedals and doing rapid turns around the lamp-posts. His shyness had evaporated; now he was a show-off. Melanie did her best to outdo him with her skills, and for me it was a pleasant few moments. Quite suddenly, Joseph decided he was unafraid of me. He halted at my side and said, 'Do you arretht naughty boyth? There are thome very naughty boyth at our thchool.'

'We only arrest very naughty people,' I said. 'We are here to help people, really, like your mum when she lost her purse or you, when somebody took your new bike.'

'I'm ten now,' he said proudly. 'I'm big now and I'm not frightened of you any more!'

'Good, then I am very pleased. Now, you must look after your bike . . .'

I gave him a short lecture on caring for his belongings and bade the family farewell. I thought no more of the incidents until, around half past five one evening, I heard a knock at my office door. I went outside to find Joseph standing there clutching a small boy by the collar.

'Thith ith a very naughty boy,' Joseph announced as the other cringed and protested beneath my gaze. 'I've brought him for you to arretht!'

'What's he done?' I asked.

'He thtole thome thweets from a girl at thchool, I thaw him,' he said. 'That ith very naughty!'

'Really, well, you'd better come in, both of you.'

I was uncertain how to cope with this development, but the other little lad, a six-year-old whose name I learned was Simon, denied the charge.

'I never,' he said. 'She gave me them.'

I lectured Simon against ever stealing sweets and congratulated Joseph on his community spirit, albeit couched in terms he would understand, and packed them off home. I wondered if he knew what was meant by the word 'arrest' – perhaps he thought it involved nothing more than a telling off by a policeman? In that case, I had done as he had expected and honour had been satisfied. Two days later, Joseph returned with another arrested child. This time it was a girl who'd torn another girl's dress in a fight.

'Thhe'th very naughty,' Joseph told me. 'Thhe'th tore Fiona'th dreth fighting when Mith Clement said not to.'

I gave Fiona a lecture about damaging the belongings of her friends, and she cried a little. I told Joseph to take her home. Now I had a problem, because he turned up with other 'arrested' children and probably thought he was doing a good job as a very special constable. I didn't want to hurt the child by telling him off, for that might destroy all his new-found confidence and the good work that had been achieved in removing his fears of policemen.

So, in an attempt to solve this little dilemma, I decided

that the easiest way was to be 'out' whenever he arrived with one of his arrests. I explained the situation to Mary and so during the following few weeks, whenever we heard his knock at the office door around teatime, she answered it. For a short time afterwards, she was confronted by Joseph and his many prisoners. On some five or six occasions that followed, she explained that PC Rhea was out on patrol and suggested that Joseph and his prisoner return later. This had the desired effect. Joseph ceased his one-man vigilante campaign, but he always spoke to me when he saw me. In fact, he matured into a fine young man and became a detective chief inspector in the London Metropolitan Police with his own lovely children. And he always pops in to see me when he's in the area – but now he doesn't bring his prisoners for me to deal with!

A farmer's eight-year-old son caused something of a flap one Christmas Eve, but it was a short-lived panic. I learned that the little boy, who was called Jonathan, had been suffering from teasing at school because he believed in Father Christmas when some of the others claimed he did not exist. Determined to settle this issue in his own mind, young Jonathan had not mentioned his doubts to anyone, not even to his parents, but after they had tucked him into bed that night, he had secretly gone out to seek Santa Claus.

I learned of his disappearance about ten o'clock on Christmas Eve when his father, Howard Sinclair, rang me. I hurried straight to the farm, which was only five minutes' drive from my own home, and was ushered into the living-room. There, with the help of Jonathan's older brother, Andrew, I learned of his worries.

Andrew told us that, at school, several of the lads in Jonathan's class were boasting that they had discovered the truth about Father Christmas and Jonathan had championed those who still believed in him. Jonathan had said, before the holidays, that he would find out for sure whether Father Christmas really existed.

'Did he say how he would do this?' I asked Andrew, an alert eleven-year-old.

'No, he never said. I thought he'd forgotten all about it, Mr Rhea, 'cos it was at school, before the holidays when he was on about it.'

At my instigation, we checked Jonathan's clothes and found he had dressed in his warm clothes which comprised a pair of small jeans, warm jumper, wellingtons, scarf, gloves, balaclava and overcoat.

'Let's search the farm buildings first,' I suggested.

'We've had a look around,' said Howard.

But if a policeman learns anything, it is how to conduct a thorough search of houses and buildings, especially for people who are deliberately concealing themselves.

I was sure the lad was out of doors, because of the clothing he had taken, and so we began our hunt. I allowed the parents to go one way while I went elsewhere, then I would retrace their steps, searching for the tiniest and most unlikely of hiding places. There was no snow yet, but it was crisp and frosty outside, so there'd be no footprints to provide any clues. After some twenty minutes of searching outbuildings, sheds and parked vehicles, I found myself in the hayloft. It was dry and cosy, with the scent of the hay filling my nostrils as my powerful torch picked out the stacked bales with hollows and passages between.

And then, as my torch beam moved across the surface of the bales, someone hissed for me to be silent.

'Sssh!' demanded the child's voice. 'You'll frighten 'em off!'

'Jonathan?' He would not know my voice.

'Who's that?' he demanded.

'The policeman, PC Rhea, we're looking for you.'

'I'm all right, leave me alone. I'm busy.'

My torch picked him out now. He was lying fully clothed on some bales of hay, peering through the loft window in the gable-end of the hayshed. The window was normally closed, having a small door to cover the gap, but now it was standing wide open. It gave him a perfect view of the farmhouse and at his side was a carpet brush and dustpan.

I knelt beside him. 'What are you doing here?'

'Waiting for Father Christmas,' he said.

'He never comes when children are awake and waiting for him,' I said gently. 'He will know you are here, so he'll keep away till you go to sleep in bed. Why do you want to see him?'

'To see if he's real,' he said simply.

'Well, as I said, Jonathan, he won't come while you are here, so you'd better come home. Your mum and dad are worried about you.'

'Are you sure he won't come?' he asked me, standing up and collecting his brush and dustpan.

'Yes,' I said, pointing the way out with my torch. 'But why have you got that brush and dustpan?'

'For reindeer droppings,' he said. 'I know Father Christmas will come to that chimney over there,' and he pointed at the house. 'And I know his reindeer like our hay, 'cos Mum and Dad said so; we always leave this hayloft window open so them reindeer'll come here for a feed. And I know how cows and horses make droppings, so I'll pick 'em up and show 'em to my pals. Then they'll know Father Christmas is real, won't they?'

'If you can find some reindeer droppings, I'm sure you'll convince them,' I said, accepting the brush from him and taking his hand. 'Come on, time for bed.'

'I'll never know, will I?' he said slowly.

'One day you will,' I told him, as I led him back to the house.

If young Joseph Myers misunderstood the meaning of 'arrest', it was understandable that little Martin Stokes, a small-built ten-year-old, should misunderstand one of this nation's best-known phrases. Most grown-ups know what is meant by 'London's streets are paved with gold' but Martin's vision of that big city was one of a glistening fairy-tale lane with golden footpaths and houses which contained everything a family could ever wish for, especially a dad.

Martin's mother had no husband. Martin was the result of a brief encounter with a young man who had vanished immediately after the act which had created Martin, and so the little fellow was reared by his loving and caring mother who was called Rosemary. She provided her sole offspring with lots of affection and as much comfort as possible.

She worked in a local shop which provided the barest of necessities, but at least she did work and she did attempt to give Martin the best that was within her very limited means. When the village primary school announced it was organising a trip to London for some ten- and eleven-year-olds, therefore, Martin said he would like to go. The trip was a form of celebration of the conclusion of their primary school education because next term, they would begin a new life at either a Grammar School or a Secondary Modern. In spite of the expense, Rosemary wanted Martin to go to London and she raided her meagre savings for his fare. Happily, a local businessman had said he would match fifty per cent of the total cost if the parents would raise the rest themselves.

The outcome was that a dozen children found themselves embarking on the trip of a lifetime. None had ever been to

London and so the teacher, Miss Clement, told them about it. She explained about the Houses of Parliament, Big Ben, the Queen and Buckingham Palace, the Horse Guards, the River Thames and all the traditional tourist sights. She showed them photographs too and a short film about London. And it was Miss Clement, in her lecture about the delights of our capital, who quoted from the poet George Colman (1762-1836), when she said,

> 'Oh, London is a fine town,
> A very famous city,
> Where all the streets are paved with gold,
> And all the maidens pretty.'

At home that evening over his tea, Martin told his mum all about the golden streets of London but she tried to explain that they weren't really made of gold. She told Martin that London was the town of opportunity, where people could become rich if they worked hard because there was a lot of money in London. It was there for everyone if they worked hard and took the opportunities to find it. Martin said he understood, and the night before the trip, she'd bathed him, got his best clothes ready and packed him an old army knapsack full of sandwiches and drinks.

'Will I be rich if I go to London?' he had asked her as she'd tucked him into bed.

'Maybe when you are grown up,' she'd said. 'If you go to London and work.' Poor Rosemary; money was so short for her that her worries about it must have made an impression upon her young son. He was always anxious to earn lots of money. 'But if the streets are made of gold, there must be some for me?' he'd said.

'No, darling, I've told you. The streets aren't made of

gold, not really. They're stone like our streets, but there is lots of money in London, there's lots of it about and people can find ways of getting a lot, earning a lot, if they live and work there.'

He hadn't quite understood it all, but had fallen into a fitful sleep, dreaming of the fabulous town he would visit tomorrow. Next morning at six, a small coach left Aidensfield for York Station where the train departed just before seven o'clock, thus allowing them a day in London under the guidance of the teachers and one or two volunteer helpers. They were all so eager to see the sights and to bring back lots of souvenirs. All had little bags containing their sandwiches and drinks, and I knew these would be full of trinkets and leaflets upon their return.

I was aware of the trip – a village bobby should know everything that is happening on his patch – but as none of my own children were old enough to join it, I was not really involved. The trip was an unqualified, if exhausting, success and my professional involvement came the following morning.

I received a phone call from Rosemary Stokes asking if I could call at the shop where she was working as she had a matter to discuss with me. Not knowing what this matter could be, I drove along to Maddleskirk where I found her behind the counter of the Post-Office-cum-grocery-store. She was alone, the proprietor having gone into York to buy his weekly stock of groceries, and the morning was quiet.

'Hello, Rosemary,' I greeted her. 'What's bothering you?'

'Would you like a coffee, Mr Rhea? I've got the kettle on?' This was a good start!

I let her make the coffee without asking more questions and she settled on a stool behind the counter as I settled on another at the customers' side. If a customer entered, she would deal with him or her, and I would enjoy my drink.

'I hope you don't mind me calling you like this,' she apologised. 'But I am very worried about Martin.'

'Why, what's he done? He went to London yesterday, didn't he? He has come back, hasn't he?' I suddenly had an awful thought that he might not have returned.

'Oh, yes, he's back. He's still asleep. He went straight to bed last night when he got back, Mr Rhea, he was utterly worn out. I've never seen him so tired,' and she bent to withdraw something from under the counter. It was a small khaki-coloured knapsack of the type soldiers used to carry for their rations and it was evidently very heavy. As she passed it over to me, I heard the rattle of coins.

'Look inside,' she invited.

Resisting its weight as I accepted it, I pulled open the stout press-studs and saw it was half-full of coins. Threepenny bits, sixpences, shillings, florins, half-crowns, pennies and ha'pennies. There was a small fortune.

'Somebody's been saving fast!' I laughed. 'Whose is all this?'

'I don't know,' and she looked sorrowful. 'Martin brought it back from London. He said he'd found it all. I didn't give him that money, Mr Rhea, nothing like that. I don't know where it's come from. I do hope he hasn't been stealing. I thought I'd better hand it in.'

I fingered through it; there were no £1 notes or ten-shilling notes, merely a large amount of cash. I didn't count it and learned Rosemary hadn't done so either, but there would be several pounds.

'Did you quiz him closely about it?' I asked.

She shook her head. 'No, he was too tired, he just fell into bed, exhausted and besides, I didn't like to upset him after his day out. I do know it's not his money and as he said he'd found it, I thought I'd better hand it in. I wondered if anybody had said anything to you about it.'

'No, they haven't,' I told her. 'I'm not surprised he was tired, carrying this around! I'll have to ask him about it.' I was worried in case he had taken it off the other children, although I doubted it. Martin was an honest little fellow, I was sure.

'He's in bed, at home, Mr Rhea. My mother's looking after him today; he's got the day off school. I didn't wake him to ask about it this morning. Should I come with you?'

'Your mother's there, so I'll be fine. I'll take the money to remind him!' I said, and so I returned to Aidensfield to have a chat with Martin.

Mrs Stokes, senior, Rosemary's mother, opened the door and was aware of the reason for my visit. She took me into her house, for Rosemary still lived at home, and said Martin was now out of bed and in the front room, playing with his souvenirs of yesterday in London. I went in. He was a happy boy, with a mop of curly blond hair and bright blue eyes, and showed no apprehension at my arrival.

'Hello, Martin,' I squatted on the carpet at his side. 'What have we got here?'

'Things from London,' he told me proudly. 'Pictures, books, flags; look, that's where the Queen lives and that's Big Ben . . . there's boats on the river and that's the Tower where the two princes were killed . . .'

I let him tell me about his journey and it was clear it had made a tremendous impression upon him. At this stage, I knew nothing of his vision of golden pavements, but when I presented the knapsack full of coins, he said, 'I got them from London, Mr Rhea.'

'Did you?' I expressed surprise. 'Where from?'

'The streets,' he said. 'Everybody said the streets were paved with gold, well, they weren't, they were stone like ours, and it was Mum who said there was money on the streets for everybody who could find it, so I found all that, Mr Rhea. I looked for it, and brought it home.'

'You mean you found all this, Martin?' I ran my fingers through the coins.

'Yes, Mr Rhea. On the pavements. I told Mum that.'

'Was all this money lying on the pavements?' I asked, surprised at the amount. Finding the occasional coin was not unusual, but to find all these . . .

'Yes, it was,' he said. 'People were throwing money down and other people were picking it up.'

'Whereabouts was this happening, Martin?'

'Oh, all over. Everywhere we went.'

'And who was picking it up?'

'Sometimes nobody, it was just left there. But those men playing music and drawing things on the pavements, they were keeping some. And sometimes, people threw it in boxes and hats and things on the pavements. I saw a lot of money thrown away like that, Mr Rhea, so I thought I'd have some.'

'You helped yourself from the boxes and hats, then?'

'Not really, 'cos I thought it must be somebody's, but I did pick some up from the pavements when it was just lying there. There was lots lying about, Mr Rhea.'

'I'm sure there was!' I had now guessed the source of his cash flow!

And so, by asking more questions, I came to realise that Martin, through the legend that the streets of London were paved with gold, had honestly thought money was being thrown on to the pavements to be collected by poor people like himself. And so, during that trip, he had picked up pounds' worth of coins from the feet of pavement artists, buskers and newspaper vendors and no one had noticed.

Martin's grandmother overheard this and was shocked.

'Martin!' she shouted at him. 'That's stealing . . .'

'He wasn't to realise that,' I said. 'But Martin, this money did belong to those people playing the music and doing the drawings. That's how they earn their money.'

I don't think he fully understood, but his grandmother asked, 'You're not going to take him to court, surely?'

'No,' I said. 'I wouldn't, not for this! But I couldn't take official action anyway, not without a complaint from those buskers and pavement artists. And I hardly think I'll get one from them!'

'What do we do with the money, then?' asked Mrs Stokes.

'I'll leave Rosemary to decide,' I said. 'She might give some to a charity, but I'm sure if those artists and buskers knew the struggle she was having, they wouldn't mind it going into Martin's Post Office Savings Account. He can always pay some back next time he's in London.'

I left, not wishing to know more about Martin's money-making but hoped he would learn that, even in London, cash was not there for the taking. It had to be earned.

On another occasion, anxiety was caused after Miss Alice Calvert retired as Headmistress of Ashfordly Primary School. Because she had served there during her entire teaching career, a matter of some forty years, her retirement created a lot of interest in the town and surrounding area, and resulted in wide local press coverage. There were presentations to her, one from her pupils past and present, and another from the governors and parents. Then, on the last day of her career, there was a social evening in the school with speeches and yet more gifts for Miss Calvert from her small staff and numerous associates, both within the teaching profession and from the townspeople.

She announced that next year she would be taking a

long holiday to tour Europe by car, and she hoped to take an extended break to visit her sister and her family in Australia. She also intended to enrol at night-school to study pottery, and promised that her retirement would enable her to undertake all those things she'd been unable to do while working.

Alice Calvert was of very distinctive appearance. Now sixty years old, she was a very tall and heavily built lady with a habit of wearing long, colourful and flowing dresses which concealed any hint of her feminine shape. Some of the crueller senior boys would call her Bell-Tent Alice, and few people really knew whether she was slim on top with big hips, or big on top with narrow hips. Almost invariably, she wore flat-heeled shoes or sandals and lots of bangles.

Her face, however, was beautiful. Embraced by a mop of pure white hair, it was round and cheerful with rosy cheeks and a constant smile. Miss Calvert radiated happiness and love and I, for one, often wondered why she had never married. She loved children and was completely happy in her work. Retirement, and the subsequent parting from the children, would not be an easy adjustment to make. But Alice Calvert could cope and would make the necessary adaptations without grumbling or self-pity.

She lived in Aidensfield, where she had a neat little bungalow not far from the church. I would see her pottering around the place at weekends, for she kept an immaculate garden full of flowers and shrubs, somehow guiding her massive bulk between the plants without causing damage. The bungalow was called Honeymead and during her long school holidays, she would ask me to keep an eye on the house whenever she was away. She was always careful to lock it against intruders. I was pleased that, during her frequent absences, she did notify me and so allow me to keep a careful watch on her property. I knew that during her longer absences overseas or indeed any other travelling she undertook in Britain, she would keep me informed when the bungalow was empty. I knew she would worry about the effect of her recent publicity, and whether this would attract undesirables who would snoop around her premises. In an attempt to offset this concern, I assured her that my colleagues and I would pay regular visits when on duty.

Knowing this background, it was with more than a little concern that at four o'clock on the morning following her farewell party, I received an urgent telephone call from her. It took a long time to arouse me but by the time I reached my cold office downstairs, I was fully awake.

'Mr Rhea,' she hissed into the phone. 'There's a man outside . . . he's been trying to break into my bungalow . . . What shall I do?'

'Is he still there?' I asked, speaking in a hoarse whisper.

'Yes and it's funny, I think he's gone to sleep outside, on the patio . . .'

'Asleep? Right, don't make a sound. I'm coming straight away. Look out for me . . .'

Pausing only to call Divisional Headquarters with an urgent request for the Police Dog Section and any other handy mobiles to be available at the bungalow in case the villain ran away or there was trouble, I dressed and hurried out. I did not take the mini-van, because a stealthy approach seemed vitally important. Instead, I used a pedal-cycle I'd just acquired and, after riding without lights for half a mile in the semi-darkness of that summer morning, I arrived at Honeymead within minutes. I parked my bike several doors away, having earlier radioed Divisional Headquarters to announce my departure for Honeymead and to inform them I was about to search for, and hopefully arrest, the reported intruder.

Calls of this kind were made as a form of security so that

if I failed to respond to radio calls in the ensuing drama, assistance would be sent. I knew the dogs and maybe other crews were already *en route*, and that gave me some comfort. I could wait for them, but I would hate to lose this prisoner; he might be frightened off at the approach of their vehicles, and so I made my move. My heart was pounding and I made sure I had my handcuffs and truncheon, my only defence against attack.

As I crept up to her back door in the near-darkness, I thought it odd that her burglar had gone to sleep, but I knew that sillier things had happened. Burglars often went to sleep inside a deserted house or even cooked meals there. Maybe this was just a drunk who'd read about her in the papers? The bungalow was in complete darkness, but in the approaching light of morning, she had seen my arrival. She unlocked her back door and opened it silently to admit me.

'Thank goodness you've come, Mr Rhea!'

I did not make the mistake of switching on my torch but could see she was enveloped in a huge flowing dressing-gown and had a heavy poker in her hand. If he'd got in here, he would have had a shock and a few bruises into the bargain.

'Where is he? Is he still here?' I whispered.

'On the patio, fast asleep. Maybe he's drunk.'

'Can I get there by going through the house?'

'No, he's lying against the French windows. You'll have to go round the side and through the garden.'

'Right,' I whispered and began my move. I knew the way. I'd been around her bungalow many previous times.

'What shall I do?' she asked.

'Stay here. Keep an eye on me from inside; it's not too dark. If I get attacked or anything, dial 999 and tell the police what's going on.'

'Be careful!' she whispered. And so I left. I crept around the side of her house, trying not to make a sound, and then, as I reached the front, I could see the dark shape of the sleeping intruder. It was a bulky man and he was huddled on the patio, lying fast asleep against her French windows. In the dim light, I could see he was very casually dressed in jeans and a sweater, and that he carried a back-pack comprising a sleeping-bag and rucksack, and this was forming his pillow. His hair was tousled and I could just discern a thick brown beard . . .

Wondering how long it would take for my assistance to arrive, I halted to take a deep breath. Miss Calvert was nearby with her poker but in cases like this, there was no knowing how a suspect would react; he might have a gun or a knife, he might be armed with a knuckleduster or a club. I began to think it would be wiser to await the dogs, but I could not flinch from my task.

I approached the sleeping form.

'Hey!' I moved his foot with my boot. 'You, hey, wake up . . . it's the police . . .'

I stood back in case of a violent reaction.

'Hmm?' He stirred but did not arouse. I kicked his boot again, shouting at him and keeping my distance.

'Police . . . wake up . . .' and now I shone my torch full in his eyes. 'Hey, come on, who are you? Stand up . . .'

In the reflected light of my torch, I could see Miss Calvert just inside her French windows, wringing her hands and wondering what she should be doing. I just hoped she did not go away – that poker might be my salvation! But the fellow was now rising to his feet, sleepily and without any sign of antagonism. He made no effort to run off, but stood there, blinking at me and apparently quite docile.

'Who are you?' I demanded loudly, hoping to penetrate

his weariness. 'This is the police . . .'

'Huh?' He blinked against the light of my torch and covered his eyes. 'Who?'

'Police,' I said. 'Who are you? What are you doing here?'

'Oh God,' he muttered and his deep voice emerged with a strong Australian accent. 'Streuth, I'm shattered, I really am . . . is this Miss Calvert's house? Alice Calvert's house?'

'Yes, it is,' I said. 'So who are you?'

'G'day. I'm her nephew . . . from Adelaide . . . Derek's the name . . . I knocked but she was asleep . . . I didn't like to rouse her so I kipped here . . . she always left a key under the stone when I was little so I could get in, but it's not there, Officer. Sorry, have I upset things?'

'You've been travelling long?'

'Couple of weeks or so,' he said. 'Flew a bit, caught ferries and hitched most of the way; I aimed to get here as a surprise, for her retirement party, do you know . . .'

'Wait there,' I said, and I knocked on her window. 'It's all right, Miss Calvert. You can put the light on and open this door.'

Even with my approval, she was nervous, but she obeyed. When the door was fully open, Derek said, 'Aunt Alice!' and threw his huge arms around her.

'Derek! It is you, isn't it? Derek!'

'Yes, it's me . . .'

I maintained a discreet distance during their dramatic reunion and then she invited me inside to have a cup of tea with her nephew. I learned it was seventeen years since she'd last seen him; he was then twelve and was now twenty-nine and approaching thirty. This had been his retirement surprise . . .

'And you're coming back to Australia,' he said eventually, delving into his baggage. 'I've a return ticket for you, starting five weeks from now. For a whole month . . .

you're coming to stay with us . . .'

I felt I ought to leave this scene of domestic happiness, but at that moment, the bungalow was suddenly surrounded by cars, flashing blue lights and lots of police officers . . .

'Oh crumbs!' I said. 'I forgot to cancel the cavalry!'

'Bring them in for a drink,' said Alice Calvert happily. 'It's a good job he wasn't a burglar!'

'It is,' I laughed. 'They'd have frightened him off!'

Half a dozen policemen and two dogs came into the house and filled the place with blue uniforms as I explained what had happened. They were delighted with the truth.

'Look,' said Alice, addressing us all in her school-ma'am voice, 'I knew you're not supposed to drink on duty, but I do have a bottle of wine . . . perhaps a glass each, just to celebrate? My nephew has come rather a long way, half-way round the world, and he did miss my party . . .'

And so, in the early hours of that morning, seven policemen and two police dogs, aided by glasses of wine, slices of her farewell cake and cups of coffee, helped Miss Calvert to celebrate her nephew's arrival. It was a lovely night's work!

As we prepared to leave, I said to my colleagues, 'Miss Calvert's going away soon, lads. Can I ask you all to keep an eye on her bungalow when I give you the word, just in case some burglar shows an unhealthy interest in it?'

'Sure,' they said. 'So long as we can have another party when she gets back!'

'That's a promise,' she beamed, hugging her nephew.

My reinforcements left in a procession of cars, doubtless rousing and puzzling the entire village, and I returned to my parked bike. Derek followed me out.

'Thanks, Mr Rhea,' he said. 'Thanks for looking after Aunt Alice. It could have been nasty, eh? A real intruder?'

'It's all part of the job,' I said, shaking his hand.

HEARTBEAT

CONSTABLE ACROSS THE MOORS
AND OTHER TALES OF A YORKSHIRE VILLAGE BOBBY

NOW AN ITV SERIES

Nicholas Rhea

Of the millions who have enjoyed ITV's popular series HEARTBEAT, none will forget characters such as Claude Jeremiah Greengrass, Sergeant Blaketon and PC 'Vesuvius' Ventress. And they will be familiar with the village of Aidensfield, at the heart of Constable Nick Rowan's North Yorkshire beat. Set in 1960s Aidensfield, this omnibus collection of stories, which together with Nicholas Rhea's other tales of a village policeman originally inspired the HEARTBEAT TV series, tells of all these characters and many more: of Claude Jeremiah's dog Alfred and his unfortunate incident with the budgerigar, of young PC Nick's first merry New Year's Eve in Aidensfield, and of the funeral of the ancient tramp, Irresponsible John. Humorous, touching and imbued with a deep affection for the Yorkshire countryside and its people, this heartwarming collection is a treat no HEARTBEAT fan will want to miss.

'Witty, warm-hearted and full of lovable rogues'
Northern Echo

Heartbeat is a Yorkshire Television series derived from the Constable Books by Nicholas Rhea

FICTION / TV TIE-IN 0 7472 4125 2

A selection of bestsellers from Headline